True Religion

An unexpected encounter with an otherworldly spirit at a holiday party in the Orenda Valley sends Seth Davis, a gay journalist from Manhattan, on a profound religious journey. Along the way, Seth stumbles into a quarreling coven of witches in the charming tourist town of Hope Springs, Pennsylvania, formerly known as Hell's Ferry, and one of the most haunted destinations in America. As Seth learns more of the town's remarkable history, he also uncovers his own shocking past, and in order to seek peace for his troubled soul, he must determine the fate of the coven, the town, and the entire Orenda Valley. *True Religion*, J.L. Weinberg's debut novel, is a genre-bending fusion of paranormal horror, spiritual therapy, American history, and New Age enlightenment.

"Brace yourself—for witches, ghosts, and unsettled souls that do way more than go bump in the night. They are out for a showdown with Seth, a determined, young spiritual seeker who is the hero of J.L. Weinberg's edge-of-your-seat paranormal thriller. This is a thought-provoking debut that will leave you wanting more!"
—David Pratt, author of *Looking After Joey* and *Bob the Book*

"Radical faerie boys and spirit guides, Old Religion and New Faith, these are the wondrous tools Weinberg uses to create a remarkable contemporary fantasy for gay readers. Whether or not God really does bless America, be assured that the prose in *True Religion* is divine, clever, and engaging."
—Steve Berman, author of *Vintage: A Ghost Story* and editor of the *Wilde Stories* annual series

True Religion

a novel by

J.L. Weinberg

Chelsea Station Editions
New York

True Religion
by J.L. Weinberg

Cover photo from Shutterstock.com
Book design by Peachboy Distillery & Designs

Published by Chelsea Station Editions
362 West 36th Street, Suite 2R
New York, NY 10018
www.chelseastationeditions.com
info@chelseastationeditions.com

Paperback ISBN: 978-1-937627-03-4
Ebook ISBN: 978-1-937627-63-8
Library of Congress Control Number: 2015945841

First Edition

*To Adam Septimus Kent,
and to my familiar spirit, Tweetie,
with all my love.*

"It is not necessary to understand.
It is necessary to believe."
Jean Cocteau, *Orpheus*

True Religion

Prologue

The Orenda Valley has existed since the beginning of time. The river which flows through it, known at first by no name, and then by many names, is now called the Orenda River. Like rivers great and small, the Orenda is an eternal presence which has triumphed over, and washed away, human follies throughout the millennia.

Water is the strongest of the elements. It may be lashed by wind, but it rarely succumbs for long. It may be filled with earth, but this is only temporary, as water will well up and find its path to the sea again. It can quench almighty fire, thought by many to be the fiercest elemental force. While electrical fire was instrumental in creating the universe, without water, no life can be sustained. The primal need for water trumps all.

The mighty Orenda River flows through five states—New York, New Jersey, Pennsylvania, Maryland, and Delaware—on its way to the Atlantic Ocean. Prior to the European annexation of the North American continent, the river was considered holy by the native inhabitants. Springs that fed the river sheltered water spirits, who were honored for the sweet sustenance they provided. The river also hosted fish, snapping turtles, and beaver, among other creatures. But what made the river holy was not anything like the gold of the *Nibelungen* stolen from the River Rhine, but a bed of quartz crystal which lies hidden beneath its stony floor. The crystal bed runs a distance of ten miles in the vicinity of present-day Banbury, New Jersey and Hope Springs, Pennsylvania, towns on opposite sides of the waterway.

Crystals have always been prized by mankind. As vessels of white light energy, they are revered for physical and psychic healing. Embued with earth elements, crystals inspire intuition, protect against negative vibrations, and aid communication with the unseen dimensions. Their natural properties, enhanced by the energy flow of a major river, make the Orenda Valley a unique place of power. The native inhabitants venerated the aqua-crystal marriage and called upon it for blessing and guidance. They understood that crystals provided psychic entrance into the spirit realm, where their guides could be contacted and asked questions about tribal life. They performed a cleansing and purification ritual in the crystal-rich river waters. They secreted crystals on their bodies to maintain internal balance and good health, and drank water in which a crystal had been suspended as an additional health benefit.

Even though the native population has long since abandoned the valley, having lost their homeland to the white man, the area continues to exert a powerful influence over those who have resided there. Souls—indigenous, European, and American— who inhabited the valley in previous lives are drawn back to work out the karma of their current life. As each human reincarnates, or comes back into the flesh after ending one lifetime, karma—the sum of each person's actions in previous lifetimes—determines the challenges of the new lifetime. Perhaps the Orenda Valley souls are tied to the energy generated by the flow of water over quartz. Or perhaps the possibility of working feats of will to alter reality—what many term "magic"—is the bond. Whatever the connection, karma and reincarnation are the twin laws that govern mankind's progress on the experiment called Planet Earth, which is overseen by a beneficent and loving universal soul, even if this is not always apparent.

The spiritual journey of one human soul who is tied to the river, the land, and its former inhabitants may help illustrate these laws in action.

Part One

Close Encounter

One

It was all he could do to keep the cascading sepia-toned images at bay, scenes of demonic possession morphing one into the next. Angelic girls transforming into blaspheming harridans; sweet-faced boys changing into gaunt men with murder in their eyes. The fiendish visions rushed forward like whitewater surging toward a precipice. From a flash of crimson flame, a man emerged. Hostile and threatening, he loomed large, assuming the aura of an evil deity come to claim the blood sacrifice due him: a young boy who had now materialized, radiantly enshrouded in light.

Father and son. Evil and death. Life and light. It was a nightmare that could not be prevented. The father stalked his son as a satyr would a faun, with one thing in mind. The father yearned for—and couldn't abide not having—the most intoxicating, most forbidden possession of all.

Waves crashed through the dream. The boy tumbled through the current and came to rest on a sodden strand of beach, where the tidal rhythms lulled him into a deathly unconsciousness. He felt only the froth of white water that rose over him and retreated in an endless cycle, threatening to wash over his head and drown him at any moment. As he was about to be covered by the brine and pulled out to sea, Seth Davis awoke with the sense that he'd narrowly escaped death. He opened his eyes and involuntarily sputtered to clear the dream's water from his lungs. A chill passed through him when he remembered he'd had this nightmare many times before.

Seth gazed at his boyfriend's long-limbed, muscular body lying beside him. Martin's face was peaceful, his ice-blue eyes unseen behind sleeping lids. A profound regard for his partner of seven years welled up in Seth, despite the cracks that were beginning to appear in their relationship. "I love you," he whispered. His words broke the dream's spell, and the unsettling images faded from his awareness.

He relaxed into the bed. He longed to fall back into uninterrupted sleep, but the damp bedclothes put him on edge. He closed his eyes and slipped into a new dream, where he sat before a tiny red-skinned man with gray whiskers drooping from the corners of his mouth and chin.

"Who are you?" Seth asked.

"I am Ketanëtuwit, but you may call me Keta."

"Why have you summoned me?"

"You have summoned *me*," Keta answered.

"But I haven't."

"You have. You are seeking direction and have asked for help. You try something, it doesn't work out, and you move on to the next something which will again be left behind," the wizened man lectured with a wave of his diminutive hand. "There's no follow through, my child."

Seth rose into the air, levitating above his body and the bed, which rippled and disappeared, leaving the sensation that he was floating above cushions of clouds. A pattern of roads appeared beneath the clouds, a jig-saw path that Seth took to be the course of his life. As his mind adjusted to the dream, he saw that the line of his life choices was held in the lines of the small man's hand. "I thought I could achieve perfection in this life, at least as far as humans can."

Keta let out an ethereal chuckle, dry as dust. "If you were perfect, you would be a Divinity," the ancient figure gently admonished.

"Are you saying that all my efforts have been wasted?"

"Don't be so hard on yourself. You must examine the overall picture as well as the details and see what they tell you."

"What they tell me is that I wasted ten years pursuing an acting career. And I've ended up as a typesetter at a magazine

I hate, where I'm not taken seriously as either a film critic or a computer professional."

"Punishing yourself will lead nowhere," Keta said with a slight nod of his head.

Seth laughed bitterly. "The whole thing's a bad joke. At thirty-five, all I've got is a life evaded."

"And what about your partner?"

"Our compatibility just disappeared."

"It leached away, undetected by either of you. One day critical mass occurred, and you were no longer in synch."

"Are you some kind of shrink?"

"Of course not," was the bemused reply.

Before Seth could respond, the old man bowed stiffly and hobbled away. After a breathless few moments, Seth opened his eyes. "What a weird dream!" he said.

Martin stirred at his side. "Are you awake?" Seth whispered.

Martin yawned and stretched. "I am now," he said. "You were thrashing about like someone possessed."

"The heat's driving me crazy. It's affecting my dreams. We should get out of the city. Maybe it will be cooler at the shore."

"You'll have to go on your own, because Miraculous wants a final draft of the script in three weeks."

"Everyone needs a break. You can take a few days off."

"I can't take time off when I'm under deadline."

"I'm under deadline every week to close an issue of the magazine."

Martin turned away from Seth and sat up, mumbling a guilty, "Look, once I hand in the script—" but was interrupted by the ringing of the telephone.

Seth jumped out of bed and raced down the hallway to the living room, past a wall of unfinished pinewood bookshelves overloaded with Martin's screenplays, art books, and classic American and foreign movie videos. He reached for the phone that rested on a rusting metal table. "Hello," he blurted into the receiver.

"Seth?" Without waiting for a reply, the voice continued, "It's Richard. How'd you and Martin like to spend July Fourth in Hope Springs?"

Seth sprawled on the captain's bed covered with a paisley East Indian spread, which served as a sofa. "What are you doing in Hope Springs? I thought you were in the city."

"It's a shame you can't keep up with an old man like me," Richard laughed. "I've been down here for a month. I'm sure I told you. I was asked to spearhead the campaign to halt construction of the Starfire nuclear power plant, and I've decided to do it."

"You've joined the No Nukes movement?"

"I'm a charter member. Listen, I'll take you to a cool Independence Day celebration. A bunch of old hippies and bikers get together and party. That guy who was famous, but now his wife's more famous, always shows up and plays guitar. I mentioned you to Beth, and she asked me to invite you."

"Who's Beth?"

"Beth and Roger Prince. They went to jail with me in Chicago. Dyed-in-the-wool revolutionaries, except Roger's now the CEO of his own software company. I think he's sold out."

"I was just talking about getting out of the city. It's hellish up here. What perfect timing."

"Not perfect—*synchronous!*" Richard proclaimed, as if revealing the secret of life. "Take the Orenda Valley Bus Line from Port Authority. Let me know when you're getting in, and I'll meet you at the stop. There's a Mobil station there. You can't miss it."

"I'll be down Sunday afternoon."

"Wait till you see the cabin I'm living in, it's right on the river." Richard gave Seth his phone number and hung up.

Martin appeared in the living room, stretching his arms over his head and revealing his brawny torso. He wore a sweat-stained white T-shirt and long-legged blue jeans despite the heat and humidity that by nine in the morning had turned the apartment into a sauna. "Was that for me?" he asked.

"No, it was Richard inviting us to a July Fourth party in Freeman County. There'll probably be substances to abuse. I don't suppose you want to go."

"Well—" Martin said, drawing out the word.

"Just say no, Martin."

"It's not like anything's going to happen over the holiday weekend."

"I told Richard I'd be down on Sunday."

"Sounds good," Martin muttered as he disappeared into the kitchen.

"Will you make some coffee?" Seth called out. He sat naked against a mirrored cushion, surprised that he hadn't had to beg Martin to accompany him. His thoughts darkened when he realized that the lure of unabashed drinking may have proved too much for Martin to resist. "When we get back, do you think we can get the air conditioner fixed?" he yelled to Martin in the kitchen.

There was no reply.

Seth lay back on the captain's bed and closed his eyes. He fell into a waking reverie akin to a flickering vision of the past. A menacing father figure again chased him. He ran into his childhood bedroom in San Francisco, now devoid of furnishings, and locked the door. Feeling the beast's malicious energy fill the room from the other side of the door, he ran through the doorway that led from the bedroom to the adjoining bathroom. He turned the lock just as the presence on the other side of the door twisted the handle. Fear for his life overwhelmed him, and he snapped awake in a panic. His heart was beating so fast he felt it would explode.

Two

Though the summer of 1988 was barely a month old, it was one of the hottest of the decade. The heat hadn't abated in the two days since Richard's call, rising to 98 degrees, with no break in sight. As Seth and Martin walked through the Port Authority bus station on Manhattan's Eighth Avenue, they stepped inside a blast furnace; the building was not air-conditioned. Apart from the flow of commuters who traveled to and from New Jersey, the site was overrun with the homeless, and populated by petty criminals, prostitutes taking a break from Times Square, and drug dealers. The close proximity of high and low, rich and poor, privileged and deprived, was one of New York City's many paradoxes. Negotiating this purgatory of lost souls, Seth and Martin dodged unwashed panhandlers and shifty-eyed grifters while walking the wide halls and riding an escalator two flights to a berth on the upper level, where the Orenda Valley buses docked. They joined the line in front of door 433 and waited in the sticky air.

The hinged doors opened, and the driver stepped through to announce, "Bus to Freeman County now boarding." The line inched forward. Seth and Martin walked through the doors to the idling bus and were hit by a gust of scorching air mixed with exhaust. They stowed their bags in the luggage compartment and climbed aboard, where they found two seats towards the rear.

"From what I've heard, Freeman County should be beautiful," Seth said as the bus navigated the concrete bowels of the terminal. "Old stone farmhouses and lots of greenery. Maybe we can swim in the river."

"I've got to work on my script. But don't let that stop you," Martin replied.

Seth's mood soured. *I might as well be single*, he thought. He accepted Martin's stone-faced concentration on the manuscript that lay open in his lap, and put a tape of Pink Floyd's *Dark Side of the Moon* into his Walkman. He fished a Jane Roberts "Seth Speaks" book out of his shoulder bag. Martin had found the book in a used bookstore downtown while browsing through shelves marked "Spirituality" and "Paranormal." Seth grabbed it from Martin's reading pile, intrigued by the allusion to his namesake. The claim that Roberts channeled a disembodied spirit who imparts occult wisdom also captured his imagination, even though he wasn't certain that such entities existed.

The bus emerged from the Lincoln Tunnel into the freeway-choked New Jersey lowlands. Seth looked up from his book, which he could scarcely concentrate on. The dreamy music coming through his headphones placed in relief the factory-fouled marshlands and eerily lit power plants that spread out into the distance. He remembered his dream about the Native American guide and the vision of his life's pattern. But as quickly as it materialized, it vanished, slipping maddeningly from his grasp. In its wake, he recalled how he and Martin Spencer had been introduced at a press screening by a mutual friend. He traced their relationship troubles back to the time, a few years later, when Martin began writing schlock horror screenplays for Miraculous Films' genre division. Under pressure of tight deadlines and rewrite schedules, Martin had turned to the bottle to unwind. His excuse was that the owner of the company was crazy, and that the deadlines were impossible. Martin always added that this gig would be his stepping stone to Hollywood, as if to justify his drink-fuelled surliness and the lack of communication that had come to characterize their partnership.

Seth shut the book and switched off the Walkman; the music seemed dated, a reminder of his lost youth. He glanced at Martin, who was engrossed in marking up his script. *What brought us together*, Seth thought, *was our love of movies, the ultimate escapist fantasy. I used them to avoid reality. Going to the movies was like getting lost in a dream.* After a moment, he mused, *I wonder what Martin's running from?* He nearly laughed when he thought, *Sex with me. And it was so hot when we first got together. Why does that always happen with couples?*

When they'd first met, Martin had a shelf of books on spiritualism—books he had collected since his boyhood—of famous possessions, mediums, and spirit-talkers. He wouldn't let Seth handle them because many of them were old, the spines broken and the pages yellowed and crumbling. When Seth asked what they were for, Martin was evasive. "They're the key to the universe," he had said without elaboration. After Martin moved into Seth's apartment, a year into their relationship, the books came with him, but were hidden away in the hall closet. Seth ascertained that some of them were magic books, and when he came home late at night from work and smelled sage and frankincense, he knew that Martin had been casting spells. He wasn't sure that Martin's spellcasting amounted to much, and viewed it as a harmless diversion. Martin continued to read New Age and occult books, some of which he passed along to Seth. Books that dealt with unseen worlds and hidden knowledge fascinated Seth. He was skeptical of the self-empowerment mantras, yet he secretly took them to heart.

The rural scenery sped past the window as they traveled deeper into Jersey's interior, leaving the suburbs behind. Green fields of silver queen corn and summer tomatoes alternated with rolling hills covered with low shrubs and grass. Varying shades of green, earth tones, and smudged purple stretched into infinity. The bus shifted into low gear and turned onto a winding two-lane road. It picked up speed, moving with a rocking motion. A succession of tiny villages with houses trimmed in red, white, and blue bunting and surrounded by white picket fences flew by. American flags flapped in the breeze on front lawns, heralding the upcoming holiday.

The patriotic display triggered another memory. Carole Silverstein, a thirtiesh filmmaking student and political activist Seth knew while attending NYU's film school, invited him over to discuss a role in her movie. When he peered into the living room of the dimly lit Bleecker Street apartment, he discovered that her boyfriend was Richard Abbey, a Sixties radical and drug guru. Even through the bluish haze of cigarette and marijuana smoke, Richard looked familiar. His unruly Jewish Afro had turned steel gray and was trimmed around his collar, and his heavy features were hidden behind a mask-like beard and gold-rimmed spectacles, yet Seth recognized the man who had protested the Viet Nam war in the papers and on television, most famously at the 1968 Democratic Convention.

Richard and Carole had parted ways over opposing definitions of monogamy, Richard's containing a catch-as-catch-can clause. The old radical remained in the Walker Street loft in Tribeca that he and Carole had renovated, where he continued to experiment with drugs. The results were books like *H is for Heroin* and *Cocaine Blues*. As their friendship became more certain, Seth teased Richard about his dedication to researching his subject, referring to him as the Tripmaster. In the last few years, Richard had grown despondent that his revolutionary politics hadn't brought about more change.

The bus veered down a tree-covered hill, rounded a curve, and glided into a town that looked like a holdover from the previous century. It wasn't until they passed through this hamlet and crossed a steel bridge spanning a swiftly flowing river that they left New Jersey. On the other side, a sign read, "Welcome to Hope Springs, PA." The bus turned onto a thoroughfare signposted River Road, which was lined with eighteenth-century mansions. It crawled along in the late-afternoon tourist traffic, past shops, restaurants, and inns. The antiquity of the place was evident. The town's colonial heritage was trumpeted from every storefront—early American antiques, quilts, and heirlooms luxuriated in tasteful window displays.

Further on, River Road became a narrow country lane shrouded by a canopy of trees that blocked the sunlight. The trees converged into a dense, primeval forest. The bus pulled to the right and shivered to a halt in front of a Mobil station. Seth nudged Martin and said, "This is it." They disembarked and collected their bags from the driver. "It's just as hot as in the city," Seth said. A staggering figure with a goofy smile approached on foot. Seth whispered to Martin, "He's tripping his brains out."

Richard rushed forward to greet his friends and stumbled. Seth grabbed his arm to keep him from falling. "I didn't see that fuckin' crack, man," Richard slurred. A sheepish grin peaked through the tangle of beard.

"From the looks of it, you're not seeing much besides swirling colors," Seth said.

"Hey, man, don't get down on me for expanding my consciousness on a beautiful summer day," Richard replied. "What do you think God made drugs for?" This drew cautious stares from the passengers who lingered at the stop. Richard patted Martin on the back and said, "Still cranking out those screenplays?"

"Yes. Thanks for having us," Martin said.

Richard ushered Seth and Martin along the sidewalk towards the center of town. He started to weave off the pavement, prompting Seth to place a hand on his shoulder to guide him. Richard said, "I want to take you guys for a drink at a cool old inn. It's from before the revolution. The *first* American Revolution."

"Do you think you need any more intoxicants?" Seth asked.

"Don't be a downer. Having a drink at the Ferry Inn is a Hope Springs tradition."

"Sorry. A drink sounds great."

They fell into a shared rhythm as they walked along the tree-lined street, their conversation punctuated by friendly pools of silence. The languid air and hazy sunlight filtering through the maple leaves gave the afternoon an authentic summer feel. The town's historical sites were interspersed with centuries-old stone dwellings. Martin stopped to read a weathered "Historical Places" plaque posted on a squat two-story building that housed a Mexican restaurant on the ground floor. "This was once a colonial inn called the Lloyd House," he said. "Aaron Burr hid in the attic during the Revolution."

Across the street was a barn-like theater with "Freeman County Playhouse" on the marquee. *The Crucible* was the current attraction. "The Playhouse was originally a grist mill," Richard said. "It was built after the town was destroyed by fire in the late eighteenth century."

Glimpses of the river appeared from the streets that intersected River Road. Seth stopped to read a banner announcing the "Hope Springs Psychic Festival."

"This is the capital of the New Age," Richard said. "Or at least an important outpost."

"I see," Seth replied, wandering a few paces along a side street to get a closer view of a metal scroll hanging from a wooden structure that read, "Hell's Ferry Boat House." "I thought we're in Hope Springs," he said.

"Hell's Ferry was the town's name before it burned down in 1780," Richard said. "Only the Ferry Inn remained standing. The town was later rebuilt as Hope Springs."

"Why was it called Hell's Ferry?" Martin asked.

"In colonial times, people regularly drowned when crossing the river by ferry. The current can be unpredictable and treacherous, especially in winter."

They walked along a stone bridge that spanned what Richard said was a canal built during the 1820s for cargo transport. There was no sign of commerce now, only verdant back lawns running down to the canal bank, which was lined with weeping willows. The slow-moving water, a smokehouse submerged in a hillside, and the white flagstone homes gave Hope Springs a lazy Southern feel that was unusual in the Northeast. The town's atmosphere of another time and place was beginning to cast a spell. Seth sensed he'd been there before, even though this wasn't the case.

Beyond the bridge stood a three-story stone mansion set back on a corner plot. The lawn that separated the house from the street was surrounded by a white picket fence. "That house was built in 1784 by Benedict Parsons, using rocks dredged from the river," Richard said. "Parsons raised Hope Springs from the ashes of Hell's Ferry. He rebuilt the mills and brought industry back. He's considered the town father, and was one of the county's earliest industrialists. That is, one of the first capitalist pigs to pillage the land, which was stolen from the native inhabitants."

Walking along the mansion's boundary, Seth said, "It's amazing how you can turn any bit of history into a diatribe against capitalism."

"Am I wrong?"

On a side lawn, a metal weathervane—a tawny figure in a loincloth—sat atop a tall pole. "What do you make of that weathervane?" Seth asked. "Historically, I mean."

"A perfect case in point. That's Chief Ferry, a Native American who lived when this territory was a British land grant. The Chief so admired the friendship extended to his people by William Penn that he adopted the name of one of Penn's administrators, Joshua Ferry."

"Doesn't that contradict your theory?"

"No. After Penn's death, the British settlers cheated the Native Americans out of their best land in an incident called the Running Purchase. The colonials offered to buy the amount of land they could run in a day and a half, then got their fastest men to participate in relays, which extended the amount of terrain they covered."

"That's a dirty trick."

"Exactly. It's the blueprint for our collective actions to this day."

The Chief was fashioned from copper and painted in an *art naïf* manner. His loincloth was an eggshell yellow with a blue and brown zigzag border. He pulled a missing arrow in a taut bow. His strangest feature was the willowy feather crown he wore, which recalled a flapper's hat rather than the headdress of a fierce Native American hunter. The grimacing copper-faced Chief appeared ferocious, even vengeful. But from a different angle, he looked as if he was laughing. Seth gazed upwards at the Chief, who oversaw the comings and goings of the town, and wondered if he was a symbol of something.

"The weathervane was made in the 1830s, and originally stood in front of the Ferry Inn," Richard said. "He was referred to as the 'Ferry Inndian.' To add insult to injury, whoever designed the Chief gave him an inaccurate headdress. No Northeast tribe ever wore such elaborate headgear. Only the Plains Indians wore that many feathers."

"You win," Seth laughed. "All of history *can* be reduced to the white man's subjugation of people of color in the name of world domination."

"Of course, you can also view history through a Freudian construct," Richard said in a mock-German accent. "Check out the cannon and pile of balls over there." Sitting in the middle of a brick square between the Parsons Mansion and an elegant inn was a cast-iron cannon with a mound of ammunition before it. "The gun commemorates the cannon that repelled the British as they forded the river before Washington's midnight crossing, which took place ten miles south."

Seth nodded, but was distracted by the angled sunlight, which had an odd density to it. He looked toward the stately inn beyond the square and caught the building in a halo of three-dimensional air. The slanting light shafts were milky, and blocked out rather than illuminated what stood behind them. The air appeared to be populated with transparent organisms.

They crossed a cobblestone street and approached the Ferry Inn. In front was an oval wooden sign bearing a reclining Chief Ferry in an odalisque pose, wearing a feathered headdress and smoking a long white pipe. To one side of the Chief, in ornate scrolled lettering, was carved, "The Ferry Inn." At the oval's top were the words, "Hope Springs' Original Inn," and at the bottom, "Superior Spirits, Food, Accommodations." The inn was painted the same pale yellow as the loincloth on the weathervane, with forest green shutters at each window. The first storey, surrounded on three sides by a covered wooden porch, was constructed of exposed flagstone, while the two upper floors were of brick and wood. Walking around the building to its side entrance, they came upon a horse-drawn buggy stationed beneath two carriage lamps mounted on the porch roof.

"That's a snapshot of the inn when it was first built," Richard said. "Travelers on the New York to Philly stagecoach spent the night here." They walked to the back and discovered a modern addition consisting of a glassed-in atrium dining room and a white latticework gazebo. "Enough of this *Architectural Digest* shit!" Richard said. "Let's hit the bar." He led Seth and Martin to the main entrance, where they passed a low-ceilinged dining room with lace curtains at the windows and tables covered in white linen. They approached a curving staircase that led to the upper floors. On the stair landing, Seth glimpsed a portrait of a dour-faced couple, and a chill went down his spine. Dressed in black, each sitter wore roses—the man sported a single bloom in his lapel, and the woman had several blossoms in her tightly-curled auburn hair.

They continued along a narrow passageway to a beveled glass door that opened into the tavern, which was paneled in maplewood. Green glass lamps hung over the copper-topped bar, and brass sconces and a brass chandelier decorated the walls and ceiling. A tall fireplace, the public room's original heat source, stood against the back wall. A muted TV was perched on an overhead shelf at the bar's far end, adjacent to a pinball machine. Two patrons exited as they arrived. They settled onto high stools at the bar.

"The first round's on me," Martin said. He ordered a pitcher of margaritas. The bartender set three chilled glasses on the bar and soon placed a frosty pitcher in front of Martin, who poured the drinks and toasted, "To an old hippie who kept on going, even though flower power has faded away." Taking a stiff swallow, he told Richard, "You're not doing badly down here. You've got a media-friendly cause, and after hours you can drink with the locals."

"It's not like I'm doing a little rabble-rousing and then unwinding at the bar," Richard said. "The Damn the Dam campaign—my name, by the way—is a huge undertaking. Now that I'm in it up to my eyeballs, I ask myself why I got involved. My stamina isn't what it used to be." He lit a cigarette and inhaled deeply. "But when I consider that a few greedy bastards could destroy a river for the sake of cooling a nuclear power plant, it makes my blood boil. Then I get a surge of energy and feel that we can win this fight."

"I never saw you as a tree-hugger," Martin said.

"The older I get, the more the blighting of nature disturbs me. When I see a tree being felled—don't laugh—it breaks my heart. If the Orenda were to be dammed, the loss of fish and wildlife would be catastrophic."

"Weren't you just going to lend your name to the cause?" Seth asked.

"That was the initial idea. But I got sucked in when I realized that if I was going to have any impact, I'd have to find out what makes the various factions tick. You've got the landowners who are promoting Blithe Point for the Starfire nuclear site. They've set up a network of shell corporations to hide their identity. Then you've got the power company executives and their well-lobbied politicians, who will do whatever it takes, even redirecting a river down the dried-up tributary at Blithe Point, to ensure that there's enough water to cool the plant."

"Is it possible to reroute a river?" Martin asked.

"If you dam it, yes. No pun intended."

"I thought that since Three Mile Island, nuclear power was in decline," Seth said.

"That's what the Reagan administration would like you to think," Richard said. "The truth is that more plants are going online every year, and we are becoming dependent on nuclear energy to provide electricity. Reagan gave a speech in 1981 saying as much. This is another one of his behind-the-scenes deals, and there's some person or persons in Freeman County who wants to cash in. Nuclear proponents love to say how clean nuclear power is. They don't mention that no one has figured out how to store the waste, except to bury it in the Nevada desert, where it will remain radioactive for thousands of years."

"Do you have allies?" Martin said.

"Yes, the old hippies who moved here in the Sixties. The constituency that's hardest to reach are the locals, who don't want to get involved. A big part of my job is to win them over."

"What are you doing to stop the dam from being built?" Martin asked.

"To raise awareness, we've organized sit-ins at the plant site. We also blocked the bridge between Hope Springs and Banbury, where we're going tomorrow for the party. I got arrested for that."

"That's so passé," Seth said. "How effective are sit-ins and demonstrations now, when people are too apathetic to vote?"

"That's not all we're doing. Our representatives attend every town meeting, and we're trying to block construction through the courts. We've also canvassed the townships to communicate what's at the heart of this, which is the eradication of a public holding to benefit a few individuals. We've used the media to our advantage by grabbing every photo op and sound bite that's come along."

"Brilliant!" Martin cried with drunken exuberance.

Seth poured another round, emptying the pitcher. He raised his glass in the air and toasted, "To the media, the all-seeing eye on top of the pyramid on the dollar bill."

"To the media," Martin and Richard joined in.

Seth ordered another pitcher, along with a platter of nachos.

"Which reminds me," Richard said, "how's your writing going?"

"In circles," Seth replied. "I have good patches, where I sell back-to-back articles, and dry spells where I can't interest anyone in anything for months. Then all I'm doing is typesetting articles at *New Day.*"

"At least you only work four days a week," Martin grumbled.

"You get to work at home," Seth said.

"Don't you think that has to do with what you offer the glossies?" Richard asked. "You shouldn't be surprised when your pitch on some smarty-pants French director is rejected in favor of an article on Hollywood's flavor of the month. All the magazines cover the same thing at the same time. It's maximum mind-control of the readership."

"I think we've had this discussion before," Seth said.

"And that's when I quote Noam Chomsky, who says that journalists with anything but a mainstream orientation will be marginalized by the media establishment. Does that ring a bell?"

"Ding, dong!" Seth sang in the lilting tone that surfaced when he was intoxicated.

A cook in starched whites entered with a plate heaped with chips and melted cheese, which he placed on the bar.

"Can I get you gentlemen anything else?" the bartender asked.

Seth noticed a glass globe the size of a tennis ball perched on a white porcelain stand next to the cash register. The globe looked like a fishing net float, but its champagne color and antiquity indicated it was something different. "No thanks," he said, tearing off a clump of chips and setting it on a napkin. "But can you tell me what that glass ball is? I've never seen anything like it. It looks really old."

"I don't know much about it," the bartender said with a shrug. "Mr. Paley, the owner, told me it's a witch's ball used to ward off evil spells."

"I've never heard of such a thing."

"Mr. Paley says it's over two hundred years old. One day it appeared in the basement. One of the busboys found it. They keep it behind the bar for good luck. The weird thing is, from time to time, it disappears. Then it appears again a few weeks later."

Seth shuddered. "Thanks," he said.

"Is there anything else?"

"Just the check."

The bartender withdrew to the far end of the bar, and Richard lit another cigarette. "That's the kind of mumbo-jumbo I hear down here all the time," he said. "A lot of the locals, and not just the addled hippies and New Agers, actually believe that shit."

"Maybe there's something to it," Seth said. "You can't deny other people's perceptions."

"There's more to it than you know," Martin said.

"I neglected to tell you," Richard said, "because I didn't think it worth mentioning, that the inn's an authenticated haunting, which means some Madame Arcati's claimed she's seen a ghost on the premises. Perhaps you'd like to hang out with the local mystics while you're here?"

"Not particularly," Seth replied. "I still feel you can't say something doesn't exist because you haven't experienced it." He helped himself to another serving of chips. "Let's blow this spooky joint."

Outside, the humid, leaf-scented air overwhelmed them. As they walked along the gravel path beside the inn, Richard's stride became a snaky weave. Seth eyed Martin, and they grabbed Richard to keep him from heading into the shrubbery. Richard stopped in front of the inn and turned to regard Chief Ferry atop his pole across the street. He pointed an unsteady finger at the weathervane and slurred, "Did you know that Native Americans considered themselves to be the caretakers of the planet?"

"You mean, like maintenance men?" Seth joked as he continued walking.

"I mean spiritually," Richard spat out, standing his ground. "They believed that protecting the Earth was their sacred duty. Whereas the invading Europeans behaved in the opposite manner. We're trying to alter the course of a river to cool man's most toxic creation, for crissakes. How much more out of whack can we get?"

Seth stopped and said, "I agree, we're out of balance."

"That Indian with the pole up his ass represents two very important things for me."

"Maybe the Chief likes having a pole up his ass," Seth said.

"Maybe *you* like having a pole up your ass. Am I right, Martin? But the Chief is not of your tribe."

Martin remained silent; he was uncomfortable with any open acknowledgment of his sexuality.

"The pole skewering him means he's been shafted big time. Just like what happened to the Native Americans. They were erased from this continent. It was a genocide, although no one calls it that. Everyone pretends the Indians went away to their reservations and lived happily ever after."

"You're right, Richard," Seth said wearily.

"And their destruction coincided with the loss of the understanding that we must nurture the Earth, since she provides all that's necessary for our survival. Instead, we destroy her at every opportunity."

Seth broke into a fit of drunken giggles and shouted, "Bravo, Richard! Another sermon to the choir."

Richard glowered, then let out a bellowing whoop of laughter. He lit a cigarette, inhaled, and said, "The Chief also symbolizes my commitment to saving something before it's wiped out. Every time I see him up on that goddamn pole, my belief in what I'm doing here is strengthened."

"That's great. Now can we go?"

Lurching forward, Richard said, "Follow me."

They walked along the deserted main street, past front yards obscured by trees and shrubs and shadowy houses with their lights extinguished. They turned off River Road onto a street that ran to the river. The night was purely dark owing to the lack of street lamps. After another block, Richard veered left onto a dirt path that led to a silhouetted structure in the distance. "Wait a minute," he called out, bounding unsteadily ahead, "I'll get the light."

Seconds later a blinding flash revealed the building at the path's end. Richard's bungalow resembled a Southern sharecropper's shack, down to the screened-in front porch with patches of mesh missing or torn away. It was a modest residence, but the rush of water over stones in the distance was soothing. A swarm of moths and mosquitoes buzzed around the porch light.

"Come in quickly," Richard commanded from inside. "The mosquitoes leave welts." Seth and Martin scurried across the wooden porch and dumped their gear onto the living room floor.

"Don't stand on ceremony, guys," Richard said. "I'm going to smoke a cigarette and hit the hay. I can't imagine how you got me so drunk." He gestured towards a threadbare plaid couch. "The sofa opens into a bed. There're sheets and a blanket on the chair. Bathroom's down the hall, one door before my bedroom. See you in the morning." He stumbled down the hallway with an unlit cigarette in one hand and an overflowing ashtray in the other and disappeared into the bedroom.

Seth and Martin made up the sofa, and Seth brushed his teeth in the bathroom, which smelled of mold. While Martin took a shower, Seth climbed onto the springy bed. Carelessly stacked piles of leaflets tucked into every corner, along with placards that read "STOP THE DAMN DAM," "NO TO NUCLEAR POWER," and "STARFIRE SUCKS" indicated that this was the headquarters of Damn the Dam. On the cluttered desk beneath the front window sat several dirty ashtrays, a heavily fingerprinted blue glass bong, and a pink marble cocaine slab, proof that Richard was planning to remain in Hope Springs for the duration of the campaign.

Martin got into bed, slightly damp and smelling of soap, and passed out, oblivious to the clattering window fan. Seth fidgeted on the thin mattress, waiting for sleep to descend in the unfamiliar darkness. He was dizzy from the alcohol, and had the queasy sensation of floating above the bed. He also felt the next day's hangover coming on. It would be a bad one, curable only by more alcohol. Meanwhile, his head was pounding as if a drill-wielding maniac was boring a hole between his eyes.

Three

Daylight streamed through the Venetian blinds that hung at a slant over the living room window. The light woke Seth as the headache of the night before surfaced. *And the party continues,* he thought. *I hope I live through this.* He climbed out of bed, swallowed two aspirin, and showered, while Richard and Martin drank coffee and ate bagels on the porch. Seth joined them outside; he was slow and achy, even after two cups of coffee.

Around one o'clock they left the cabin for Banbury, following a circuitous route into town. Flagstone cottages and wood-and-brick homes lined the residential streets. Each house included an ample front and back yard with long-established shrubbery and shade trees. The structures had the weathered patina of buildings that had been standing for centuries. The town was perfectly preserved, as if under glass, making it an ideal tourist destination.

Richard directed them down Ferry Street, which led to the bridge that spanned the river between Hope Springs and Banbury. At the foot of the bridge was a ramshackle, Sixties-style head shop called Past and Present, with tie-dyed T-shirts, smoking paraphernalia, and Fillmore East and West posters in the window. Seth pressed his face against the glass and said, "What a flashback to Haight Street! Maybe we can stop in on the way back."

"If you're still standing," Richard replied.

Crossing the bridge, a cantilevered jade-green structure with a metal roadway, Seth and Martin got their first uninterrupted look at the river. From the middle of the span, where they stopped to admire the view, the Orenda was nearly as majestic as the Mississippi. They stood at the epicenter of the Orenda Valley, which the water had carved out from the surrounding low mountains. Looking downstream, the sinuous river spread out before them, with tree-ladened fingers of sequential hillsides appearing into the distance. The vista was reminiscent of the tiny outposts of civilization surrounded by menacing forests in a Hawthorne tale.

"The Native Americans believed the river had magical properties because it flows over a bed of crystals," Richard said. "They called the river the Orenda, which means 'magic power.' The local tribe took the river's name as their own. There's a spring upstream where the tribe performed sacred rituals. When the white settlers arrived, they named it Hope Spring, although few knew the exact location."

Seth lingered mid-span while Richard and Martin walked ahead. He imagined General Washington's troops crossing the river on Christmas Day 1776 to surprise the Hessian mercenaries at Trenton. Staring into the blue-green water, he felt the past was present in some unspoken way.

On the far shore, they crossed a set of railroad tracks that paralleled the river, and walked along Bridge Street in Banbury, the New Jersey town the bus passed through the day before. They strolled past dusty antique shops, used book stores, and a run-down hotel with a rusted wrought-iron balcony that, across the river, would have been an upscale inn. There were several antiquated brick dwellings bearing historical plaques, but these buildings were unkempt. At the end of Bridge Street, they crossed a trestle that spanned a shady canal and tow path. Just past the canal was a wooded hill with roofs of houses rising above the foliage. They took a road that ascended the hill's steep right flank.

"Angelica Heights is the ritziest part of town," Richard said as they climbed. "The Yuppies have staked their claims here. In ten years, this side of the river will be as pricey as Hope Springs. No one's more of a Yuppie these days than Roger Prince, who's counting on making millions once his computer software company goes public."

At the top of the incline, Seth peered into a tangled wall of shrubbery. He jumped back when he saw a cluster of bats hanging from the branches. "Those things make my skin crawl!" he said.

"What do you expect? You're in the country," Richard replied. "They're God's creatures, like the rest of us. That is, if you believe in God."

"Yes, but they're an evil omen."

"You're sounding like the locals," Richard chided. "The Princes' house is up ahead. I should warn you that this party's notorious."

"Seth said this wouldn't be a traditional July Fourth picnic," Martin responded.

They turned onto Mandrake Road. Set on a corner plot was a two-story red brick structure with pointed eaves and diminutive windows. The main section of the house looked old, with two discernible additions tacked on to either side. The appendages provided the sprawl of a suburban home, although the tri-part disjunction suggested a structure with a split personality. Richard led Seth and Martin through a high wooden gate at the front of the house that opened into a hedge-enclosed yard. Voices shouting in laughter and conversation over booming rock music came from the rear of the house.

"Check out the view," Richard said.

Seth and Martin turned to find a sea of green hills that sloped down to the river. The Orenda snaked across the valley floor, crowned by a limitless blue sky. A faraway church steeple topped with a glinting gold cross lent a religious cast to the living painting before them. The steeple was bathed in the same opaque light Seth had seen at the Ferry Inn.

"C'mon guys," Richard said. "Let's party!"

Richard led Seth and Martin into a side yard where, upon a sloping lawn that rose toward a ring of tall oaks, revelers cavorted. They made their way through the crowd, skirting a whirling enclave of dancers whipped into a frenzy by the electrifying falsetto refrain of "Sympathy for the Devil." There were so many people milling about that they were forced to stop to orient themselves. Seth took in the scene from a spot half-way up the sloping lawn. He hadn't encountered this many beaming hippies since the Summer of Love in San Francisco, when he was a fourteen-year-old teenybopper. Back then, everyone was young, and the eccentricities of fashion and behavior were a revelation. Flowered shirts and capes on men, along with shoulder-length hair, exploded gender expectations. Braless women in paisley granny dresses, laughing and smoking a joint, seemed the epitome of human liberation. Now the once slim, sunshiny hippie chicks were bursting out of their appliquéd jeans and halter tops, looking more like their middle-aged, middle-class mothers than they'd care to admit. And the men, formerly reed thin from a rigorous diet of drugs, sported paunches that could no longer be hidden behind their tooled leather vests. The unguarded, smiling faces, lined and grown fleshy with age, were painful to behold, even as Seth felt a bitter nostalgia. The Sixties in San Francisco had traumatized him, although pleasantly so. Seeing the Airplane and the Dead, coming unexpectedly upon two men kissing while walking along Haight Street, driving home stoned from the Fillmore West through the fog, had shaped who he was. That moment in time had given him a sense of joy and unbounded love that was missing from his family life. From then on, he kept returning to that era by way of music, politics, and his stubborn refusal to conform. That decade was his touchstone. Yet watching all these people stuck in a bygone era was like gazing into a mirror and seeing the cruelly aging face of his own past. *I don't want to cling to the past*, he thought. *I want to live in the present, no matter how drab it may seem by comparison. There's got be to something meaningful to discover at every stage of life.*

Richard led Seth and Martin towards a free-form swimming pool full of bathers. "I see Beth in the water," he shouted over the din. From the pool's edge, he called to a sweet-faced brunette, "Hey, Beth, look who I brought! My gay friends from New York!" The guests within earshot pretended not to hear, but the curious averted glances indicated that the words had registered. Seth squirmed, and Martin looked furious.

Beth swam to the side of the pool and extended a dripping hand. "Glad you could make it," she said. "I'll get out and show you around." She blew Richard a kiss and swam to the deep end, where she climbed the ladder and grabbed a towel from a lawn chair. She wrung the water from her sun-streaked hair as she crossed the stone patio that surrounded the pool. Her wide moon face, with its long, aristocratic nose and gold-flecked almond eyes, opened up as she smiled at the newcomers. She looked younger than her years, not like Richard's contemporary. "I was wondering when you'd get here," she said. "The party begins at noon, but the doorbell rang at eleven. Roger's buddies from Davistown couldn't wait."

"We drank too many margaritas last night, and Seth couldn't get out of bed," Richard said.

"So that's your poison," Beth said. She led them to a long cafeteria table that served as a bar at the back of the house, navigating between the guests and two food-laden picnic tables. After instructing the bartender to use the Cuervo, Beth handed each man a drink. She raised her glass in the air and said, "Here's to wrecking your health."

"Hair of the dog that bit you," Seth replied.

Beth regarded Seth and Martin with an inquisitive smile. "I'd be happy to introduce you to my friends," she said.

"They'd love a guided tour," Richard said. "I'm going to excuse myself to do a little canvassing. Plus, there's this woman—" He turned and disappeared into the crowd.

"If you don't mind," Martin said awkwardly, "I'd like to find a shady spot where I can work on my screenplay," which he indicated by shaking the contents of his canvas shoulder bag.

"There's a table and chairs under the oaks," Beth said. "You can keep an eye on us from up there."

"I'm going to make the rounds with Beth and go swimming," Seth said evenly.

Martin gulped his drink and got a refill from the bartender. "See you later," he said before heading to the top of the yard.

Beth grabbed Seth's hand and led him through the crush of people. They were nearly to the brick barbeque on the far side of the pool when a woman who was sitting and nursing a drink at a lawn table jumped up and squealed an unintelligible greeting. "I've been looking for you all day!" she exclaimed in clearer tones. Her agitated state had left her breathless.

"Jesus, honey, calm down," Beth said. "You know how crazy it gets throwing this party. So shut up and give me a hug." The women rocked back and forth in each other's arms until Beth broke the embrace and said, "I've got someone I want you to meet. This is Seth. He's a friend of Richard's."

Seth extended his hand as Beth said, "This is Christy Swann. She's my oldest friend."

"What do you mean, oldest?" Christy demanded. "I am *not* your oldest friend. Richard is, or some of those gray-haired hippies, but not me!"

"I meant oldest in terms of how long I've known you. We went to high school together."

"Oh my God, how embarrassing," Christy said, turning red and fidgeting. "Nice to meet you. How do you know Richard?" She burst into peals of laughter that seemed closer to hysterics. She composed herself and blurted out, "So what if I'm drunk. It's a friggin' party and I can drink till I pass out if I want to."

"Honey, don't be so defensive," Beth said. "Just enjoy yourself. No one's keeping track of how many drinks you've had."

"I don't know about that. Every time I ask the bartender for another screwdriver, he looks at me like I've had enough. That son of a bitch also made fun of my hair. But I told him it was prematurely gray, that it came from the stress of my divorce and worrying about whether I could support my girls."

There was a discrepancy between Christy's youthful face and the wavy red hair streaked with gray that fell past her shoulders. Her cornflower blue eyes had a wildness to them that both attracted and repelled. Her simplicity of attire—a cotton peasant dress, a white stone heart on a gold chain around her neck, and leather sandals with straps that criss-crossed up her calves—gave her the look of a shepherdess or a priestess from another age.

"You shouldn't pay that bartender any mind," Seth said. "I like your hair. It's exotic."

"Gee, thanks. Who do you know here?"

"Seth's a friend of Richard's, remember?" Beth said.

"Oh yeah. I got confused." Looking intently as Seth, Christy asked, "Are you a militant revolutionary drug addict like Richard? You should know that I'm totally bourgeois, and you're never going to change me, so don't even try."

"I'm not a militant revolutionary anything."

"Then what makes you so special? Richard only hangs out with special people. I've certainly been made to feel that I'm not cool enough for him to notice."

"Maybe it's because I'm a writer and Richard's a writer. Or maybe it's because I came here with my boyfriend, and Richard specializes in social misfits."

"You're gay? What a waste of a good-looking man!" Christy screeched. "Where's your boyfriend? I want to see which one of you is the woman."

Beth glared at her friend. "Honey, I'm going to kill you."

Ignoring Beth, Christy insisted, "I want to know why such a cute guy would be wasting his time with a man when he could be having proper relations with any woman he wanted?"

"Let's put it this way," Seth said, "I've had sex with women and I've had sex with men. Over time, the men won out."

"Wow, I didn't realize you were once normal," Christy said, sounding flustered.

"I'm not finished yet. It's really none of your business what I do in bed. But you should give me credit for comparison shopping, which is more than straight people do when they put down gay sex without having tried it."

"I feel we're being cheated," Christy said with a nervous laugh. "There's a shortage of available guys. Of course I believe in your right to a sexual preference different than mine. I mean, one of my best friends is gay."

"No one says that anymore," Beth said. "You're really dating yourself."

"You're damn right I'm dating myself!" Christy exclaimed. "All the cute men are gay and I can't find a half-way decent guy to do me. So who the hell else am I dating but myself?" She erupted into a torrent of lewd laughter, which dissolved the tension in the air. She reached out and grabbed Seth's arm, saying, "Don't mind me. I always speak before I think."

"You might try it the other way around," Seth replied.

"I'm an amateur astrologer. I bet you've got a lot of water in your chart."

"Christy—" Beth interjected.

"How can you tell?" Seth asked.

"I have a certain psychic gift. But your emotionality and passionate nature are obvious. You should let me do your chart."

"I've had it done. I'm a Cancerian, with Pisces Moon and Scorpio Rising. But you probably knew that already."

"I'm a Cancerian, too," Beth said. "What a coincidence."

"I'm not sure how coincidental it is," Seth said, "since there are only twelve zodiac signs."

"It feels very coincidental to me. Synchronous, almost, to use Richard's word. But let's go for a swim. The humidity's killing me."

"Where can I change?" Seth said.

"Behind that tree, if you're so modest."

"I'm going to get another drinky-poo," Christy said. "I'll be right back."

Seth swapped his cut-offs for his swim trunks behind a Japanese dwarf maple. Leaving his clothes beside Beth's towel on a lawn chair, he followed her to the pool's edge. Beth jumped in, and he followed. "This feels great," he said. "Refreshing on such a hot afternoon."

The pool was nearly forty feet long, but was too crowded to swim, so they treaded water at the deep end. Christy joined them, settling herself poolside with a sweating plastic glass in hand. She removed her sandals and dangled her feet in the water, splashing unsuspecting bathers if they came too near. She was both vivacious and reckless as she clutched her cocktail, rousing herself to fetch Seth and Beth fresh drinks from the bar. She returned and set their drinks on the concrete lip of the pool.

Beth took a sip and said, "I can see everything from here!" She scanned the yard and giggled, "Christy, look who's coming over—Timmy Paley."

A lanky man dressed in a white linen shirt and matching slacks approached. His chiseled features and dark hair that fell rakishly over one eye suggested a model endorsing a men's cologne. The man's refined but wasted look appeared to be carefully cultivated, yet the dissipation seemed genuine. As he drew nearer, he appeared almost skeletal.

"Over here!" Beth yelled.

The man knelt at the pool's edge. He extended a hand to Beth, who rose out of the water and kissed him on the cheek. "I'd like you to meet Seth," she said. "He's from New York. Seth, Tim owns the Ferry Inn. He's my former employer."

Christy mouthed an obligatory "Hi," in Tim's direction before taking another swig of her cocktail.

"We had drinks at the inn last night," Seth said. "The bartender makes a mean margarita."

"I'm so glad you enjoyed the spirits," Tim said in an affected British accent. "You should come by and have a drink with me while you're here. I'd *love* to compare notes about New York. I go there every chance I get. Uncle Charlie's is a particular favorite." The last remark was accompanied by a hot glance.

"Thanks, but my friend Martin and I have to leave tomorrow."

"I see. And where, if I may ask, is your friend?"

"Under the trees being anti-social."

"Perhaps I'll walk over and introduce myself."

"Please do. Maybe you can bring him out of his shell."

"I love a challenge."

"With Martin, you'll get one."

"And how long have you two been *friends*?"

"Martin's my lover of seven years."

"Oh, I see. That's very interesting. Because if he's as handsome as you are, I'd really like to meet him. I'm always curious to see how people match up."

"Martin looks more like a straight jock. He's got the most intense blue eyes and a delicious little nose, and he's built like a linebacker."

"Oh, I *see*," Tim said, straightening the creases in his linen. "I'll just be off to the top of the yard then."

As Tim disappeared into the crowd, Beth said, "I cannot believe you had that conversation! You appear and he drops his guard and flirts like there's no tomorrow."

"I wasn't flirting," Seth said. "Maybe he just likes beautiful men, and couldn't help himself."

"Let's not be so modest, missy," Christy cracked. "We wouldn't want it to go to your head, now, would we?"

"I think it's already gone to his head," Beth said. "I'm just not sure which one."

Christy rocked back and forth with laughter, nearly spilling her drink into the pool. Pretending to be insulted, Seth splashed Christy, soaking her shift.

"Okay, that's enough," Beth said. She waved to her husband, who was stationed behind the barbecue pit. "Roger's sending the Grimmsleys and Delia over," she said to Christy. "I'm sure Raven will praise our patriotism for throwing the party. She says the same thing every year."

An elfin woman with closely-cropped brown hair and tortoise-shell glasses trailed behind a couple in their late-fifties. The wife wore a crimson silk dress. A black cape, with an oily sheen to it, covered her sturdy shoulders. Luxurious gold-orange hair curled down over the cape. The woman's emerald eyes, along with the red lipstick that was drawn across her wide mouth, heightened her odd appearance. In contrast, the husband, tall and thin, was clad in khaki trousers and a cream-colored cotton shirt. With his graying temples and fading matinee-idol looks, he was a dapper older gent.

"Beth, my dear, what a lovely patriotic gathering!" the woman called out in a theatrical sing-song. "I'm touched you thought to include us old fogies. After all, we don't exactly fit into your set. And we certainly don't indulge in *whatever* like your friends."

"I'm so glad you could make it, Raven," Beth replied. "This wouldn't be a real Independence Day without you and Stone. After all, you represent the Orenda Valley at its most historic."

"Are you saying we're relics, my dear?" Raven asked.

With an arm draped over the side of the pool, Beth answered, "Not at all. It's just that your families have lived here since the Revolutionary War, so you're a link to the past."

"Actually, we go back before the Revolution, but I suppose I know what you mean."

Playing the hostess, Beth asked Raven's husband, "Are you having a good time, Stone?"

"Yes, fine," Stone grumbled. "It's just too goddamned hot."

"How about you, Delia?" Beth asked the elfin woman. "Perhaps you'd like to take a swim?"

"No thanks," Delia replied. "I'm just a little concerned about Stone. You know he has his dizzy spells." She paused, then said, "I had a glass of that punch you're serving and nearly passed out. What's in it, anyway? You should mind that the seniors don't get hold of it."

"Thanks for letting me know."

"Aren't you going to introduce Seth?" Christy whispered.

"Of course," Beth said. "I'd like you to meet a friend of Richard Abbey's who's visiting from New York."

Raven stiffened at the mention of Richard's name. She leaned towards the pool and extended her hand. "How nice to meet you," she said.

Seth grasped her hand; she gripped his hand firmly before releasing her hold. He glanced into her glittering eyes, but was distracted by her jewelry. Each finger on each blue-veined hand brandished a ring of precious stones in gold settings. She wore antique silver bracelets on both wrists. A pear-shaped crystal the size of a chandelier drop hung from a filigreed gold chain around her neck. The crystal and chain appeared to be old, perhaps handed down through generations.

Raven, in turn, scrutinized Seth with a curious gaze, even though most of his body was under water. A glimmer of recognition flickered across her face. The look changed to shock, then to fear and anger. She regained her composure as she straightened herself up. "Yes, how very interesting to meet you," she said. "You remind me of someone. Now I must see my mates before we leave." She motioned her retinue to follow as she marched towards the house.

"What an unusual woman," Seth said.

"That's one way to describe her," Christy replied. She lifted her legs out of the water, rose unsteadily to her feet, and said, "I need another drink."

"Raven lives across the river in Upper Dark Hollow," Beth said. "She's the Hope Springs town historian. She's written two books of Orenda Valley ghost stories. I think they're called *Spirits in Our Midst* and *More Spirits in Our Midst*. She's also the leader of a Wiccan circle. Their mission is to protect the valley's ecology. She does good works for the Earth and the local community, but I'm never sure where I stand with her. One minute she's friendly—charming, actually—then out of nowhere she can turn on you. Roger's in her circle, and he told me she lost her mother as a teenager. She was not allowed to grieve or even cry. He thinks that's why her emotions are so repressed and unpredictable."

"I wonder who I reminded her of," Seth said.

"God knows. I should help Roger behind the barbecue. You're on your own now. Just mingle. Everyone's friendly." Beth hoisted herself out of the pool, grabbed her towel from the lawn chair, and left a wet trail on the stones as she crossed the patio.

Seth downed his drink and swam to the pool's shallow end, where he climbed the steps and wove his way through the crowd to the bar. He glanced at Martin sitting under the trees, marking up his script as if he were the only person in the yard. With a fresh margarita and a plate of pasta and salad in hand, he returned to the lawn chair. He ate and sipped his drink, while the sun dried him. But the humid air soon became oppressive. He carried his glass back to the pool's edge and set it on the concrete lip. He dove into the water and came within inches of landing on top of a swimmer. He surfaced, and the man who'd been behind the barbecue demanded, "Don't you look before you dive?"

"I'm sorry," Seth said. Treading water, he asked, "Aren't you Roger?"

"Yes."

"I'm Seth Davis, Richard's friend."

"If it were anyone else, I'd be angry," Roger said in a friendlier tone. "But I'll make an exception." He looked Seth in the eyes as he spoke.

"Why?"

"Because I wanted to meet you. You're a native New Yorker."

"I'm not a native. I grew up in San Francisco."

"You know what I mean. You live there. Everyone in the boonies wants hear stories about the wild life in the Apple, even in difficult times." Roger's handsome features grew animated as he spoke. His face, with its Roman nose and carnal lips was framed by a crown of dripping auburn curls that hung to his shoulders. Sporting a full beard, he resembled a youthful Bacchus. Like his wife, he looked a decade younger than Richard.

"It's not for everyone," Seth said. "At least you're not starved for nature down here."

"We're starved for other things. There's always a trade-off." The conversation slipped away until Roger said, "How about we do a few laps? Then you can tell me about the Apple."

They shoved off the deep end in unison, leaving a translucent blue wake behind them. Roger swam ahead, bathers clearing to the side as he went. It took Seth a nearly a length to synchronize his breathing with his flailing arms and legs. He caught up with Roger on the third lap, finally able to pit himself against his host. His hand touched the lip at the shallow end; he turned around, planted his feet on the floor, and dove through the air, gaining a slight lead. Roger increased his speed, and the two men swam neck and neck for another length. Seth propelled himself along, gasping for breath as his arms clawed at the water. The friction of the water against his sides drove him forward, and the waves coming off Roger's body urged him on. They kept up their pace for another two lengths until Roger cut his speed. He grabbed the pool's side and stopped, hanging on and panting. Seth's hand hit the edge at the same instant, and both men, as if they read each other's minds, ended the race.

"It's a tie," Roger gasped. "I'm surprised I couldn't beat you. Maybe you're tougher than you look."

"I am," Seth wheezed. "And don't forget it."

"I wouldn't have guessed it." Roger climbed out of the pool and shook the water from his limbs. He stroked his torso and arms with an outstretched hand, then performed the same ritual to his muscular thighs and calves. He lay alongside the pool in front of Seth, who remained in the water, his arm slung over the side. "Will you keep me company?" Roger said. "I want to catch my breath."

"Of course."

An uncomfortable silence descended. Seth reached for his glass, which Roger had placed in front of his belly, and took a sip of his cocktail. He locked eyes with Roger, who was staring at him in a detached yet forceful way, as if trying to peer into his mind. Seth averted his eyes to the dusting of dark hair on Roger's chest. He followed the trail down to the forest that swept upwards from Roger's red swimsuit, which clung to his body like a second skin. Seth's penis thickened inside his trunks. They gave each other sly, wordless smiles before Roger closed his eyes to block out the late-afternoon sun that was shining in his face. Pitched slightly forward on his side with his head resting on an outstretched arm, Roger seemed to be offering himself up as the main course on a feast table. The crotch of Roger's nylon briefs began to expand. As the heft of Roger's penis strained the brief's capacity, Seth's cock hardened. When his member couldn't get any bigger without escaping the swimsuit, Roger opened his eyes and stared at Seth. The sun glinted off his brown orbs, igniting leaping reddish flames in his pupils. He growled,

"It's yours whenever you want it," then rolled onto this stomach, suppressing his erection from view.

Seth did not respond. Roger smiled and watched a woman with long white-blonde hair parading around the pool in a Day-Glo orange bikini and gold mules. She stopped every few feet to lean provocatively over the water. Whenever a swimmer invited her in, she purred, "Not in this suit, sweetie," and moved on.

Roger sat up and waved his hand, calling out, "Diana!"

The woman terminated her latest dalliance and sashayed over. Towering above Roger with legs akimbo, the blonde Amazon knelt down and gave him a lingering kiss. She regarded Roger's crotch as she broke their embrace and cooed, "If I'd known you were that happy to see me, I would've come over sooner."

"That's all right," Roger said coolly, his look signaling Diana to be more discreet. "You're here now, and that's what matters." Roger turned to Seth, his cock still standing at attention, and said, "This is Diana Spector. She's my gal Friday."

"Actually, I'm his computer operator and telephone answering slave," Diana sniffed in a low voice.

Roger eyed Seth and whispered to Diana, "Remember that three-way we've been talking about?"

"Ooh!" Diana gurgled. She gave Seth a hurried once over and said, "I'm going to get a drink. See you later." With a shake of her shapely rump, she sauntered off towards the bar.

"She's a handful," Roger said. "She's a demon in bed, and she'll try anything."

"I guess you've met your match," Seth replied.

"I'm getting closer," Roger said with a wink. "There's a lot more to Diana than meets the eye. You'd never guess that she's the best spirit caller in the county."

"What's that?"

"Someone who summons spirits to do their bidding."

"You're joking."

"No, I'm not. When you call spirits, they come. They're waiting in the wings to be summoned into the physical realm. Diana's highly skilled at contacting them."

"You can't prove that."

"Watch the fireworks tonight. After that, I won't have to prove a thing."

"You're awfully cocksure of yourself."

"Damned straight," Roger replied. He reached over and forced his index finger inside Seth's mouth before Seth could pull away. "I've got to make sure Diana stays out of trouble. Catch you later, buddy." He rose, adjusted the contents of his swimsuit, and disappeared into the crowd.

The sweet smell of marijuana wafted across the yard as the guests milled about on the lawn. *How did I stumble into a rural soap opera?* Seth wondered. *What is it about life in the sticks that makes people come so unhinged? Either they drink too much, do too many drugs, or become pansexual athletes.* He watched the guests eating, drinking, and smoking in a flurry of circular motion, caught up in an eddying pool of time. *Do the same people come back year after year? And do they do the same things over and over again?*

ℋ

Seth climbed out of the pool, retrieved his clothes, and refreshed his drink at the bar. He joined Martin, who sat in a white Adirondack chair in the shade of the oak trees annotating his *Trick or Treat* screenplay.

"You've been gone for hours," Martin said, barely looking up from his script, a knock-off of *Halloween*.

"I met some strange characters," Seth replied.

"Like whom?"

"Beth's friend, Christy, who can drink you under a table." Martin gave Seth a sharp glance, but said nothing.

"Then I swam laps with Beth's husband Roger, who got a hard-on and told me it was mine whenever I wanted it."

"He did no such thing!" Martin said. "You're just trying to distract me."

"I can't believe you're worried about being distracted in the middle of a party." Lowering his voice, Seth added, "Roger really did proposition me."

"I suppose you took him up on it. There're plenty of bushes around here. Does he have a big one?"

"As a matter of fact—" Seth said, dissolving into a fit of laugher.

"I'm glad you think it's funny, but I don't like that I can't trust my boyfriend."

"And I don't like you implying that I'm some sort of tramp."

"From what I know of your past, anything's possible."

"That's crap, and you know it." After a moment, Seth said, "You better get some food before it disappears."

"I'll get another drink while I'm at it."

Seth changed out of his damp swimsuit into his cut-offs and Hawaiian shirt. Martin returned with a plate of food and a margarita, and Seth sprawled on the lawn at his feet as he ate. The clammy moistness of the grass penetrated his clothing, each blade welcoming him back to the earth. As day faded into twilight, a calm settled over the party. The sun, momentarily suspended above the treetops, suffused the sky with a salmon-colored glow that placed everything beneath it—trees, shrubbery, and houses—in stark silhouette. A celestial energy, which belonged to neither day nor night, was revealed.

"Look at the sunset," Seth said.

"It's beautiful," Martin replied and leaned down to discreetly kiss Seth on the cheek.

"I almost forgot," Seth said. "Did Tim come by?"

"I don't remember his name," Martin said between mouthfuls of potato salad, "but I glared at him, and he went away."

"Good job. That was the owner of the Ferry Inn."

"Oh, well."

ℋ

Richard spent the afternoon stumping for Damn the Dam. He shared an occasional joint as he canvassed the guests, and made several trips to the bar. He kept an eye out for the woman who worked as the cashier at the New Age bookstore in Hope Springs. He'd seen her around town, but had never had a chance to meet her. As the sun set, he spotted her talking to Beth. He extricated himself from his latest conversation and hurried through the crowd.

Beth smiled as he approached and said, "There you are. I hope you haven't done too much damage."

"Not nearly enough," Richard replied.

"Have you met Blanca Naughton? She works at Bell, Book and Candle."

"Pleased to meet you," Richard said.

"Likewise," Blanca replied.

"Richard is spearheading the Damn the Dam campaign."

"So I've heard," Blanca said. She wore tight faded jeans and a flimsy halter top. Baby's breath was wreathed into her long, flaxen hair, and the scent of patchouli emanated from her. She flashed a guileless smile at Richard and turned her buoyant bust in his direction.

"I'll let you two get acquainted," Beth said. "I've got to check on the food."

"I'm all talked out about Damn the Dam," Richard said, smiling through his beard.

"Sorry to hear that. I'm a member of a group with a commitment to ecology, and we may be able to lend support."

"Which group is that?"

"The Circle of Light coven. Raven Grimmsley is our leader."

"I've heard of the local coven, but never knew much about it. You don't put curses on people, do you?"

Blanca laughed. "Don't be silly. We don't curse anyone. We're Wiccans who worship nature and the seasons. The magic we practice, which is a form of prayer, is positive, for the benefit of humanity and the planet. Our group is dedicated to saving Mother Earth."

"Then we have similar interests."

"I think so. We serve the Orenda Valley community. One of our members is a teacher of parapsychology at Davistown University. Tim Paley owns the Ferry Inn. And Roger, in case you didn't know, is a member. He breeds an endangered species of salamander to keep them from vanishing."

"I had no idea."

"We've helped turn the valley into a tourist destination. We sponsor the Hope Springs Psychic Festival, as well as the ghost tours and haunted hayrides. Five years ago, we fought to stop construction of a shopping mall that would have destroyed a park on the outskirts of town."

"That's impressive. Would your group support an anti-nuke cause?"

"Of course. We've celebrated sabbats and performed magic to that end, pouring earth over maps of nuclear power plant sites and waste dumps to psychically cleanse them and return them to their rightful purpose."

"Right on!"

"I can't speak for the coven as a whole, but I'd like to learn more about the issues. Once I have a better understanding, I can present it to the group. It may be possible to get the support of the Wiccan community behind Damn the Dam."

"That would be terrific!" Richard said, beaming at Blanca. "I've been trying to build local interest, and this could help, especially if Circle of Light is so highly regarded."

"Do you have any literature?"

"I handed out my last flyer. Why don't I stop by the bookstore? Are you working tomorrow?"

"Yes. We're open until six."

"I'll come by at closing. Maybe we can get a bite to eat and I can give you some background then."

"I'd love that."

"So would I."

ℋ

Around nine o'clock, the orange sky dissolved into a muddy sea of clouds, and night fell over the yard. Paper lanterns embossed with red, white, and blue flags flared to life on the patio. Guests circulated with lit candles, which they placed around the pool, the barbecue pit, and the dance area on the side of the house. Roger planted two Tiki torches at the back of the lawn, retreated inside, and reappeared carrying a box of fireworks. Through the darkness, two figures approached Seth and Martin at the top of the hill.

Clutching a glass in one hand, Christy said, "We looked all over for you."

"How's the work coming?" Beth asked.

"Not bad," Martin replied.

"We should move down to the lawn," Beth said. "You don't want to miss the fireworks. Roger always puts on a good show."

Martin stowed his script in his shoulder bag, and they clambered down the incline and stationed themselves in front of the torches, which gave off oily tongues of flame. Diana steadied the rocket launcher so Roger could pound it into the lawn with a wooden mallet. Wearing cut-off jeans and a white T-shirt knotted under her breasts, she appeared subdued— she'd switched on another personality. Roger mounted a candy-striped rocket into the launcher, and Diana retreated into the blackness that fell beyond the torchlight. When the torches sputtered flame in her direction, her closed eyes were cast heavenward, eyelids fluttering like moths.

"Friends, it's time for the fireworks!" Roger announced.

A slow migration of people commenced from the house and front yard. Some guests picked up candles and used them to illuminate their way, like pilgrims heading to a shrine. When everyone assembled on the lawn, Roger said, "Beth and I would like to thank you for coming. This is the first time we've held the party in our new home. We hope you enjoyed the pool!"

The crowd whooped and whistled its approval.

"Without further ado," Roger said, "let the fireworks begin!" He leaned over and lit the fuse on the candy-striped rocket, which lifted off with a whizzing sound and disappeared into the starless sky. Nothing happened, and a dissatisfied murmur passed through the crowd. The rocket suddenly burst into a galaxy of gold sparkles that expanded outward in several rings from its nucleus, and the startled guests dutifully applauded.

Roger positioned a rocket with "Red Devil" stenciled on its side into the launcher. He lit the fuse and the rocket took off, seconds later emitting a loud double-boom along with a hail of red sparks. As the fiery embers cascaded to earth, the backyard was bathed in an infrared glow. The guests cheered their approval. When the hooting died down, Roger said, "The Red Devil never fails to satisfy."

"Just like you, Roger!" a woman's voice cried out.

Martin nudged Seth and whispered, "You've got competition."

Roger fired another missile, which burst into a halo of sapphires and diamonds. He launched two more rockets in quick succession, then said, "That about wraps up the main event. I've got one more rocket and some pinwheels you can nail to the trees at the top of the yard. As an accompaniment to the grand finale, Diana will hand out sparklers."

Roger placed a red, white, and blue missile with "God Bless America" emblazoned across its nose into the launcher. Diana distributed sparklers and matches, and returned to his side. He told the crowd, "Light your sparklers and hold them overhead, like the Statue of Liberty."

"That's so goddamn hokey," Richard yelled from across the yard.

"It's only for effect," Roger replied.

Diana slipped into a shut-eyed trance as Roger lit the fuse. The rocket rose into the air and, moments later, a deafening explosion filled everyone's head with confusion. In the instant following the blast, a brilliant white light flashed across the sky, creating the impression of broad daylight. The effect lasted only seconds, but during the pulsing of the white light, time—and people's hearts—stood still. A cold terror descended upon the crowd, as if they'd been transported to Hiroshima when the atomic bomb was dropped.

The night sky flashed brighter than day once again. As Seth's eyes adjusted to the light, an image appeared before him of a man angrily approaching him. He moved through the night with force and fury, ready to attack. As the man reached Seth, he stretched out an arm, as if to grab Seth by the collar and pull him to the ground. Seth's heartbeat quickened, but there was no pain, and just as fast as the man appeared, he vanished. Seth blinked, assuming his eyes and the light were playing tricks on him, but a stench hovered in the air around him. He looked down at his feet, thinking he stepped in something, but his sandals were clean. When he remembered how much he'd had to drink, and how bright the explosion was, he banished the notion of spectral hallucinations from his thoughts.

Time started up again as the rocket burst overhead, sending out red, white, and blue sparks that shot towards the heavens before gracefully falling through the warm night air. The explosion brought the guests back to their senses, a reminder that this was a homemade fireworks display, not an atomic blast.

"Hey, Roger, how'd you do that?" a voice called out.

"Trade secret," Roger replied. He glanced at Diana, who looked like she was shaking off sleep. She gave him a cursory smile as her face twitched.

Murmurs of "I wonder how he did that?" and "That scared the shit out of me" ran through the gathering. A line of guests bearing candles meandered towards the house, the party's mellow spell broken by the fearful explosion. "See you later, Roger," some said, while others found Beth in the darkness and hugged her good-bye. Cries of, "Meet us at the inn in half an hour," indicated the party would continue into the night.

Seth said to Martin, "Let's find Richard and go."

"Before Big Boy really blows something up," Martin replied.

"I'll check the yard," Seth said. "You look in the house. I'll meet you inside in ten minutes." He waited until Martin had gone before approaching Roger, who was handing out pinwheels and sparklers to the remaining guests.

"What on earth caused that explosion?" Seth asked.

"What do you think of spirit calling now?" Roger said.

"I don't believe a spirit caused that blast."

"Of course a spirit caused it. I could never buy fireworks that powerful. Diana asked the fire elemental that lives in the yard to add a charge to the rocket. As you saw, the explosion was supernatural."

"That's one explanation. Anyway, thanks for an eye-opening party."

Roger extended his hand. Seth shook it, and Roger drew him close and tried to kiss him. Seth wrestled himself free. "See ya," he said shakily, stumbling towards the house.

Seth found Martin in the white-tiled kitchen chugging a beer, avoiding a circle of partiers sharing a joint. They walked through the darkened dining room and entrance hall into the candlelit living room, which was populated by people standing in groups, drinks and cigarettes in hand. Two black-leather sofas were placed at diagonals in front of a stone hearth. Over the mantle, illuminated by votive candles, hung a painting of a sprite swathed in diaphanous drapery. Richard sat hunched over a bong on one of the sofas. He looked up at Seth in slow motion. "You've got to try this shit," he croaked in a smoke-roughened voice. "It'll blow your mind."

"No thanks," Seth said. "Are you about ready to go?"

A pained expression peeked through Richard's beard. "I can't believe you're crapping out on me," he said. He passed the bong to Martin, who rebuffed the offering. Turning to Seth, Richard cajoled, "Have a hit for the road then."

"All right," Seth said. "What harm can it do?"

Richard handed the bong to Seth and rasped, "Knock yourself out."

Seth put his thumb over the carburetor hole, brought the bong to his lips, and sucked in the smoke, a mixture of high-grade marijuana and hashish. His lungs expanded, and he felt an instantaneous buzz as he exhaled. *The perfect end to a surprising day,* he thought, as his legs buckled. He handed the bong to Richard and collapsed onto the sofa.

"Are you okay?" Richard asked in a bleary voice.

Seth gave Richard a woozy look. He slumped against the back of the sofa and sank into the cushiony leather as both his stomach and his mind spun out of control. The room faded to black. When he came to seconds later, he said, "It's time to go." He stood up, only to fall back onto the sofa. He emitted a sickening gasp and spewed the contents of his stomach onto a coffee table littered with plastic cups, plates, crumpled napkins, and half-eaten hors d'oeuvres.

Beth, who was ushering guests out the front door, raced over. "Honey, what happened?"

"I'll clean it up in a minute," Seth said with a sickly grin.

"You'll do no such thing. July Fourth isn't complete until someone pukes. It's like waiting for the Fat Lady to sing." She ran to the kitchen and returned with a bucket and some rags. As she sopped the mess into the bucket, a stream of pale green liquid flew from Seth's mouth, narrowly missing her. "That's it, buster," she said. "You're obviously not capable of walking, and I won't have you vomiting all over my car. You can sleep here on the futon."

Seth was so nauseated he couldn't object.

Beth retrieved a packet of incense from the mantelpiece, lit several sticks, and placed them in the potted plants around the room before taking the bucket into the kitchen.

"Do you mind if I leave?" Martin asked. "You'll be fine here, right?"

"Go ahead," Seth said sullenly.

"Meet me at Richard's tomorrow and we'll catch the noon bus back."

"If I can walk."

"Poor, poor boo," Martin murmured. He and Richard said good-bye to Beth and left.

When the last of the guests departed, Beth said, "Let's get your bed ready." She unfolded a futon that was nestled in an alcove next to the hearth, and made it up with bedding from the hall closet. Roger walked through the living room and climbed the staircase to the second floor, avoiding eye contact with Seth. Beth fluffed the pillows and surveyed the wreckage of her party. "I can't deal with this mess tonight," she said. "I'll clean it up in the morning. There's a bathroom off the front hallway. I left the light on."

"Thanks," Seth said. "I'm sorry I ruined your table."

"Don't worry about it. You'll feel better in the morning." Beth walked to the sofa and gave Seth a sisterly kiss on the forehead. "Sleep well."

As Beth mounted the stairs, Christy materialized from the darkened dining room. "Where is everybody?" she asked.

"Where have you been?" Beth said, leaning over the railing.

"Looking at the stars," Christy replied. "They finally came out."

"Party's over for this year, hon. Good night."

"I'll call you tomorrow," Christy said. She regarded Seth slumped on the sofa and slurred, "Looks like you had one too many drinky-poos," before hurrying out the door.

Seth rose unsteadily, crossed the room and, without undressing, collapsed onto the bed. He rested his head on the pillow, which gave off the stuffy smell of a cedar closet, and relaxed into the futon pad. He closed his eyes and fell into a black vortex that swallowed him whole.

ℋ

Violent coughs woke Seth in the middle of the night. He opened his eyes, but couldn't distinguish anything in the darkened room. A terrible hacking penetrated the gloom; Beth was making the choking sounds, as if her breathing had been cut short. She cried out, "Hester's not here anymore!" followed by a silence so deadening it seemed that the pulse had gone out of the world.

An edgy awareness jolted Seth fully awake. His heart raced as something glided down the stairway from the second floor. He couldn't see anything, but sensed an energy moving towards him. Then he smelled it. The acrid odor of burnt, dead leaves forced its way up his nostrils, singeing his mucous membranes and the back of his throat. The same smell he had detected earlier on the lawn. Tears sprang from his eyes, and he began to cough. The sulfurous scent was so sharp, so piercing, it seemed three-dimensional. *It's not of this world,* he concluded before the burning stench expanded inside him, closing his windpipe. He thrashed about trying to catch his breath, and a heavy dampness that carried the smell of dank graveyard earth and rotting shrouds blanketed the room. *The walking dead,* he thought, as his heart beat faster.

The silent intruder drew nearer, its tingly electrical energy chilling Seth. The force field prickled his skin like a traveling patch of nettles. His body grew numb. He told himself, *Empty your mind. Think of nothing that will identify you.* But the *thud* of his heart pulsed wildly inside his chest, and his heartbeat could betray him. Lying paralyzed on the futon, there seemed to be no body of flesh and bone between his soul and the thing that was three feet away. *I'm dead if it finds me.*

The spirit force glided past him into the dining room. As the prickly energy dissipated, Seth lay motionless, terrified to move. Only when he relaxed his clenched muscles did he realize, *The alcohol's been shocked out of my system. I'm sober. I'm awake. I didn't dream this.* In a horrifying flash of intuition, he understood, *That was a ghost. An old, powerful ghost.* He sat upright. *It was a man, the one I saw in the yard. And he was looking for something he couldn't find.* He wondered if Beth could hear his thoughts and would pad downstairs to minister to her guest. But no light flashed on upstairs. *The stench is what made Beth choke. The spirit was upstairs with Beth, then down here with me. He became disoriented and left.*

Every nerve in his body was alive, and he jumped at the unfamiliar house's creaks and groans. With eyes now accustomed to the dark, he scanned the room for movement. Nothing stirred, and he understood that the ghost wouldn't return. He stifled a hysterical laugh at the idea of going back to sleep.

An hour later, as the dawn cast a pale light through the sheer curtains that hung at the living room windows, his eyelids grew heavy, and he sank into the sweat-drenched mattress. He drifted into his second sleep with a queasy feeling in his stomach. His nausea came from the thought, *The ghost was looking for me.*

ℋ

Seth awoke to the sound of running water coming from the kitchen. The ghost sprang back into his mind and his body jerked at the memory of its harsh odor. Not wanting to give the incident too much credence—although he didn't disbelieve it—he dismissed it. He got out of bed to wash up in the bathroom and found Beth in the kitchen, arms immersed in a sink full of suds. "Thanks for taking care of me," he said. "That was kind of you."

"Even though you puked all over my living room," Beth said, flashing a smile.

"So this is my last July Fourth party?"

"Don't be silly. I'm sorry you got sick. But I'm glad I met you. You're always welcome to visit. Just give me advance notice."

"Thanks. I always forget to get out of the city before it drives me crazy."

Beth mentioned that she had followed the news reports of recent demonstrations, gay activists targeting the large pharmaceutical companies. Seth nodded, acknowledging that it added another layer of fear and complexity to big city life, as he recalled the loss of a co-worker the year before. They exchanged phone numbers, and Roger bounded into the kitchen dressed for work in a beige sport jacket and brown slacks. "We never talked about the Apple," he said. "Maybe next time."

"If there is a next time," Seth said.

"I'd drop you at Richard's, but I'm going in the opposite direction," Roger said as he walked out the kitchen door.

Beth escorted Seth outside to the street. She pointed him towards Hope Springs, and he waved to her as he descended the hill.

H

Seth entered the screened-in porch where Martin was drinking coffee and reading the *Freeman Patriot-Times.* Martin glanced up from the paper and said, "Welcome back from the dead."

"Where's Richard?"

"I don't know. He walked me back last night, then took off. He said if he didn't return before we left, he'd call us in the city."

"Where does he get his stamina?"

"Drugs."

They packed their bags, and Seth scrawled a note for Richard on a Damn the Dam flyer, which he placed under a magnet on the refrigerator. After securing the screen door behind them, they headed down the gravel path and turned onto the street, walking through patches of shade and sun. Already the air was heavy, and rivulets of sweat ran down their faces.

On River Road, they passed the colonial tourist traps that ran the length of Hope Springs. "Don't you think there's something distasteful about exploiting America's heritage, especially now, with all the greedy materialism out there?" Seth asked.

"There's nothing wrong with making a buck," Martin replied.

"To me, it's false patriotism. The Reagans embody the notion of money and social position as the pinnacle of American ambition."

"What else is new? Money and social standing have always bought influence. You just need to be the person with the money to buy what you want."

"Arts funding has been cut under Reagan, and homelessness has exploded. Artists and people who fall through the cracks are considered outcasts and failures. Just sweep them aside, as if they don't exist."

"Art is a business, Seth. Don't be naïve."

They reached the Mobil station and crossed the street to the New York-bound bus stop, demarcated by a green wooden bench. The Orenda Valley coach pulled up a few minutes later.

They boarded, and the bus crossed the Orenda and entered New Jersey. After climbing a steep grade and leaving Banbury, they traveled along a two-lane road for several miles. Seth observed the countryside fly by the dusty windows. The green hills and farmland lulled him into a trance that rendered the landscape unreal. As he was about to slip into an open-eyed slumber, that *thing* popped back into his memory and punched him awake. He glanced at Martin as he listened to *The Magic Flute* through his headphones. He wanted to tell him about the ghost. But Martin's response would be: "That weed was soaked in acid. You were hallucinating. That's why I never smoke dope."

Seth spent the remainder of the journey debating whether or not the encounter had occurred, until the looming spires of Manhattan brought him out of his reverie. The island of skyscrapers, looking like a real-life Oz, was a majestic vision which always drew him back.

❦

Seth and Martin moved underground through vast subway corridors and along the Forty-second Street platform. A train pulled into the station, and they sat in discomfort in a car without air conditioning. "There's no place like home," Seth said.

It was no cooler upon entering their apartment—the moist, stagnant air was so thick it was difficult to breathe. Seth threw his weekend bag onto the captain's bed and took a cold shower before getting ready for work. An hour later, while sitting on an uptown F train, the unexpected strangeness of the Orenda Valley and its colorful inhabitants returned. *How ridiculous*, he reasoned, *if I believe that ghosts are real, then I also have to believe in goblins, sprites, trolls, and gremlins. I might as well embrace "A Midsummer Night's Dream" as a waking reality. The next thing you know, I'll believe in the bogey man.* As he walked into *New Day*'s lobby and pressed the elevator button, he erased all experience of gliding phantasms from his mind.

Four

The night following the July Fourth party, Raven Grimmsley paced the living room of her home in the sunless woods of Upper Dark Hollow on the Pennsylvania side of the Orenda River. Dressed in a gray shift, and wearing her crystal pendant, she turned on two Chinese lamps with blue and white porcelain bases on either side of an L-shaped sofa. "Darkness usually helps me concentrate," she muttered, "but tonight it's too gloomy to bear." Although she was approaching sixty, her skin was as clear and unlined as that of a woman half her age. Her luxuriant red-gold hair, inherited from her mother and grandmother before her, had hardly any gray.

Raven was a hereditary witch who could trace her lineage, and the accompanying psychic skills, back several centuries. She was descended from a family of Scottish witches, the McWyckes, from Auldearne, in Morayshire. Her ancestors were astrologers, herbalists, psychics, and mediums, all highly skilled in the occult arts. She was fond of pointing out that she was a *real* witch, not a new-fangled Wiccan. One of her ancestors, Polly Andrews, had been tried for witchcraft during the witch hunts. Her family were devotees of the Old Religion, Europe's pre-Christian faith that worshipped nature and the seasonal cycle. The Goddess and the God—Diana and Faunus—were revered as the dual powers of the universe, akin to the Chinese Yin and Yang. Also similar to Eastern philosophy was the Old Religion's belief in reincarnation and karma. One's actions, good or bad, returned three times over in this lifetime and determined one's next life. Seeking religious freedom, members of her family emigrated to the New World in the late seventeenth century after securing a land grant from William Penn, and had remained in the Orenda Valley. They maintained the Circle of Light coven through the centuries; Raven was the current High Priestess. The coven was devoted to sustaining nature's equilibrium, and in the current century sought, through spellcasting, the protection of Mother Earth from the hazards of the industrialized world. More and more they felt they were fighting a losing battle.

Raven had known adversary in her life, challenges which she had always surmounted. The death of her mother when she was a teen. The abandonment of an infant under difficult circumstances. And the steady loss of what was once a family fortune, until she and her husband were forced to survive precariously on loans and credit cards. As she approached the stone fireplace, where her pet raven, Rah-wing, slept on a perch, his head tucked beneath a pitch-colored wing, she said, "I hate to disturb you, but I need your insight."

The bird peered out of one eye as if to say, "I sleep, my lady."

Using the telepathic powers that had been taught to her from an early age by her father, Raven formed her thoughts and mentally projected them toward Rah-wing. The transmission was akin to broadcasting a radio signal to a receiver. *I've never had such a shock. Help me sort this out. What have I done to deserve such difficult karma?*

As Raven's animal familiar, Rah-wing had a unique relationship with his mistress. Raven raised him from a chick, and he bonded with her as a child does with his mother. The energy link between them was based on absolute trust and mutual love. That link proved to be psychic. Raven could mentally tap into Rah-wing's biology, using his avian spirit to magically attune with the Goddess and the rhythms of nature. She could communicate telepathically with her pet, and the bird understood most of what she said, both aloud and mind-to-mind. In response to her request, the bird mentally replied with his own desires, *Give me drink and grubs, I am hungry.*

Raven went to the kitchen and prepared the bird's food and water cups. She returned and mounted them in their holders on the perch. Rah-wing devoured a worm as Raven said, "I saw someone yesterday at the party. I can't be sure, but it could be him."

Who is him?

"This is silly. I'm making myself sick over nothing. I must have been hallucinating from the heat. Or maybe it was the punch. How would I know what he looks like now?"

Despite their psychic connection, Rah-wing was unable to respond to the ramblings of his mistress, vacillations which preceded every decision. There had been many such uncertainties lately, given the Grimmsleys financial worries and the protracted struggle to lease a parcel of McWycke land to Orenda Power and Electric for the Starfire nuclear plant site.

"When I saw him in the pool and shook his hand, a chill passed through me. I knew it was him. My intuition is rarely wrong."

Who is him?

"If I say it out loud, perhaps I'll know I'm wrong and can forget the whole thing."

Ajax?

"Of course not. Why would a spirit appear in a pool? Even if he can materialize under water, what would be the purpose? I sent Ajax to investigate last night, but he came back with nothing to report."

Rah-wing nibbled on a worm and took a sip of water.

Raven sighed and said, "I think I met my son."

Rah-wing cocked his head. *I am your son.*

"Yes, my pet, you are my son. But many years ago I gave birth to a child and had to give him up. I'm sure I told you."

Don't remember. Not important.

"It's very important. Why would he come back now? And why through the Princes and Richard Abbey?" A stricken look passed across Raven's face, causing her to frown. "I've had so many difficulties, I can't bear a new one. Isn't trying to maintain a traditional Dianic coven enough of a battle? Constantly fending off the mates who want to introduce neo-paganism and radical faerie Wicca into the circle is exhausting. The Old

Religion will not be bastardized! And the money worries are draining. We are barely scraping by. Selling the plots of land will help. Leasing the land to the power plant is the long-term solution, but construction could be blocked. Can't anything ever run smoothly?"

Stone the father?

"No." Raven regarded her familiar with tears of frustration forming in her eyes. She grew defiant, and said, "The father is—"

Rah-wing looked expectantly at his mistress.

"Someone I had an affair with when I was too young to know better. My father and aunts and grandmother guided me so carefully in my studies, and I nearly threw it all away. I was rebelling, I suppose. In a way, I chose well, but dangerously. The man was a magical adept. He taught me things that, given the slightest imprecision of will or direction, could veer off into black magic. That both terrified and fascinated me. Back then I referred to him as the 'dark stranger.'"

The Beast?

"Aleister Crowley?" Raven laughed skittishly. "My family knew him, but no, he was too old and perverted. Someone close to him. A master of the Kabbalah, among other disciplines. I never told him about the child. I disappeared to San Francisco to give birth." Raven clutched the crystal and closed her eyes in an effort to focus her thoughts. "I always wondered what powers our child would have."

No worries, my lady. He'll not return.

"But that's just it. He may return at any time. It's worrisome that he's connected to Richard Abbey. I won't have him joining the movement to muck up the power plant." Raven held out her hand for Rah-wing. The bird hopped on her finger, then jumped to her shoulder, where he nestled against her cheek. "The problem is also a secret. I gave up my son for adoption because he was born out of wedlock and I was too young to keep him. But the real reason I got rid of him—killed him off, you might say—is that he's the rightful owner of the family land. He would have inherited all the property at twenty-one. This is family law. Even back then, I knew enough to see that our dwindling finances wouldn't last. I needed to secure the future for myself, and didn't want any heirs coming into my entitlement."

Not your son, Rah-wing declared.

"I hope you're right. In any event, he's been dead to me all these years. This sounds horrible, but he must remain dead." Raven stroked her pet's neck, massaging the inky feathers as Rah-wing bent his head. She sat down on the sofa. "There's no use jumping to conclusions. Perhaps the man in the pool had a similar vibration to my son. What are the odds he would turn up?"

I see something, past and future, Rah-wing said.

"What, my pet?"

Glowing child with golden hair. Radiant boy, youthful and fair. Mother took his life away. If child returns, mother pays.

Raven sat back, stunned. "Radiant boy, radiant boy—" she mumbled. "That's not the radiant boy. The radiant boy is a glowing spirit who appears in the middle of the night. Whoever sees the boy becomes wealthy, then dies a sudden death. What does a mother have to do with it?"

What I see, mistress.

"That makes no sense. The more I think of it, the more I know the man I met could not have been my son. It's too improbable. My perceptions were off. I've spooked myself for nothing."

Glowing child with golden hair. Radiant boy, youthful and fair.

"Don't taunt me! I'm sure it wasn't him. You're a bad boy, scaring me with silly rhymes."

Glad we could talk, mistress. Sleepy time now. The bird's eyes drooped shut and he lost his footing, nearly slipping off Raven's shoulder.

"Go to sleep, sweetheart."

Raven rose and returned Rah-wing to the perch. She paced the living room, uttering a makeshift prayer while shutting off the lamps. "O Great Goddess and Wise Lord Pan, guide me in these treacherous times. Shine your merciful Light on me. Let me pass through the gates of wisdom again and again. Blessed be."

She lapsed into a melancholy silence. The late hour was catching up with her. She slipped down the hallway to her bedroom at the rear of the house, shutting the door behind her. She and Stone had slept separately for years, another troubling aspect of her existence. After drawing the heavy damask curtains, she took off her shift, hung it in the closet, and placed the crystal on the night table beside her. She slipped into a cotton nightgown, climbed into bed, and nestled beneath the sheets. She soon drifted into an uneasy sleep.

In her dreams, a spirit child surrounded by a halo of light reached out to her. The naked angel had emerald eyes that matched hers and flowing red-gold hair. Raven extended her hand to touch the boy. She received an electric shock and pulled away. She stirred and opened her eyes, then settled back on the pillow.

The boy approached again, encased in orange and green flames which rose up from a crescent moon. His body glowed bright through the flames, diminishing them with his aura. "The coming of a fairy boy, radiant in visage and true to himself, brings great fortune and a sudden fall," the boy whispered.

Raven tossed in her sleep. "I didn't kill you. I saved you," she murmured.

The boy wailed pitifully, and blue flashes of light shot from his hands. A blue halo framed his face as he said, "You birthed me and killed me and buried me in the forest to hide your shame. Or was it to gain my share?"

"No, child," Raven replied, "if I had you now, I would feed you and dress you and shelter you like the most loved of children."

"You murdered me!" the boy insisted.

"For your own good," Raven mumbled in her sleep. "You could never know your father. Too dangerous."

The boy loomed upwards and emitted sapphire sparks and orange flames from his body. "If the child returns alive, beware, the mother dies!" he said.

Raven sat up wide awake, her heart pounding. She held her hand to her chest, trying to catch her breath. The one thing in the world she didn't want to accept she now knew was true.

Five

Over the next week, the heat wave abated, and temperatures fell into the mid-80s. The Northeast had endured a trial by fire like the one that climaxes *The Magic Flute*. Whenever Martin blasted that opera from the living room stereo, Seth was reminded that Mozart was a Freemason, an adherent of an arcane, mystical belief system that practiced secret rituals and revered a Supreme Being. Seth knew a little about Freemasonry, largely what Martin had told him when discussing Mozart's opera. Even so, trials by fire, the existence of a Deity, and realms beyond the visible world baffled him. If he was ever forced to confront these issues, he would have no foundation upon which to build a reliable response.

One part of Seth rejected religion outright, as he'd come to reject the Reformed Judaism in which he'd been raised by his adoptive parents. Another part of Seth—the one that read Martin's occult books with a sense of wonder—reasoned that the notion of God was something that had eluded him. Following his Bar Mitzvah and confirmation, he abandoned Judaism. He knew that if he'd been brought up Christian or Muslim, he would have rejected those faiths as well. Organized religion seemed small-minded. There were plenty of rituals and rules, but nothing of the divine mystery—the sacred flame—that must lie at the heart of all faith.

As a teenager, he'd undergone a spiritual awakening that pointed him towards something more nebulous, a belief system that was being established by the counterculture and the New Age movement. If Judaism had anything to offer, he imagined, it must lie in the hidden teachings of the Kabbalah. But no one gave him access to these mysteries. It didn't matter that Jewish law forbade the teaching of the Kabbalah to anyone under forty; he felt unfairly excluded from true revelation, and offered only an empty ritualistic shell in its place.

Now, as he looked back, he wondered if he'd missed the boat across the River Jordan to Paradise because he'd been too busy rejecting social conventions to allow something as numinous as the Divine to make its presence known. In renouncing all that society imposed on him, he had automatically dismissed the supernatural. If he hadn't been so thorough in his rebellion, he might have possessed a belief in something.

ℋ

One evening about three weeks after his visit to the Orenda Valley, Seth lay in bed beside Martin, unable to fall asleep. *Where did the fire go?* he despaired. *It was so hot at the beginning, then everything became routine. The passion vanished.* He blamed Martin; life's simple pleasures became a casualty to his screenwriting career. He never blamed himself, yet hadn't he started to look longingly at other men? At what point did his harmless flirtations begin to diminish his desire for Martin? And at what point did his constant need to test his attractiveness shunt Martin into the background?

He recalled Beth's invitation to visit. He was certain she was only being polite. It would be awkward if he got in touch, yet the idea of returning to the Orenda Valley was appealing. Beth's pool and the river beckoned. A swimming weekend would tide him over until he and Martin traveled to England in September. *It'll be weird seeing Roger again*, Seth mused. *Not that I'd ever cheat on Martin. But—* He nodded off in the middle of the thought.

ℋ

Seth dialed Beth's number the next morning. Roger answered the phone, and without identifying himself, Seth asked to speak to Beth.

"Hi, it's Seth Davis." he said when Beth picked up.

"Hi," Beth replied, sounding confused.

"Remember me?"

"Of course," Beth said with a laugh. "I was wondering just last night if I'd ever see you again. Are you in town?"

"No. I'm in the city. How's everything?"

"Good as can be expected."

Seth paused before saying, "I was hoping your invitation to visit is still open."

"Absolutely. When did you have in mind?"

"I don't want to sound like a pushy New Yorker, but how is next week? We have an early close at the magazine, which means I'll have a four-day weekend."

"Let me think. Yes, that should be fine. Roger's always off doing his thing, so it will be you and me and Christy, if she isn't on call."

"I'm looking at the bus schedule. I can be down Thursday around noon."

"Great. We can go tubing down the river."

"I was hoping to swim in the river."

"It's a blast. Bring some old tennis shoes. You'll need them to walk on the riverbed."

℀

The bus ride to Freeman County was a mirror image of Seth's first visit, except this time he was alone. He observed his face reflected in the bus window, with the blur of greenery outside superimposed on top. The odd double-vision of his sea-green eyes, auburn hair, full lips, and strong cheekbones set against a verdant natural mirror captivated him. He imagined himself older, with a beard of leaves, his lean, six-foot frame shrunken with age. He was reminded of Jean Cocteau's cinematic Orpheus, who enters the underworld by touching his rubber-gloved hand to a looking glass. At his touch, the magic mirror turns to water, allowing passage into Death's realm.

The Orenda Valley bus pulled up in front of the Mobil station just after noon. Seth stepped outside, and Beth came forward and hugged him. Standing behind her, Christy said, "I hope you appreciate that I took the day off work to be with you."

"After lunch we're going on a three-hour tubing expedition," Beth said as they walked to her blue Malibu, which was parked off River Road towards the center of town. They drove across the bridge to Banbury and up the hill to Beth's house, where she showed Seth to his bedroom at the end of the second floor hallway. He unpacked, placed his toiletries in the adjoining bathroom, and walked downstairs to the kitchen. Beth stood at a butcher-block island preparing a chef's salad. Christy sat at a table in the corner sipping a beer. The women had been gossiping, but Beth cut short the conversation and said, "We've been experiencing some poltergeist activity in the house lately."

Seth looked at her blankly. The memory of that *thing* stirred, but did not fully rise to the surface of his awareness.

"The corners of mirrors are breaking off, and glass over pictures is cracking. I've been meaning to get some smudge sticks at Bell, Book and Candle, but every time I'm in Hope Springs, I forget."

"How do you know that what's breaking the glass is a poltergeist?" Seth asked.

"The glass has been hit by a specific force," Beth said as she set the table. "This force breaks off pieces in exact shapes—triangles and circles. The glass covering the picture over the mantle looks like it was hit by a BB, which is another manifestation. Since prankster spirits do this sort of thing to call attention to themselves, I'm guessing that a poltergeist is to blame."

"I believe you when you say you think you have poltergeists, but I find it hard to accept that such a thing exists."

Christy remained aloof, silently serving the salad. "I wanted you to know," Beth said, "in case you notice anything out of the ordinary. And I should tell you that Roger and I are splitting up. We've filed the divorce papers and we're going to put the house on the market as soon as we spruce it up."

"I'm sorry," Seth said.

"Don't be. This has been a long time coming, and I'm relieved now that the decision's been made."

"Are you sure the glass isn't cracking from the hostile vibes between you and Roger?"

"No, it's poltergeists."

After lunch, Christy went upstairs to change, while Seth and Beth lounged on the leather sofas in the living room. Beth put on the new Prince CD, *Lovesexy,* saying, "It's about the place where sexuality and belief in God meet, with a dose of the supernatural thrown in."

"Prince is a genius," Seth said.

"I agree."

When, after three songs, Christy hadn't materialized, Beth strode over to the staircase and yelled, "Get a move on, Swann! We're going to miss the three o'clock bus!"

"Be there in a minute," Christy hollered. "You can't rush beauty."

Seth joined Beth at the staircase and shouted, "Especially if it's not there in the first place!" He let out a wicked laugh and smiled at Beth.

"You should be nice to her," Beth said. "She's had it rough."

"I'll try, even though she's a homophobe."

"She's been through a lot, working and raising her girls on her own. Nursing's a tough profession. It's taken a toll."

An eerie hush fell over the house. Seth looked at Beth, and she returned his perplexed expression. They seemed to be standing inside a bell jar with all the oxygen removed, cut off from the world of the living. Sounds were amplified to an unbearable level—the intake and outflow of breath was like the ocean's roar. A weighty book entitled *Secrets of the Realm* that was lying on the stairs slowly rose into the air without any visible means of support. Beth eyed the levitating volume and held out her hand. After flipping over in slow-motion, the book landed with a gentle thud in her outstretched palm. Beth glanced at the book, then at Seth, and said, "See what I mean about the poltergeists?"

H

Beth parked the Malibu in a rock-littered dirt lot reserved for Blithe Point tubers. Clad in swimsuits, loose T-shirts, and beat-up tennis shoes, Seth, Beth, and Christy walked towards a cluster of red barns. Glimpses of the Orenda appeared through breaks in the tall grass and trees that lined the riverbank. They stopped in front of the central building to select innertubes from a mountain of rubber resembling a tire graveyard. Lulled by the waves of humidity that came off the river, they boarded a dusty yellow school bus and steadied the tubes between their legs.

The driver, a frat boy wearing cut-offs and a muscle T, gunned the engine and turned onto River Road, which above Hope Springs became the more prosaic Route 10. The bus careened along the frequent bends of the river at a dangerously high speed. They penetrated a forest of giant maples, red cedars, and mossy apple trees that allowed the sun through in sprinklings of mottled emerald light. A patch of flowering dogwoods and a copse of white oaks gave way to weeping willows that dipped their limbs into the river.

The bus pulled off the road and stopped in a muddy clearing. "Everybody off!" the driver yelled. "Have a good trip!" They disembarked and scrambled down a slippery hillside to the pooling water of the riverbank.

"Three hours on the river, with the hole in the ozone, can give you a nasty burn," Beth said as she passed around a tube of sunblock.

They waded into the water and struggled to position themselves inside the innertubes. Following Beth's example of throwing herself rear first into the tube, soon all three floated downstream, caught in the river's lazy current. They paddled towards the middle of the river, and the craggy cliffs that demarcated the valley came into view. The riverbanks were awash in green foliage. The water was clear enough to see the mossy rocks and pebbles at the bottom, along with schools of tiny fish.

Seth recalled an episode that he couldn't explain when it occurred a year earlier. "Do you want to hear a dream I had?" he asked.

"Sure," Beth said, steering her tube in his direction.

They reached the center of the river, which widened dramatically, creating the illusion that they were adrift on a substantial lake. "First of all, you should know that I'm adopted," Seth said.

"If you'd let me do your chart, I could tell you the karmic reasons for that," Christy said.

"When I was in high school, I made a half-hearted attempt to obtain my birth records, but they were sealed, so I gave up. I figured I could live without knowing my birth parents."

"Weren't you curious?" Christy asked.

"Yes, but I accepted that I'd probably never find the truth about my origins. What else could I do?"

"Was it difficult being adopted?" Beth said.

"Yes, for all the obvious reasons."

"Such as?" Beth asked.

"It bothered me that I didn't resemble my parents or my sister. I felt like I didn't belong anywhere, since I had no identity. Not being grounded in a bloodline made me feel invisible. When I visited my parents in San Francisco last summer, my father said he wanted to talk to me. He took me aside and told me about his stretch in the army during World War Two and how it had been the most meaningful time of his life. Then he asked me to keep the medals he'd been awarded, including two Purple Hearts, and I realized that this was the reason for our conversation."

Seth was distracted by a floating branch that butted into his tube. He grabbed the wood that bore a few leaves and flung it off to the side. "Out of the blue, my father asked me if I'd ever consider using 'Seth Van Wyke' as a pen name. Wondering where that came from, and knowing I didn't want to be named after an expressway, I said no, I was content with my given name. He said, 'I mentioned "Van Wyke" because that was the name of your birth mother." I was so stunned I could hardly breathe. I felt like I'd been punched in the stomach."

"Were you aware he had that information?" Christy asked.

"No. Both my parents denied knowing any details about my birth parents."

"That's bad karma," Christy said, "pulling something like that."

"Later that night I dreamt I was four years old, back in the dining room of our house in San Francisco, which had wall-to-wall carpeting. I ran the carpet sweeper back and forth over the same spot in a repetitive motion. Something snapped, and I stepped through a hole in time and entered another dimension. Are you following me?"

"Yes!" Christy exclaimed.

"The instant I entered this other dimension, an entity hurtled through space and crashed into me with such force I thought I was going to die. I let out a scream that woke me, and I was moaning as I came back into consciousness. Even though I was awake, the dream continued, and I understood that the entity had crashed into me to kill me. But my essence was stronger than it anticipated, and the entity obliterated itself against my energy field, my aura."

"That's heavy," Christy murmured. "I once read a book that said that adopted children are more susceptible to hauntings and possessions than children raised by their natural parents."

"Why is that?" Seth asked.

"Because they have no one of their own flesh to protect them from the evils of the world."

"What's really heavy is that as the dream continued, I realized the entity was my birth mother. I saw bits of her floating down from the sky. She'd turned into perfect little flames, the kind in Tibetan religious paintings with three orange fingers blazing out of a semi-circular base. The flames fell through the sky like ashes, hit the horizon, and burned out. When they were all extinguished, my mother was gone. I had killed her."

An uneasy silence descended, broken only by the gurgling water and the overhead snap of branches that, a few seconds later, plunged into the river. They drifted along aimlessly, surrendering to the sun's warmth and the current's liquid embrace.

"Do you think that was an out-of-body experience?" Christy asked.

"I'm not sure what it was," Seth said. "But it did feel like I'd crossed into another realm. Are there other realms of existence?"

"Of course!" Christy said. "They intersect with our reality all the time. What do you think astrology is? It charts the invisible influence of the planets on our lives. It's as real as you and me tubing down this river. And as real as the universally accepted fact that the moon governs the tides. If human beings are made up of seventy percent water, wouldn't it only make sense that the moon exerts a strong pull on us, too?"

"I suppose," Seth replied.

The river narrowed as they traveled downstream, strengthening its flow. Sitting astride the tube, Seth slipped into the water. He slung one arm through the tube's center and unfurled his body in the river, riding the current as he glided past the shoreline.

"Want to hear my story?" Beth asked.

"Is it a dream?" Seth asked.

"No, it's the story of this river. It will give you a better appreciation of the Orenda Valley if you know its history. For example, are you aware that this was one of the first inhabited areas of the country? Inhabited by Europeans, that is, since the Native Americans were always here."

"Sounds like something Richard would say," Seth said.

"It's common knowledge that William Penn established land grants here, and that English settlers arrived in the middle of the seventeenth century. But the first Europeans to reach the area in the early 1600s were the Dutch and the Swedes. They traveled upstream to what became the Orenda Valley. What they found was a wilderness full of buffalo, black bear, panthers, foxes, timber wolves, and bobcats. Most of which have been hunted to extinction, analogous to the Native Americans, who were last seen here at the end of the eighteenth century."

"How do you know all this?" Seth asked.

"When Roger and I were looking to buy a house in Banbury, I read up on the area. The Dutch and the Swedes prospected for iron ore, silver, and gold. This continent has always been seen as an El Dorado, to be ransacked without concern for its inhabitants or its ecology. Of course no one had heard of ecology back then, but the Europeans' avarice is shocking. And the greed that brought them here continues today. Look at Yuppie culture, which my husband has embraced. It's all about driving a stinking Mercedes and becoming a millionaire by the time you're thirty, without regard for whom, or what, you destroy in the process."

"What a wide-ranging reading of history!" Seth teased.

"I think it's interesting," Christy said.

The trio fell silent, captivated by the river grass and stooped willows that slipped past, along with the cliffs that towered overhead. Seth struggled back into his tube and trailed his hands in the current.

"Is there more to your story?" Christy asked.

"It's worth mentioning," Beth said, "that since William Penn was a Quaker and a peaceful man, he treated the native inhabitants fairly."

"That's bully for him," Christy said, "but the men who came after did an about-face."

"You're right," Beth replied, "because the last forty Orenda Indians of the Black Bear clan moved westward to the Ohio River Valley in 1775. Their homeland had been bought out from under them."

"I will concede," Seth said, "that it saddens me to think an entire population was wiped out to make way for a civilization whose apex is the shopping mall."

"Thank you," Beth said.

Christy and Seth maneuvered their tubes to face Beth. "You're forgetting something," Christy said. "At the end of his life, Chief Ferry witnessed the Running Purchase and had a premonition of what was to come. He cursed this area, making it a place of doom for anyone who settled here. Right after the Native Americans left, that fire they're always talking about burned Hell's Ferry to the ground."

"With the natives out of the picture," Beth said, "Freeman County became one of the cradles of the American Revolution. Many battles were fought here, and countless soldiers are buried in the fields and cemeteries around the county."

"Which is why the area is so haunted," Christy said. "Those soldiers died violent deaths, and their souls were never properly put to rest. I read a newspaper article that said Hope Springs is the most haunted place in America, and the Ferry Inn is Ghost Central."

"After the Revolution," Beth continued, "Freeman County became a beehive of industry, all of which exploited the area's natural resources. Trees were felled, tied into rafts, and floated down river to market. Quarries were dug to unearth the limestone, flagstone, and granite that's so abundant here." Beth took in the vista of water, weathered cliffs, and sky and said, "I think you'll agree that this valley's a beautifully preserved haven where parts of the primeval forest still exist. But you're wrong to think that nature's protected here. Because this river used to be full of bass and trout and terrapin turtles, but where are they now?" When no one responded, she said, "Depleted by overfishing and pollution, that's where. So I applaud Richard for trying to stop the dam, which would destroy whatever life remains in the river."

"You've brought history full circle!" Seth said.

"That's just the way I see it."

"You left out the river's occult aspect," Christy said. "The Native Americans were aware that a network of spring-fed streams flowed into the Orenda. They also knew there was an abundance of spirits here, and believed the Orenda Valley was a magical place. Spirits need energy to manifest in our world, and water makes it easier for them to cross the veil between their realm and ours. The river, streams, and canal are sources spirits use to reveal themselves. The native inhabitants worshipped a

water elemental—Ariel, I think—who lived in a cavern beneath the Great Spring, what's now called Hope Spring."

"But what specifically makes the river magical?" Seth asked.

"Crystals. The combination of a major river flowing over a crystal bed that runs for ten miles makes this a monumental place of power. The Orendas considered crystals to be a sacrament from the earth. They ground them into powder and baked them into a kind of bread. They felt that by ingesting crystals, they'd absorb their psychic and healing properties. They also wore crystals to protect against negativity and to balance the body's energy flow."

"I think the river's psychic power affects dreams," Beth said. "As soon as we moved to Banbury and I started working at the Ferry Inn, I had these recurring violent dreams about a little girl. In them, I walk up a staircase with a woman who's related to the girl. I open the door to a bedroom where the girl is sitting in an old-fashioned high cradle. When she sees us, she rants and rages. She's livid. She hops out of bed and picks up a rifle. She hides in an alcove and starts shooting. It's all we can do to dodge the bullets."

"That's the entire dream?" Christy asked.

"That's what happened at first. It progressed to another stage where I tell the girl, 'You'll be all right. There's a place you can go where you'll be happy again.' I ask her if she wants to go there. Finally, she says yes, so I tell her that if she puts down the gun, I'll help her get there. She looks at me with a tearful expression and throws the gun to the floor. I take her by the hand and we walk outside, where we stroll along the river that runs in front of her house. I look up and see her standing on the other side of the river. She waves good-bye and vanishes. After that, I never had the dream again."

"You helped her cross into the Light," Christy said.

"Perhaps. I picked up the girl's surname, which came to me in a combination of consonants and vowels. Consonant, vowel, double consonant, vowel, consonant. 'Middleton' or 'Chatterton,' or something like that."

"Do you think the girl was once a living person?" Seth asked.

"After I had the dream for about a month, I mentioned it to Tim Paley. He said, 'Oh, don't you know? The inn's an authenticated haunting, and one of the ghosts is a little girl. She's led several people to their deaths in the canal behind the inn. They follow her, she pushes them in, and they drown.'"

"What a charming little miss!" Christy said. "Did you know that Groves Corner, twenty miles south of here, was the Philadelphia League of Spiritualists' summer resort in the nineteenth century? Countless ghost-hunters, séance-holders, and table-lifters came to the Orenda Valley to commune with the spirits. It doesn't surprise me that Raven's coven found a home here." Glancing over her shoulder, she added, "We're about to head down the rapids ass-backwards."

They spun around to face downstream as they sped towards a line of rocks that, from a distance, barely broke the river's surface. The far-off whoosh of water rushing over stone could be heard. The current slackened, depositing them in a shallow pond in front of the protruding rocks. They drifted until they reached the first of the huge river boulders and were pulled forward by the cascading water.

Sitting inside his tube with legs held high, Seth was tossed into the air by the leaping water, only to fall back into the current, aerated tide churning against his bottom. He bobbed down the rugged course for several hundred feet. The rushing water tossed him about; if he was thrown from his tube, he'd be smashed against the jagged boulders. He hung on, and the falls deposited him back into the current, spinning in circles, as the river resumed its normal flow. "That was fantastic!" he called out, laughing.

The current eased once they rounded the next bend. The river opened into an expansive bay. Seth scanned the water and woodlands and said, "This landscape is a natural wonder."

"Which is why it shouldn't be destroyed," Beth replied.

They drifted further into the bay, and Seth was overcome with a peacefulness induced by the watery environs. He slipped into an open-eyed reverie and saw the Orenda as the Black Bears' holy river, like the Ganges is holy in India. He imagined that bathing in its waters had purified him, and perhaps blessed him. The trip was a baptism, an initiation, into the river's secret realms. The water, vegetation, cliffs, and roiling rapids had each revealed their mystery. It was now up to him to understand what he had been shown.

The red buildings of the Blithe Point tubing facility came into view. "Land ahoy!" Beth said. They struggled to their feet in the knee-deep water, upended their tubes, and waded towards the shoreline thirty feet away. This was the most difficult part of the excursion, since walking on the slippery river rocks was treacherous.

ℋ

Beth drove to a roadside farmers market and bought silver queen corn and vegetables for the frittata she'd planned for dinner. When they returned to Angelica Heights, the sun was hovering above the treetops. Seth squeezed limes and made margaritas, while Beth started cooking. Christy excused herself, saying she wanted to get home before dark. She hugged her friends and drove off into the twilight. An hour later, with drinks and plates in hand, Seth and Beth went outside to the poolside patio to eat. Seth positioned a ring of citronella candles around the wrought-iron table, lit them, and said, "I've got some hash upstairs if you want to smoke."

"I don't do drugs anymore," Beth replied. "But go ahead if you want to."

"I don't really need it. I'm pretty mellow from the river. After your party, I should probably lay off drugs altogether." Relaxing into his chair and sipping his cocktail, he said, "Can I ask you something?"

"Sure."

"Are you a vegetarian?"

"I try to be. But I slip up occasionally."

"I'm a veggie, too. I've lost my taste for meat, so I don't slip up."

"I figured you were vegetarian from what you ate—and threw up—at the party."

"There's something else I'm curious about."

"I hope it's not as personal as your last question," Beth said with a laugh.

"How'd you end up in Banbury?"

"I had a connection to the area. I grew up in Davistown, which is the county seat of Freeman County. My father taught economics at the university there."

"Richard mentioned that he met you at the Chicago Democratic convention."

"That was a lifetime ago. I've blocked a lot from that era, because my brother, who introduced me to Richard, went underground and disappeared. I haven't seen him in seventeen years."

"It's hard to imagine you as a radical."

"At this point, *I* can't even imagine it. I realized after that phase was over that I defied my parents before I defied political authority. I was a wild teenager. I gave birth to my son Kit out of wedlock when I was seventeen. That's his room you're staying in."

"That's pretty young."

"To add fuel to the fire, Kit's father was a Hell's Angel who abandoned me and the baby."

"Your parents must have loved that."

"They convinced me to put Kit up for adoption, but at the last minute I couldn't go through with it. I literally got sick and knew I had to keep him no matter what. That's why I was curious about your being adopted. I don't see how it's possible to give up a child."

"Kit's lucky you kept him."

"It wasn't easy. I raised him on my own until I met Roger."

"At least he knows who his mother is. I've always felt abandoned, and as a result, I regard myself as unlovable. Otherwise, why would I have been given up? At some point

I realized that all the people I've chosen as romantic partners have been incapable of returning my love. So it becomes a self-fulfilling prophecy."

"If you're aware of it, you can change it."

"It's not that easy. When I was younger, I filled the void with lover after lover. But I saw that that was a bottomless pit, and there was nothing that could ever satisfy my longing for love. Not a thousand lovers, or ten thousand. Sex is an addiction that keeps you coming back for more."

"And now there's all the danger involved."

"No one ever said it was going to be easy. Now, it's just more complicated."

Beth nodded and turned to the table, saying, "Don't let the food get cold."

"I'm sarcastic to cover up what a shrink would call my congenital wound. Being flippant about things keeps the pain of rejection at bay—and inflicts pain in return. Just ask Martin. He thinks I'm a bitch." Seth tasted the frittata and said, "That's delicious! Where'd you learn to cook?"

"I've always been an instinctive cook. To get out of the house, I've taken kitchen jobs, which is how I came to work at the Ferry Inn. But Roger's old-fashioned about his wife having a career."

"I'm surprised."

"There's a lot about Roger that would surprise you. His thing about me not working makes me wonder how much of the Sixties actually registered with him. I think he was just out for a good time. Instead of confronting him on the work issue, I became what I call a spiritual housewife. I did psychedelic drugs, transcendental meditation, Rolfing, est, A Course in Miracles, you name it. Hell, I even did bodybuilding!"

"All in the name of enlightenment."

"Absolutely! Now that Kit's away at college, I'm studying reflexology and homeopathy. I can prescribe an herb that soothes sprained muscles and alleviates constipation, which is great if you're ever crippled and shitless at the same time." Beth let out a hooting laugh like a tropical bird's call.

The kitchen door slammed, and Roger approached through the shadows. "I ate at the office," he said.

"I'm sure you did," Beth answered with a trace of sarcasm.

Roger shook Seth's hand and excused himself to change clothes. He reappeared wearing a black silk shirt and black linen trousers. He pulled up a chair next to Seth and said, "How's New York?"

"Stressful."

"Where's your boyfriend?"

"He couldn't make it. He's on deadline."

"We've got Seth all to ourselves, honey," Beth said. "Isn't that nice?"

"It's what I've always wanted," Roger replied. He abruptly rose, saying, "I'm going to meditate," then receded into the darkness. Seconds later the kitchen door slammed.

"That's about the extent of our communication lately," Beth said. "I was hoping he'd move out of the bedroom and onto the futon downstairs, but so far that hasn't happened."

Seth walked inside to refresh their drinks, while Beth served another helping of the frittata. They lingered over the meal, planning an excursion to Hope Springs in the morning. They brought the dinnerware to the kitchen, and Seth retired to Kit's room, where he brushed his teeth in the adjoining bathroom. Before getting into bed, he turned on the fan that rested on an old steamer trunk at the foot of the mattress. The fan rattled loudly, but he dropped off to sleep, his relaxed body carried along on the soothing currents of the Orenda into the land of dreams.

Six

All Seth could see was a man being strangled in close-up. A gurgling sound of water or blood bubbling through a constricted passage accompanied the image. Wavy black hair and dark, fathomless eyes flashed out of a tangle of rushes beside a riverbank. The face, twisted in agony, was distorted beyond recognition. Two hands encircling the neck were the sole evidence of an assassin.

Seth saw a boy dressed in knee pants and a brown jerkin standing helplessly by as the hands tightened, forcing the eyes to bulge out of their sockets. The mouth gaped open in an attempt to breathe and scream, but released only a choking rattle. A blistering terror coursed through Seth's veins, scalding him from the inside. Feverish and damp, he twisted in the bedsheet. The stabbing pain of strangulation broke through the heat and wracked his body. It felt *sharp* to be murdered, like being stuck with a battery of knives. As the pain reached a threshold beyond endurance, his flesh convulsed in a series of contractions.

The unknown victim reappeared, the face a mask of pain, only to surrender his will to live. He went slack and collapsed to the marshy ground in slow-motion, an untethered scarecrow returning to the earth. As he fell, Seth's agony dissolved into a peaceful nothingness. He snapped out of the dream as the man was about to die. Instantly awake, a cold sweat rose over his body. He opened his eyes and scanned the bedroom, but could not distinguish anything in the dark. He fumbled for the lamp on the nightstand and switched on the light. Nothing appeared out of the ordinary—the fan hummed loudly at the foot of the bed; the clock read a few minutes past four. He got up, walked into the bathroom, and urinated. He climbed back into bed, turned off the light, and pulled the moist sheet over himself.

As soon as he fell back to sleep, an acrid, burning odor jolted him awake. A tingling energy like prickly pins-and-needles spread across his body, nauseating him. The blanket of nettles came from a different vibrational level altogether; it was heartlessly cold. But it was the sulfurous stink of moldy, dead leaves which singed Seth's nostrils, teared his eyes, and contracted his windpipe that indicated he was in the presence of a ghost. Not just *a* ghost, but *the* ghost that had previously glided through Beth's living room. Only now the apparition was hovering over the length of his body. Lying prone on his back, he was trapped—paralyzed and mute. The spirit's pungent, burning vapor began to choke him. He gasped for breath, but refused to open his eyes, for an intuition welled up and warned, *Seeing that thing will scare you to death.* The ghost pressed downwards, wrapping him in its otherworldly chill. Invisible hands forced his legs apart and caressed his inner thighs. He nearly swooned as an immaterial finger slid inside him, stretching and burning his anal canal.

A sulfurous wind scorched his nostrils and stung tears from his eyes as he sank into an airless void. Stinking breath grazed his ear, and a disembodied voice inside his head hissed, "So, you've come back, my boy!" He jumped, and was pushed deeper into the mattress by the ungodly energy. His breathing was impaired by the monumental yet weightless strength exerted against him. His breath, when it came, was in tight little gulps. *It's trying to suffocate me.*

"Breath of life, my boy?" the voice inside Seth's head inquired. "You'll draw breath again only if you serve me—and save me."

Seth guessed that the ghost could read his thoughts. He screamed inside his mind, *Go away! Go away!* The spirit only laughed while continuing to flatten him into the mattress. He thought the sound of his voice might frighten the ghost away. But when he opened his mouth to scream, he emitted a low-pitched rasp: "Ahhhh! Ahhhh!" he squeaked, no louder than a mouse in a trap. *Go away! Go away! GO AWAY!* he hollered in his mind.

He mouthed the words at the same time, eventually getting his voice to work, though the words croaked out haltingly. "GO AWAY! GO AWAY! GO AWAY!" he shouted. *Beth and Roger must hear me. Why don't they come to see what's wrong?*

Yet he wasn't certain whether he'd actually screamed, or if he'd merely spoke inside his head. He couldn't tell on what level of reality he was functioning as he tried to summon up something he wasn't sure existed. Was he hoping to access a hidden resource in his soul that he'd never needed before? Or a previously untapped power that would well up? As he lay quaking in the dark, he accepted his own psychic strength and spit out a fierce "GO! A—WAY!" The command engendered a split-second impression of Keta, the Native American guide from his dream.

The spirit rose off Seth's body and glided to the other side of the room. Its stench wafted away, allowing Seth to breathe. He opened his eyes, raised his head on the pillow, and saw a play of glowing amber lights against the far wall next to a chest of drawers. The fuzzy light shafts came together in random, abstract patterns, like light refracting through a prism. *GO! A—WAY! GO! A—WAY! GO! A—WAY!* he yelled in his mind, while the ghost flickered across the room.

"Gladly, boy, once you help me over," the voice inside Seth's mind replied. "If you fail, I will obliterate you, as my mistress desires."

But I mean you no harm! Seth pleaded, now certain the spirit could read his thoughts.

"You've caused me nothing but harm!" the ghost said, twisting Seth's body from within with a stabbing rancor. "How amusing that fate brings us together again. How fortunate for me."

I mean you no harm, but go away. I mean you no harm, but go away, Seth chanted inside his head. The spirit's breathing, like wind rustling river reeds, accompanied Seth's words. *I mean you no harm, but go away. I mean you no harm, but go away. I mean you no harm, but go away.* The mantra soothed Seth, and silenced the ghost—the menacing breathing diminished.

He glanced across the room and watched the eerie lights fade in and out. The spirit vanished momentarily before the lights pulsed back into view. The lights dimmed and reappeared until, all at once, there was nothing there.

Seth's heart pounded as the first light of day peeked through the corners of the shades that covered the dormer windows. He lay motionless, transfixed by the intersection of the two worlds he'd witnessed. *Thank God I didn't smoke any hash!* he thought. *I don't know how I would have dealt with that thing stoned.* The lingering scent of sulfur kept him on the brink of nausea. He struggled to sit up and observe the rosy dawn illuminate the bedroom, accompanied by sporadic bird calls. He was weakened, as if he'd been enchanted by the spirit. He had to piss badly, but was too frightened and queasy to get out of bed. He sank back into the mattress and lay motionless for an hour. The old house creaked and moaned, but no sounds came from Beth and Roger's bedroom at the opposite end of the hallway.

If the ghost induced the dream—and was the entire episode a dream?—what had broken it? Seth wondered. *Could it have been my plea 'I mean you no harm' that sent the spirit away? Like calling on God in my hour of need? Is there a logical explanation for this? 'I mean you no harm' comes from a basic human goodness that protects us from evil. Because if there is a God, that thing wouldn't exist in the first place.*

Sunlight filtered through the shades and set the room in high relief. The eye-like windows stared at Seth, accusing him of madness. The whiteness of the bedsheet that shrouded his body blinded him. The clock on the nightstand ticked as loudly as a bomb, and the fan screeched. The light that penetrated the shades bent at crazy angles, mimicking the prismatics of the ghost's ethereal body.

He buried his face in the pillow. Dry coughs tore his throat and shook his body as he lay in a bed he could not leave. He curled into a fetal ball, longing for the oblivion of sleep. Rolling onto his belly, he drifted from a jagged wakefulness into the initial stages of slumber. As he lost consciousness, he was shocked awake by the thought, *It's following me.* Then he passed out.

Keta materialized in his dream. "Gentleness, mercy, and love expressed from the heart can vanquish any evil," the shriveled creature intoned in a wispy voice. But Keta's revelation slipped from Seth's mind as he embraced the narcotic sleep of the dead.

Seven

Seth started awake. The bedroom was flooded with daylight. He raised his head from the pillow; *I've got to get out of here* ran through his mind. He climbed out of bed and rifled through his duffel bag, searching for a pair of cut-offs and a fresh shirt. He hurriedly dressed as a hint of the ghost's energy returned. The cold, tingling sensation and faint whiff of sulfur confirmed that this was the same spirit he'd encountered on his first visit. He sat down on the window seat, uncertain how to react to a haunting. He put on his sandals, walked down the hallway, and descended the stairs.

He found Beth in the kitchen grinding coffee beans. She greeted him with a smile and asked, "How'd you sleep?"

"I had a visitor in my room last night," Seth said over the whir of the electric grinder.

Beth released the button and looked at him with a startled expression. "Don't tell me Roger came in," she said.

"Your poltergeist was in my room. Except it's not a poltergeist, it's a ghost. It hovered over me and tried to kill me."

"Oh, my God!" Beth gasped.

As she spoke, Seth thought, *If God is the positive energy of the universe, then the ghost is the ultimate negative energy.*

"It's freaking me out that the manifestations are increasing," Beth said. "Now you're in danger."

"What can we do to get rid of it?"

"We'll go into Hope Springs and buy some smudge sticks," Beth said in a voice drained of emotion. Moving like an automaton, she dumped the coffee into a plastic filter, which she slid into the coffeemaker.

"What can smudge sticks do against an evil spirit?"

"They can cleanse the house of bad energy."

"I need more protection than that. I yelled for it to go away. Didn't you hear me?"

"I heard someone calling, but I thought I was dreaming."

"You believe me, don't you?"

"Of course," Beth sighed. "I feel it's my fault."

"How so?"

"Being so goddamn passive allowed this shit into my life. It's one of our worst Cancerian traits. I'm aware of it, but I can't change it."

"That's what I was saying last night. But how does it account for a ghost?"

"If I'd put my foot down the first time Roger—" Beth struggled to maintain her composure.

"The first time Roger what?"

"Never mind. It's too late, anyway. We've got to figure out how to protect you." Beth walked to the phone on the wall beside the refrigerator and dialed Christy's number. "I'm so glad you're there!" she said when Christy answered, then relayed the news of Seth's visitor. Dialing the phone again, Beth said, "I'm calling my friend, Rose. She's a psychic, and she knows how to deal with these things."

Seth sat down at the kitchen table. He was torn between protecting himself from his spectral visitor and packing up and leaving.

"Okay, we'll burn smudge sticks," Beth said. She looked at Seth and recited, "Sleep with garlic around his bed to ward off spirits. Pray to summon the white light of God for protection. If a demon appears in a mirror, he shouldn't try to question it or fight it."

Seth jumped to his feet. "What's next?" he asked. "Roger appearing out of thin air and hissing, 'I vant to suck your blood'? I'd better go."

"I'll call you back," Beth said. She put down the receiver and walked over to Seth. "Everything will be fine once we smudge the house."

"I should catch the next bus to New York," Seth said, but as he gazed into Beth's eyes, his resolve weakened. He was stuck in place, trapped by the haunting.

"If we get rid of the spirit, you'll be able to enjoy the weekend," Beth reassured.

"I don't know about that. But if the ghost follows me, I'll be in danger wherever I go. Running away may not be the solution."

"We should deal with it here, where the ghost has manifested."

The thud of a car door announced Christy's arrival. Through the kitchen window Seth saw her approaching the house. She briskly knocked on the door and stepped inside. "Don't worry, Seth. We'll help you get through this!"

Caught in Christy's embrace, Seth said, "What if it happens again? I need protection from that thing."

"Let me get dressed and we'll go into Hope Springs," Beth said.

Beth went upstairs, and Christy called in sick to work. Hanging up the phone, Christy poured herself a cup of coffee, sat down at the table, and asked Seth to describe what had happened. When he finished, she said, "There's something about the way the ghost keeps contacting you that reminds me of your birth mother."

"What're you suggesting?" Seth asked.

"I'm not suggesting anything. But this may be more than a run-of-the-mill haunting. So keep that in mind in case things get weird."

"They're already weird! Any weirder and I'm out of here. Provided I'm not pinned to the bed and ravished by my spirit-lover, or whatever you want to call him."

"I didn't say lover. You did."

"For a minute I thought he was going to rape me. But that's impossible. Spirits can't have sex with humans."

"Oh, yes they can. And from what I hear, it's a supernatural fuck."

"That's absurd."

"There are male and female demons called incubi and succubi that have sex with humans in erotic dreams they produce. Maybe your ghost is a flamer who thought you were hot and wanted a piece."

Seth deflected his annoyance by studying the white stone heart that hung on a gold chain around Christy's neck. *Heart of gold*, he thought, yet he refused to voice his feelings to her. When he considered that she had rushed to help him, his glare dissolved into a reluctant smile. "Not to compliment a homophobe, but that heart's beautiful."

"I wear it to guard against whatever bad energy's out there. Given what's happened, you should look for something, too."

Beth bounded into the kitchen wearing white tennis shorts and a pale-blue man's dress shirt. "Let's go," she said, giving her hair a quick brushing as she headed out the door.

Christy drove her Toyota into Hope Springs and turned onto River Road. They crawled along in tourist traffic until they reached the Mobil station, where Christy saw a car vacating a space and maneuvered into the spot. They strolled back into town with the mid-morning sun blazing through the trees, passing the Freeman County Playhouse and the Lloyd House. The leafy canopy and flagstone homes triggered a sense of *déjà vú* in Seth, as they had when Richard guided him and Martin along the thoroughfare.

They approached a low-slung wooden bungalow set ninety degrees off the street facing a brick courtyard. Standing in the side entrance, which opened onto River Road, was an elderly woman dressed in a flimsy summer shift. Her white hair was unkempt, and her pinched face looked like wrinkled shoe leather. Her eyes darted about. When she noticed the group, she fixed them in her sights. Nodding at the woman, Christy said, "Hello, Marsha," which was met with silence. The woman continued to stare as they moved past. Seth and Beth looked at each other in confusion, and Seth grew queasy in the old woman's presence.

"And good morning to you, too," Christy mumbled. "She wasn't like that when I tended her in the hospital or bought aromatherapy oils from her at the fair."

They turned into the courtyard, where a cauldron-shaped sign with flame-red letters across its belly read, "Bell, Book and Candle—Home of the New Age." Delia Hazard, the store owner, stepped outside to hang a placard announcing a "Murder and Mayhem Mystery Weekend" on the corkboard next to the entrance. She mouthed a greeting to Beth and Christy and scurried around the corner of the building.

Beth opened the front door, which set off a tinkling bell, and entered the store with Seth and Christy in tow. They were engulfed in slurry New Age muzak and a heady blend of incense and aromatic candles. Beth approached the cashier's station along the rear wall. "Hi, Blanca. Do you have any smudge sticks?" she asked.

Blanca pointed to a far corner, where a carved East Indian table housed an array of incense displays. Beth walked to the table, and Christy led Seth to a jewelry case adjacent to the cashier's desk. A heavy-set woman loitered at the bargain book table in the middle of the store. The woman's body was encased in a pink polyester pants suit that was too small for her, causing rolls of fat to cascade beyond the confines of her misbuttoned white blouse. The woman's poorly-dyed brown hair was tousled, as if she'd forgotten to brush it. Her unruly hazel eyes, squashed nose, and slack mouth looked as if they'd come through a time machine, each feature reassembling at a slightly different interval. Her skin, pale as milk, hung in puffy clumps. Orange lipstick was smeared beyond the contours of her lips. She had the distracted look of someone who hadn't slept in weeks.

Beth called out to Blanca, "I don't see any smudge sticks."

"They're underneath, my dear," the woman in pink answered as she shambled over to Beth. "What do you need smudge sticks for?"

"I've had some poltergeist activity in my home."

"Perhaps I can help," the woman said. "I teach parapsychology at Davistown University, and I authenticated the ghosts at the Ferry Inn." She extended a pudgy hand, saying, "I'm Julia Sutherland."

Beth smiled and shook her hand. "Oh, yes, you're in Roger's circle. Thanks, but it's nothing a few smudge sticks won't take care of." She turned her back on Julia and rummaged through the boxes secreted beneath the table.

"Have you experienced any other entities besides poltergeists?" Julia asked. "A ghost, perhaps? I sensed a disturbance last night. A strong past-life reconnect, if I'm not mistaken."

"No, it's really nothing at all," Beth said coldly. Julia shuffled back to the bargain table.

Seth and Christy perused each pendant in the display case. Among the amulets were a black stone dagger; a clear icicle-like crystal; a turquoise obelisk with a filigreed silver cap; a burnished silver pentagram; and a fat-bodied female fertility figurine cast in white gold. Seth found it hard to concentrate on the jewels—the store's air was heavy with electricity, like the atmosphere before a thunderstorm. As he and Christy reached the bottom row, they noticed a gold double-sided crescent moon. At the top, where the two crescents intersected, hung a small crystal. The left crescent bore a grinning man-in-the-moon face, and the right featured a swirling pattern that evoked the dark side of the moon. Excitedly pointing her finger, Christy said, "That's perfect!" Seth agreed. The ornament was an exact representation of his changeable Cancerian nature, the outwardly smiling side coupled with darker, moodier aspects.

"What kind of crystal is that?" Christy asked Blanca, who leaned over the desk and said, "Herkimer diamond."

"I've heard of Herkimer diamonds," Christy said, "but I'm not sure of their properties." She walked to a shelf marked "Crystals" and pulled out a hefty gemstone encyclopedia, thumbing through it as she returned to the cashier's desk. Steadying the book on the counter, she read, "Herkimer diamonds. These rare crystals are found in only one location in the world—Herkimer,

New York—hence the name. Their properties connect with the unconscious and encourage the transference of knowledge from the unconscious to the conscious mind through dreams."

"That's even more perfect!" Christy said as she closed the book. Beth joined them, holding three packets of smudge sticks, which looked like dried green herbs.

"Could I see the double moon pendant?" Seth asked. Blanca opened the glass-topped display with a tiny skeleton key and withdrew the charm. "How much is it?" he inquired as she handed it to him.

"A hundred and sixty dollars plus tax, without a chain."

Julia noisily rummaged through a pile of *Mystic Fire* videos on the bargain table. Addressing Blanca, she said, "I don't see the *Ring of Fire* tape I asked you about. It's imperative I find it to show my students. If you can't be of assistance, I'll go directly to Delia."

Seth considered the pendent in his palm. "I hadn't planned on spending so much money," he said.

"I can put it on my charge card and you can pay me back later," Beth said. "I have an old gold chain that was my brother's that's perfect for that charm."

"Thanks. It's just so close in here, I can't think." As he spoke, Julia inched her way along the bargain table, picking up and putting down books and tapes as she drew nearer.

"You can pay me back in installments," Beth said.

Seth was about to accept Beth's offer when he swung around to find Julia, her face a pasty white mask, rubbing her upper thigh and crotch against his leg. The friction of Julia's flesh against his body created a foggy forcefield. He allowed her to continue until her unseeing eyes and half-parted lips forced him to gasp in disgust and step away. Julia peered at Seth through slitted eyelids and moved towards him again. He sent her a mental *Stay away!* which froze her in place. Massaging her temples, she turned her head in circles until her eyes popped open like a doll's. She gave Seth a measured look and slunk off to the opposite corner of the store, feigning interest in books on ancient Egypt.

"Are you all right?" Beth whispered.

"I want to leave. I can hardly think in here."

"I know what you mean," Beth said, taking the smudge sticks to the counter. As Blanca rang up the sale, Seth said, "I'd like to buy the pendant. Would you mind charging it?"

"Of course not. I'm glad you're getting it. It's a good omen."

A good omen in Hope Springs might be a bad omen anywhere else, Seth thought.

Blanca took several minutes to process the charge for the pendant and wrap it in tissue paper. On the way out, as the bell over the door jingled, Seth caught Julia giving him a final inspection. When their eyes accidentally met, Seth saw a glint of madness in her gaze and turned away.

ℋ

Seth, Beth, and Christy walked along River Road, silenced by what had taken place in the bookstore. As they passed the well-kept homes and historic landmarks, Seth's vision altered. He saw the town as if viewing a photograph with its negative superimposed on top. Hope Springs' colonial glamour peeled away to show what lay beneath—the carcasses of old houses built upon a landscape cursed by a powerful Native American shaman. A veil of thinnest gossamer lifted before his eyes, allowing a better detection of the two realms that had momentarily blended. One was the physical world, while the other revealed the theft of native lands and the destruction of the environment upon which Hope Springs was founded. The gauzy world of hidden truth bled into the material world, their intersection marked by fuzzy light shafts that blurred his eyesight.

He fell into a waking dream, while his friends receded into a background mist, two indistinct bodies floating through space. Keta appeared and moved his whiskered lips, but no words came out. He planted his meaning directly into Seth's brain as an infusion of understanding, or gnosis. "I am Ketanëtuwit—'Great Spirit' in the Orenda tongue. I exist in all living things,

100

whether they be flesh, tree, or stone. Manitowuk, the lesser nature spirits, cry to me that this land is poisoned by the spell of a righteous chief. It didn't used to be this way. My people were gentle, existing harmoniously with each other and the natural world. They lived simple lives, and were content with what I provided. No one owned the land—the Earth, our Mother. Now the Earth is parceled out and ripped open, her insides taken for profit. Our Mother is in the process of dying."

The bustling colonial settlement of Hope Springs materialized in Seth's vision, reflected in the pooling waters of the Orenda. Leaning on his staff for support, Keta raised his hunched body and sternly pointed a long-nailed index finger towards the ground. A clear understanding came to Seth: "The curse on Hope Springs must be lifted, or the town and the river will be destroyed."

Keta continued, "Ghosts and magic are real, not a figment of the imagination. As a result of the chief's curse, black magic is easily practiced here by those foolish enough to be tempted by its rewards. The old woman who stared at you is a wise woman of considerable powers. She knows the use of roots and herbs as deeply as my people do. Julia is a medium who's manipulated by spirits as well as by those who seek her skills. To assess your psychic gift, she needed to make physical contact with you."

The nausea that overwhelmed Seth in the presence of the ghost and the old woman returned and forced him toward the pavement. He stumbled and righted himself, subliminally aware of the grip of his friends' arms upon his. Keta said, "You are powerful because you sent the spirit away. Your power threatens others who are not as innocent."

Why? Seth asked without speaking. *I have no power.*

A shimmering rainbow appeared, fusing the blurry light shafts that been tormenting Seth's eyesight into a luminous prismatic globe. Keta presented the globe to Seth, then touched Seth's forehead. The old guide's wrinkled face relaxed into a crooked grin as he said, "The rainbow of psychic wisdom and understanding, and the ability to receive messages from the spirit world, this is my gift to you."

The veil began to fall, a curtain descending across an enchanted landscape. Seth's dual vision snapped back into sharp single focus. He saw the trees and the street and Christy's Toyota ten paces ahead. His friends released their steadying grip on his arms so he could climb into the car. While Christy drove down River Road and the hot breeze blasted through the open windows, he understood, *My power is about to change my life.*

ℋ

Christy turned the Toyota onto a county road that brought them to a modern shopping mall on the edge of a forest. They wandered the aisles of a supermarket, emerging thirty minutes later with fresh pasta, salad fixings, and three bulbs of garlic. On the drive home, Beth suggested that they smudge the house, then have a calming afternoon by the pool.

Beth put away the groceries, and Christy paraded upstairs and down waving smoking smudge wands that smelled like burning sage and cedar. In a makeshift ceremony, she said, "Unbidden spirits, begone! Trouble this house no more!" Afterwards, she cleansed Seth's moon pendant by dipping it in salt water. She fastened it around his neck on the gold chain that had belonged to Beth's brother, saying, "In the name of the Light, may this protect you from evil."

They went outside to sun themselves on the patio, and swam to cool off. The phone rang around four-thirty, and Beth emerged from the house ten minutes later to say it was Rose offering additional suggestions. "Now don't panic," Beth said, "but Rose feels you haven't seen the last of the ghost. She stressed the importance of surrounding yourself and the bedroom with the white light of God before you go to sleep. She said not to forget the garlic, which really does keep spirits at bay. And she said that if the ghost returns, you should demand of it, 'Do you walk in the name of God? If not, then leave at once!'"

"How can I ask for protection from a God I don't believe in?" Seth said.

Christy, who was lying on a chaise lounge with her eyes closed, replied, "You will search your soul until you find the place that believes in God, because now is the time to start."

"You can't switch on belief like a light," Seth argued.

"I know, but God doesn't have to be an old man with a beard, or a saintly Christ figure. God can be the essence of goodness and love that you find within yourself. Take whatever makes you comfortable and use it, because you're going to need to *believe* to make Rose's suggestions work."

"I'll try."

As twilight fell, Beth went inside to start dinner, while Seth and Christy took turns showering in Kit's bathroom. During the meal that followed, Christy said, "I'm spending the night. I'm going to sleep in Seth's room in case anything happens." A growing sense of dread raised Seth's heartbeat and flushed his cheeks. The kitchen screen door slammed and Roger appeared, proceeding upstairs without greeting anyone. They moved into the living room and settled on the leather sofas, where they watched the TV news. A little before midnight, Seth climbed the stairs clutching the three bulbs of garlic, with Christy and Beth trailing behind. On the landing, Beth kissed Seth on the forehead and said, "Call me if you need me." She walked into her bedroom and left the door ajar. A light shining through the frosted glass doorway between the two bedrooms indicated that Roger was in his office.

Christy changed into one of Kit's T-shirts and draped herself seductively across the double bed while Seth distributed the garlic around the room, placing one bulb on the trunk next to the fan, one bulb on the night stand, and one bulb under his pillow. He got into bed, and Christy tickled him and pulled the cotton blanket and sheet away, eliciting nervous titters from them both. "You better watch out," Seth said, "because I'll spoil you for any other man."

Christy laughed and said, "The sex isn't important. What really matters is that I'm here to help. You know that."

"I appreciate it. And you know *that.*"

Seth turned off the bedside lamp, and Christy burst into peals of laughter. A few minutes later her uneven snores punctuated the darkness. He closed his eyes and tried to visualize the white light of God, but experienced only an emptiness in his soul. Years before, a superstitious friend had insisted he white-light an airplane to ensure a safe flight. The memory soothed him. The light no longer seemed foreign, and he could imagine the presence of a higher power through his prior connection to it. He asked this power to defend him against ghosts, and a flicker of Divine light materialized in his mind. The light began as a spark—a small, intense glow from a flinty match—that flashed and went out again. The glimmer of it heartened him. He visualized the spark again, and as he concentrated on the light, made a deeper connection to it. The light stayed lit in his mind, a crude fire kindled from twigs against the darkness of a forest. The light became a full-fledged fire, blazing upwards with a golden glow that seemed holy. The golden aura was the spirit behind the light. He concentrated on the glow, isolating it from the surrounding flame. When his mind was filled with the golden light, he tried to discern its pure energy, which revealed itself as the fiery white light of—God? His imagination? He wasn't sure, but he refused to stop and analyze it.

Pregnant with the light, he pictured a gleaming whiteness running from the top of his head to the tip of his toes. He projected a glowing white laser beam over the bedroom's walls, ceiling, and floor. He saw himself as a monk in a cell trying to keep the Devil at bay, and understood that this white-light projection was the equivalent of praying. He began to actively pray, in a primitive fashion, for the first time in his life. *I don't know if there's a God, but if there is, I'm asking for protection against whatever's threatening me. I'm not sure why you should help me since I've never been a believer. But please protect me from harm, if you will.* That he'd sunk to the level of prayer he took as a sign of madness. Exhausted, he rolled onto his stomach. After repositioning himself and fidgeting with the garlic under his pillow, he drifted into a light slumber.

He was awakened an hour later by a mysterious singing. The notes were high-pitched and clear; the melody was composed of Middle Eastern trills and melismas. To Seth's sleepy mind, the words were, "Save me! Rescue me!" The singer stopped, then launched into another sinuous refrain. Sweat rose over Seth's body as he tried to ascertain whether the serenade came from inside or outside the house. His instinct told him this was a woodland spirit's song, something that would only be heard in the deepest forest glade. He shook Christy awake. She snorted and opened her eyes, appearing disoriented. "Listen to that!" he said in a hoarse whisper.

Christy sat up irritably, pushing her hair away from her face. "I don't hear anything. Go back to sleep."

The siren singing began again. "That's what I'm talking about," Seth said. "What on earth's making that sound?"

Christy cocked her head and listened. "That's just a cat howling," she said.

"Cats don't sound like they're singing from the other side of the grave. That's a spirit."

"It's a cat, Seth. Go back to sleep."

A beating of wings and piercing squawks sounded outside the dormer windows. "What the hell's that?" Seth whispered. "A sparrow?"

"It's probably a hawk. We're out in the woods, you know." Christy threw off the sheet, saying, "I'm going downstairs to get a glass of water. Do you want anything?"

"Water's fine."

Five minutes later, Christy burst through the door with two glasses held precariously in her hands. "I saw the ghost!" she said breathlessly, handing Seth a glass. "It's in the living room. I accidentally brushed against it and all the hair on my body stood on end. I went into the kitchen, and on my way back I told it, 'Your daughter's not here. She's crossed over.'" Christy set her glass on the chest of drawers and paced the room. "Its energy was horrible," she said in a nerve-torn voice. She hugged herself and cried, "Ugh! Ugh! Ugh!"

Seth sat up in bed. "Did you see what it looked like?" he asked.

"Yes," Christy said, as she rocked in place with her arms about her.

"Is it male?"

"Yes. It was wearing a long, dirty garment like a shroud. From what I could see of its face, it looked like Jesus walking under the weight of the cross. A tortured, ghostly Jesus." She let out another guttural "Ugh!" and retrieved her glass from the dresser. She took a sip of water, got into bed, and pulled Seth to her. "That's the worst energy I've ever felt."

"But the white light and garlic must be working because it hasn't come upstairs. *Yet.*"

They settled under the sheet, and Christy dozed off. Seth stared at the ceiling and heard faint footsteps on the stairs. His heartbeat accelerated as the footfalls advanced. They sounded sodden, as if dripping water from the river on the carpeting. Christy slept obliviously by his side. He considered calling out to Beth, but instead surrounded himself, Christy, and the bedroom with the white light of God. The footsteps reached the bedroom door, stopped, and advanced no further. He lay still, his heart pounding. The stench of sulfur stung his nostrils, but there was no further evidence of an intruder. The first light of dawn penetrated the window shades. The footfalls retreated down the hallway and descended the stairs, growing more distant until, several minutes later, they ceased altogether.

♒

Christy woke at eight and jostled Seth's shoulder. "I've got to run," she said. "Thanks to you, I've got a twelve-hour weekend shift." She climbed out of bed and slipped into her jeans. "I'll call you when I get home from work tonight."

"Thanks for staying with me," Seth said.

"Any time." Christy dashed out of the bedroom, and moments later her car pulled away from the house.

Seth sat up and considered the events of the last two days. He couldn't stay in Banbury any longer. The level of fear he'd initially experienced was becoming constant. He would have breakfast, walk into Hope Springs, and get the bus to New York. On his way to the kitchen, he peeked through the office door and saw Roger tangled in the sheets of a fold-out sofa. When Seth passed Beth's vacant bedroom, he remembered she had a reflexology workshop that morning. *I can't worry about leaving without telling her*, he thought. *I'll call her once I'm home.*

In the kitchen, he fumbled with the coffeemaker until he got it to work. Roger approached through the dining room, wearing a pair of gray gym shorts held precariously around his midriff by a loosely-knotted drawstring. "Coffee's almost ready," Seth said. "I'm going to leave. I don't feel safe here."

Roger gave Seth a sympathetic leer. "Beth mentioned you had a ghost in your room the other night. Did he come back?"

"Yes. Christy saw him in the living room. Don't be offended, but I've got to go."

"If there was something that disturbed you, why didn't you come to me?"

"There was nothing you could've done," Seth replied. He sat down at the table and poured out a bowl of granola, which he doused with milk.

Roger went upstairs, returning with a book. "I think you should take this," he said. "It's Beth's, and she'd want you to have it."

Seth leafed through the volume, entitled *Psychic Self-Defense: A Guide to Protection Against Spells, Curses, and Psychic Attack*, noting its herbal remedies and antique drawings of medieval sorcerers expelling demons from naked women. He surmised that this was Roger's book, and wondered why he should want to pass it off as Beth's.

"Thanks," Seth said, handing the book back to Roger, "but I can take care of myself."

"I know Beth would want you to have it."

Seth reluctantly accepted the book. He placed his dishes in the sink and went upstairs to pack. Upon returning to the kitchen, Roger, dressed in black jeans and an AC/DC T-shirt, handed him a brown paper bag and said, "Beth would want you to have this."

Seth took the bag of six ears of silver queen corn and said, "Will you tell Beth I'll phone her tonight?"

"Of course. Put your things in the Beemer and I'll drive you into town."

"I don't mind walking."

"I don't want any guest of mine feeling uncomfortable in my house. It's the least I can do."

They crossed the front yard and passed through the wooden gate into Mandrake Road. Roger opened the passenger door of his black BMW and motioned Seth inside. He climbed into the driver's seat and popped a heavy metal tape into the cassette deck. They descended Angelica Heights with blistering guitar licks and a singer screaming about the fire in his loins coming from the speakers. "I love the same things I did as a teenager," Roger shouted. "Fast cars, loud rock and roll, and beautiful women. I'm working as hard as I am to get the best that money can buy."

Beautiful men, too, Seth wanted to add. Instead, he said, "Do people come with a price tag?"

"Everyone has their price. That all-you-need-is-love crap won't put a roof over your head or money in the bank. You can make millions if your computer software hits. And mine's about to."

"I guess you've lost your youthful idealism."

"And good riddance to it. Richard's a tired anachronism. This decade's about making your own reality, using whatever means necessary. You'd be surprised how exercising a certain type of mental power can attract money."

They crossed the river and turned onto River Road. The Saturday morning traffic was heavy, and they moved along at five miles an hour. Roger eventually pulled into the Mobil station and parked. He and Seth got out of the car and walked to the wooden bench that served as the bus stop. Scanning a faded schedule posted on a light pole, Roger said, "You're in luck. The next bus is at ten-twenty." Seth looked up and saw the Orenda Valley coach approaching on the opposite side of the street. He grabbed his bags and dashed into the traffic. On the far sidewalk, he turned and saw Roger wave. As he raised his arm in reply, Raven Grimmsley drove past, her red-gold hair visible above the steering wheel of a battered black Impala. She nodded at Roger and continued driving.

The bus doors opened and Seth boarded, handing the barrel-chested driver a ticket. He stowed his duffel bag and the corn in the overhead rack and, like a frightened schoolboy, sat down behind the driver. The bus lurched forward into traffic. Seth sank into his seat, relaxing enough to allow the adrenaline that coursed through his body to wrack him with shivers. His stifled fear, rising to the surface, left him lightheaded. Each thumping beat of his heart told him he'd never up and left someplace, fleeing for his life. As the bus crossed the river and climbed the bluff in Banbury, a puzzling memory surfaced of a boy fleeing through the woods. No name, no face, just a blurry figure on the run.

He observed the succession of rural towns slip past the window. Leaving the Orenda Valley was a relief, yet the knot of tension in his throat tightened until he had to will himself to breathe. There was still something wrong, even as the Jersey farmland gave way to suburbia, and the distance between Banbury and the bus increased. The thought, *Will the ghost follow me?* took root in his mind. An overwhelming dread both chilled and fevered him. *Was the ghost real? Or an hallucination like Keta? Will the ghost help me or torment me? Will Martin be safe?*

Visions of a shadowy spirit trailing the bus brought Seth to the brink of tears. He coughed repeatedly to keep his emotions from overwhelming him, and passengers turned to stare, whispering to each other. An elderly lady leaned across the aisle and asked, "Is everything okay?" to which Seth replied, "Yes, I'm fine. Nothing to worry about."

The bus coursed through the Jersey lowlands, and the glittering spires of Manhattan loomed above the marsh grasses and the overhead web of electric power lines. As the bus began its spiral descent into the Lincoln Tunnel, Seth was comforted by the thought that Manhattan's density might hinder the spirit from tracking him. With any luck, he could remain anonymous among the crowd. Idly fingering the double-moon pendant that hung around his neck, he prayed that his aura would become unreadable once he entered the Babel he called home. Only when the bus entered the tunnel did he realize he'd been so frightened, he'd forgotten to call Richard to tell him he was in Banbury.

Eight

Seth set his duffel bag and the sack of corn on the living room floor of his apartment. He dumped the contents of the bag onto the captain's bed, hastily sorting through his clothes. He knew it was a ridiculous thought, but what if some trace of the ghost remained, some cloud or force that had traveled with him? He noticed nothing until he thought of the bag itself, which had been on the window-seat a few feet from the ghost's twinkling body. He opened the zippered side pockets and turned the bag inside out. As he did so, he felt a prickly radiance against his skin. Certain that this was the ghost's numbing energy, he flung the bag into the foyer.

Next, he considered the corn. There was something about its aliveness that disturbed him. *Could the corn be tainted? Weren't sheaves of dry corn stalks set alight to celebrate a pagan harvest day?* Once he made this association, he wanted the corn out of the apartment, too. He tossed the crumpled paper sack in the direction of the duffel bag. Three ears spilled out onto the bare wood floor in a tangle of wilting husks and gold silk.

He noticed Roger's book lying on the captain's bed, half-hidden beneath his shaving kit. *That thing's cursed. Roger put a spell on it to track my movements.* He threw the book into the foyer, where it landed with a thud. He didn't stop to determine whether he was behaving rationally as he stuffed the book and the corn into the duffel bag and carried the contaminated items downstairs and into the street. Eyeing the garbage cans next to his building, he thought that dumping the duffel bag there would be like sending a signal to whatever was pursuing him, so he walked down Carmine Street to Sixth Avenue and headed north. As he strolled, he dropped the corn, an ear at a time, into the wire trash receptacles along the avenue. He recalled the trail of breadcrumbs left by Hansel and Gretel as they advanced into the forest. When he remembered that the crumbs did nothing to prevent the children from getting lost and ending up in the witch's clutches, his heart began to pound.

He dropped the last ear of corn in front of Balducci's market at Ninth Street. He crossed the street, checking to make sure no one was following, and continued walking north until he came to Famous Ray's Pizza. Two metal trash bins guarded the front doors. Eyeing the counter staff to make sure they weren't watching, he fished the book out of the bag and pitched it into the nearest bin. *If I throw the bag in, they'll think I'm some crazy homeless person or criminal.* He pretended to scour the street for an unseen landmark and, when no one was looking, stuffed the duffel bag into the other bin and fled down Sixth Avenue.

I've gone mad, he thought, as he observed the person he used to be behaving in ways that made no sense. "Who's making the decisions?" he wondered aloud. "Who's in charge?" Not knowing made him shudder. He stopped and steadied himself against the Jefferson Market Library stair railing. Sadness forced him to the stone steps, where he sat hugging his knees. He lingered there staring at the ground, feeling the eyes of passersby burning into him, then flitting away as soon as he looked up.

He resumed walking down the avenue. He was certain his movements were being monitored by some all-seeing force. He was also convinced it was only a matter of time before a spirit arrived to destroy him. He longed to dismiss his fears as mere paranoia, but they would not diminish; instead, they manifested as a giddy, sinking feeling in the pit of his stomach. He decided it would be best to sequester himself in his apartment for the remainder of the weekend. He didn't have to be at work until Monday afternoon, which meant he had two days to pull himself together. He stopped at the market at the end of Carmine Street to buy provisions—several bulbs of garlic, three white votive candles, and a bottle of garlic supplements. He swallowed a handful of the capsules as soon as he entered his apartment.

𝓗

The ceiling fan in the bedroom whirred overhead, forcing the air around in hot little flourishes. Seth lay on the bed in a T-shirt and frayed pajama bottoms, telling himself, *Just relax. When you've quieted down, you can figure out what to do.* The thought kept him from becoming hysterical, but did nothing to alleviate the dread that overwhelmed him. He sought some rock to cling to that would ground him in reality, but found nothing. The one idea that haunted him was how helpless he was in the face of what he'd seen.

Fatigue and the sticky afternoon heat brought him to the brink of sleep. After drifting in and out of consciousness, he slipped into a river of slumber. The sky was so close he thought he could touch the orange clouds and blue firmament overhead. He soared through the heavens like a disembodied spirit, flying so fast his eyes teared and his stomach reeled. He remained weightless as long as he kept his eyes focused on the horizon. But the instant he looked down, a sickening vertigo seized him, and he spun out of control. Spiraling to earth, he saw not ground, but a swirling vortex below. As he plummeted toward the black maelstrom that opened to receive him, he cried out from the depths of his soul, "Save me, Jesus!" He awoke as he was about to be sucked into the whirlpool. "Save me, Jesus!" he mumbled. "Save me, Jesus!" he continued against his will.

Where did that come from?

He lay prone on the bed, astounded that he'd called upon Jesus. Yet his plea had a calming affect; he'd unlocked a door that let in a single ray of light. His intuition told him that if anyone could save him, it was Jesus, not the stern Jewish God who didn't hear anyone's pleas, and who wouldn't necessarily respond if he did. He roused himself and sat against the wooden headboard, surveying the bedroom cluttered with Martin's rumpled clothing. His body flushed hot as he saw himself as the drowned man, an image on some ill-fated Tarot card, who briefly glimpses the Divine and perishes. *Only dying men are desperate enough to open themselves to the Divine. They're blinded by the dazzling light of God and die.* As the drowning man, he would be pulled into the whirlpool just as his arm broke the waves and reached towards heaven.

He relaxed into the damp bedclothes and fell asleep. Keta appeared in his dream holding a carved yak-bone staff with a Yin-Yang medallion at its crest. "Balance is the law of the universe," the guide informed him. "If nothing balanced the disparate forces of nature, the Earth would fly apart and be scattered across the galaxy. The ghost's negative energy has its opposite—God, Goddess, Jesus, Buddha, Allah—whatever you wish to call it. Male and female, good and evil, positive and negative, black and white all exemplify the attraction of polar opposites that hold the world in place. Each extreme balances and defines the other in a perfect equilibrium of opposing energies. In each opposite lies a tiny piece of its inverse, since the inverse determines, through sheer opposition, what it essentially is."

Keta held out a polished black box with a small white dot on its lid. Seth reached out and accepted the gift. He lifted the lid, and in a leap of faith, sought to discover the spark of Divine light that would pull him to higher ground. As he peered inside, the dream faded to nothingness.

❧

The hum of the city outside the bedroom window roused Seth. He opened his eyes and drew his knees to his chest. Was Keta's ongoing presence in his dreams, along with his calling on Jesus, a sign of mental deterioration? *Jesus is an approachable God,* he told himself, *a man who underwent the trial of spirit made flesh that all humans endure.* Jesus' message of love appealed to him. *I believe in love above all else. Love is the highest power. So if Jesus preached, 'Love your enemies. Turn the other cheek. Offer love in the face of hate and revenge,' then I'm all for it. Maybe Jesus really was the first hippie. And maybe I've really lost my mind.*

He fell into a light slumber and was awakened in the early evening by the sound of the dead bolt turning on the front door. He heard Martin's footsteps in the living room and called out, "I'm in here."

Martin walked into the bedroom and switched on the light. His sun-reddened skin and wavering gait indicated he had taken his habitual Saturday trip to Fire Island with a thermos of gin and tonic as his companion.

"I suppose you're wondering why I'm back early," Seth said.

"Why are you lying in the dark?" Martin asked. "You didn't vomit all over the Princes' house again?"

"No, it was much worse than that."

"Well?"

"There was a ghost in my bedroom that pressed down on me while I slept. It was trying to kill me."

"You're kidding."

"No, I'm dead serious. Yesterday Beth, Christy, and I went into Hope Springs. In the New Age bookstore, a medium rubbed her crotch against me. After that, I had a vision that Hope Springs was cursed by a great magician."

"Jesus, Seth."

"Last night I heard singing that came from a woodland spirit. The ghost was in the house again. Christy saw it in the living room, but it didn't come into the bedroom because I surrounded myself with garlic and the white light of God."

"You've seen too many vampire flicks," Martin said, suppressing an inebriated smile. "It's like something I would write myself."

"When I finally understood the danger I was in, I got the first bus home. I'm worried the ghost's followed me." Seth paused before saying, "That's why I'm back early. Oh, I almost forgot. Beth and Roger are getting a divorce."

Martin looked at Seth with dismay in his ice-blue eyes. "Poor, poor boo," he said. "Did Richard slip you more drugs?"

"I didn't see Richard. And I didn't hallucinate, dream, or imagine any of it."

Martin's features hardened. "Are you sure what you saw was a ghost?"

"Aren't you the one who's read all those magic books? And didn't you tell me that all occultists believe in the existence of spirits?"

"Of course. But spirits can be imagined when they aren't there."

"What I saw was real," Seth insisted.

Martin grew thoughtful and asked, "Did something happen that triggered an image of a ghost to come into your mind?"

"No," Seth sullenly replied.

Martin sat on the bed and drew Seth to him, cradling him in his arms. "Is it possible that what you saw was a manifestation of Beth and Roger's bad relationship?"

"No! I don't know why you can't accept what I said at face value."

"Poor, poor boo," Martin murmured, as Seth relaxed into his arms. "I accept it. I just want to make sure you're right."

"I'm glad you're back," Seth said, for Martin was the tangible other who would restore him to the world as he had previously known it. He surrendered to Martin's embrace and hugged him tighter.

ℋ

That night before going to sleep, Seth set a bulb of garlic and a votive he'd placed in a sea shell on the bookshelf beside the bed. He lit the candle and stared meditatively into its flame, trying to visualize the light of God. Without a word, Martin shut off the bedside lamp. Seth placed a bulb of garlic under his pillow, blew out the candle, and slipped beneath the sheet. He lay on his back, visualizing himself encased in a bubble of white light, and began to pray. *Dear God, I know I don't deserve your help, but if you'll send me your light, I'll be forever grateful. I'm sorry to seek protection out of desperation. I know I should have sought you out all along. Please bless me with your light, if you will.*

Thank you for hearing me in my darkest hour of need. He silently implored, *Save me, Jesus! Save me!* again and again.

A trigger went off inside his head before dawn. He opened his eyes and glanced at the clock on the bookshelf. It was the hour when the ghost had left Kit's bedroom two nights before. The early morning quiet confirmed that no spirit was present, only the memory of one.

Sunday passed in a haze. Martin polished his *Trick or Treat* screenplay in preparation for a meeting the next day, while Seth read the *Times* and cat-napped. By the time he remembered to phone Beth, it was late. The machine picked up, and he didn't leave a message.

In bed that night, with Martin's body turned away from him, Seth said his clumsy prayers. He was thankful he'd survived the previous night without a supernatural visitation, but was certain the ghost would appear at any moment. He passed out and slept soundly until he snapped awake at the hour when the ghost had pressed down on him.

ℋ

Martin got up at seven the next morning. Seth slept on, although he was aware of footfalls and the sound of a chair scraping the living room floor. He heard a noise at the front door, rose out of bed, and walked to the foyer. Opening the door, he saw Keta dressed in a tan cloak made of animal hide. A leather band around his forehead held red turkey feathers, which rose from his forehead, giving him the look of an ancient bird. A leather wallet hung around his neck, suspended from a strip of hide.

"I've come to live with you," Keta announced as he stepped across the threshold. "You have called me, and I have come."

Martin gave Seth a peck on the cheek, interrupting the dream. Seth heard the front door close, then watched himself rise out of his body and rush to the foyer. "You keep saying I've called you, but I don't remember," he said.

"You must remember everything," Keta replied. "I am your guide, and have been for many lifetimes. You are seeking direction and have asked for help."

"I need to keep a ghost at bay. Can you assist with that?"

"I cannot tell you what you must learn for yourself."

"Then what good are you? I need protection from God or the Light or whatever can shield me."

"That is true. But you must find it yourself. Your karma demands it. You are being challenged. You must question what you have seen and what it means. Your conclusions will direct you forward. You cannot run away or recede into non-action. That will no longer work."

"So I'm on my own?"

"Yes, but I will support you. Being an adopted child is part of your karma. You must resolve the past-life issues you carry forward."

"Can you be more specific?"

"Bring your father into the Light. Your mother has returned from the dead. Beware!"

Seth looked questioningly at Keta, but the guide said nothing more. He reached into the pouch around his neck and extracted a gleaming crystal in the shape of an arrow head. He handed the crystal to Seth, who opened his hand to accept it. The crystal emitted a rainbow of light as it settled in Seth's palm.

"Come in," Seth said. Keta hobbled inside, and Seth turned the dead bolt, glided into the bedroom, and slipped back into the body that lay sleeping on the bed.

Part Two

The Magickal Empire

Nine

The Circle of Light coven was founded on the shores of the Orenda by Raven Grimmsley's Scottish ancestors when they emigrated to the New World in the late seventeenth century. At the end of the Burning Years, the centuries of witch trials that began in the Middle Ages, one branch of the McWycke clan had had enough of secrecy and persecution. They secured a land grant from William Penn and set out for a continent free from religious harassment. For that was what their Celtic witchcraft was—a religion as old as time itself, practiced throughout Europe. The Old Religion worshipped nature, the seasonal cycle, and the elements of the earth. It was as basic, and as elegant, as a religion could be. The forces that affect daily life—wind, water, earth, and fire—were believed to be alive with the Divine Fire, the energy that animates life and intelligence throughout the universe. These forces were honored not only for sustaining life, but for imparting wisdom through their very existence. Focusing upon the elements during worship granted Old Religion adherents a connection to the Divine in everyday life and allowed them to seek the balance necessary to be a proper witch.

As with many early faiths, the Old Religion, or the Craft of the Wise, honored the Female Creator, the Goddess. Her counterpart, the Father God—Pan, Sylvester, Faunus—was also important, but it was the Goddess who gave birth to all life and who dominated the pantheon. Still, the Life Force derives from polar opposites coming together to spark existence, so the female and male principles were each given their due.

Four seasonal celebrations, the Great Sabbats, serve as the basis of the Old Religion's calendar. April thirtieth, August first, October thirty-first, and February second mark a time when communal rites reestablish man's connection to nature and the universe. This is necessary so mankind may live in harmony with the environment, and in balance with other men and women. These celebrations, along with the lesser esbats, which mark the coming of Spring and the bounty of Summer, define the natural cycle, the cosmic wheel upon which all life spins.

Karma and reincarnation are the twin foundations of the Old Religion. A true witch is aware of the effect of his or her actions, on others and on oneself, in this lifetime, and in lifetimes to come. Cause and effect—which determine karma—are the interactive laws of the universe. What you create returns to you. Witches embrace reincarnation as the mechanism through which each individual attains greater spiritual achievement, lifetime by lifetime. For this reason, a witch is bound to act morally and in balance with nature. Unethical behavior, including the selfish practice of black magic, will come back to the practitioner three times over. A good witch knows it is not worth short-term gain in this life for a degraded existence the next time around.

The Circle of Light's early years in the Orenda Valley were challenging, since, like all European settlers, they were pioneers. Living in the wilderness was harsh, particularly during the cruel winter months, but the coveners persevered and helped found Hell's Ferry. They were integrated into the town's life as inn owners, grist mill operators, seamstresses, wise women who nursed the sick, and farmers. Given the Craft's centuries-old knowledge of flora, they excelled at agriculture, providing much of the valley's hay, maize, and potatoes, along with medicinal herbs.

The early coveners soon discovered that the location of their new home was auspicious for the working of magic, that is, for summoning the natural forces required during worship. The Orenda River, which runs over a bed of crystals for several miles, generated a rare psychic energy. Water flowing over crystals enhanced the coveners' clairvoyant powers, facilitating contact with the elemental spirits that animate natural phenomena. The fertile land of the Orenda Valley provided not only sustenance but secluded groves and dense forests for Sabbat gatherings. The valley was the ideal spot for worshipping—and eventually protecting—the natural world, the Goddess' greatest gift to mankind.

As herbalists and seers of faerie—the wee folk who live invisibly in the natural world—the coveners found kinship with the Native American population, who shared their pantheistic beliefs. Every rock and stone, flower and tree, creek and stream had its animating genie in both the native and Old Religion world views. The coveners came to know the natives, and learned about the hidden Great Spring with its ruling water spirit. The native population shared with them other places of power that were propitious for the working of magic. While these spots were sacred to the natives, the coveners could frequent them with permission. The natives also shared their crystal lore, allowing coven members access to the river's crystal cache. When the last natives fled the valley in the late eighteenth century, the coveners mourned their departure.

Over the years, the McWyckes watched with mild distress, and then a deeper horror, as the valley's resources were mined for profit. At first, the depletion was barely noticeable. Forests were gradually logged and cleared, streams were stripped of their aquatic bounty, quarries were dug and mined, and wilderness was transformed into parcels of farmland. Coven members were partially at fault in the last regard. While they continued to revere nature, they participated in its destruction through aggressive farming. They always thanked the Goddess for the use of the land, but as time passed, the devastation mounted. The final shock came when nuclear power plants started to appear in the Pennsylvania countryside. Such power, they knew, was unclean, and would poison vast swathes of the landscape if an accident occurred. The Three Mile Island meltdown, which took place in Dauphin County, Pennsylvania in 1979, confirmed their worst fears. The release of radioactive waste water into the

Susquehanna River was a harbinger of what could happen to the Orenda should its shores ever host a nuclear power plant.

The coven did not exist in a vacuum. Although generations of McWyckes provided the core membership, the family, by necessity, intermingled with and married other valley residents. At first this was problematic, since the common view of witchcraft was one of evil spellcasting and consorting with the Devil. It was often difficult to convince an outsider that the rites the circle performed were meant to honor nature and a Goddess who predated Jesus Christ. But since many settlers brought over their own Celtic connection to the Goddess, appropriate members were found. The Grimmsley clan, of English background, proved an early ally, as they were also a family of hereditary witches, although not as disciplined and distinguished as the McWyckes. The Grimmsleys and the McWyckes joined forces, thereby strengthening both families and providing an active gene pool with clairvoyance and second sight as prominent traits.

The danger of allowing outsiders into the coven remained a concern. The need for discretion was not always respected, exposing the McWyckes to periods of social banishment. On several occasions they were run out of town. Those who sought out the coven as a haven for black magic posed the biggest threat, since they were looking for wealth or the death of an enemy; there was no interest in the worship of the natural world. Such seekers were politely dismissed. Yet there were black magic practitioners who penetrated the coven, and who performed dark deeds under the coven's auspices. According to family lore, such episodes were rare and unfortunate, and were resolved quickly.

Because the Old Religion venerates the Goddess, a woman is appointed to direct the coven—a High Priestess presides over coven affairs and ceremonies. Since the McWyckes were a family who passed down traits of clairvoyance, second sight, mediumship, and telepathy to each generation, the role of High Priestess was usually drawn from their ranks. (A High Priest, who facilitated connection with the Father God, existed from time to time, and served in a secondary capacity.) Mavis McWycke was an early High Priestess of legendary powers. It was she who sought out the natives in order to learn about the valley's psychic powers. The portion of the river fed by the Great Spring drew her interest. She presided over the coven during an episode of black magic gone awry that resulted in a haunting that continues to this day.

The current High Priestess, Raven Grimmsley, was a repository of McWycke family traits and magical totems, including the crystal pendant she wore around her neck at all times. The pendant was handed down from High Priestess to High Priestess. Centuries old, it was mined from the Orenda River bed. Legend has it that it was given to Mavis McWycke by an Orenda chief, possibly Chief Ferry. Like a crystal ball, it bestowed clairvoyant powers on the wearer, and aided in contacting the spirit realm.

Raven was schooled by her father in telepathy from an early age. (In hereditary witch families, occult knowledge is passed from mother to son and father to daughter.) Her father devised telepathic exercises of increasing difficulty in order to develop the child's sixth sense. By the time she was ten, her father could implant an action or task in her mind, and Raven would do it without any prior visual or verbal communication. Raven's grandmother taught her the art and science of astrology by drawing astrological symbols on index cards and quizzing the girl on their meaning. As a young woman, she became renowned for casting horoscopes and divining from them the subject's personality, psychology, and bodily strengths and frailties. She could even see past-life traits and problems in a chart.

Apart from animals, particularly birds and reptiles, her greatest love was the study of herbs. After her mother died, she convinced her father and grandmother to let her travel to the New Forest of southern England to live with the resident gypsies and study herbalism. Under the gypsies' tutelage, she learned how to use nettles, horehound, willow bark, and coltsfoot for medicinal purposes. She cultivated mint, chamomile, ginger, and jasmine for soothing teas. While she was reluctant to take on the wise woman/healer role upon returning to the United States, she could, upon request, prescribe an herbal remedy that more often than not worked. She also learned which herbs, roots, and barks were toxic, and which could be used in magic ritual to cause death. This was important information to have, but she vowed never to put it to use.

Her vow was significant, for she had to be on guard against a turn toward evildoing. It was not that she was inherently bad, but something in her character, a bitterness at being abandoned by her mother in death, perhaps, caused her to have sinister thoughts. And when these thoughts rose to the surface, prompting her to action, she could be dangerous. Her Scorpio nature made her inherently vengeful, an impulse she tried to suppress. At her bleakest moments, she felt the pull of black magic, the immediacy of casting a spell to hurt, maim, or destroy an enemy or rival, and this allure was enhanced by her association with the dark stranger, the father of her son. In the stranger's presence, she saw what was possible by working black magic, and ever since had to fight the urge to gratify her lower desires. Though she recognized that black magic was a debased practice, this knowledge was not enough to squash temptation. She could readily draw upon the malevolent energy engendered by Chief Ferry's curse on the valley, a further enticement to evil.

As High Priestess, she understood magic to be the working of an intensely focused will used to shape reality to her intentions. Oftentimes she requested a beneficial condition to be manifested from the Goddess, such as sending healing energy to parts of the Earth damaged by industrial processes. The request was invoked and supplicated, never demanded. A black magician, on the other hand, will summon the spirits under his command to do his will, treating these disembodied entities as slaves. The black magician knowingly chooses evil over good without regard for the long-term karmic consequences. The black magician dominates the powers at his command, while the Old Religion practitioner seeks out these powers, pays homage to them, and worships them as the forces that underlie all natural and supernatural phenomena.

ℋ

On the day of Seth's departure from Hope Springs, Raven called a meeting of the coven, twelve of the region's best psychics, spirit-callers, mediums, and New Age Earth worshippers, all of whom set out for her home in Upper Dark Hollow. One member, who lived in New York City, made a special trip to attend. As darkness fell, a caravan of cars turned into the Grimmsley's unmarked driveway off Route 10. The whoosh of tires on the winding asphalt drive broke the forest's silence, preventing Raven from transforming her fears into tranquility.

She needed to determine if her abandoned son had returned, at whose invitation, and for what purpose. The idea that he knew of his inheritance, a large swath of Orenda Valley land that included the Starfire allotment, tortured her. Given her financial difficulties, there could be no rightful heir suddenly appearing in her life. This would undermine the plan for solvency that Starfire represented. The project would be particularly lucrative, as she had negotiated not only the leasing of the land to the electric company, but a percentage of the ongoing revenue generated by the plant. Since she was the chief architect and beneficiary, it gave her autonomy from her husband Stone; she would no longer be beholden to him for support.

The notion of an income stream lulled Raven into a calm which never lasted long. She had a fear of running out of funds, of having no food, nothing new to wear. For this she blamed the McWycke's genteel poverty. The clan had always had stature in the occult world, but they had never recovered their Old World wealth, and Raven felt like a beggar when she married Stone. It was a valuable alliance, one which would provide stability, for at the time the Grimmsleys were flush. Yet even when she had the means to buy an extravagance or two, it meant nothing. Filling her closets with clothing and her pantry with food still left her feeling poor. She had a hoarder's mentality—she couldn't throw out what was old or outdated. In the end, all the treasure in the world would not remedy her sense of emptiness. And the idea of sharing what she did have, in this case with her presumed son, was anathema. She would cling to what was hers, even if she destroyed herself and those around her in the process. She didn't know what she would do if this stranger was her son. Thoughts of eliminating him rose up in her mind, only to be pushed down, knowing that the karmic results would be dire. Yet the notion that her son had inherited his father's magical powers terrified her; could he destroy her if he chose to?

She had hoped to extract this information from Ajax, her spirit familiar, a ghost passed down from one High Priestess to the next, whom only a High Priestess could summon. Twice she had commanded him to appear, but he refused to materialize. Her familiar could not resist a third command. He was obliged to appear by the Law of Three that ruled all magical practice—a spell repeated three times, a thrice-murmured prayer, and the threefold law of karmic returns. As High Priestess, Raven had three familiar spirits who enhanced her connection to the supernatural realm—Ajax; Rah-wing, her beloved pet and psychic guardian; and Astarte, the water sprite who ruled the Great Spring, bound to the coven two centuries before against her will. Once she'd questioned the coveners and Astarte, she would summon Ajax, if further clarity was needed.

Raven greeted each of the mates, as she referred to her fellow witches, as they entered her home, a three-story gothic structure with carved oak front doors. The once elegant house, the seat of the McWycke family for a hundred and fifty years, had fallen into disrepair. Paint pealed from the walls and ceilings, window panes were cracked, wallpaper pulled away from the walls, and pieces of the oak wainscoting were damaged or missing. Despite the drabness of her abode, Raven acted the hostess, ushering the mates inside with exaggerated cheer. She wore a simple blue caftan and her crystal pendant. Her red-gold hair was pulled away from her face and tied into a ponytail with a green silk scarf.

Stone stood behind the cocktail trolley at the entrance to the living room. "What can I get you?" he asked each guest in a voice that betrayed he'd downed several shots of whiskey. His conservative navy blazer, white shirt, striped tie, and gray slacks were the uniform of a small town real estate broker, a pursuit in which he dabbled and had limited success. Although he came from a family of witches and was a coven member, he looked incongruous in his wife's milieu.

"Stone, people can drink later," Raven said as she joined the mates in the living room. She positioned herself before the glassed-in fireplace built from Orenda River stones. Despite the summer heat, Raven had lit a fire that framed her figure with leaping tongues of vivid orange flame. Fire heightened the spiritual powers of a witch, as it invoked the mystical wisdom of the Divine Fire. She had a personal affinity for this element, often wearing scarves and dresses embellished with the flames found in Tibetan art.

The mates, who had settled onto the threadbare sofa, arm chairs, and folding chairs grouped in a circle, included Marsha Washington, a practitioner of herbal potions; Frank Grant, the president of the Orenda Valley Historical Society and publisher of Raven's books; Delia Hazard, owner of Bell, Book and Candle and Raven's acolyte; Julia Sutherland, a parapsychologist; the former owner of the Ferry Inn, Andy Ritter, detached and gentlemanly; Tim Paley, the current owner; and Roger Prince and Diana Spector, cuddling on the sofa. Blanca Naughton, Bell, Book and Candle's cashier, and Wanda Morrigan, Delia's ghost tour assistant, sat beside each other on an oversized easy chair, whispering and giggling.

Ivy McBroom, the mate from New York City, was the curator of a parapsychology foundation and library established by her great-grandmother. Given her family pedigree in the paranormal, she was second only to Raven in her ability to communicate telepathically. Dressed in a stylish linen pants suit, she seemed out of place with the other mates. She belonged to a "country" coven precisely because it was outside the big city, where a deep connection with nature was difficult. In the

Orenda Valley, she could exercise her telepathic powers to their fullest, communicating with the nature spirits that governed the countryside.

The Circle of Light coven was an established presence in the Orenda Valley. While Raven used discretion regarding the location of the seasonal celebrations, she was proud of her religion and refused to act as if it was something to be ashamed of or kept hidden. Those interested in joining her group did not have to search too hard. Raven kept the coven to the traditional thirteen members, and when an opening became available, either through a mate resigning, moving, or dying, Raven vetted the candidates carefully. She required absolute tact, a demonstrable sympathy for the Goddess as the giver of life, and a passion for the natural world. The current mates were active in the local ecological movement. Tim sponsored a comprehensive recycling program out of the Ferry Inn. Delia did the same from Bell, Book and Candle. Blanca and Wanda worked on an Orenda River cleanup campaign. The "Save Mother Earth" focus of the coven drew local praise, for which Raven took much of the credit. But a threat loomed—Richard Abbey's Dam the Damn campaign could eventually shine an unflattering spotlight on Raven for leasing her land to the Starfire nuclear power plant. The mates knew of Raven's involvement and were shocked that a piece of the natural world under her jurisdiction would be sacrificed to something so destructive. "Like TV reruns, the money keeps rolling in, helping our group stay afloat," she had explained, but it did little to ease the mates' mistrust of the plan.

Raven cleared her throat and began, "Thank you for gathering at such short notice." A flapping of wings and loud caw-cawing erupted. She smiled as Rah-wing flew in from the darkened dining room and landed on her shoulder. "Isn't that sweet," she said, stroking the bird's glistening neck. "He wants to be here, too." She set the bird on his wooden perch beside the fireplace. "Which reminds me, I should summon Astarte." She closed her eyes, held out her hands at waist level, and chanted, "Astarte, Astarte, make yourself present, water sprite of mine!"

There was no response. "Come forth at once, beauteous undine, magnificent ruler of rivers. Now here be! Astarte! Astarte! *Astarte!*"

The sound of rushing water and the splash of waves against rock ricocheted off the living room walls. The atmosphere became as damp as a swamp. A soft, disembodied voice rose in pitch and volume, yodeling in an incomprehensible tongue.

"It's good of you to come!" Raven said. "Will you remain present while we discuss the matter at hand?"

The voice billed and cooed, making most in the coven smile and nod. Translating for the mates, Raven said, "Thank you, my lovely, for granting us your time." Astarte's response, which only Raven and Ivy understood, was, "I had no choice, did I? I am here against my wishes. It has always been so." Assuming a serious demeanor, Raven said, "Let's get down to business. The reason why I've called you here is to discover the identity of a stranger who recently came to the valley."

"Many people visit the valley," Frank said.

"This person is not a tourist," Raven replied. "He is a friend of Roger's, so perhaps we should start there."

Roger sat up on the sofa and withdrew his arm from around Diana. "I don't know who you're talking about," he said nervously, as he'd been unexpectedly singled out.

"Your houseguest," Raven said, "the one who sent Ajax away like Casper the Friendly Ghost. I ordered Ajax to investigate this stranger, and he returned shaken and defeated."

"Beth had someone down from the city. He said there was a ghost in his room. I'm surprised it was Ajax."

Raven looked expectantly at Roger, but said nothing.

"Beth and I met him at the July Fourth party. His name's Seth Davis. He's a friend of Richard Abbey."

"That explains it! Abbey is planting spies to undermine the Starfire project."

"With all due respect," Roger said, "that's absurd. Inviting Seth to the party was a coincidence. He has nothing to do with Starfire. The subject never came up. You know we all don't see eye-to-eye with you on the nuclear plant, but no one here would oppose you."

"So that's all you know about Mr. Davis? Any idea of his background or where he's from?"

"He lives in Manhattan. He's from California. Other than that, I know nothing."

"Is that the man you introduced me to at the party? The one in the pool?" Diana asked.

"Good memory, dear," Roger replied.

Raven settled on the sofa beside Julia. She regarded the mates and said, "Let me level with you. This individual may be a threat to the existence of the coven." She let the words hang in the air before continuing. "I know you're aware of the precarious state of my finances. Without going into too much detail, both the McWycke and Grimmsley legacies have dwindled to nothing." Glancing at her husband, she said, "Stone's real estate business is barely breaking even. We're in desperate straits."

"Is there anything we can do?" Julia said.

"You can lend me your support in finding out if Mr. Davis is—"

"Is what?" Andy prompted.

"Is someone who could claim the Starfire land. Because that's what's at stake. If Mr. Davis is the rightful owner of the land, then I will lose it, and all hopes of financial security will be dashed. The ability of the coven to continue as it has for centuries would be challenged. Stone and I may have to sell the house and move, to where I have no idea."

"How could Mr. Davis own the land unless he's a relative of yours?" Tim asked. "And in that case, a witch like yourself."

"There are many ways an individual can lay claim to land," Raven said cryptically. "As for being a witch, if he can repel Ajax, you may be on to something."

Blanca cleared her throat and said, "While I don't want to work against you, Raven, I am in touch with Richard Abbey. I've learned about Damn the Dam from him. Perhaps I could ask him about Mr. Davis. Would that be useful?"

Raven regarded Blanca harshly, then softened her stare. "Why, yes, it would."

"I'll see what Richard can tell me. But I have to say, the more I hear about the effects of damming the Orenda, the more it goes against our principles of protecting Mother Nature."

Raven fidgeted with her pendant and replied, "We've discussed this before. Given my circumstances, there is no alternative. We will release the land to the power plant during an upcoming sabbat where we thank the Great Mother for her bounty and request the land for nuclear use. I think the Goddess will understand. She *must* understand."

"Did you know that when a nuclear plant draws water from a river to cool the reactor, fish are sucked into the plant and killed in the process?" Blanca asked. "And when the water is released back into the river after cooling the plant, it has been heated to an unsafe level, which can then destroy fish and plant life."

"No, I hadn't heard that," Raven sniffed.

"The heated water also contains trace amounts of radioactivity, which poisons the river and its wildlife."

Raven flushed with anger. "Get me scientific proof! Until you do, I will move ahead with my plans. I think you've been talking too much to Mr. Abbey."

"If what Blanca says is true," Wanda interjected, "you should reconsider leasing the land. We can't harm the Earth in pursuit of profit, no matter how much it's needed."

"I agree," Ivy said, "although I understand your needs, too." Ivy habitually tried to bridge the gap between the coven's factions; she always jockeyed for position within the group.

"I met Mr. Davis at Roger's party," Tim said. "He was charming, with the most penetrating green eyes I've ever seen. Just like yours, Raven."

"The luminous eyes are a McWycke trait," Raven murmured. "Did you find out anything about him?"

"Just that he lives in New York and has a boyfriend."

Raven said nothing. She was ambivalent about homosexuality. Although it was well-known that throughout the millennia, gay priests and priestesses served important functions in many religions, she struggled with the notion of homosexuality in her coven. She'd had to rebuff Tim and Andy when they suggested adding a radical faerie component to their worship.

"I may have helped Mr. Davis buy a pendant at the store yesterday," Blanca said. "He came in with Beth Prince. He appeared to be agitated."

"I met him, too," Julia chimed in. "His psychic energy is through the roof."

"He must be the man I was introduced to at the party," Raven said. "I had an odd reaction, which I should have trusted. Before we determine a course of action, let me consult Astarte. My precious, can you tell me what you see from the other side?"

Astarte's vocalizing transformed the oak-paneled room into a murky deep sea cavern. The coven quieted, listening to the eerie sounds. Translating the aria, Raven said, "Yes, my precious, you're saying that Set, as you call him, is a water child? And that in this incarnation his watery Cancerian nature is intensified by a Scorpio Ascendant and a Pisces Moon? The chart's almost all water. Is that correct?"

An emphatic arabesque trill rang through the room. "I will take that as a 'Yes,' " Raven said, as the yodeling continued. "You're saying that Set's connection to the Moon, since that heavenly body rules Cancer, makes him a natural servant of the Goddess? That he's predisposed towards the deity we serve?"

The singing intensified into a piercing bird-like trill.

"Then perhaps we can form an alliance with him since he's constitutionally predisposed to Our Goddess of the Moon."

An elongated "Neueueueueueueuh" reverberated off the walls.

"Why not?" Raven asked. She relayed Astarte's response: "Because his soul has commanded spirits through many lifetimes, and he will not serve only the Goddess."

The members of the coven shifted their postures in response. Raven gasped for air and said, "He won't serve only the Goddess? Then he's not one of us."

Astarte's trilling trailed off. "So that's all you can tell us, my sweet?" Raven said. "You may go if you wish."

The sound of rushing water filled the room. The atmospheric density lifted and the air became dry. The mates continued to look at Raven for guidance. "We haven't got to the heart of the matter," she said. "I will summon Ajax."

Raven directed the mates to form a standing circle inside the ring of furniture. She shut her eyes and moved her hands in front of her. Feeling the mates' collective will mass around her, she began a metrical chant: "Now here be, Goddess triple-faced the of name the in! Once at known presence your make and mistress your of bidding the do! Ajax thrice-called, spirit, me to come!" She sung her invocation twice more, ending with an emphatic, "Come!"

A burning, sulfurous scent permeated the room. The outline of a tall man dressed in a ragged, mud-caked shroud appeared in the dining room, the flickering cast of his face set off by a helmet of wavy black hair, a neatly trimmed mustache, and muttonchop sideburns. He had a long, narrow nose, frowning mouth, and sunken black eyes that expressed an infinite sadness which touched Raven and the other women of the coven. "So you've finally made an appearance, my man," Raven said. "What took so long?"

While the spirit could hear Raven, he did not possess the power of speech in the physical world. Instead, he implanted his thoughts directly into Raven's mind as he glided into the living room. *I have much which occupies me on the other side.*

You didn't used to stay away so long, Raven silently responded through an eye of psychic communication she had opened. "You have been summoned to explain why you failed to ascertain the identity of the stranger," she announced aloud, for the others to hear. "How could you be dismissed so easily by a human?"

The mates sat speechless in the chiaroscuro room. They watched Raven's face for news. Her expression changed from admiration for her familiar to disbelief as Ajax said, *Mistress, be not so harsh with me. I've never encountered such power in all my years in spirit. I cannot say what happened. I knew your secret thoughts and acted upon them by trying to crush the life from the man—or at least giving him a good scare—when suddenly I was flung across the room. I could not cross back to save my lost soul.*

How could a mortal disarm you? Raven silently demanded. *Only the mightiest of magicians could do so. I hope you're not lying—*

What I said is the truth, Ajax interrupted.

Then can you describe the force you encountered? We know the stranger is human, but is he possessed by a demon who acts through him? Tell me, what was his power like?

His power, Ajax began, *was as still and deep as a subterranean lake that is the source of a mighty river. Once it became active in the chamber, it buffeted me about, and there was no combating it. If you'll allow me to compare it to your gifts, mistress, it was smooth, effortless, and boundless. Whereas your labors are sometimes strained, constipated almost—*

Enough! You needn't insult me. Should I recount the fall that brought you to your present condition?

No.

Tell me what you could glean of his background. Is he an adept in a magical society? Or were his skills passed down mother to son?

He was a guest of the Princes. That's all I could read from his aura.

Surely you noticed something more pertinent than that.

Nothing else came through, Ajax insisted. *Perhaps he shielded his thoughts from me.*

Or perhaps you're not telling me everything you experienced.

I swear, mistress, that's all I picked up.

If that's all you have, you are dismissed.

Ajax dematerialized, and Raven motioned the mates to be seated. "Damn that spirit!" she said. Eyeing the assembly, she briefed the others on her conversation with Ajax, adding, "The stranger's challenge to his authority has rattled him. Once he's calmed down, he'll tell me the entire story."

Of course I know the man who dismissed me, Ajax said from his dematerialized space. *The jolt of recognition would have killed me if I weren't already dead.*

A reedy cackle inside Raven's head made her jump. Either Ajax was playing with her or revealing something of what had occurred. She stood in front of the coven appearing distracted.

What luck to find the agent of my demise, Ajax said. *He can break the curse. He can set me free!*

"Silence!" Raven cried to the air around her.

My freedom is at hand!

"Enough!" Raven grew dizzy and disoriented. The room swirled before her as if she were on a carousel. She watched the coveners speaking in words she could not understand. She focused on their lips, trying to calm herself. Waving her hands, she cried, "Let's not all talk at once!" She steadied herself against the back of a chair and grasped her crystal pendant to restore her focus. "We can now proceed to the next step," she declared. Drawing herself up to her full height and turning to Blanca, she said, "You will discreetly gather information about Seth Davis from Richard Abbey. I'm not thrilled by your association with him, but it may prove useful."

"Yes," Blanca murmured. A defiant look in her gaze indicated she was weighing her commitment to the coven against her burgeoning love for Richard and his cause.

"Roger, if you don't already have it, get Seth Davis' address and phone number from your wife without making her aware of what you're doing."

"Yes, Raven."

"Ivy, once I have this information, you can do some investigating in New York. Perhaps the Society has access to a database you can use."

"There's LexisNexis," Ivy replied. "What will I be looking for?"

"Mr. Davis' parents, family background, life history, whatever you can find. If you discover anything, I will scrape together the money to pay for a private detective, although I will need a miracle from the Goddess for that. I must find out the stranger's identity."

"Chris at the Association for Psychic Investigation may be able to help. His brother-in-law is a high-level police officer who has access to everything."

"Good thinking," Raven said.

Blanca waved her arm to get Raven's attention. "I can't deceive Richard, even for the good of the coven," she mumbled.

"You must do this, Blanca. It will benefit us all."

Blanca's hand fell back to her side, and a look of tight-lipped resignation clouded her face.

Raven scanned the mates, who wore concerned expressions. "Stone, turn on the lights," she said. "You can serve drinks now."

"Yes, ma'am," Stone said as he rose and shuffled towards the cocktail trolley.

Raven strode to Rah-wing's perch and held out her hand. The bird hopped onto her finger. "I'll have a Bloody Mary," she said.

"Yes'm."

"Make it a double!"

Ten

Seth scrutinized his face in the bathroom mirror, trying to detect a physical transformation that corresponded to his supernatural awakening. *Keta was only a dream. An idea of my mind. Not something real.* His eyes stared back at him, wide with fear and anticipation, the startled eyes of a madman. Yet his appearance was unchanged; other than the tense lines around his mouth, he looked the same. As he gazed deeper at his reflection, his face shattered into a thousand slivers of glass. Shards containing an emerald eye, a nostril, an ear lobe, a lock of cinnamon hair, and a partial upper lip clattered noisily to the floor, splintering into smaller fragments. He looked down at the splinters that surrounded him. Cuts on his feet bled like razor nicks. When he returned his gaze to the empty mirror frame, there was nothing there but a space where his face had been.

Spooked, he retreated to the living room. He picked up a copy of *New Day* and sat on the captain's bed, distractedly leafing through the pages. He tried to focus on going to work later that afternoon. His job would get him out of the apartment, which had become as claustrophobic as a prison cell. He kept returning to the notion that something unusual had happened. He needed advice, paranormal counsel, from someone he could trust, not some card reader on Bleecker Street. There were friends he had known in San Francisco who might help, among them Clara Cooper. Clara had introduced him to astrology. She was accurate when she read his birth chart, knowing, without him telling her so, that he was adopted. He hadn't seen her in years, but her phone number was in his address book. He took the phone from the metal table beside the captain's bed and dialed the number. After several rings, Clara's bell-like voice answered.

"Clara?" Seth said uncertainly.

"Yes, who is this?"

"It's Seth Davis. Remember me?"

"Of course! We haven't spoken in ages. Are you still acting?"

"I gave that up years ago. How're you doing?"

"I'm incredibly busy. I can't believe you got me in. I'm finishing my Masters in psychology, and I'm never here."

"That's a switch from astrology."

"Not really. Read Jung—you'll see. I'd ask how you are, but I can hear it in your voice. Is everything all right?"

"Well—" Seth said. The tension that lodged at the back of his throat constricted his speech. He paused, then said, "That's why I'm calling. I need your help. I was visiting friends in the country and was nearly suffocated by a ghost. The next day I had a weird encounter with a parapsychologist and experienced an unsettling vision. The ghost came back the next night. I was so scared I got the hell out of there. I know I sound ridiculous, but I'm not into dark energy or anything like that. I've accepted the existence of God pretty quickly."

"Sometimes events come to us so we can open ourselves to the Divine. I'm reminded of Jacob wrestling with the angel, asking for blessing."

"I need advice on how to protect myself. I'm terrified the ghost has followed me."

There was a prolonged silence on the line. "Clara, are you there?" Seth asked.

"Yes. Are you sure it was a ghost?"

"It was—"

"A spirit? A force?" she interrupted. "Ghosts can travel, and contrary to the old legends, they can cross bodies of water. But a ghost traveling a long distance is unusual. You might have disturbed a force and that disturbance has followed you. For the next three days, meditate while burning white candles and incense. You need to open your heart chakra to the experience, while asking the universe to help you get through whatever's been triggered. You should also ask that anything you need to learn from the experience be revealed in a dream or a flash of intuitive understanding. Keep in mind that a sepia-colored dream may indicate a past-life connection."

"Is that type of revelation possible?"

"Of course. I think what you've seen will turn into a profound awareness of God. I'm getting the impression that this was a reconnect to a past life. You should be open to that possibility, and address that when you meditate."

"You think the spirit is related to me?"

"That's what I'm seeing. And judging from your chart, you know as well as I do that such things can happen."

Seth hesitated before saying, "I'll give it a try. Would you mind looking at my chart to see if it's a good time to travel? And would you take a peek at my boyfriend's chart, too? I'll call you back with his time of birth."

"I'm really jammed now, but since this is an emergency, I'll send something on cassette within a week."

Seth gave Clara his address and phone number and hung up. He wanted to meditate, even if it made him late for work. He dressed and walked to the Waxen Image candle shop on Christopher Street, where he purchased two boxes of white votives. He also bought three packets of sandalwood incense sticks, the same scent as the essential oil he wore.

Back in the apartment, he confiscated shells from Martin's Fire Island collection and placed the votives inside. "I hope to Christ this works," he mumbled, as he stationed the lit candles on the bookshelf beside the bed, on Martin's computer desk, and on the floor at the four corners of the room. He put two incense sticks in a wooden holder he'd had since college, and placed several more in the plants on the window sill.

He lay on the bed and rested his head on a pillow. Closing his eyes, he visualized the white light of God, as he'd done for the last three days. He sent the light to his heart chakra—the region between his breasts that he was only now conscious of—and imagined his heart opening to receive it. A golden warmth spread through his chest, both calming his heart and inflaming his blood. The radiance coursed through his body, prompting him to pray, "Dear God, dear universe, please grant me your guidance in getting through this encounter." His prayer was too simple, and he was ashamed of his lack of eloquence, but he would not be deterred. Asking again and again for clarification, he deepened his concentration with each appeal. He spun his prayer like golden floss on a spinning wheel, each turn of the wheel infusing his cry for help with a keener urgency. As he asked for revelation to be sent in the form of a dream, and as he considered whether his haunting could be past life-related, he felt like he was burrowing through layers of soil and rock to the earth's core, or opening successively smaller boxes to find some kernel of truth deep within. When he emerged from his trance an hour later, a sense of relief stemming from his ability to pray heartened him.

❦

Seth meditated each day before going to work. The night of his third meditation, he dreamt that his apartment was expanding and contracting like a living organism. The squared-off walls became elastic and tensionless as the borders of the material plane flexed to intersect with another reality. His living room transformed into a Dali painting; the coffee table liquefied and slumped over, its joints no longer able to support it. The pinewood bookcase flew apart at the seams, sending Martin's videotapes and screenplays to the bare wood floor in slow-motion. The dining table and chairs vaporized and fell to the ground as dust. Martin's magic books with the gold tracery on their spines blew out of the hall closet and danced on the floorboards.

The remaining furniture dissolved into the floor and the apartment assumed the contours of a rain-soaked cardboard box. Ebony eyes and a twisted mouth filled his dream. A tormented face flickered in silent movie close-up. The visage was blurry, with the unsteady quality of an old photograph re-animated back to life. Sepia light bathed the anonymous features in a reddish-brown glow. A young boy was pulled through river rushes by an elderly gentleman wearing colonial clothing—a long black waistcoat, knee breeches, and buckled leather shoes. The boy stood by as the old man cornered, and then began to strangle, a limping man dressed in similar vestments. The limping man succumbed, his eyes bulging from their sockets as he expired.

"He was your father," Keta's disembodied voice whispered. "That's all I can tell you."

ℋ

On Friday evening, Seth walked up Seventh Avenue. He hoped to run into friends at the Dew Drop Inn, as he did most Friday nights. He passed the triangular Village Cigar Store opposite Sheridan Square and the Riviera Cafe with its bustling outdoor tables. Weaving through the weekend crowd, he couldn't shake the feeling that Martin was going to die. The loss, a dizzying black emptiness, crept coldly under his skin, causing him to shiver despite the warmth of the night. He grew lightheaded but pressed onward, stopping outside the bar to stare through the windows into the crowded interior. *Go easy on the booze. You're already out of control.*

Inside, he scanned the smoky room, only to see that no one he knew was there. He took the sole unoccupied stool at the bar next to a woman dressed entirely in white. She looked out of place, an angel at a Christmas pageant in July.

Seth greeted the bartender, who wore a permanent grin, and ordered a margarita. As he looked around for familiar faces, the woman in white turned to him and asked, "Do you believe in miracles?"

"I'm not sure," Seth replied.

"Well, I've just had a miracle," the woman announced.

"I hope it was a good one," Seth said, dismayed that he was being pulled into conversation with a stranger.

"I just found a fifty dollar bill at the bottom of my purse that I didn't know I had. I was wondering how I'd pay my tab." She nudged Seth in the ribs and laughed, "Washing dishes, like they did in the old days."

He sipped the drink that had been placed before him and said, "It's a good thing you found the money."

For someone not able to pay her bill, the woman was well-dressed. She wore an exquisite silk sheath embossed with Chinese hieroglyphs, and matching white silk pumps. A pentagram inlaid with diamonds hung around her neck, while diamond bracelets adorned both wrists, and a diamond-encrusted band shone on her ring finger. The pale skin of her face and shoulders was dusted with freckles. Her golden ringlets and dainty features were those of a porcelain doll, yet her face had a hardness to it. She looked both childlike and far beyond her thirty-five or so years.

"Bush, if he's elected, and he will be, will only serve one term," she said. "I have inside information about this."

Seth searched the packed bar, but saw nowhere else to sit, or even stand comfortably.

"You know the eye above the pyramid on the dollar bill?" the woman asked in a hushed, conspiratorial tone. "That didn't used to be there. The founders of this country were all Freemasons, and originally they had an open-ended pyramid on the dollar bill. When Roosevelt was in office—he was a Freemason, you know—he added the eye to the top of the pyramid." She glanced around the room, as if she were about to reveal state secrets, then reached into a canvas bag that lay at her feet and pulled out a purple vinyl binder. She ceremoniously placed it on the bar and opened it. The right pocket contained a large color photocopy of the eye on the dollar bill, while the left pocket held a reproduction of the dollar's eagle insignia and the multi-starred Glory that floats over it. The woman pointed to the pyramid and translated the Latin inscription beneath it, saying, "New Secular Order." She placed her finger on the eagle and said, "This symbolizes the spirit, one step removed from the Deity above it. The spirit grasps the laurel branch of peace and the arrows of war, just as a nation does. These are all Masonic symbols, you know."

Seth glanced at her quizzically.

"All this points to the fact that we're living at the end of an era. The two thousand year reign of Christ, the Piscean age, is over. That epoch brought with it the rise of science, materialism, and the machine to the exclusion of all forms of intuitive knowledge, including faith in God—and the Goddess. That's why the dollar bill's the perfect symbol for our materialistic age."

Seth took another sip of his cocktail, remaining defiantly silent.

"The era we're ushering in now, the New Age, will be much more spiritual in nature. When we move completely into the New Age, the all-seeing eye on the dollar bill will supplant the pyramid as a symbol of the Divine watching over everything."

"Where did you learn all this?" Seth asked, both annoyed and intrigued.

"It comes when you study the old ways," the woman said. She extended her hand while sizing up Seth with a steely blue stare. "I'm Ivy McBroom, the curator of the Paranormal Society on East Thirty-Eighth Street."

"Seth Davis," Seth said as he shook her hand. He instantly regretted giving his name.

A slight smile crossed Ivy's lips as she said, "I thought you were special the moment you sat down."

"How do you mean?"

"That you are receptive to the hidden realms. Am I right?"

"Well—" Seth hesitated. "I've recently become aware of the presence of ghosts."

"Yes, that, and the ability to cast spells and practice magic."

Seth tensed and blurted out, "I'm not a witch!"

"There's nothing wrong with being a witch. I'm a witch, if you care to know. Your energy tells me you have a penchant for the spirit world. Perhaps even a hereditary connection."

Seth considered paying for his drink and leaving. "This is all new to me," he said. "As for any family link, I'm adopted, so I have no hereditary background that I'm aware of."

Ivy gazed into Seth's eyes. "You could benefit from a group I belong to in the Orenda Valley. I'm a Goddess worshipper, someone who reveres the Earth. Spells don't hold up in the concrete and steel of the city, which is why I practice my religion in the countryside. Besides, the covens here are too cocktail-party chic for my taste. My group already has thirteen members, but I'm sure you would be welcomed."

Seth stood up and placed a twenty-dollar bill on the bar. "Are you following me?" he demanded. "How did you know I was here? Did Beth tell you where I live?"

"Wait, Seth," Ivy said, placing her hand on top of his. "There's nothing to be afraid of."

"Then why are you following me?"

"Our meeting is a lucky coincidence. But now that we know each other, I'm wondering if you have any family connections to the Orenda Valley? Any connection to the land itself?"

"None that I know of. I was there recently visiting friends, that's all."

Ivy reached into a white clutch purse and extracted a business card. "You can reach me at the Society's offices. Stop by whenever you like. I can help you. Honestly. You may be able to help me as well."

"I'm not sure how I can help you or what else we need to discuss." Seth hurriedly paid for his drink. As he said good-bye to the bartender, Ivy slipped the purple binder into the canvas bag and placed it back at her feet, a faint smile lingering on her lips.

He walked down Seventh Avenue and, for a moment, grasped the significance of Ivy's talk about the Piscean Age winding down and the dollar bill's metamorphosis. And just as quickly it slipped from his understanding. He wondered how this woman had found him among the millions of people in New York City. It was a bad omen.

♈

Martin was sitting in front of the boxy computer in the bedroom when Seth returned. "I think I'm going crazy," Seth said.

Martin reluctantly turned away from the screen and asked, "What now?"

"I don't know how else to explain it," Seth said, sitting on the edge of the bed. "This ghost experience has taken over my life. I just met someone from the Orenda Valley in the Dew Drop, completely out of the blue. Man, she was strange! And I keep thinking you're going to be killed to punish me for seeing the ghost and the medium and the vision of Hope Springs."

"That's nuts," Martin said, swiveling around in his chair to face Seth.

"Do you feel like you're in danger?"

"No, I don't."

"I'm terrified you'll be taken from me."

"Don't you think if I were in danger, I'd know it?" Martin asked impatiently.

"I don't know."

"I can protect myself."

"Are you sure?"

"Yes, I'm sure."

"But how do you know?"

"I'm protected, Seth. Stop worrying." Martin turned back to the computer and said, "Now let me finish this."

Eleven

Moving like a stranger through his life, Seth lived as he always had—going to work, pitching articles to magazines, and stealing shared moments with Martin. His nightly typesetting job gave him the flexibility to attend daytime press screenings and, when he got an assignment, to interview the director or actor who was the subject of his article. But he was no longer enthusiastic about something as inconsequential as a movie. Summoning the energy to conduct an interview and write it up seemed a waste of time. Instead, he fantasized that his trip to England would climax with a fatal haunting. Gruesome scenarios played out in his head, destroying his concentration. Whether he was strangled, suffocated, or frightened to death, he—and possibly Martin—would meet a supernatural end. At risk was losing his deposit on the charter airline tickets, but he refused to pay the balance until Clara's reading arrived.

His equilibrium slipped away; spiraling lower, he contemplated the nature of God when he prayed himself to sleep. This was a dire countermeasure, but he couldn't stop himself. He despaired that the only rock he could find to cling to was the Divine. Yet the more he tried to dismiss the concept of God, the more it took hold.

A flood of metaphysical memories surfaced. He recalled that as a six-year-old, he'd lie awake at night trying to fathom the limits of the universe. *How deep is infinity? Where does the universe begin and end?* His childish intellect insisted it had to end somewhere. *But what's beyond that point?* He struggled with the notion of infinity until he could no longer comprehend where the universe stopped. His interior questioning abated and rose, but no matter how he tried, he could never picture what contained space itself. The notion that God is a boundless energy source that encompasses everything in the universe was never satisfactory.

That memory sparked another. As a boy, sick in bed with a fever, he'd dream that he was lying on the strand of Ocean Beach in San Francisco about to be covered by the tide. The tide would rise, slowly recede, and rise again, only to reach a higher point on his body with the next inflow. When he was on the verge of drowning, a Red Indian would appear in his bedroom. The towering, naked figure stalked Seth, so terrifying him that he'd climb out of bed and hide behind the bedroom door. Years later, in one of Martin's books, he learned that Ayurvedic medicine posits that demons invading the body are the source of all illness, and that pneumonia is caused by a red demon made of fire. As he considered this, he understood that the Red Indian was a supernatural being. *Which means I've seen spirits all my life. Was one of my birth parents psychic? Did I inherit this trait?*

ℋ

Seth lay twisted in the sheet, unable to sleep. Dreams and reality were indistinguishable. *What if my ghost was real?* He inched out of bed, careful not to disturb Martin, and went into the living room. He found the telephone directory and searched the listings for "Supernatural," "Paranormal," and "Psychic" until he came across "The United States Association for Psychic Investigation."

At midday, he walked along a tree-lined block in the West Nineties to a brownstone with a brass plaque above the doorway bearing the Association's name. He shook off his anxiety, climbed the stairs, and pushed open the glass and ironwork door to step inside a high-ceilinged lobby, bare except for a desk at the far end. He approached the receptionist, an elderly woman who wore a gold Celtic cross around her neck and glasses that magnified her pale eyes, and asked if he could view the collection before becoming a member. "Certainly," she said. "The librarian's name is Chris. He can answer any questions. He's here Mondays through Thursdays. The weekend librarian is on duty Friday and Saturday. We're closed Sundays." Directing Seth up a curving flight of stairs to the second floor, she added, "Chris is the best person to consult. He knows the library inside-out."

Seth took the curved marble staircase to a sunny chamber lined with bookshelves. A graying, bespectacled man in his late fifties sat at a desk at the back of the room. Approaching the desk, Seth said, "I'd like to see what the library has before I become a member."

Chris eyed Seth from behind a pile of books, one of which he was rebinding. "What kind of material are you interested in?" he asked.

"I'm trying to understand what happened," Seth began. "I experienced a ghost in the Orenda Valley."

Chris coolly appraised Seth. "You can start by looking up Hope Springs and Banbury in the card catalog. I'm not sure how much we have, though."

"How did you know I was there?"

"Just a good guess," Chris replied, a smile spreading across his thin lips.

"I'm also looking for books on haunted inns, past lives, and witchcraft," Seth said.

Assuming a professional demeanor, Chris said, "Again, consult the card catalog. Some of the paranormal journals contain useful information, so don't overlook them. Keep in mind that the collection extends down the hallway and into the front room. Ask if you can't find anything."

Seth turned to the card catalog behind him and pulled out the "H" drawer. He carried it to a Formica-topped table, sat down, and took a notepad and pen from his shoulder bag. Looking through the drawer's contents and seeing nothing on Hope Springs, he decided to compile a list of books under "Haunts and Hauntings." He methodically jotted down titles and Dewey decimal numbers, squinting from the glare of the fluorescent lights overhead.

As Seth worked, Chris said, "Excuse me, but something just occurred to me. Were you the only person to experience the ghost?"

Seth looked up and asked, "What difference would it make?"

"If more than one person sensed the manifestation, it's grounds for scientifically proving the existence of the entity."

"A friend said she saw it in the house the next night."

"Then with her corroboration, you could prove the ghost exists. You'd be adding to the scientific literature. Paranormal science is in its infancy and needs all the help it can get in authenticating the spirit realm."

As Chris finished speaking, a book toppled from a high shelf across the room and hit the floor with a sharp crack, startling them both. Their eyes met in surprise. The question, *Was that a ghost?* telegraphed from Seth's brain to Chris'.

The librarian laughed nervously and said, "Oh, no, it's not what you think. That happens all the time. The books are packed so densely that when you take one out, they tip over by themselves."

Seth rejected the explanation. He decided the book was the resident spirit's way of calling attention to itself.

Chris resumed his bookbinding, while Seth flipped through the catalog tray. Regarding Seth over the top of his glasses, Chris said, "Before you make a decision about joining us, you should check out the Paranormal Society on East Thirty-eighth. You don't need to be a member to use their collection. I can call the curator and tell her you're coming over."

"It couldn't hurt to see what else is out there."

"They close at five, so you'll have a few hours. Shall I make the call?"

Seth nodded, and Chris dialed the black rotary phone on his desk. When a woman's voice answered, Chris said, "Hello, Ivy? It's Chris at the Association. I'm sending over a young man who's doing some very interesting research on the Orenda Valley. I thought you might be able to help."

Seth checked the address Chris had given him against the card he extracted from his wallet. *It's the same.* He hesitated before pressing the ground floor doorbell of an elegant townhouse. The door buzzed, and he walked into the Paranormal Society's dimly lit vestibule. He was greeted by the woman in white from the Dew Drop, who waltzed, rather than walked, on dangerously high heels. She wore a form-fitting aquamarine taffeta dress that flared into a full Fifties-style skirt. "I thought I'd see you again," Ivy said, extending her hand. "If you'll sign in, I can help you find whatever you're looking for."

"Is this another lucky coincidence?" Seth said.

"No. It's fated, if you believe in such things."

Ivy escorted Seth down a hallway lit with ceiling spots to a register on top of a card catalog. He paused at the register, reluctant to print his address and phone number in the ledger. Glancing at the register once he'd finished writing, Ivy pushed a golden ringlet behind her ear and said, "Chris mentioned you're looking for information on the Orenda Valley. Is that a coincidence?"

"No. That's where I encountered a ghost. I'm told the area, particularly Hope Springs, is haunted."

"Yes, the inn has quite a history. Whatever we have on Hope Springs will be listed in the card catalog. The shelves are labeled by subject, which is another way to explore the archive." Distracted by a toddler's squalling, Ivy said, "I've got to check on my son. Make yourself at home. I'll be right back." She hurried up a steep spiral staircase at the end of the hallway, heels clicking against the metal as she climbed.

A basement recreation room housed the Society's books; the holdings were small compared to the Association's. Sparsely-filled bookshelves lined the walls, while a substantial mahogany table absorbed the remaining space. Only the glass doors that led to a leafy back garden alleviated the room's claustrophobic atmosphere.

Books on witchcraft comprised most of the collection. Seth pulled several volumes from the shelves and sat down at the table to take notes. In a book titled *Wicca Regained*, he came across the following entry: "Adherents of witchcraft, or the Old Religion, were the builders of Stonehenge, not the Druids. The monument was a temple of astronomy intended for Goddess worship, not for anything as nefarious as human sacrifice, as has been widely speculated. It should be emphasized that the Wicca people did not engage in human or blood sacrifice. That came with the Druids from pre-Hellenic Greece."

He put the book aside and turned to *Witches, Ghosts, and Hobgoblins*, a catalogue of witch lore. Flipping through the pages, he read of instances where a cat or a rabbit was really a witch in animal form. He also read that when the family cat and mice share a plate of food, the woman of the house is a witch. *A bunch of old wives' tales*, he thought, annoyed that he was wasting his time. He skimmed the Table of Contents and Index, found nothing further of interest, and closed the book.

When he opened *The True Pracktice of Witchcraft*, an antique leather-bound volume with delicate gold tracery on its cover and spine, a flowery perfume wafted through the room. Seth looked to see if the scent had blown in from the garden, but the sliding glass doors were shut. The exotic fragrance, as heavy and intoxicating as lilies in a mortuary, had emerged from the open book. The sweet bouquet made him dizzy. He perused the text, trying to make sense of chapters in a section on "Black Magick" entitled "The Proper Use of Curses" and "Understanding When to Take a Life." Yet he couldn't comprehend the words, which blurred in and out of focus. Instead of absorbing information, his mind was clouded by the scent's tendrils. As his vision dimmed, he lost consciousness. He blacked out, but snapped awake as he was about to slump forward onto the table. A reflex prompted him to close the book, and the scent faded, dispersed by an undetected breeze.

The clack of Ivy's heels on the staircase roused Seth. She carried a tow-headed toddler with a food-stained bib around his neck. "This is my darling Ali," she said.

Seth stared glassy-eyed at the boy and mumbled, "He's sweet."

Ivy settled into the chair beside Seth, cradling Ali in her lap. She glanced at the books on the table and said, "You said you were adopted. It's possible your birth parents are witches. You would do better to research hereditary witchcraft."

"How do you know that?" Seth said, recovering his focus.

"Just a hunch. If I may ask, do you know the name of your birth mother?"

I can't believe I'm having this conversation with a stranger, Seth thought. "I think the name is Van Wyke."

"Any idea where your mother came from?"

"No. I was born in San Francisco."

"You should research that name in the Orenda Valley counties. Try different permutations—Van Dyke, McWycke—move the letters around like an anagram."

"I can access LexisNexis at work."

"Use it. Look for land deeds connected to the names. You might be surprised by what you find."

"Why are you telling me this? What's in it for you?"

"I think we can help each other."

"But how? You barely know me."

"I may know your birth mother."

Seth was speechless. Finally, he said, "It seems like a long shot."

"You must trust me. You could be entitled to an inheritance."

"How does this help you?"

"It may allow me to get something I've wanted for a long time."

Seth looked at his watch. "I've got to get to work."

"Do the research and call me."

Seth rose and returned the books to the shelves.

"I'll be in Hope Springs next week," Ivy said as she walked Seth down the hallway. "Let's talk before then." She let out a mysterious laugh that made Seth stop and turn to face her. She took his hand and said, "McWycke."

At work that night, Seth was distracted and had to be told several times to implement edits to a closing story. He tried to get on the LexisNexis terminal, but it was continually occupied. He went home, undressed, and climbed into bed, blaming his low energy on the narcotic odor from the witchcraft book.

During a fitful slumber, he dreamt he saw Ivy draped in a brilliant red toga. She stood on a marble column, frozen in place like a statue of a goddess. Her face looked young, but part of her toga was a cowl that covered her head, so it was difficult to discern her true appearance. Ivy broke her pose and assessed Seth with a penetrating gaze. "So you're a—" she said, invoking an esoteric magical title.

Seth met her stare but said nothing.

Ivy threw off her drapery and transformed into a stooped old woman. Seth turned away, unable to look at her gnarled limbs and shriveled face.

"Friend or foe?" he demanded. "Truth or lie?"

She glided over to him, put her hand on his arm, and kissed his cheek, saying, "You must go back to move forward." Throwing her scarlet cowl over her head, she hobbled off.

Seth awoke and looked at the wall clock across the room. It was ten in the morning. He got out of bed and walked to the kitchen, more tired than when he went to sleep.

"Raven, it's Ivy."

"Have you found out anything?"

"I did some snooping and met him in his local bar."

"And—"

"He's adopted."

There was silence on the line.

"Raven?"

"Yes, I'm here. Does he have a clue about his birth parents?"

"No, other than the fact that his birth mother's name is Van Wyck."

Another silence. "The name's close enough. Ivy, do you think it's him?"

"My instincts tell me yes."

"So do mine. This is not good news. Does he know anything about his birthright, the land?"

"He didn't mention it. He's unclear about his origins."

"Even so, there's the danger he could find out. Someone could tip him off."

"Who would do that?" Ivy asked with exaggerated innocence.

"I don't know. Richard Abbey, if he ever discovered the connection."

"That's unlikely."

"Still, they're friends."

"What should I do now?"

"Are you in touch with him?"

"Yes. He came to the Society."

"Befriend him and keep tabs on him."

"Okay."

"See you at the sabbat. We'll need to be focused. No near misses with the spell."

"Of course not."

"Between you and me, I may add something extra. One can never be too careful."

"I understand."

"There's a book I'd like you to bring along."

ℋ

The next night at work, Seth sat down at the LexisNexis terminal. He tried to look as if he were on official business as he typed "Van Wyke & Orenda Valley" into the database. His initial entry yielded no results. After two more attempts, he remembered the name Ivy gave him and keyed in "McWycke land & Orenda Valley." An archived newspaper article appeared on the screen, entitled "McWycke Clan's Land Sell-Off."

The article began, "Members of the venerable McWycke family, longtime Orenda Valley residents, have recently put several parcels of land up for sale. Landholders since pre-Revolutionary times, the allotments have been in the family for centuries. The sale represents a historic opportunity for the right buyer. The family has also decided that one parcel, used long ago for fishing and logging activities along the Orenda River, will be leased rather than sold."

Seth scrolled down the screen to read, "A McWycke descendent, current family matriarch Raven Grimmsley explains the sale this way: 'The clan has dwindled from a large extended family to just my husband and myself, with a few relatives scattered across the county. Managing the holdings has become cumbersome and time-consuming, so we've decided this is the right time to divest.'"

Surprised to see Raven's name, Seth read on. "Mrs. Grimmsley claimed that an old custom also prompted the sale. 'According to a revered McWycke tradition, the oldest heir inherits the family landholdings at age twenty-one. Since my husband and I are, unfortunately, childless, there is no one to pass along the land to. Selling seemed the best solution.'"

Seth stared at the screen in disbelief. *McWycke instead of Van Wyke. 'I may know your birth mother. You could be entitled to an inheritance.' Is it possible? Is Raven Grimmsley my mother?*

ℋ

Seth's extended work hours during a double-issue week and surreptitious LexisNexis searches for McWycke land left him anxious and drained. The notion that he'd taken information from a stranger in a bar and accepted it as truth disturbed him. All the years he'd considered looking for his birth parents, and then given up on finding them, forced him to challenge his judgment. What was the likelihood that coincidental visits to the Orenda Valley and the Dew Drop would produce his long-lost mother? The fact that she was a witch might explain his connection to the spirit world. But still—he was both skeptical and intrigued.

Since LexisNexis revealed nothing further, he decided to revisit the Association. Perhaps a clue to his patrimony was buried in their archives. At least he had something to go on, a family name and location. He also knew he would have to ask Ivy for as much truth as she could provide.

The late nights and diminished sleep had another affect—he saw things move out of the corners of his eyes. Shadows and gauzy lights, giving an impression of a ghost's body, flitted across his field of vision. He was only free of these affects once he came home from work and removed the double-moon pendant from around his neck. He became convinced that the pendant was to blame for his blurry vision, rather than the consistent three a.m. closes. *Something about the Herkimer diamond isn't right,* he thought. *It's attracting negative energy instead of keeping it at bay.* The crystal, with its extreme clarity, seemed to inspire the strangest musings, both awake and asleep—thoughts of God and the Devil, and of ending his life out of fear for his soul. When he got home at dawn on Friday morning, he removed the charm from around his neck and placed it in a covered china dish on the living room bookshelf.

Once he stopped wearing the pendant, he wanted something religious to wear. *I've seen the Light,* he told himself. *I must show the world that there's a God.* That night, a Yin-Yang of white light and darkness materialized in his dreaming mind. The serpentine halves spun around, creating a whirl of grayish energy, while Keta declared, "The fundamental truth of the universe is that there's a spark of God in the blackest evil, and a stain of darkness in the purest good. Embrace this mystery and you will comprehend the need for good and evil in the world. Only by experiencing the black hole of negativity called hell and the shining light of divinity known as heaven can you come to a complete awareness of God."

A glowing cross made of light, with a molten white sun at its center, appeared. Keta said, "The cross represents the tree of life, the oldest symbol of earthly existence. To this tree mankind is nailed, sacrificed to the dimensions of space and time. As spirit made flesh, man undergoes an inevitable death.

But accepting the cross—and one's demise—brings a spiritual life that transcends mortality." The cross was succeeded by a golden star of interpenetrating triangles surrounded by blazing Hebrew letters. Even in sleep, Seth resisted the symbol of his spurned religion. But when Keta said, "David's Star is born of a union of holy opposites, and represents the divine light of God in both its male and female forms," Seth accepted the star as he had the cross and Yin-Yang.

On his way to work on Monday, he passed the pushcarts of street vendors along University Place. By the time he reached Union Square, he'd purchased a yak bone Yin-Yang, a silver cross and Star of David, and a braided silver chain. He strung the talismans on the chain while riding the subway to Forty-Second Street, then fastened the chain around his neck. The emblems hung directly above his heart, which he thought was a good omen.

ℋ

When Seth got home that night, he turned on a lamp in the living room to read. Martin, a light sleeper, called out from the bedroom, "Come to bed!" Seth undressed and brushed his teeth. He climbed into bed next to Martin, who grumbled something unintelligible before withdrawing to the bed's far side.

Seth lay on his back; with his arms outstretched across the top of the bed, his body assumed the shape of a cross. He marveled at his descent into faith. What he'd once considered the ultimate crutch, he now rushed to embrace. The constant *thwack, thwack, thwack* of the ceiling fan lulled him into a stupor, and his belief stirred. He tried to visualize God first before asking the Creator of All That Is for the protective white light. The Westernized Jesus, a bearded fairy-tale prince with shoulder-length blond hair and merciful doe eyes, appeared in Seth's mind. *He looks like a piece of kitsch calendar art. Who could take this version of the Lord seriously?* The fair-haired Jesus was supplanted by a medieval portrait of Christ that Seth had noticed as he'd hurried past the Catholic church on Sixth Avenue and Washington

Place on his daily errands. This clean-shaven Jesus had dark hair and a dark complexion. His long, thin face, full lips, and angular features were those of a Semitic nobleman. Large ebony eyes evinced all the pity in the world, even in the flat, iconic rendering that dominated the church's display window. *If Jesus is at all portrayable, this is what he'd look like. A swarthy Semitic prince.* He struggled to memorize the portrait's features, and pleaded, *Merciful God, bless me with your light.* The medieval Jesus emitted a pinpoint of light from the veiled third eye in the middle of his forehead. The white dot expanded until it covered Jesus' face, blotting out his human countenance.

The medieval Jesus reappeared from behind the glowing white mask attached to a body. Like the Cristo Redentor of Rio, he opened his arms to embrace the world, his staunch legs planted firmly on the ground. The outreaching Jesus transformed again into a Christ with a shining star for a face. In a blaze of diamond-white light, Jesus' arms and legs disappeared. What remained was pure God energy, the quintessence of life. Jesus' revealed third eye of supreme cosmic consciousness was a point of shining white light enclosed in a pulsing golden nimbus.

"Thank you, Lord," Seth murmured, "for being here in my hour of greatest need." He surrounded his body with the shimmering gold-white light, imploring, "Please protect me from evil spirits and evil humans." He visualized sending the light, coupled with his own energy, back to God. The circle was now complete—an electrical conduit switched on with energy flowing from the Source to the outlet and back to the Source again. The sideways figure-eight of infinity hovered in Seth's mind like a singular cloud in a clear blue sky.

ℋ

The following night Seth had difficulty envisioning the light. Sweat rose over his body, and he tossed and turned until he dropped off to sleep, only to be startled awake by the words, "God is in your heart!" which resounded throughout his being. He drifted back into a restless dreamstate, and a blinding white light contracted and sent forth a newborn baby glowing with its own radiance. The light also gave birth to a cascade of fleeting pictures, bits and pieces of himself. An occasional likeness, held in freeze-frame, registered—a length of rope, a diminutive child's arm, an antique medicinal vial containing a forest-green tincture. Keta's voice chanting, "Let it go! Let it go! Let it go!" accompanied the images.

"How much of my life should I let go?" Seth asked.

"All of it!" Keta replied.

"Do I have to let go of Martin, too?"

"You are allowed to take someone along. You take him on your path and he takes you on his. So long as you love each other, nothing can separate you. But before you can proceed, you must understand that God, who is inside us, also exists outside our souls as a distinct energy form."

A spiral pathway of golden light crystals appeared. Out of the pathway erupted a swirling cosmos of stars that arched into deepest space, transforming into a tiny human hand. Keta said, "The swirling image of the cosmos is contained in each human fingerprint. As children of God, we're all stamped—*imprinted*—with this likeness. Remember, the universe is one vast emanation of love. When you act against the outflowing of love, you remain trapped on the material plane. To move beyond, you must align yourself completely with the powers of love. Only then can you transcend the physical plane."

A blazing orange ball obliterated the hand from view. First expanding, then contracting, like a star being born—or dying—in the distant reaches of the galaxy, the sphere flickered intensely and vanished, as if someone had turned out a light.

When Seth awoke, he grasped that something else was present in the dream. He drew himself up against Martin's sleeping body, and the dream's residual feeling returned. *Each God and Goddess is the same*, he thought. *They're called by different names, but each deity is an aspect of the one true God. This is the universe's great secret, and now is the time to reveal it. All the Gods are One.*

Twelve

Blanca Naughton spent most of her time away from Bell, Book and Candle working with Richard on Damn the Dam. She helped him stuff envelopes for a mailing campaign and soon became his constant companion. Like a good political wife, she was the woman behind the man at several spontaneous demonstrations along the Orenda River. She performed civil disobedience by lying down with fifty other protesters to prevent the Starfire construction crew from surveying the ground for the plant. When she was arrested, she raised a clenched fist and shouted, "Death to environmental rapists!"

Her conversion to Richard's cause came at a time when she needed rejuvenation, similar to her initial dabbling in witchcraft a decade earlier. As the counterculture faded in the mid-seventies, she'd filled the void with the Craft. Since the Old Religion venerated Mother Nature, and the hippies were all about ecology, the transition made sense. Now she was devoted to Damn the Dam, but her commitment betrayed Raven's trust. She was working against the venture that would save Raven. Her interactions with Raven grew strained; the perceptive High Priestess detected Blanca's shift in loyalty.

Most surprising was that, well into her fourth decade, Blanca was falling in love. Richard treated her like a lady and was deferential to her wishes. They ate dinner together and then said goodnight several times before she invited him into her hillside apartment above River Road in Hope Springs. That first time, and every time thereafter, had been so tender and yet so vigorous. Because she couldn't tolerate the mildew scent of Richard's cabin, she asked him to move in with her. He complied, and made her apartment his home.

"I've been reading the publications from the anti-nuke think tank," Blanca said as she poured Richard a second cup of morning coffee. "I'm amazed at how dangerous nuclear power is. It has the potential to destroy the world."

"The more I learned about it, the worse it seemed," Richard replied. "That's why I got involved." He reached up and cupped Blanca's cheek in his hand, pulling her down to kiss her.

"Your beard tickles," Blanca said, giggling.

"I'll give you something to tickle you. Tonight after the town meeting."

Blanca caressed his face and sat down at the table. Sipping her coffee, she said, "It shocked me to read that we don't know how to store toxic waste. Up until 1970, fifty-five-gallon drums of nuclear waste were dumped into the Pacific and the Atlantic. The containers leaked, sending radioactivity into the ocean and the fish, which were then consumed. We've built plants in earthquake zones. If a big quake happens, who knows the degree of damage that could occur. Radioactive water leaking into a river or ocean would contaminate drinking water and fish stock. Radioactivity would be released into the air and soil. This is a disaster waiting to happen."

"And it will happen. The Starfire plant has the potential to contaminate the Orenda River from here to Delaware."

"The problem is that radiation is invisible. We don't immediately see the effects. Bottom line, our drinking water is at risk. If an accident happened, the water for millions of Americans could be impacted. The sources of drinking water for many major cities are within fifty miles of a nuclear power plant. No one has thought this through."

"It's like the old Harold Lloyd movie—'Safety Last!'" And you know what always comes first and drives the whole enterprise? Greed. Greed on the part of the electric and nuclear industries and their lobbyists without a care for the well-being of people or the planet."

"I agree. As radioactive liquid enters the environment through leaks and accidental dumps into lakes and rivers, the water supply becomes compromised. This is occurring on a global scale. We are literally poisoning ourselves. Our water will give us cancer before we know it."

"That's why we're fighting." Richard regarded Blanca tenderly and said, "You've really done your homework. I'm glad you're with us. You're giving me the strength to keep going. My energy was flagging."

"Happy to be with you, my love."

♍

One evening after dinner, Blanca and Richard sat on the sofa in her living room. "How do you know the gay couple at the Princes' party?" Blanca asked.

"I hope you're not homophobic," Richard said.

"Of course I'm not homophobic. Two of my neighbors work at the gay club near the highway and I've been to plenty of their parties."

"Seth is as politically astute as they come," Richard added. "He's veered off into queer culture by reviewing for some gay weekly, but that's his way of raising political awareness. He's always writing something extra about equal rights or AIDS causes."

"I was wondering if you knew anything about Seth's background?" Blanca asked. "From what I saw of him in the bookstore, he has a strong connection to the occult. As a Wiccan, I can usually sense this."

"Apart from astrology, I've never known him to indulge. He's not a witch like you."

"What about his family background?"

"He's adopted. He doesn't know much about his birth parents. Why are you so interested?"

"He seems like an intriguing character. You should invite him down. I'd like to get to know him."

"Next time I talk to him." Richard lit a joint, leaned back on the sofa, and said, "I discovered some interesting information today rooting around for land deeds in the county museum."

"Really?"

"Did you know that two families founded Hope Springs—the Parsons and the Grimmsleys?" Richard said, passing the joint to Blanca. "Hmm. Good shit!"

"That's common knowledge. All that's left of the Parsons is that mansion." Blanca regarded the joint in her hand. "I really shouldn't smoke. Raven says it interferes with our ability to contact the higher realms during ritual. No pun intended." She cautiously inhaled and held the smoke in her lungs, then coughed upon exhaling.

"Ever wonder why the Parsons died out?"

"Not really. Maybe they moved away?"

"According to the monograph I read, in the 1720s the Grimmsleys joined forces with the McWyckes, who'd emigrated from Scotland, to keep the Parsons from sharing in the valley's natural wealth. It took a century of collusion, swindles, and backroom deals, but they achieved their goal. Isn't that fascinating?"

"I suppose. I thought the McWyckes were more concerned with practicing the Old Religion. Shows how much I know."

"It proves that wealth is the motivating force, no matter how religious you are. I've been trying to find out who owns the Starfire site. Even though the information should be public, all I've come up with are the names Craftwise Realty and Enchanted River Enterprises, which are shell corporations set up to hide the owner's identity. Our lawyers haven't been able to crack this yet."

"People here do like their privacy." Blanca hesitated before adding, "There was an article in the paper saying that Raven Grimmsley is selling family land. Didn't you see it? One of the plots along the river is being leased."

"I wonder if that's the Starfire site. Why didn't you mention it before?"

"I'm caught in the middle, Richard. I'm dedicated to our cause, but Raven is my friend, too. She's mentored me in the Craft for ten years. I feel like I'm betraying her in her time of need."

"She's needy?"

"The family money is gone. That's why she's selling the land. Although no one's supposed to know. You mustn't let on that I told you."

"I should try to reason with her about leasing the land before it's a done deal. Tell her she shouldn't be associated with damming the river and destroying the environment. Especially as a nature worshipper!"

"You can try, but she's desperate. I already spoke to her and got nowhere."

⟨H⟩

"Blanca?"

"Hi, Raven."

"Just calling to remind you to arrive an hour earlier than usual for the sabbat. We will drive from my house to an outdoor location. This will be a special invocation of the Goddess, and we need to be in nature."

"Where are we holding it?"

"It's a secret," Raven said in hushed tones. "All I can say is that the site is sacred. It should aid our concentration in releasing the land."

There was silence on the line.

"Blanca, I realize you've been dabbling in politics with Mr. Abbey, but I need to know that you are with me."

"Yes, Raven, but—"

"No buts. We must stand together. The coven's existence is at stake."

"I think it's more a case of your finances, if you want my opinion."

"If I wanted your opinion, I would have asked for it. Now, what have you discovered about Seth Davis? After all, that's why I encouraged your association with Mr. Abbey."

"Not much, other than the fact that he's adopted."

"Yes, so I've heard."

"I've asked Richard to invite him down."

"That could be useful. Keep at it, and see what else you can find."

"Yes, Raven."

"And remember to be punctual on Sunday. The sabbat must run like clockwork."

"Yes, Raven."

Thirteen

"Merry meet!" Ivy cried as she opened the front door and walked into Raven's house. She arrived at two in the afternoon, three hours prior to the coven's convergence for the Lammas celebration. The August First sabbat to honor the summer season, when the earth's bounty is at its peak prior to the harvest, had been moved ahead a day to Sunday so all the mates could attend.

"Merry meet!" Raven said, rushing into the foyer. She embraced Ivy and asked, "Did you bring the book?"

"Of course." Ivy reached into an oversized shoulder bag and extracted a leather-bound volume covered in gold tracery called *The True Pracktice of Witchcraft.* "You haven't told me why you wanted this particular volume."

"There's a chapter I need to consult before the sabbat."

"Which one?"

" 'Understanding When to Take a Life.' "

"But I thought we will release the land at the sabbat."

"We will," Raven said firmly.

A look of dawning awareness animated Ivy's delicate features. "Have you thought this through? Seth may have some value to us, as one of us."

"I have made my decision."

"And you expect the others to go along with it?"

"They will do as I tell them. As will you."

"Raven, I really think—"

"That's enough! I won't have my concentration rattled by an argument."

"I can't guarantee everyone will go along with you. Why take such a drastic measure? The sabbat's magic will go from white to gray to black if you're not mindful."

"I am mindful! This is what I must do. I can't lose the chance to lease the land because some old hippie, who opposes Starfire, has a friend who is possibly my son."

"If your son doesn't know he's your son, what difference does it make? And if you're not sure, I would use caution. The karma involved isn't worth it. The spell may reverse and kick back against you, three times over. You could harm yourself more than anyone else."

"I appreciate your concern, but I know what I must do. Now let me study the book in peace."

♓

The mates arrived at Raven's house singly and in small groups, and by five o'clock everyone had assembled. A faint double-haloed moon hung low in the summer sky; there was an intensity in the air, a crackling psychic energy, that was palpable. Raven emerged from her bedroom and greeted the coven. In a businesslike manner, she announced, "Stone, Frank, and I will drive to the location. Delia and Tim are already there. Load your regalia into the trunks to keep it out of sight. Let's get started." Due to centuries of persecution, Old Religion rites—and the garments and tools that accompanied them—were practiced in secret, even in the tolerant Orenda Valley.

Ivy and Blanca drove with Raven in her black Impala. Rah-wing perched on her shoulder. The other cars followed at a discreet distance. As they turned onto Route 10, where it wound along the banks of the Orenda, Blanca asked, "Can you tell us where we're going?"

"We'll be there soon," Raven said. "It's a sacred spot, helpful to appealing to the Goddess and God and the spirits of stone and water." As High Priestess, Raven oversaw all rituals and determined their location. During ritual, she went into trance and became the living embodiment of the Goddess.

"Have we worshipped there before?" Ivy asked.

"Not in my lifetime, but my ancestors knew of it. We are going to the Great Spring. Legend has it that Chief Ferry shared the location with my ancestors to show his respect for our practices. So much of how we worship is the same. Both religions are primeval faiths based on the rhythms of the natural world. Native American shamans astral project into the ether to bring back knowledge from their guides, which is what I do as well."

"I didn't realize anyone knew the location of the Great Spring," Blanca said.

"In a few minutes, all the mates will know. It must remain a secret, as must the fact that Astarte is the spring's guardian spirit. Mavis McWycke had a falling out with the Chief when she borrowed Astarte for the coven."

The Impala rounded a succession of curves, driving deeper into Freeman County's forested reaches. The summer sun, still strong as evening approached, cut through the overhead branches that shaded the roadway and mottled the windshield with bursts of light, forcing Raven to concentrate on the road. After navigating several bends, she slowed down at a stone bridge that traversed a creek which ran from the opposite hillside to the river. Just beyond, she made an abrupt left turn into an abandoned country lane, overgrown with weeds. A chain barrier had been disengaged and lay across the path. The car inched forward along a rutted dirt road, with the two other vehicles following. Climbing a hill through dense brush and towering trees, Raven drove cautiously until she pulled into a clearing at the top. Level ground was covered with unkempt grass and weeds and was surrounded by white birch trees, sacred to Mother Earth in Old Religion belief. The river was visible through the tree branches. At the back of the clearing, a stone outcropping exposed a narrow entrance to a cave. Water bubbling from beneath the earth could be heard.

Delia and Tim stood in the center of the clearing beside a stone altar they had spent the afternoon erecting. Two stones of equal size formed the base, and a more substantial flat stone comprised the top. On the altar, Delia had placed the regalia, the ritual equipment required for sabbat observance. Among the items was a sword made of tempered steel, used to draw the magic circle; Raven's athame, a black-hilted ceremonial knife; a white-handled knife, employed for utilitarian purposes; a willow wand, which extends the arm raised to summon the four guardians; a waxen pentacle containing a five-pointed pentagram, the symbol of magic; a censor; four candlesticks holding white candles; a ceremonial scourge make of knotted sisal; and ribbon-like multi-colored cords, representing the sacred laws to which all coveners are bound. In addition, two silver chalices held water and salt. Beside the altar, another stone was placed to house the sabbat offerings of flowers, fruit, cakes, red wine, and honey. Additional white candles, for purification and protection, dark blue candles for change, and green candles for money, as well as hand drums, shakers, and tambourines were kept here. Red clay urns holding sprays of wildflowers, along with sheaves of river wattles bound with scarlet silken cords, stood at each corner of the clearing. A makeshift perch of birch branches stood behind the altar.

The mates got out of the cars. "Merry meet!" Raven said.

"Merry meet!" the mates replied.

Raven placed Rah-wing on the perch and said, "This is the sacred site of the Great Spring. The location must never be revealed. You are all sworn to secrecy."

The mates looked around in wonder. "I didn't think this place was real," Andy said.

"Neither did I," Julia added.

"I've gathered wild herbs near here, but never stumbled upon it," Marsha commented.

"It's sacred to the native residents, and we should respect their presence, though they've long since left the valley," Raven said.

All murmured their consent.

"We must purify the space," Raven said. "Let's change into our robes."

The mates retrieved their ceremonial garb from the car trunks. They donned long, loose-fitting black robes over their light summer clothes—black representing the summation of all color vibrations and the primordial darkness of the universe. The men wore simple silver bracelets on both wrists. Roger, as Faunus, wore a horned mask that covered his eyes and the top of his skull. The women added more elaborate ritual jewelry. Ivy donned a necklace of antique amber beads. Diana wore a silver crown set with four crescent moons. Blanca sported an Egyptian ankh around her neck, while Wanda wore a silver pentagram. Julia and Marsha positioned wreaths of ivy around their heads, into which Marsha had woven sprigs of lavender. In addition to her crystal pendant, Raven wore two gold wrist cuffs. She slung a leather pouch over her shoulder, which contained three candles in glass containers, an herbal offering to the Goddess of her own making, and quartz crystals from the Orenda River.

"Let us synchronize our breathing to achieve a singular mind," Raven said. The mates formed a circle in the clearing and joined hands. With eyes shut, they breathed in and out for several minutes, gradually finding a shared rhythm. When they breathed in unison, Raven opened her eyes and said, "With quiet and serene focus, let us prepare the circle. Delia, do you have the incense I prepared?"

"Yes, Raven," Delia replied.

"A mixture of rose, sandalwood, gardenia, frankincense, and cinnamon should please the Summertime Goddess. Add it to the censor, please."

Delia walked to the altar and placed the scent on the unlit coals.

"Mates, clear the area so I may draw the circle."

The coveners disbursed to the back of the clearing, and Tim handed Raven a broom which he had fashioned of heather bound to a freshly cut sapling. With her features hardened into sharp focus, Raven swept the clearing from front to back to clean the ritual space. While she worked, she sang in a resonant alto:

We are all drops of water

Wee drops from the rivers
That become the rain showers
That replenish the Earth.
Only to return
At the end of our journey
To the sea of the Goddess
Ruled by the Virgin White Moon.
Bless you, Great Goddess
Bless you, Great Goddess
Bless you, Great Goddess
All glory to you!

She handed the pouch to Delia and retrieved the sword from the altar. She walked counterclockwise, tracing a circle nine feet in diameter along the ground with the point of the sword. Delia followed, reaching into the pouch and sowing the crystals like seeds into the earth, points facing outward to amplify the energy. To demarcate the magic ring in three dimensions, both women visualized a gossamer globe of silvery-blue light. When Raven reached the circle's cardinal points—North, West, South, and East—Blanca, who quietly joined the procession, positioned a lit white candle to mark the spot. She then lit the white, blue, and green candles on the stone beside the altar.

Raven approached the altar. She took the silver water chalice in one hand and the athame in the other and said, "In the name of our Mother, the Goddess, and our Father, the God, I purify this water." She touched the athame to the water as she spoke. She set down the water and picked up the salt container. She touched the athame to the salt and said, "In the name of our Mother, the Goddess, and our Father, the God, I consecrate this salt. Let only good things enter here, while casting out all that is bad." She walked the circle counterclockwise sprinkling the water from the chalice, while Delia followed sprinkling salt. "Circle of power, the boundary between man and spirit, I conjure thee!" Raven said. "With the blessing of the Goddess, I purify this ring for the working of magic. For the North, we offer the Earth, our Mother." She placed the wax pentacle Delia handed her next to the North node candle. Moving with Delia in tow, Raven said, "For the West, the chalice of water, sustainer of life." Then, "For the South, my fiery knife, Magicka." Keeping the athame in hand while completing the circle, she said, "For the East, the magic wand, ruler of air."

She stopped, placed her feet apart, and held her hands out, palms away from her body, her elbows bent slightly. In the Goddess position, she raised the athame and cut a pentacle in the air, saying, "Guardians of the four quarters, esteemed Lords of the Watchtowers, grant us the blessing of your presence, and protect and consecrate this circle." She held her fellow witches in her gaze and said, "Let the work begin! Mates, enter the circle through the South node gate."

Delia scurried to the southern point of the circle and held out her arm to indicate an invisible doorway. The mates solemnly filed in. They turned and stared at the idyllic outdoor spectacle as if witnessing the Lammas rite for the first time. The sun had waned, and the tall birches cast long shadows that hastened the night.

Responding to a look from Raven, Delia lit the censer and traversed the inside of the circle counterclockwise, dispersing the floral incense as she went. After walking the circle three times, she placed the smoking censor on the altar and returned to Raven's side.

"The circle is now ready for magic!" Raven said. She placed the athame on the altar. "O Triple Goddess! Maiden, mother, crone! We are grateful for the crops and for all that comes from the earth. But without the God, our Father, nothing would grow. O Faunus, Sylvester, Pan! We thank you for warming the Earth, you who are the sun, the giver of life. You who are the animating spirit in trees, woods, and waters, bless us with continued sustenance. O Loving Goddess! O Boundless God! We give thanks for the bounty of the earth."

The mates chanted, "Diana, Hecate, Isis! Come hither! Cerridwen, Artemis, Athena! We await you! Great Goddess of the Moon, we adore you! Mistress of the Green Earth, bless us!"

Roger and Diana retrieved the hand drums, shakers, and tambourines and distributed them. The group started a slow tattoo to establish the dance rhythm, accompanied by a wordless chant of a medieval-sounding dirge. As they sang, Raven moved to the center of the circle and addressed the coven. "Friends, we are here on Lammas Day not only to celebrate the fruits of the earth, but to honor the river which flows through our valley. The river which brings life to all. There is a part of the river, a dried-up tributary at Blithe Point, which needs our attention."

"Yes!" chanted the mates, before resuming the dirge.

"Let us focus our thoughts on sending life-giving water to this section of the river so it may be revitalized and released from nature's dominion for the production of electricity."

"Yes!" the mates cried. Blanca and Wanda were less exuberant than the rest.

"Let us celebrate the river and the electricity that comes from harnessing its energy. It's a small sacrifice of water and land we request, so that nuclear power will sustain us in the future."

Blanca eyed Wanda, as if to say, "Count me out."

"Let us say a proper goodbye to this part of the river to ensure that no crime against nature occurs, only a gentle borrowing that will benefit all. Let the dance begin!"

The dirge picked up speed and volume as the mates set down the instruments and began a counterclockwise spiral dance around the altar. They joined hands and performed the grapevine move—side step, step behind, side step, step across— which was repeated as they spun around. The dirge became a song:

O Great Goddess
Come amongst us
Bring our goal
To light of day.
Return the water
To the stream
And bless the land
To make it pay—Hey!

The singing grew more strident and the pace increased. The mates fell under the spell of the pungent incense and the flickering candlelight, the only illumination in the clearing, and their collective vision blurred. Their breathing, though labored from the dance, remained in synch, and their minds became as one. A silvery-blue electrical current radiated upwards from the ground as the dancers whirled. The cone of power was raised. A spell could now be cast. Not a spell for evil, but a prayer, a projection, a thought.

As the ethereal blue current rose over the mates' heads, Raven stepped away from the dance. "Mates, join your minds in unison," she commanded before chanting:

River rock and river grass
If thou wilt
Come to pass
Release the Blithe Point land for me
To Starfire's realm
Blessed be!

The mates increased the dance to a sprint. Raven continued:

Rushing waters
Diana's bath
Wend the valley
Carve the path
Crystals bright
Bring to me
A river of money
Flowing free
Make my life a comfort be
Bay leaf, cedar, apple, oak
Rain down prosperity's
Velvet cloak
Wrap me in the garment fair
Cash and coins for my red hair
Come to me, flow again
Banish all tormenting pains

The dancers spun faster. Raven regarded the mates with a satisfied smile and said, "Focus and—"

Holding hands as they danced, Blanca and Wanda looked at each other and acknowledged their refusal to join the group mind.

"Release!"

The mates raised their hands in the air, sent an outrush of collective breath towards the sky, and fell to the ground, signaling the end of the dance. Raven remained standing, hands extended in the Goddess position. Rather than winding down the ritual, she retrieved her leather pouch and took out three black candles. These she set on the altar and lit. The mates roused themselves and sat upright, while Raven moved to the center of the circle. She regarded the strobing candle light and inhaled the rich incense, then closed her eyes and looked inward, summoning a frenzy of fear, which turned to furious hate, necessary for what she must do.

She fell into a trance used to contact her spirit guides. Yet she moved in a different direction, not summoning Astarte or Ajax, but seeking a demon of the darkest powers that would carry out her request. She invoked Chief Ferry's curse on the land, and a beast appeared in her mind's eye—wet, shiny, covered with wartlike bumps, a glistening tube of black energy. She opened her eyes, her orbs glinting sinisterly in the candlelight, and silently acknowledged the spirit's presence. In a startling basso profundo, she croaked, "Balsam bitter, baneberry, roux. Bryony, dropwort, foxglove, too. Nightshade deadly, poppy white, end a life on this fair night!"

The mates gasped and looked at Raven in confusion.

Ivy glanced up at the High Priestess and a shudder passed through her. " 'An' it harm none, do what ye will.' Raven, you will harm someone!" she exclaimed.

Roger said, "Seth's not a threat—" but Raven's stone-faced stare silenced him.

"Radiant boy, who mother shunned, why do you return again?" Raven continued. "To murder me, legend tells, but I will send you straight to hell!"

Ivy rose and approached Raven, grasping her arm. "Stop before the spell is cast!" she implored.

Raven shook her off and said, "Bitter hemlock, drink it down. Choke the throat, round and round. Twist and turn in painful sight. End a life on this sweet night!"

"Raven, stop!" Blanca pleaded. Wanda shook her head in agreement.

Raven cast her eyes to the black starry sky and commanded, "Forces of the darkest night, serve me now without delay! Find and kill my only heir. In desperation, murder's fair." She addressed the conjured beast with, "Blast it! Choke it! Damn it! Evil! Blessed be, thy wondrous devil." She cast the thought of Seth lying dead in his bed into the world with a screeching yelp before collapsing to the earth, her robe billowing around her.

The clearing fell silent. Only the rustle of birds in the trees and the clicking of crickets could be heard, along with the gentle bubbling of the Great Spring. The mates climbed to their feet, mesmerized by the ceremony, but shaken by Raven's conjuring. They were ashamed to regard her as the silvery-blue cone of power dissipated at their feet.

Raven met them with a look of triumphant defiance. To earth the power that had been raised, she retrieved the dish of poppy cakes and passed them around. She poured the wine, infused with cinnamon and cloves, into earthen mugs and distributed these. As the mates ate and drank, she strode to the center of the magic circle and began the closing rites by singing:

Goddess and Horned God
Nature sprites, too
Along with the powers
Who've paid us their due
The hour has come
To bid you adieu!

She took the athame from the altar and walked the circle clockwise, making the sign of the pentagram in the air as she moved. She paused at each cardinal point to blow out the demarcating candle and continued her benediction:

Goddess, Consort, Elementals all

If your will be it so
Please answer our call
Free the land for new use
And end my freefall.
Goddess and God
And Guardians Four
We thank you with praise
And humble amour!

She moved to the stone beside the altar and snuffed out all but the three black candles. With only this light to work by, she poured the remaining salt into the water chalice and handed it to Ivy, who regarded her with a look of undisguised horror. Ivy poured the salt water into the earth behind the altar, muttering an invocation of forgiveness to the Goddess.

Raven retrieved the heather broom from beside the altar. The mates rose and joined hands, resuming the wordless chant that had started the ceremony. Though they were shocked by what had taken place, they were obliged to complete the ritual. As they sang, Raven swept away the remnants of the magic ring. Delia followed, picking up the crystals and placing them in the pouch. Raven walked to the opening of the Great Spring and placed a large maple leaf before it. On the leaf she scattered herbs and flowers from her garden known to draw prosperity—basil, chamomile, clover, bergamot, marjoram, and snapdragon. The offering to Mother Nature would dissolve into the earth or be blown away on the wind, leaving no trace of the sabbat, and no destructive imprint on the environment, though this seemed of dubious importance now. She turned to the mates, and in the darkening clearing, raised her hands above her head and sang:

Magic works in twenty-one days
Or not all
That's what is said
Now it's time to gather up
Magic's regalia
And off to bed
When thou wake

In early morn
Remember tonight's spree
All join hands and wish each well
With a hearty "Blessed be!"

ᚻ

Ajax hovered in the birch branches during the sabbat, a murky ball of energy. Had the mates not been so caught up in the proceedings, they might have seen him twinkling, occasionally throwing off amber light. But Raven had not required his presence, nor had he been called upon at the last minute to assist in the evening's unforeseen magic. He was thankful his mistress hasn't ordered him to kill Seth, for Seth's power could send him back to the Light. The fact that Seth was Raven's son in their current lifetime was an irony too incredulous not to ponder. Fate worked in strange ways! It was almost as if Ajax had impregnated Raven, and Seth was the offspring, a manifestation of the curse—and the possibility of breaking it—that tied Ajax to the coven.

Ajax had memories of his last life as a man. He recalled the forests that surrounded his town, the rushing river full of fish and turtles, the inn he operated, and his family—a wife, two daughters, and a son. He also remembered, though not willingly, the deeds that had cost him his life and soul. It was a bad dream he endured again and again. Ambition. Greed. Black magic spells for prosperity. And the most painful memory of all, which nagged at his soul—his son.

He lived in a timeless void—an eternal moment—neither past, present, nor future. His world was composed of mists and miasmas, thin gray fogs that cloaked him in a shroud of nothingness. He had lost track of his time as a spirit; the absence of something to anchor his existence made him confused, and then afraid. He thought he would never be able to leave his limbo. He served a succession of McWycke priestesses who could require him to perform feats against his wishes; this was horrible to him. The sole notion that occupied him was the idea of being freed, of being sent into the Light. Being sucked to the dark side for the misdeeds of his last earthly life was his greatest fear.

Lacking a material body, Ajax was an energy form that could take on the appearance of his last human existence. He could also manifest as an aura of amber light. As pure energy, he could float in the air and fly through walls. He could appear and disappear in the human world at will, revealing himself to some people and not to others as he preferred. He could move objects to call attention to himself. Most importantly, he could materialize anywhere he chose simply by concentrating on the location. He could even cross bodies of water and appear under water, contrary to old superstitious beliefs.

A newly born earthbound has much to learn about his ghostly powers. Ajax dimly recalled his first moments as a spirit. It was like being a baby, confused and helpless. He was barely able to negotiate the lack of physical laws and the novel abilities granted him in the spirit world. At the moment of his death, he was bound to an earthly mistress; as a result, his contact with the material world remained constant, as he was required to act as an emissary and guide to his realm. The McWycke mistresses commanded him to carry out tasks, some for the good of the coven, and some for selfish gain. With each base act he committed—a haunting to scare off a rival wise woman, a suffocation or strangulation to destroy a financial competitor— his spectral powers increased thricefold. He could flit from one corner of the valley to another in the wink of an eye; he could enter a person's dreams and scare them nearly to death; and he could serve as a conduit to the black energies that his mistresses sometimes sought. As his ghostly powers grew, something peculiar happened—he developed an odor. His olfactory sense was gone, but he heard it in the reaction of the living. "Sulfuric," "gassy," "rotten eggs," "stink," and "burnt leaves" were used to describe his presence. In his last life as a human, he had been fastidious as to his person, so this dismayed him. What bothered him even more was that, although his human existence has been far from perfect, he never intended to harm others. In the eternal now in which he lived, his presence terrified people. He dwelled on the menacing acts he'd been commanded to perform and saw that instead of moving toward a release into the Light, he was going in the opposite direction. He would remain in the swirling mists of timelessness, and gradually move to the dark side. Already he could feel those forces beckoning him, telling him to hate the human world, to be jealous of those who had not been caught in the net of evil, and to be angry at his plight. Unseen voices urged him to increase his power by creating chaos in the world of the living and then feeding on the bedlam that resulted. These voices tormented him until he understood that he was living in a perpetual hell, his punishment for his previous life's actions. A fresh torment was the feeling that he'd never break free of this cycle. He couldn't remember the last time he'd seen a ray of the Light, a glimpse of God's mercy, in his world.

Seth did not appear to be a radiant ray of light when Ajax first encountered him. He was a helpless human who could scarcely protect himself against Ajax's otherworldly energy. But how quickly the shock of recognition occurred! The Light works in unexpected ways, for Seth was his ray of hope, his passage out of hell.

Ajax took advantage of the sabbat time, in his world where there is no time, to forge a plan of escape. He would find Seth and compel him to cross him into the Light. Seth could do this. His shamanic powers carried over through lifetimes. They had to; once attained, such illumination stayed with a soul through each incarnation. Ajax knew Seth lived in New York City, but his exact location was a mystery. He saw himself soaring above the darkened New Jersey farmlands, casting an infinitesimal shadow across the dazzling face of the moon as he flew through the sky. He crossed the mighty Hudson River—easy!—and found himself in a forest of concrete structures, the likes of which he'd never encountered. The electricity of the city, the energy generated by so many people and machines, was daunting. It confounded him, leaving him a disoriented speck of energy blown about the avenues on a humid breeze. He couldn't materialize in an unknown location because he had nothing on which to base his thoughts. But he could think of Seth, and he could hold the image of him in his imagination. He thought of his son, he remembered his lover, and he visualized himself materializing in Seth's apartment.

He thought it, and it was so.

Fourteen

A young boy with dark hair, black eyes, and pale skin wandered through Seth's dreaming mind. Moving in a flickering sepia haze, the child clambered up trees and hid in hedgerows in a colonial town. "I put it in my mouth 'til the thing exploded," the boy murmured. "He said that's what men do."

The boy, now accompanied by a tall man wearing a black frock coat and knee breeches, entered a stable at the back of an inn. They ascended a ladder to a hayloft, where the man withdrew his penis from his breeches. He coaxed the boy into fondling it, then forced the child's head down.

If only I can restore the child's innocence, Seth thought. The thought reversed and became, *I can restore the child's innocence if only I—*

In a fog-shrouded ring of trees, the man fucked the boy while black-clothed celebrants danced and chanted around them. The boy, drugged or unconscious, gave off a radiant glow that expanded to fill the grove as the rite reached its peak. At the moment of orgasm, a smoky demon emerged from the night air and hovered overhead.

Seth awoke with an erection. He lay next to Martin in a daze. He drifted back to sleep and slipped into a dream which began with the sensation of something floating above him. An indistinct form loomed overhead, straddling his body. He opened his legs to accommodate a probing finger and embraced the form's torso with his legs, while the invading finger slid in. "We haven't had sex in the middle of the night in years," Seth whispered.

The unseen lover entered Seth with an expert maneuver that mixed burning pain with a deeper pleasure. "Did you have a dream, too?" Seth asked. There was no answer, and he could not locate his paramour's eyes. The invader gathered Seth up and kissed him; their lips locked together, and Seth met his partner thrust for thrust with his undulating rear. A cat's tongue to the neck drove Seth into a bucking frenzy. "It's as good as it used to be," the lover whispered, as he pumped deeper, pistoning Seth's cock with his fist. Steaming breath came in short, rapid gasps, and moist heat singed Seth's face, drawing him upwards in search of another fiery kiss. Greedy lips devoured his mouth. The two moved in synch like one mindless organism until Seth let out a fantastic groan and shot a shower of cum into the air. The paramour rose up like a majestic bird of prey and shivered as he came inside Seth, who looked up and detected no reflection in his ravisher's gaze. The shadowy visitor cocked his head heavenward and let out an icy laugh. Seth's panting body froze upon hearing it.

"As good as it used to be. But that's not why I'm here."

Seth jolted awake. He saw Martin's sleeping body next to him and sat upright. A play of amber lights floated beneath the ceiling fan. Before he could leap out of bed, a voice inside his mind said, *Yes, son, I've found you.*

Seth reached over to wake Martin, but the spirit restrained his hand. *This is between you and me. No one else need be involved.*

Seth's heart raced. He couldn't move his lips to speak. He said in his mind, projecting the thought outwards, *I mean you no harm. What do you want from me?*

The Light.

What do I have to do with the Light?

You must send me there. You are responsible for my present condition.

Who are you?

In this state, I am Ajax, named by my first mistress for the mighty Greek warrior. What a mockery! I have no power except to follow orders. The name means "mourner," appropriate for one who longs for his former existence. I had another name when I was your father.

Are you the spirit who haunted me in Banbury?

Of course.

I have no means to send you to the Light.

You have the ability; you must find it.

Why did you try to kill me?

Find out what you need to know to help me. Otherwise, I will— The scent of sulfur and decaying leaves filled the bedroom as the twinkling amber lights dimmed and vanished.

Seth searched the room for signs of the ghost. When he saw nothing, he jostled Martin and said, "Honey, wake up."

Martin roused himself. "What's that smell?" he asked.

"The ghost's found me. His name is Ajax."

⚘

Seth rang the Paranormal Society's bell a little before noon. The door buzzed open, and he was greeted by Ivy. "Come in," she said. She led him into the main room and gestured for him to take a seat. She looked at him intently and said, "You're alive."

"Are you surprised? The ghost I mentioned has contacted me. I need your help. Can you prescribe some sort of protection? A spell, perhaps."

"I can direct you to some books. But you are in greater danger from other quarters. Did you research your birth family background?"

"Yes."

"What did you discover?"

"An article on Raven Grimmsley and McWycke land that is passed on to the first-born heir."

"Then you know," Ivy said with a mysterious smile.

Seth leaned back in the chair and let out a weary sigh. "I never thought I'd find my birth mother. Why are you helping me?"

"You may be of assistance to me. Without jeopardizing my standing in the coven, I can't say more except that your life is in imminent danger. The ghost is the least of it."

"The ghost tried to kill me, and may try again."

"You need to protect yourself from something else." Ivy walked to a shelf labeled "Witchcraft" and pulled out two books. She opened *The True Pracktice of Witchcraft* and turned to a chapter called "Spells to Break Spells." "Write this down," she said.

Seth took a notepad and pen from his shoulder bag.

"Place a tall black candle in a large black bowl. Heat beeswax and use it to fix the candle to the bottom of the bowl. Add water to the bowl, filling it to within an inch of the top of the candle. Breathe deeply for as long as it takes to clear your mind. Light the candle and meditate on the flame, visualizing the spell's power emanating from the flame."

"What type of spell should I visualize?"

"A death spell."

Seth put down his pen and looked at Ivy.

"Quietly contemplate the candle and the spell's power as it burns brightly in the flame. Watch the candle burn down until the flame comes in contact with the water. As the flame sputters and dies, the spell is dispersed. Visualize the spell's power dwindling to nothingness. Pour the water into the ground, or into a natural body of water. Bury the candle alongside the water."

"You can't be serious?"

"Dead serious. For good measure, here's another spell. It's antique, but effective." Ivy opened the second book, called *Folk Magic and Witchcraft*, and read: "Historically, practitioners of the Craft have used urine to cure bewitchments and curses. One such curative calls for a lock of the victim's hair to be boiled in his own urine, which is then thrown onto a fire, breaking the spell. A variant is to boil the sufferer's urine in a pot with crooked pins."

Seth scribbled down the words. "You advise performing both spells?"

"Yes. You need everything you can muster."

"My mother's trying to kill me?"

Ivy put her hand on Seth's. "Put these spells into practice, that's all I'll say. Call me if you sense you're in danger."

"Thanks," Seth said, rising unsteadily. "I've got to get to work."

"Do this sooner rather than later."

♓

Seth headed home. He didn't have time to implement both spells, but he could perform one before going to the office. He stopped to buy a box of straight pins and bottled water, drinking one bottle before he reached his apartment. He went to the kitchen, where he extricated Martin's spaghetti pot from the tangle of crockery above the stove. He placed the pot on the linoleum floor and chugged a second bottle of water. In the bathroom he found his haircutting shears. He pulled a wavy lock of hair from his temple and snipped it off.

Returning to the kitchen, he dropped the hair into the pot and began bending the pins into a V-shape and sticking himself in the arm. His own blood, added to the mixture, would enhance the brew's power. He downed the third bottle of water while tossing the bloodied pins into the crucible. The pain in his gut shot deep into his intestines, forcing him to open his fly and release a stream of urine that splattered and frothed as it hit the sides of the pot. When he was done, he hoisted the slopping mixture to the stove and nearly retched at the sight of his hair floating in a sea of urine and pins. He lit the flame beneath the pot. While the concoction simmered, he composed a charm. "Bubble, bubble, toil and trouble, reduce my mother's life to rubble."

The urine boiled, sending a bitter stench into the room. He devised a more suitable incantation, intoning, "With this potion, which contains my essence, I return your spell. May the vapors defend me and carry your curse back to you three times over." He didn't hear the front door open as Martin entered the apartment. Nor did he notice his partner standing in the kitchen archway observing his benediction over a vat of boiling piss. When he finally saw Martin's lurking figure, he jumped. Their eyes locked, and Martin yelled, "What the hell are you doing?"

"I'm boiling my urine to break a death curse."

"Did you find my magic books?" Martin shouted, his face flushed with confusion. "I told you never to touch them! No one's energy should be on them but mine."

"I didn't touch your books. I have my own sources."

"I'll know if you used them."

"Why are you so focused on your books? Aren't you concerned that someone's trying to kill me?"

"Of course I am. I can help you, if you'd only ask. But I'm moving out if you touch my books. Only one magician can use those books."

Seth regarded Martin with a preternatural calm and said, "I'm not a magician like you. And maybe you should move. You'd be safer elsewhere."

⅍

As Seth sat at his ATEX terminal at work, Keta whispered inside his head, "If you're going to save the world, you must save every single soul. Which means redeeming the highest and the lowest, not just souls who've achieved enlightenment." Another communication arrived when he climbed into bed that night. "Jesus' mission was to offer salvation to every soul on the earthly plane. Salvation that comes through love of God, love of humanity, and love and acceptance of ourselves."

Why are you telling me about Jesus? Aren't you Native American? Seth silently inquired.

"That is my tradition, yes. But you must know where you stand in the historical present, and where that present leads. The world's fate hangs in the balance. The physical world will be saved—or not—as the new millennium progresses. Salvation is predicated upon whether mankind can restore the planet's ecology."

So you're saying that as man moves closer to destroying the planet, either everyone will be saved in the effort to salvage the environment, or we'll eradicate the world as we know it?

"Precisely," Keta replied. "At this moment in history, humanity's existence is an all or nothing proposition."

The next morning at breakfast, Keta commandeered Seth's mind by saying, "As the Piscean Age winds down, Jesus is making himself known to certain people. These individuals are meant to carry forward the seeds of love and compassion that Jesus preached, and plant them in the faith that emerges in the Age of Aquarius. This is what's meant by the Second Coming of Christ, which occurs when Jesus' consciousness returns to usher in the next level of spiritual evolution."

Keta went on, "As a result of Jesus' renewed contact with the world, the veil between the visible and the invisible realms is thinning. This thinning grants humanity greater access to the spirit world, and promotes increased interaction between the living and the dead."

That's what caused my ghost experience, Seth thought.

"That, and karma," Keta asserted. "As the Piscean Age ends, the God associated with it will die. That God is Jesus—the Piscean fish—whose worship defined the era."

Is it sad to see an old God die? Seth wondered. *Or should we celebrate Jesus' demise as if he were an ancient king sacrificed for the continued life of the tribe? Does the predominant religion die at the end of each two-thousand year cycle, only to be reborn with a new name and a fresh conception of the Divine? Isn't that what happened to Judaism as Christianity displaced it? And now Christianity's the dying religion, whose remnants will be incorporated into the next emerging faith. Am I right?*

"Many questions, my child. Your task is to find the answers."

I'm taking assignments from a voice inside my head. Isn't that a sign of insanity? Or spirit possession?

"No need to be facetious," Keta scolded. "Remember, you summoned me. I am here to offer guidance."

Following Keta's lead, Seth entertained notions of a new religion. He concluded that the religion's founding tenet would be no more blood sacrifices. Abraham will no longer be commanded to offer up Isaac. God the Father will no longer nail his only begotten Son to the Tree of Life for the redemption of mankind. The new religion will not be based upon a father slaying a son; rather, it will be life-affirming. The life-denying faiths of the past have brought Earth and its inhabitants to the brink of extinction; these ways must end.

Seth devised a name for his new faith—the True Religion. "True," because every faith that came before had not been able to save mankind from itself, and the True Religion, by necessity a compendium of the truth of the ages, must do so. To discover and reveal this truth, there must be a direct communion with God—a fundamental gnosis—to help mankind evolve past the need to sacrifice life in order to connect with the Divine. No more lambs—actual or in the guise of the Son of God—would be slaughtered.

ℋ

Seth went to Weiser's occult bookstore on East Twenty-Fourth Street and bought several New Age books. He justified the expense by convincing himself that the key to his new religion was somewhere in the books. Every day he dipped into the volumes before and after work. One night as he sat at the dining table reading while Martin slept, he was struck by a passage in a book titled *Renewed Faith: How to Believe in the New Age.* It read, "The great lesson of the new era will be that the three major religions derive from the same source—the One God. This unified godhead will be the foundation of the new faith that arises." *Judaism, Christianity, and Islam all stem from the same root,* Seth thought. *That's obvious. Is there something I'm missing?* He touched the medallions that hung around his neck and considered adding a Muslim crescent and star. *While you're at it, why not add every other religious symbol? You wouldn't be able to walk.*

The next morning, waiting for the coffee to brew, Keta spoke inside his head. "Your life mission is to reveal that all the Gods are One." Seth's fervor was inflamed later that day by an astrological treatise on the operation of karma across lifetimes that he skimmed before going to work. The book suggested that the New Age religion would be founded on man's elemental connection to the earth's ecology, along with the evolution of humanity's psychic powers. *That sounds like paganism,* he thought. *Maybe aspects of that religion will be carried forward, too.* When he read, "The chart represents one of the old-soul children who are reincarnating now to help usher in the New Age and its religion," he grew certain he was one such soul. He bounded into the bedroom where Martin was staring at the dialogue on his computer screen and read the passage aloud.

Martin turned away from the monitor and shouted, "Seth, listen to me! You're not an old-soul child. You're not a prophet of a new religion. You're a struggling writer who may or may not have seen a ghost."

Seth started to object, but Martin cut him off with, "If you keep going on like this, people will think you're nuts. You can't walk around talking about ghosts and new religions and assume that's normal."

"I know what I saw," Seth insisted. "And I will tell people, because I must."

Martin scowled, prompting Seth to retort, "Better a holy fool than just a plain old fool."

"Better not to be a fool at all," Martin coldly replied.

ℋ

Seth received a package from Clara in his mailbox. He tore open the padded envelope and read the scrawled message as he rode the elevator to the sixth floor: "Hope this is helpful. Note what I say about travel. Any questions, call, although I'm never home." He popped the cassette into his Walkman, put on his headphones, and pressed *Play* as he sprawled across the captain's bed. After twenty minutes, Clara signaled her summation by clearing her throat. Her disembodied voice said, "Now I don't want you to be alarmed," at which Seth's stomach tightened, "but judging from the chart, it is not, I repeat, *not* an auspicious time to take an extended trip. I suggest you cancel any major travel plans and remain within your usual environment until the end of the year. You and Martin can take weekend trips, but nothing more complicated than that. I looked at Martin's chart, and he should also abide by what I'm saying."

Seth tore off the headphones. "Martin," he sputtered.

"What's up?" Martin called from the bedroom.

"Clara says we shouldn't travel. I've got to cancel the flights, otherwise we'll lose the deposit."

Martin walked into the living room. "That's fine. Now I won't have to kill myself finishing this rewrite."

"I thought you wanted to go."

"I don't like to travel. You know that."

"But England's wonderful. I've been looking forward to this trip all year."

"I was looking forward to the beer."

"Jesus, Martin."

"I'm being honest."

"I was hoping we'd have an adventure."

"Well, now that the stars say we *can't* go," Martin said caustically, "I can tell you why I agreed to go."

"Why?"

"Because I knew you'd be disappointed if I didn't say yes."

"I should have known."

ℋ

Seth was startled awake by percussive thumps issuing from the air around him. A voice floated through the room, distant and unfathomable. An angry man's voice. "I can't believe it," Seth muttered. "Now I'm hearing ghosts." The thumps turned into the heavy clattering of furniture dragged across a wooden floor. He sat up, staring into the darkness for any sign of movement. A sharp rapping commenced on the wall behind the bed. He heard the sounds, yet they hadn't disturbed Martin, who slept by his side. The banging accelerated to a steady military cadence, which became a pounding, as if someone were using both fists to break through the wall.

A mist materialized over Seth's head. Dull gray and vaporous, the miasma glided to the foot of the bed. A rotten stench filled the room, and Martin stirred in his sleep and rolled over. Blurry amber lights bounced off the ceiling and walls. A vortex of invisible energy swirled around Seth, closing in like a vice tightening. Before he could cry out, a voice whispered inside his head, "Are you ready?"

Seth's heart beat frantically, pushing blood through his body at twice the normal pace. He sent his thoughts into the cocooning energy. *What do you want from me?*

"Send me to the Light!"

I have no idea how that's done.

"You do. Learn anew or remember what you know. Otherwise, you will learn the hard way."

Who can teach me?

"You will find someone. I am outside time, but you can't wait much longer. You are in danger. Save yourself to save me. Quickly, before time runs out. There are books about the process. Remember Egypt."

Egypt?

"Remember the past. Also remember that I cannot shield you from those who would harm you. I can warn you, that is all."

The gray vapor dissolved upwards into the ceiling and the sulfuric stink diminished. The amber lights twinkled on and off. Seth lay down, his ragged breathing the only sound in the room. He embraced Martin and whispered, "Help me, Martin. The ghost returned."

Martin groggily mumbled, "I smell it. Is it still here?"

"It's gone. You've got to help me."

Martin turned away and said, "Maybe I can summon it. I'll figure out something in the morning. Now let me sleep."

Seth relaxed into the bed and stared at the ceiling. *Should I return to the Association and research crossing over a spirit? I wonder if Ivy knows how to do it? She's a witch, after all.* He slipped back into slumber, dreaming that something hovered over him. Keta's voice boomed, "Seth!" "Yes!" Seth cried, responding to his guide's summons. A luxurious breathing caressed his body while a mysterious alphabet floated before his eyes. The flaming letters, circumscribed by an antique box of gold-painted wood, looked like Hebrew or ancient runes. Keta said, "You are chosen by God either to continue to reincarnate, or to end your soul's journey with a particular lifetime. Those whose journey is terminated have remained low on life's scale, failing to meet their higher goals. These souls will never achieve union with God, which ends the reincarnation process." A bodiless hand materialized and, with a wave, erased the floating words. Keta went on, "You've been selected to continue your journey. The selection process includes a numerical reckoning—a small division or multiplication—which determines how far a soul will travel on the path towards God. The calculation slips you through the gates into new lifetimes." The floating letters reappeared, spelling out the transaction required to pass through the gates. "Twice more," Keta translated. "Two in this lifetime, too. Mother and Father, into the Light." Seth awoke with the final words.

Fifteen

A week after the Lammas sabbat, the phone rang in the Paranormal Society's foyer, and Ivy raced down the spiral staircase to answer it. "Hello?" she said breathlessly. "Paranormal Society."

A voice blared out, "Ivy, is that you?"

"Of course, Raven. Who else works here?"

There was an indignant silence on the line. "Sorry to bother you," Raven sniffed, "but I'm calling to get an update."

"About what?"

"You know very well about what. Must I spell it out for you?"

"I'm almost done compiling the books you requested. I'll bring them down next week."

"That's not what I'm talking about!" Raven said.

"What, then?"

Another angry silence. "I'd rather not say. You never know who's listening." Raven paused before whispering, "Did the spell work?"

"Oh, of course. How silly of me."

"Well, did it?"

"He was here earlier this week to find a protective spell against ghosts. So, as of then, it hadn't."

"Is there any way to get an update?"

"I could call him, see if he answers, and hang up if he does."

"Ivy, your tone concerns me. You don't seem to take seriously the fact that the spell has twenty-one days in which to work. If it fails, we're back to square one."

"You're back to square one. You're the one who benefits from Starfire. I would never have involved the group in casting such a spell."

"As High Priestess, I'm entrusted with the coven's well-being. I wouldn't have taken such an action unless I was certain it was the only choice. Not only for myself, but for us all. As one of the oldest covens in the country, we must survive, and we cannot if I don't have the means to live. It's as simple as that. Dark magic exists for precisely these circumstances."

"If I were in your shoes, I would have met with your son, if that's who he is, and come to an agreement. The karma involved in that spell is too heavy, as is the potential kick-back to you. If it doesn't work, some of those present psychically opposed it."

"Did you?"

"For your own sake, I tried to stop you. Now if I were High Priestess—"

"Well, you're not! I hope that you trust my judgment. If not, perhaps the group is not the right one for you."

"I cherish you as our priestess, and I respect each of the mates. I just would have acted differently."

"When you bear the burden of leadership, perhaps you'll understand my decision. Until then, I would appreciate your cooperation."

There was no response. "Ivy, are you there?"

"Yes."

"Two things. Would you mind overnighting the books to me? I'll reimburse you for the expense. I can't wait until next week."

"Of course."

"And follow up on the spell. I must know if it's taken effect. Call me the moment you have any information."

"Yes, Raven."

⏾

Sitting on the living room sofa, Raven opened a parcel containing three books from Ivy. She leafed through *God/dess Androgyne:*

197

Invocations of the Goddess and God, put it down, and examined the Table of Contents in *Magic Mirror, Magic Mind*. She opened *Crystal Magic: Defensive Spells and Incantations*, checked the Index, and turned to page sixty-four, where she read: "The use of crystals in spells amplifies the energy of whatever you are trying to achieve. During self-protection work, crystals fortify an individual's aura. When working spells to implement a specific goal (prosperity, career success, love) the proper inclusion of crystals forcefully propels the desired outcome into the universe. On the darker side, crystal energy can be used to end a life by helping the practitioner visualize the victim and the goal, as if seeing the result in a crystal ball."

Raven looked up to find Ajax staring at her. She jumped, spilling the books onto the floor. "Why did you sneak up on me?" she asked, steadying her trembling hands. "I didn't summon you."

There's something I would ask of you, Ajax telegraphed into Raven's mind. He stood motionless, draped in the shroud in which he was buried, his dark eyes burning.

And what might that be? Raven asked, sending her thoughts into Ajax's consciousness. *Can't you see that I'm busy?*

A favor.

Raven cocked her head. *Make it quick.*

Ajax hesitated before asking, *Haven't I faithfully served you and all those who came before?*

As you are bound to do. Don't waste my time, Ajax.

In my state, there is no time to waste. And yes, that's the bargain your ancestors extracted from me.

Picking up the books and placing them on the sofa, Raven answered, *It was a mutual agreement.*

Haven't I fulfilled my part of the agreement?

For the most part, yes.

Then, Ajax said, drawing out the word, *can you find it in your heart to release me from servitude and send me into the Light?*

Raven regarded her familiar with a bemused look. *Haven't we had this conversation before? And what has my reply always been?*

That I am bound by ties that cannot be severed, Ajax sighed. *Nothing short of a miracle can set me free.*

Then why must you persist in making this request? Raven asked. *Could it be to badger me into submission?*

Have you no pity for me, locked in a limbo between death and another chance at life? After centuries of service to the McWyckes—guiding the priestesses through the realm of spirit and lending my energy to their spells, good or ill—all I ask is to be freed.

Raven rose and paced the room. *Need I remind you of how you came to this state?*

Ajax remained silent.

Surely you recall that as the Horned One who served your own son in ceremonies that defied and defiled Old Religion protocol, rites that were debased magic performed with the coven's outcasts, you damned yourself. Even so, you were able to remain in Mavis McWycke's circle, which I will never understand, since you tried to kill her. It was only her stronger magic that prevailed. You pretended to follow coven laws, yet repeatedly broke them. Your little offshoot group veered into magic for selfish gains, something forbidden by our faith. You requested that if you died an untimely death, you be drawn back into the clan's service.

Performing the Great Rite with my boy was done only to raise power. It was a necessary sacrifice to contact the spirit realm. The gods required it.

The gods required nothing of the sort, and you did this outside coven jurisdiction. You make it sound so selfless, but you couldn't keep your hands off the child, and it was fortunate for you he was blessed with such a gift. While homosexual rites may be useful in some traditions, the repeated rape of a son by a father is not. Truth be told, it was greed that propelled you back into the coven's service. Having lined your pockets with the wealth magic brought you in life, you couldn't bear to surrender it in death. *How could you not have known that when a disincarnate soul is bound to a master, it forfeits rebirth? It forfeits the Light, you fool!*

It's true, I miscalculated my lot.

Then you must also recall that my ancestors hexed you. As Mavis McWycke summoned your soul into service, she decreed: "You may be released from these bonds only when you make amends with your son." And how is that possible? You had just died, the child is long since dead, and you will never see him again.

That is not true.

Are you calling me a liar? Raven said.

No. All I meant is that it may be possible to see my boy again.

Unless you're able to reach across lifetimes to find your son, you don't have that option.

Ajax looked intently at his mistress. *You might be surprised to find that what was once impossible is now within reach.*

I'm sure I don't know what you're talking about. Without a miracle, a karmic intervention from the Goddess, you are doomed to an eternity of service.

Mavis did not look far enough into the future to see how karma works across lifetimes.

You will never know your son again. She saw that clearly enough.

Ajax's tattered shroud vanished, revealing a transparent silhouette roiling with oily black smoke. He advanced and backed Raven against the picture window that looked out onto the forest's gloom. Bearing down upon her, he shrilly demanded, *So you will not free me?*

Never! Raven said. *You are doomed to your fate.* She stood firm and commanded, *Away with thee! Leave me to my books.*

The hulking spirit glided away and disappeared into the dining room.

"I'll summon you when I need you." Raven called after him. She walked down the hallway to her bedroom, where she retrieved her leather pouch containing the river crystals, along with four black candles in black glass containers. Returning to the living room, she walked to a wall of books, climbed a step-ladder, and withdrew *The Black Arts: A Necessary Evil* from the highest shelf. Blowing dust off the cover, she settled on the sofa, turned to a chapter called, "The Sorcery of Death," and began reading.

ℋ

Raven closed *The Black Arts* and placed it alongside her open Book of Shadows on the coffee table. Night had fallen, and she sat alone in the darkened house, the only light coming from a lamp beside the sofa. Rah-wing perched on her shoulder, and she rubbed his head as he bent his neck for further attention. She perused the notes she had jotted in the Book of Shadows, a compendium of the spells, invocations, and blessings to which she was partial. During the afternoon she had added a spell, the darkest curse she'd ever considered casting. She was irreversibly crossing a line into the world of black acts, yet she wouldn't consider the consequences. Her thinking was narrow yet clear, focused on one thing—the elimination of the radiant child. He was the sole obstacle to financial security, which would make her existence comfortable again. She could repent later by casting beneficial spells for the Earth and Mother Nature and turn around her karma. It was never too late for that.

She rose from the sofa, settled Rah-wing on his perch, and switched on the television, something she rarely did. She needed to clear her mind, and TV would do that, filling her head with foolish entertainment and useless information. She picked up Stone's remote and settled back on the sofa. She shuffled through the channels, rejecting a comedy show, a nighttime soap opera, and a PBS special. Surfing through the Orenda Valley TV universe, she nearly passed a public access show until she heard, "—Starfire nuclear plant would be an environmental disaster in the making." She stared in disbelief at the screen. Sitting around a table in a community television studio were Richard Abbey and Blanca Naughton, fielding questions from Clive Barrons, a local news show doyen.

"Mr. Abbey, can you back up that statement?" Clive asked.

"Actually, I can," Blanca jumped in, looking at Richard for the signal to proceed. He nodded.

"I'm new to the anti-nuke movement," Blanca began, "but I've done enough research to know that putting more nuclear power plants online will lead to potentially devastating pollution of our land, air, and water."

"Please elaborate," Clive said.

The camera zoomed in on Blanca. "Water drawn from a local source, in this case a tributary of the Orenda River, will be used to cool the waste heat produced by the plant. When the water is drawn into the plant, fish are also sucked in and killed. When the heated water is pumped back into the river after use, it elevates the river's temperature, jeopardizing aquatic and plant life."

Raven sat back on the sofa, mortified. Here was a member of her circle bashing her in public.

"Then there's the problem of how to dispose of the radioactive waste produced by the plant. There is no safe way to get rid of this material, which can remain radioactive for thousands of years. You can't keep dumping it in the Nevada desert or out at sea, since the canisters have a history of leaking. There's something inherently flawed with a technology when you can't figure out how or where to safely store its byproducts."

"If an act of God like a flood or earthquake damages a plant, radiation will be dispersed into a river, an ocean, the soil, and the air," Richard said. "Think about the Three Mile Island meltdown and Chernobyl, the worst nuclear accident in history. Another such event could contaminate the air and drinking water for millions of people. We shouldn't be taking chances with our lives and the health of the planet."

"Let me play devil's advocate," Clive said. "Isn't nuclear power considered to be clean energy, with no pollutants created in its production?"

"It's clean until it leaks and destroys the environment," Blanca said. "There are other types of energy, such as wind and solar power, which should be developed instead of a technology that can end life as we know it."

"Our time's almost up," Clive said. "Can you tell our viewers how they can learn more and become involved if they want to?"

"We are asking all concerned citizens on both sides of the Orenda to join us this Saturday at a demonstration at Blithe Point to stop construction of the Starfire plant," Blanca said. "We will have informational material available, along with suggestions about how to end this madness—"

Raven snatched the remote and shut off the TV. She looked at Rah-wing, resting with his head under his wing, and said, "Well, I never! There's a turncoat if ever I saw one."

Rah-wing stretched his wings and flew to Raven, landing on her outstretched finger. "Yes, my pet," Raven said. "I know you support me." She opened the pouch that lay on the coffee table and examined the river crystals. "You must help me guide the energy," she said, "since there's no one else at hand, and I don't trust Ajax to come to my aid."

Rah-wing caw-cawed in response, and Raven stroked his neck. She opened the Book of Shadows to the latest entry: the Revenge of the Raven curse. She perused it and rose off the sofa, clearing away two armchairs and an end-table to make a working space. With Rah-wing on her shoulder, she donned the pouch and walked a counterclockwise circle, stopping every foot to deposit a crystal, point facing outward, on the floor. She lit a black candle at the four cardinal points and, as she moved, visualized a gleaming three-dimensional circle of blue-black light. Once the circle was described, she walked to the center and assumed the Goddess position, with one arm holding Rah-wing aloft. Closing her eyes, she breathed deeply for several minutes, summoning the valley's cursed energy. She opened her eyes and, in a guttural voice, chanted:

Agents of darkness
Evil and Death

Find my victim
As he draws breath
Cause him discomfort
Self-loathing and fear
Bring him despair, sadness, and tears
Dim his power and resolve
Writhe him, twist him
As Earth revolves
Drain the energy from his core
Deny him life
Evermore!
Return him to the Goddess' wheel
Round and round
Nevermore!

Raven fell to her knees with a deep exhalation of breath. Released from her finger, Rah-wing flapped in the air over her head. Her breathing and the bird's fluttering persisted until she held out her hand to her pet, who landed gracefully. Raven climbed to her feet and surveyed the circle. The black candles flickered, and the crystals glinted in the subdued light. She focused her mind on sending out the death curse and screeched as she released it towards her victim, her son, who had returned to destroy her.

Sixteen

Seth awoke feeling lightheaded. He walked into the bathroom and vomited into the toilet. He sank onto the tile floor and remained there for several minutes, unable to rouse himself. The strength had been sapped from his body; he wondered if he was coming down with the flu. But in August?

Martin walked in and asked, "What's wrong?"

"I'm nauseated. I feel like the life's been drained from me."

Martin helped Seth up and took him to the bedroom. "Do you want anything to eat?"

"Just water. Maybe tea with honey."

Seth called in sick to work, and Martin ministered to him between writing sessions on the computer. Seth's strength returned as the day wore on. He worried that the spells Ivy provided hadn't worked.

"Martin, do you know how to repel a spirit?"

"Stay away from magic, Seth. It can be dangerous if you don't know what you are doing."

"But can it be done? Can a spirit be repelled?"

"You may need to attract the spirit before it can be repelled. Magic isn't like a light switch. You can't turn it on and off."

What other options are there? Seth remembered the Association for Psychic Investigation and decided to visit it the next day before work. He would try to find information on crossing a spirit into the Light while he was there.

M

Seth entered the Association, stopping at the receptionist's desk to pay his membership dues and collect a temporary ID. He walked upstairs and was greeted by the weekend librarian, a middle-aged woman with a sour expression. He told her he'd been there before, had conferred with Chris, and needed no further assistance. He combed the shelves, pulling out books on curses, spells, protective magic, and spirit lore. He jotted down several death-repelling remedies in his notebook. He came across a book called *Spectral Evidence,* which contained an anecdote that recalled his ghost encounter. "The spirit induced a nightmare of a grizzly stabbing murder, then woke his prey by hovering over him and pushing him into the bed. The pressure was so extreme the victim thought he would die of asphyxiation before the spirit moved away and disappeared into the night." He entered the passage in his notebook, telling himself, *So my ghost isn't a figment of my imagination.*

When he returned to the Association on Saturday, he was drawn to books on the history of European witchcraft and the underground continuation of Old Religion traditions, along with the pagan presence in the American colonies. The more he read, the more it became apparent that Europe's religious dissenters brought to the New World every type of creed, including a belief in magic and the supernatural. Old Religion adherents sailed to the colonies in search of a more tolerant atmosphere in which to practice their faith, just as the Puritans had done. English, Irish, Welsh, and Scottish settlers who arrived in the seventeenth and eighteenth centuries transported their Celtic folk traditions, which included a belief in a female Creator. The practice of herbal medicine, the ability to command spirits, and a pantheistic awareness that the Earth is alive with sprites that govern flora and fauna were also ferried across the Atlantic. In the Celtic tradition, it was common for an elder spinster to heal the sick with herbal potions and the laying on of hands. These women, referred to as *wiccas*, were also called *witches*, meaning "wise women."

A voluminous witchcraft encyclopedia attracted Seth's attention. A passage on curses read: "It has long been believed that water which runs in a southerly direction has magical qualities. Water from a south-flowing stream is valued by wise women for medicinal use, as well as for the breaking of enchantments." When Seth recalled that the Orenda River ran southwards over a bed of crystals, he decided to ask Ivy for a sample of river water, along with a corresponding spell. The book fanned its pages of its own accord and stopped at an engraving of three witches on broomsticks flying over Salem, Massachusetts. The bird's eye view revealed that Salem is situated at the convergence of three south-flowing rivers.

He read the Salem précis, and found several theories purporting to explain the witchcraft hysteria that ravaged the Massachusetts colony in 1692. One long-standing notion held that the young female accusers had dabbled in the occult as an amusement, only to be taken over by powers they couldn't control. A more recent explanation postulated that the 1692 wheat harvest was tainted with a mold that caused psychedelic hallucinations. In the hushed back room, Seth muttered, "Feed your head," and smiled at thinking of Jefferson Airplane's "White Rabbit" in this context. *Could the accused witches have actually been practicing witchcraft?* he wondered. Hadn't he read that the first settlers brought their Old World magical beliefs with them? If true, then why couldn't the events in Salem be seen as an eruption to the surface of such practices? The resulting hysteria would have been a by-product of genuine witchcraft activity and not people simply imagining it. Salem and Hope Springs became twinned in his mind. He pictured each town with a contingent of witches to rival any community left behind in Europe—they were the two occult centers of colonial America.

On Monday before work, Seth pulled a book from the shelves entitled *A Compendium of Spooks,* by Ben Raines. He scanned the Table of Contents, turned to a chapter called "The Most Haunted Inn in America," and found a photograph of the Ferry Inn with the caption, "Spirits of all ilk make this country inn their residence." According to Raines, the inn was built in 1727 as a stagecoach stop midway between New York and Philadelphia. Originally called the Hell's Ferry Inn, it served as a town meeting hall, court, and post office, in addition to its functions as a tavern and rooming house. Revolutionary War officers, including General Washington, planned campaigns in its dining hall. Aaron Burr and General Lafayette, as well as Hessian and colonial soldiers, were said to haunt the place. As one of the oldest inns standing in the United States, the inn was listed in the National Register of Historic Places. Further along, Seth read, "In the late 1960s, an antique witch's ball turned up in the inn's cellar. The bartender displayed the yellow glass ball behind the bar, where it remains to this day—except when it disappears for weeks on end. Witch's balls were used in the colonial period to deflect spells cast upon the inhabitants of a residence." *That's what I asked the bartender about,* Seth recalled.

On the next page, former Ferry Inn owner Andrew Ritter described a painting on the stair landing. "The wedding portrait depicts Ambrose Pennington and his wife, Patience, who once owned the inn and who, some say, met a tragic end. Over the years, guests have noticed the smell of roses coming from the picture. They thought we scented it, since Ambrose is wearing a rose boutonniere and Patience has rosebuds in her hair, but we never did. I've no idea where the odor comes from, except that it's strongest at the full moon."

Raines closed the chapter with, "The Ferry Inn, authenticated as a haunting by several psychics and mediums, has two verified spirit residents. They are an adult female and a girl, most likely mother and daughter. Legend has it that the mother was hanged, for what crime no one knows, and the girl drowned either in the Orenda River or in the canal behind the inn. There's a third ghost, a male, who's said to inhabit Room Eighteen, but who has so far eluded authentication. Locals believe he was executed for some barbaric offense, and those who've encountered him say he's hostile. A burning scent of dead leaves signals his presence."

Seth closed the book and cradled his head in his hands. For there it was in black and white: *a burning scent of dead leaves.* That was his ghost. That was his father in a previous life.

The next day, as Seth surveyed the books in the witchcraft section, he noticed a title he'd never seen in the card catalog. When he pulled *The Gospel of the Moon: The Decline, Fall, and Resurrection of the Old Religion* from the shelf, he was puzzled by its appearance. Bound in black leather, with the title and author's name etched in ornate silver script on the cover, the book looked both old and new. He opened the volume and saw a publication date of 1986. But there was no publisher listed, only a "© Hugo Champion," who was the author. He sat down and read the Introduction, where Champion stated, "I will chronicle, and thereby attempt to account for, the degeneration of Europe's Old Religion over the past millennium. Also under consideration will be the unexpected rebirth of paganism in the twentieth century." Skimming passages at random, Seth couldn't decide if the author possessed a profound understanding of his subject, or if he was a crackpot spouting a wacky historical thesis. He turned to a chapter called "Losing the Light" and started reading.

"In the centuries following the death of Jesus," Champion wrote, "Christianity came to prominence by the shrewd tactic of subsuming aspects of the religions of the day into its own canon. For example, the Church founders aligned Christ's divine attributes with those of the Roman Sun God to make their Savior palatable to the Roman emperors. The most blatant instance of such purposeful correlation is the Church's celebration of Christ's birth on December 25, the same day as the Roman birthday of the Sun. Christianity also acknowledged the massive Goddess cult with the figure of Mary, Mother of Jesus. This Goddess, in a new, yet still virginal guise, went on to have a following nearly as great as that of the Christ himself. The Church fathers made certain their faith had something for everyone, so the scales of belief would tip in their favor. Perhaps Christianity was the first religion born of a primitive demographics, or just the latest in a long line of cut-and-paste faiths."

Seth skipped ahead to read, "During the late Middle Ages, at the height of the Inquisition, Old Religion blessings, consecrations, and seasonal celebrations were actively suppressed, along with the legitimacy of the pagan clergy. These notorious persecutions were a calculated necessity in order for Christianity to secure its position as the dominant religion. Since being burned at the stake was a martyrdom most pagans did their best to escape, the need to practice their rituals in secret arose. Forced to worship in deserted woods and countryside, often under cover of night, the pagan clergy gradually lost sight of their role as consecrated servants of the Goddess. (Although pagan ceremonies had always been held outdoors in sacred groves and stone rings, the imposition of secrecy added a corrosive element of danger.) Rather than conducting prayer to honor the Goddess, the God, and the natural world, always with the communal good in mind, wise men and women began to work 'magic'—blessings, spells, and healings—on an individual basis. Over time they become nothing more than journeymen selling their skills.

"As the blight of witchcraft hysteria, wrongful trials, and thousands of executions gripped Europe (later to be transferred to the American colonies), wise men and women came to practice *magic for magic's sake*. They were forced to wield their powers defensively, and eventually used their skills to control others, both human and spirit alike. Pagan priests and priestesses also began to exert power against their oppressor, the Catholic Church. A moment of critical mass occurred when the spurious magical practices of this degenerated priestly class jibed with the accusations leveled against them by the Church. They *had become* conjurers, sorcerers, and witches who consorted with spirits, evil demons, and possibly even the dark power known as the Devil himself. (In its most ingenious borrowing from earlier faiths, the Catholic Church took the Old Religion's phallic deity, the Horned God, and turned him into the personification of evil. This effectively vilified the older faith, since Inquisitors simultaneously stoked the public's fear of Old Nick. Such devilish bait-and-switch strategies have been employed throughout the ages amongst competing religions.) When it became clear that those loyal to the Old Religion would not embrace Christianity, the Church branded these dissenters 'agents of the Devil.' Once again, being accused of anti-Christian sentiment made staunch pagans more anti-Christian than they already may have been. How could they not become anti-Christian when they were actively persecuted by the Church?

"The myth of the witch as we know it arose as Old Religion priestesses were cut off from their rightful place in society. Instead of an herbalist, healer, midwife, or conduit to the Goddess, the priestess became a caster of spells who worked magic for revenge against her oppressors and/or for her own selfish gain. Once again, historical realities helped forge the emerging notion of the witch, for Old Religion priestesses were forced to practice their craft in isolation, or with one or two acolytes, since their very lives were at stake (no pun intended). This cultural excommunication fostered the modern image of the witch as a caster of the evil eye, who, if she focused her thoughts on you, your child, your cattle, or your home, could induce sickness or even death. She became someone to be feared, rather than revered, an ostracized outsider who shunned, and was shunned by, polite society. Over time, the image of the hatchet-faced hag with a croaking laugh and a predilection for evil-doing became entrenched in the popular imagination, and the transformation from priestess to wicked witch was complete."

Seth turned to a chapter on witchcraft in the twentieth century, which began, "The practice of the Old Religion—currently termed 'witchcraft,' 'the Craft of the Wise,' 'paganism,' or 'Wicca'—has come back above ground as a living faith. Such a surprising resurrection, at the dawn of the New Age when Christianity is dying and the Old Religion was presumed long dead, first became apparent in the 1920s. It was then that British anthropologist Margaret Murray postulated that a European witch cult had existed underground since the Inquisition. Although Murray's theories have gone out of fashion, the Old Religion came out of hiding in the 1960s when the counterculture shook the Judeo-Christian establishment to its foundations. Among the numerous paths of belief that emerged from this seething psychedelic stew was the reborn Wicca religion, which honored nature and Mother Earth. Given the rise in ecological awareness that took place during the Sixties, the attraction of an earth-based creed seems obvious.

"It is important to note that the mid-century search for alternative lifestyles was fueled by a desire for an experience of the Divine in everyday life. While gnosis induced by hallucinogenic drugs and free love proved elusive, the anti-materialist hippie movement's experiential quest inspired both the women's and gay rights movements, to mention just two of the many liberation struggles that arose at the time. The hippie movement also set the stage for the millennial spirituality known as New Age. The earliest manifestation of the hippie movement in San Francisco contained seeds of Wicca, although I am not suggesting the two were synonymous. What I *am* suggesting is that there were direct links between the two trends that cross-pollinated one another. So, for example, the counterculture's interest in homeopathic medicine stimulated an investigation into the Old Religion and helped revive the herbalism at the heart of the Craft. The hippie movement contained additional seeds of witchcraft, black magic, and even Satanism, although I again stress that the counterculture was in no way synonymous with these practices. However, in such a revolutionary climate, the exploration of alternative faiths, like the experimentation with drugs, took place at a fever pitch.

"Of all the counterculture offshoots, the women's movement was the most fecund ground for Wicca's reemergence. Born in the 1960s from centuries of oppression, Women's Lib had its hands full reclaiming equal status for women in what was a man's world, counterculture or no counterculture. As free-thinking women started to investigate Wicca in covens that sprang up like mushrooms after a rainstorm, what may have begun as a rebellion against male domination soon turned into a long-overdue revival of the feminine aspect of the Divine."

Jumping ahead, Seth read, "Since the mid-sixties rise of 'neo-paganism,' there has been a constant debate, both within its variegated ranks and from skeptical outsiders, as to the

morality of certain practices that may or may not be taking
place in American covens. Those who suspect Wiccans of black
magic activity—the summoning of spirits to harm others and/
or to realize material wealth; the enslaving of both human
and disembodied souls; and malicious misdeeds for the sake
of personal advancement—when voicing such concerns, have
always been met with: 'We absolutely do not engage in black
magic. We practice positive white magic for the good, never
the harm, of all. We don't worship the Devil, since the Goddess
predates Christianity. And we don't rebel against Christianity
as Devil-worshippers do, so we have no need to glorify Satan.'
These denials come in the face of centuries of confusion between
the Craft and Satanism, and one can understand why Wiccans
would not want to be associated with the worship of a base
fallen angel. Nevertheless, doubts and suspicions remain. Is the
'white magic only' mantra a cover-up for what some imagine to
be an occasional dabbling in the black arts? Could this sanitized
New Age witchcraft be a neat public relations gimmick to mask
dubious practices? After all, moral boundaries are fluid, and one
person's pragmatic hex upon a business rival might be termed
a black act by a witch who engages only in healing magic.
Likewise, summoning spirits to do one's bidding is regarded by
some initiates as evil, since none but the most evolved Masters
should interfere in God's realm. This bleeding of black and white
into a murky gray may, in fact, best characterize uncensored
coven practices.

"As for today's politically-correct covens, which 'are out
to change the world into a greener, more peaceful place,' one
hypothetical scenario lingers. What if Margaret Murray was
right and Europe's witchcraft cult has steadily endured? What,
then, would Craft practices be like as a result of centuries of
oppression? As I theorized earlier, rituals that once venerated
the Goddess degenerated into acts of self-protection and
self-advancement. If this is indeed the case, wouldn't it be
possible that the covens that enjoyed a rebirth in the Sixties
might be the very groups that practiced debased magic for
centuries? And in the case of the American covens formed at

the dawn of colonial life, isn't it likely that as went the United States, so went the pagans? That is, their original quest for religious freedom suffered the same decline that other sectarian communities endured, a gradual *loss* of faith, and a supplanting of religious piety with the materialistic concerns that grip our society today. The obsessive lust for wealth and power in society at large may mirror an equivalent deterioration of the Craft's spiritual objectives."

Seth flipped to the final chapter to read the concluding paragraph. "The New Age and its amalgam of flaky beliefs and pseudo-philosophy will either produce a new religion of profound consequence or a Disneyland of meaningless faiths and idiosyncratic rituals."

Chris approached and whispered, "Ten minutes until closing."

Seth nodded and returned *The Gospel of the Moon* to the shelf, wishing he could take it home to study. As he descended the curved staircase to the lobby, the book falling to the floor on his first visit flashed through his mind. A wheezy voice went off in his head: "My gift to you. You must not give up your search. There's more, if you look." The resident spirit had spoken.

ℋ

On Wednesday, Seth entered the Association's main chamber and looked around for evidence of his invisible research assistant. No falling books or mind-messages materialized. He retrieved Champion's book and turned to a chapter called "Freemasonry: The Secret Constitution?" where he read, "Lest we forget our origins, many of America's founding fathers were Freemasons whose spiritual beliefs and practices derived from the magical/hermetic tradition of Renaissance Europe. Three out of five framers of the Constitution—George Washington, Benjamin Franklin, and Edmund Randolph—were active Freemasons who, by definition, believed in a Deity and in realms beyond the one we see before us. A discussion of Freemasonry may seem like a digression, but I present it, along with the suggestion that the

United States was, from its inception, an empire founded upon and steeped in magical and religious thought. This is significant when pondering the rise of evangelical (born-again) Christianity that is taking place in the current decade, as this movement promises to be a cultural and political force to be reckoned with for years to come.

"While I don't wish to suggest that the American government has been infiltrated by a secret brotherhood of Freemasons, it's worth noting that at least twelve other Presidents besides Washington were Freemasons. At the same time, I can offer proof (see illustration) that the basis of the United States government, the separation of power that checks and balances the legislative, judicial, and executive branches, is consciously modeled on the three pillars found on a Masonic tracing board, a visual aid that depicts Masonic principles. Furthermore, the entire structure is conceived as 'a nation under God'—a Masonic ideal—even though conventional wisdom has it that the United States enjoys a clear separation of church and state."

Seth examined a diagram depicting the division of the "nation under God" into its three main branches, which were further subdivided into federal, state, and local levels. All six divisions were overseen by the Masonic God's Eye from the dollar bill. As Seth compared the diagram to another illustration of a symbol-laden tracing board dominated by three white architectural columns, Chris approached and cleared his throat. "Excuse me," he whispered sharply, "where did you get that book?"

"I found it in the witchcraft section," Seth replied.

"It hasn't been catalogued yet. I'm sorry, but I'm going to have to ask you to return it. You can read it once it's been catalogued."

Seth reluctantly closed the book and handed it to Chris, saying, "This is a membership library that doesn't lend its books, so why can't I read this particular one?"

"I don't make the rules," Chris sniffed before returning, book in hand, to his desk. "This is a work of dubious scholarship, and we keep it only for archival purposes. I'm not sure it should even be on the shelf. The Association must uphold a certain level of erudition."

Seth packed up his notebook and pens. The same wheezy voice said inside his mind, "He makes no sense. Follow your instincts. You are Egyptian. You can help us all into the Light."

ℋ

Seth entered his apartment building feeling depleted. He'd left work early; his energy was low, and he couldn't concentrate. He'd been this way all week. Normally a good sleeper, his slumber was consistently interrupted. He'd bolt awake from a dream of being devoured by a black bird, and frenetic nightmares of his destruction would pursue him into the early morning hours. When Martin wasn't home, he cast the protective spells he'd found at the Association, but nothing changed.

He opened the apartment door and stepped into the foyer, where the scent of burning sage and frankincense greeted him. Green, red, and gold candles flickered in the darkened living room. Martin, sitting in the worn leather armchair, had his eyes closed. He rose and, turning his back to Seth, chanted:

Spirit servant
Spirit bright
Come to me
This very night
Serve me now
With green and gold
Help me call my screenplays
Sold!
Guide me well
To L.A.'s coast
An A-list writer
Will I boast.
Spirit guide
Of Seth's acquaint
Causing him to
Fear and faint

I, your master
Truly be
Forsake him now
And come to me
Ajax
My true warrior be!

Martin turned and started. "What are you doing here?" he yelled.

"I'm exhausted. I came home early."

"You should have called."

"Why? So I wouldn't find you casting a spell?"

"I'm doing this on your behalf."

"It doesn't sound like that to me."

"You came in in the middle. I'm contacting your ghost to ask him to leave you alone."

Seth regarded Martin suspiciously. "I'll have to take your word, then. Maybe when you're on the coast you'll have more privacy."

"You've ruined that part. I hope the first part sticks."

"Do you really think magic will bring you success?"

"Of course."

"Aren't you afraid to invoke Ajax?"

"I've summoned more powerful forces."

Stunned, Seth said, "Really? And did they do your bidding?"

Martin stared at Seth, refusing to answer.

ℋ

The next morning the phone rang. Seth picked up the receiver. "Hello?"

There was silence on the line.

"Hello? Who's calling?"

No response.

As he was about to put down the receiver, a voice said, "Don't hang up."

"Who is this?" Seth demanded.

"Ivy McBroom. Just calling to see how you're doing."

"To see if I'm alive is more like it."

"That, too," Ivy admitted.

"Now that you have that information, what else is there to say?"

"How are you feeling?

"Drained. Weak, like I have the flu."

"I'm not surprised. Did you perform the spells I gave you?"

"Yes. They haven't had an effect. I did a few others, but the fatigue hasn't stopped. Can you get me some Orenda River water?"

"Whatever for?"

"I read that it can break enchantments."

"Perhaps, and the river crystals are powerful, but if what I'm thinking is true, you need more gris-gris than that."

"Can you give me a stronger spell?"

"You may require something cast on your behalf. Let me look into that."

"What should I do in the meantime?"

"Meditate. Visualize white light surrounding you at all times, forming a protective armor that only goodness and love can penetrate."

"I'll try."

"I have another idea—consider returning to the valley with me. I may be able to broker a truce."

"What's in it for you?"

"Peace in the valley. And taking on a role I've had my eye on."

"I'm terrified of going back. I have to think it over."

ℋ

When Seth returned to the Association, *The Gospel of the Moon* was neither listed in the card catalog nor on the shelf. Thinking of Keta, he decided to investigate Native American ghost lore. Listings in the card catalog were scant, but he found another uncatalogued book as he browsed the shelves. "For your edification," the wheezy voice said. He sat down to read *Native American Shamanism and Journeys of the Spirit,* by Geraldine Wood. An explication of gays in Native American culture caught his attention. "In the majority of tribes, gay people were integrated into daily life, serving as peace negotiators and oracles, in addition to fulfilling the more artistic (and female-defined) duties of pottery-making and basketry. Gay male transvestites were so revered as medicine men that gays often constituted an ongoing priesthood. In most tribes, male and female homosexuals were allowed to cohabitate with members of their own sex. Gay marriage was even sanctioned in some tribes. Contrary to the name given to cross-dressed Native American men by European settlers—'berdache,' from the French, meaning 'slave boy,' 'boy sex slave,' or 'boy prostitute,' a term bearing no relation to the roles gay Native Americans played in their own society—tribal members largely held their gay brothers and sisters in high regard.

"Such esteem stemmed from the fact that gay transvestite shamans often conducted the tribe's most important rituals, those which contacted the spirit world. Since every tribal custom was governed by its relation to the spirit world, those who communed with the invisible realms wielded significant influence. It was thought that something in the nature of the cross-dressed male made him a potent channeler of spirits. It is my contention that the 'half-man, half-woman' can more readily access the world of spirit, since liberation from traditional gender roles opens one's vision to other levels of reality, in the same manner that psychedelic drugs do. So the cross-dressed gay man, in touch with his intuitive 'female' side, is more likely to perceive the invisible realms than is his heterosexual counterpart, whose role is to hunt, protect the tribe, and sire children.

"It was their otherness that gave gays the ability to promote the tribe's spiritual well-being. This, in turn, provided gays with their valued standing within the tribe. There's a lesson to be learned regarding tolerance for the differences between people, for it's often these very differences that account for the true value of an individual. It's a double tragedy, then, that Native Americans have been obliterated from the North American landscape, and that their enlightened grasp of human nature has been lost with them."

Seth turned the page and discovered a charcoal portrait of a familiar aboriginal subject. When he read the caption—"Chief Ferry of the Orenda Nation, one of the most revered gay Native American shamans"—he recognized the face. The enigmatic half-smile and lewdly crinkled eyes belonged to the figure that graced the Ferry Inn sign. He resumed reading: "Chief Ferry was regarded as one of the greatest walkers between worlds the Human Beings—as the Orenda natives called themselves—had ever known. Famed for his protracted vision quests, the Chief prepared for these journeys by fasting and remaining celibate. After ingesting ceremonial psychedelics, he went into a trance and roamed the spirit world out-of-body, communing with his guides and seeking advice on whatever concerned him at the time. Once he received the necessary wisdom, he returned to the material plane to relate his revelations to the tribe. As Chief Ferry's contact with European settlers increased, he grew distressed by what his guides showed him. He returned from the spirit realm accompanied by increasingly dark moods. When asked to explain what troubled him, the Chief's answer was, 'No man can stand in the way of the Great Being's design.' Many thought the Chief had witnessed the destruction of the planet on the astral plane. All he would acknowledge was, 'The world as the Human Beings know it is no more.' His moodiness infected the tribe and led, in 1775, to their departure for the Ohio River Valley, which had not yet been colonized by the British."

Under the heading "A Natural State of Being," Seth read, "Chief Ferry was not shy in declaring his preference for 'bucking braves.' He accepted his orientation as natural, one which he became aware of through dreams he had during adolescence. In one of these visions, the Chief met his spirit guide, Ketanëtuwit, or Great Spirit, a Native American soul. The guide, a small, thousand-year-old man, offered the Chief a feathered headdress, saying, 'If you accept this, you will be able to travel between your world and mine. You will desire your own sex and identify with the feminine half of creation.' The dreaming Chief reached out and took the headdress, and was blessed with second sight. As for his domestic life, over the course of seventy years the Chief cohabited with at least three men from his tribe, the last such union enduring for twenty years."

The chapter concluded with, "According to Freeman County legend, before Chief Ferry led his tribe westward, his final act was to curse the area. Never a hostile magician, the Chief was driven to extremes when he could no longer hide from himself the certainty that his people would lose their homeland. While doing research for this book, I discovered a text which purports to be the Chief's curse. Although my source must remain secret, I am at liberty to print the hex. 'To those who put a price of ownership on the Earth, which sustains all life and on which there is no price or ownership, and to those who break the bond between my tribe and its home—I curse this valley. May its occupants draw no sustenance from the land. May the fish and turtles and river creatures vanish, and may the river produce poison instead of quenching thirst. May the crystals from the riverbed work black magic, even when intended otherwise. And may the new inhabitants tread the empty path of greed for the rest of their days, moving ever away from the love of the Great Being. Remember this: each time the land is sold for a price, this curse will increase threefold.'

"Given the Orenda Valley's rich forests, waterways, and farmland, it seems that the Chief's curse proved an empty one. Even so, there are those who believe that his spell lingers in the valley's viscous sunlight and in the perpetual gloom of its wooded glens. These same people insist that the light which penetrates the gloom comes not from above, but from below, the glow of ghastly supernatural forces that only a mighty shaman could summon into being."

Seth glanced at the clock above Chris' desk and saw that he was late for work. He put Wood's book back on the shelf and dashed out of the Association.

ℋ

Seth climbed the staircase to the Association's second floor. He was winded and weak, though he had more stamina since he'd taken Ivy's suggestion and began visualizing white light. He searched the shelves in the main room, but could find neither *The Gospel of the Moon* nor *Native American Shamanism*. He paced the chamber, frustrated and trapped within the confines of the book-lined walls. The fluorescent lights glared down from the ceiling, giving the room the harsh look of a prison; the shelves of books loomed overhead, an impenetrable fortress of withheld knowledge. He was about to pack up his notebook and pens when the wheezy voice went off inside his head, "Past lives. The answer lies there."

He pulled the "P" drawer from the card catalog and flipped though the entries. The Association had a small number of books on previous lives, all seemingly inconsequential. Recalling Ajax's admonition to remember the past, he withdrew the "E" drawer and leafed through the cards until he found "Egypt: Guidance to the Next Life." He located a volume on a high shelf entitled *Life Beyond Death: Journey to the Next World* and sat down. The book was illustrated with hieroglyphic drawings and depictions of animal-headed gods performing rituals involving prone bodies swathed in burial linen. One illustration showed a dead human weighed on a balance scale against his heart in a canopic jar. Presiding over the ritual was Osiris, the god of the underworld, brandishing a grail and ankh. The caption read, "Weighing the karma of a lifetime." He leafed through the pages and came upon the following passage: "After the heart and lungs were removed and preserved in separate jars, the priest anointed the dead body with sandalwood oil while saying a prayer for the soul of the deceased. Acting as a guide, the priest visualized the soul traveling unimpeded to the underworld, where it would begin the process of reincarnation, if that was its fate. Only the priest was entrusted with this sacred rite, for which the pharaohs revered him."

As Seth examined the illustrations, the tinkling of a crystal bell sounded inside his head. Along with the silvery chimes, he heard a faint message. "The Chief is your brother," Keta whispered. "I watch over you both, two offshoots of the same vine." A dry laugh sounded, and the chimes diminished.

He returned the book to the shelf and the drawer to the card catalog. He picked up his shoulder bag, passed through the hallway, and descended the curved staircase. Walking along the street to the subway, he saw in his mind's eye the weathervane on the Parsons Mansion lawn rising into the air and shooting like an arrow across a night sky. It exploded into a starburst of white light as "You must remember!" resounded inside his head. "You should be past-life regressed as soon as possible." He couldn't be certain whether Keta, Ajax, or the Association's resident spirit had spoken.

Seventeen

Seth entered the steel-gray lobby of a building on West 61st Street at a quarter to two in the afternoon and took the elevator to the fourteenth floor. As he rode in the dimly-lit Art Deco cab, the dream in which Keta whispered, "He was your father," popped into his consciousness. Perhaps Ajax had been his father, and perhaps a shuffle through his previous lives would elucidate the connection. And perhaps nothing would come of it, no connections would become apparent, and no past lives would show up. How would he know that his father in a past life had become Ajax the ghost? He wasn't sure at all.

He took a seat in the plant-filled waiting room of the office of Selena Moore. He was given Selena's name by a co-worker who met her at a cocktail party in the Hamptons. Selena, he was assured, was the best regression therapist in New York. A door on the far side of the waiting room opened, and a woman in a beige linen suit and pink silk blouse emerged. She smiled and introduced herself. He followed her down a long hallway with a gleaming marble floor before entering what was little more than a walk-in closet with a humming air conditioner in the window. Strips of light cast by wooden Venetian blinds gave the room a *film noir* look. Selena motioned him to take a seat in a black leather recliner positioned opposite her more compact armchair. The only other furnishing was a tiny desk tucked beneath the window.

As he settled into the recliner, Selena said, "We talked on the phone about what you're looking for, but I'd like to review what you can expect from the regression experience. Today I'll put you under light hypnosis for an hour." While she spoke, her blonde hair rippled in soft waves, framing a Pre-Raphaelite face with curved lips and a nose that came to a crisp point. A barely perceptible tension in her neatly crossed legs suggested a disparity between her prim exterior and something more brazen below the surface.

"Different people get different impressions," Selena said. "Some receive ideas of events, some see them visually, and a few get vivid Technicolor scenes. Many can access their entire life history, even though they enter a past life at a specific age."

Seth nodded while studying Selena for signs of therapeutic or spiritual incompetence. "Will you tell me again what you're seeking?" she asked. Her refined enunciation cast a spell over the room.

"I had an encounter with a ghost in the Orenda Valley who may have been my father in a previous life. I'm hoping to go back to that lifetime to see what transpired between us."

"How would the ghost know that you, in your current incarnation, were once his son?"

"That's a good question," Seth said. "I don't know."

"We can work with that as an objective. But it's best to approach this process with an open mind and go with whatever comes through."

"I understand."

"Then let's begin. Please make yourself comfortable."

Seth took off his shoes and placed his feet on the ottoman in front of the recliner, while Selena dimmed the lights and set up her tape machine to record the session. "I want you to relax all the muscles in your body," she instructed.

Seth nestled into the padded chair. When he stopped fidgeting, Selena said, "I want you to imagine yourself encased in a warm, golden, protective light. And I want you to imagine that this light also exists between you and me. I want you to imagine a very high mountain. You're standing at the base and there's a trail leading to the top. Before you climb to the top, I want you to envision a large jar beside the trail. I want you to put anything you don't wish to bring on this journey into the jar. You can retrieve whatever you've left there afterwards."

Seth placed his preconceived notions and disbelief into the terra-cotta vessel.

"I want you to begin climbing the trail. And I want you to understand that by the count of ten you will be at the top of the mountain. One."

Seth navigated uncertainly along a steep, rocky path.

"Two."

Gaining momentum, he looked around and saw a forest that covered the mountainside.

"Three."

He grew winded from his brisk uphill pace.

"Four. Five."

On the trail midway up the mountain, the trees were sparser, with low scrub taking their place.

"Six."

His conscious mind crashed through. *This is bullshit. You're wasting a hundred dollars, which, by the way, you can't afford.*

"Seven."

He was above the tree line. The air grew thinner with each step.

"Eight."

Craggy boulders cluttered the mountainside like rubble.

"Nine."

His hands grabbing at rock, Seth pulled himself up the slippery gravel trail.

"Ten. You are now standing at the top of the mountain."

Seth bounded off the trail. He straightened his body and stopped to catch his breath.

"I want you to look around," Selena said, "and tell me what you see."

Seth scrutinized a top-of-the-world vista similar to the Tibetan Himalayas. The snow-capped peaks were turquoise and purple in the rarefied light. "I'm standing on flat, rocky ground," he said. "I see blue sky. Below me are trees that look like match sticks. The air is pure and cold and tastes like water." His voice had slowed down and deepened. He had no perception of his body or Selena's office. He was all mind.

"That's good," Selena said. "I want you to call upon your higher source, what some refer to as a spirit guide. Ask your guide to come forth, and tell me what form he or she takes."

A mechanical click sounded as Selena started the tape recorder. In the silence that followed, Seth glimpsed an entity who seemed part human and part spirit. "The guide is a little hunched-over man carrying a sack on his back and walking with a tall staff," he said. "He's Native American. His name is Keta."

"What impression do you get of his face?"

"His face is wrinkled. He has gray whiskers and wispy white hair. He seems really old."

"Does your instinct tell you that you can trust him?"

"Yes. He has a lot of knowledge. He's visited me before."

"Please thank him for coming. Then ask him if he's willing to help you explore a past life that would be beneficial for you to know about."

Repeating Keta's words as they resounded inside his head, Seth stated emphatically, "He says that's what he's here for."

"Then we're in business. He will lend protection, support, and wisdom. Now take a few slow, deep breaths. I want you to imagine that as you look up into the sky, there's a little white fluffy cloud. Imagine that you're very light and can float up to the cloud and that it can support you. As you float on your cloud, tell it to follow the direction of your higher self and your guide. Tell it to take you to whatever time and place is appropriate for you to explore. I'm going to count backwards from five to one while you imagine that you're drifting through space and time. Five. Easy and calm and relaxed and flowing. Four. Easy and calm. Three. Imagine that you're going back, and it's easy to do because you're an eternal being. Two. On the next count, imagine that the cloud has set you down and you're becoming aware of a different environment. Let it be whatever it is."

Selena snapped her fingers and said, "One. The idea of a different setting comes into your mind. Tell me what it is."

Seth glanced down and saw that he had stepped into someone else's body. He was wearing a white robe and brown leather sandals. He looked up and examined his surroundings.

"I see sand," he spoke slowly. "A desert. Palm trees. There are pyramids here."

"I want you to become aware of whether you're male or female."

"I'm pretty sure I'm male, but I could also be female."

"You can clarify that later if you need to. Where you are?"

"I'm outside the residence of the king, awaiting permission to enter. Eventually I'm allowed into a courtyard with a babbling fountain."

"How old are you?"

"Forty years."

"On the count of three, I want you to go to where you live."

The numbers, along with Selena's compelling finger snap, propelled Seth forward. "I live in a cloister that houses the high priests. I see a young man, a novice, who smiles devotedly at me. I teach him the mysteries. He will leave me when his training is complete, and I will instruct another in the craft of—" Seth stumbled over his thoughts before saying, "In the sacred craft of guiding the souls of the dead into the next world so they may continue their journey."

"Let's return to the time you enter the king's residence." Snap! "Why are you there?"

"A terrible misfortune has occurred. The king's first-born son has died suddenly, there are rumors of poisoning, and I'm required to guide his soul into the Light. I'm escorted to the prince's chamber, where he's laid out in golden vestments looking like the Sun God except for the grimace which none of the royal physicians can correct. My acolyte arrives carrying sandalwood oil and the necessary amulets. I commune with the prince's spirit, which hovers above his lifeless form. The dead boy is furious, shouting that he's been poisoned by his jealous younger brother. Speaking mind to mind, I calm him, then instruct him in the ways of the afterlife, assuring him he'll incarnate again if that's his path. Once his spirit is soothed, I anoint his body with oil and send him back to the Source. I see his transparent soul soar into a spiraling tunnel of light and merge with the radiance on the other side."

"What's your name?" Selena asked.

"Set. In honor of the god who presides over those sacrificed to the mystery of death. An appropriate name for one who escorts souls to the afterworld, don't you agree?"

"Yes, Set, your name rings true. Now I want you to move to a defining event in your life." Snap!

"Years later, I'm the king's confidant. A priest who envies my skills seeks to destroy me. You see, my knowledge of the mysteries draws phantoms to me. The mightiest of spirits serve me for the chance to be crossed into the Light. My rival sends an army of deadly thought forms to attack me. Caught unaware, I nearly succumb."

"What's the outcome?"

"Fearing I'll lose my life, I foolishly resort to black magic, forgetting that it would be better to die than to violate the authority of the gods. With the low cunning of a sorcerer, I conjure up a red-bellied scorpion and send it to my rival's chambers. I become one with it, injecting my own venom into my sleeping enemy and reveling in his death throes. Having defeated my adversary, I live out the remainder of my life in peace."

"I want you to move forward to the time of your death." Snap! "What do you see?"

"I'm hovering above my body, which has fallen across the stone floor of my cell. I'm content to leave the flesh behind for I know my soul will incarnate again. The battle with my rival is my only regret. As I rise into a sky emblazoned with golden hieroglyphics, the handwriting of the gods, I understand that the taking of a life through black magic is a gross misdeed. I fly toward the Divine radiance and perceive that I will carry my transgression as a tainted legacy that must be cleansed. I see the spiral. I see the light. I'm in the—" Set's voice trailed off until the only sound in the room was Seth's steady breathing.

"It's time to begin your return journey." Selena said. "I want you to imagine that you're going back down the mountain. When you get to the bottom, if there's anything you put in the jar that you wish to retrieve, do so now."

Seth descended the mountainside. He approached the jar, but left behind his preconceived notions and disbelief in order to return to the present unfettered by a narrow judgment that was no longer his own.

"I'm going to count from one to five as you come back integrated, mind clear, energy flowing through the body. One. Mind clear. Two. Energy flowing. Three. Your focus returns to the present. Four. You come back a fully integrated being. Five. You are back in the present." Snap!

Seth opened his eyes and looked at Selena, who regarded him with a slight smile. As his senses re-engaged, the mass of his body returned to the chair. While he was under, he'd been weightless, floating in another realm. Yet he remembered all he had recounted.

"How do you feel?" Selena asked.

"I have a buzz, like a drug high. I feel like I've touched a place where I've never been."

"As indeed you have," Selena added. "We don't have much time left, so if you want to continue, we'll need to schedule another session."

"The Egyptian lifetime answered many questions. But I'm disappointed that I didn't find the ghost."

"I can put you in a deeper trance, and we'll see what comes to mind."

ℋ

As the clock on the death spells wound down, Raven grew more disturbed and fearful. What could be stopping the hexes from working? Had she lost her mojo and issued stillborn curses? Was Seth protected by an unknown guardian with extraordinary powers? Had someone tipped him off and advised him to cast a counter-spell? The last notion seemed the most likely. If there was a traitor in her midst, she couldn't be sure who it was. Roger, a friend of Richard's and Seth's? Not likely. Roger was out for himself, and what little loyalty he had was to the coven.

Ivy, who'd had the most contact with Seth? What could she gain from such a betrayal?

The phone rang, and Raven answered with an agitated, "Hello!"

"It's Ivy."

"You've been on my mind. Why haven't you called?"

"I've got nothing to report."

"That's impossible! Surely the spell has worked by now."

"Not as far as I know. It's awkward for me to keep phoning and hanging up when he answers."

"Does he answer?"

"Yes."

There was silence on the line. "Then something's gone dreadfully wrong. That was the darkest spell I've ever cast. It should have worked like a charm." Raven didn't mention the Revenge of the Raven curse, which only Rah-wing witnessed.

"Maybe you miscalculated the spell. Or your skills."

"How dare you!" Raven responded. "My skills are nonpareil."

"All I meant was that since this is a spell none of us normally cast, perhaps you underestimated the concentration required for its success."

"Don't try to wriggle out of it. You show no respect for my leadership, for which I've been groomed all my life. That concerns me."

"I hold you in utmost esteem. But I don't think you should resort to black magic, even if you feel it's justified."

"As I've said before, until someone takes my place, my decisions are not to be vetted by you or anyone else."

"Then we have a dictatorship instead of a democracy."

"No! You and the mates must trust my wisdom, that's all. Otherwise, I'll step down."

"Who could ever replace you?"

"You, perhaps?"

"I'd never want the responsibility."

"But you've thought about it, I see. Ivy, have you—"

"Have I what?"

"Advised Seth that his life is in danger?"

"Of course not! Why would I do such a thing?"

"I don't know. But I will find out. Now call me tomorrow, whether or not you have any news." Raven slammed down the phone and turned to the bookcase. She climbed the stepladder and took *The Black Arts: A Necessary Evil* from the top shelf. "Something's not right," she muttered. "Someone's helping him, that much I know."

$\mathcal{H}$

Blanca kissed Richard and walked down the hill to sit behind the cash register at Bell, Book and Candle. Compared to helping Richard strategize Damn the Dam, her job was pointless and dreary. Working to educate the community—at town meetings, demonstrations, and on TV and radio talk shows—was far more stimulating than directing customers to books and wrapping candles and jewelry. She helped Delia open the store at ten and sat idle for an hour without serving any customers.

At eleven, the bell over the door tinkled and Raven marched in. She approached Blanca and said, "I need to speak with you." Delia entered carrying a handful of packages. "Can you spare Blanca for a few minutes?" Raven asked.

"Of course," Delia replied. "I'll watch the register."

Raven motioned Blanca to follow her to the storage room at the rear of the store. Raven closed the door behind them and said, "Let's cut to the chase. I saw you on that cable show. You've embraced the other side. Are you aware of how that hurts me?"

"I don't intend it to. But once you see the right side of an issue, it's impossible to be neutral. You were the one who forced me to get involved with Richard."

"I didn't tell you to become an anti-nuke mouthpiece!" Raven said. "You had a job to do, and I've yet to see that you've accomplished it. What can you tell me about Seth?"

"Nothing much."

"Exactly! You've taken on Mr. Abbey's cause, and most likely fallen in love with him, while abandoning your mission. Most would consider you a traitor."

"I won't discuss my personal life."

"So it's true, then. Your loyalty to me and the coven is now secondary."

"I'm committed to our work for the benefit of the planet, which is why I'm campaigning to stop Starfire."

"I can't trust you. You conspire with the enemy, and who knows if you've told Seth about the death spell."

"I don't reveal coven secrets. Wasn't that part of my oath?"

"Oaths don't matter to you, otherwise you would hold my concerns in greater esteem."

"I should get back to work. I think we know where we both stand."

"We certainly do. Only I warn you, if word gets back to Seth about his patrimony, I will hold you responsible. You, via Mr. Abbey, are the direct link to him."

"I don't reveal coven secrets," Blanca reiterated as she opened the door.

"Wait a minute!" Raven said. "I'm not done."

Blanca turned and faced her interrogator with a look of cold disregard.

"How much does Mr. Abbey know about the Starfire land lease?"

"I haven't mentioned that you are the landholder," Blanca said cautiously, "but I can't guarantee he won't figure it out."

"Make sure he doesn't. At least not until the lease is finalized and ground is broken. Can I ask that much of you?"

Blanca mumbled, "Yes."

"Now get back to work." Raven bounded out of the room before Blanca could respond.

❧

When Seth returned to Selena's office, she again instructed him to envision himself floating on a fluffy white cloud. Then she said, "I want you to become so confident of your ability to travel through the sky that you rise up off your cloud and let your body float."

Seth accepted the suggestion that he could fly, and hovered above his cloud.

"As you rise into the air, the sky becomes a black dome with stars and planets overhead. And as you drift through the far reaches of the cosmos, in a dominion outside space and time, I want you to ask your higher self and your guide to direct you to a lifetime that's of utmost importance to you. By the time I count from ten to one, I want you to be in that lifetime."

Selena counted backwards, and Seth hurtled through space in a dizzying downwards motion, which forced his stomach into his throat and sickened him. He struck the earth with a reverberating thud. He lay motionless on damp ground before rising and looking around. "I see a forest and a river," he said without prompting. "Pristine wilderness." A wave of energy passed into his body, rippling his flesh. His torso expanded, the skin pulled in every direction. Rapid, uncontrolled contortions turned his face to putty. His mouth moved to speak, and was stretched into a mutating frown. A sharp contraction brought his body back to its natural state, but his wide-eyed, childish expression indicated that someone else was present. He looked down to examine his mode of dress. "I'm wearing a woolen jacket, knee breeches, and leather moccasins we got from the red men," he said in a high-pitched child's voice.

"Are you male or female?" Selena inquired.

"What a silly question! I'm a boy," Seth replied, speaking with a flattened British inflection that might have been current in colonial America.

"How old are you?"

Seth's features moved unguardedly as he declared, "I'm ten years old."

"Can you tell me your name?"

"I'm called Samuel, miss. My surname is Pennington. Father calls me Sammy."

"Samuel, would you like to play a game? You describe your surroundings, and I'll guide you to the next place I'd like to see."

"I love games!" Samuel cried. "I play them with Father and the parishioners."

"Is your father a vicar, Samuel?"

"No, silly, he's an innkeep. But he plays with the parishioners in the woods, which is a secret, so don't tell anyone."

"I won't tell a soul. Now look around and describe what you see."

"I see a river. I was fishing until my pole broke."

"Very good. Now would you go to where you live?"

"Yes, miss. I'm walking through the woods. It's dark, even at midday. Am I playing properly, miss?"

"Yes. Now tell me what you see once you leave the forest."

"I'm on the stagecoach road. It's hot and dusty. I'm crossing the bridge over the mill stream. The inn where I live is just ahead. Father says it's the grandest building in town. Three stories, with green shutters at each window."

"Very good. Can you move forward in time and be inside your home?"

"Certainly, miss. We live in a cottage behind the inn with a hearth room and two bedchambers. I share a room with my sisters, Hestia and Prissy, who order me about because I'm the youngest. Mother's cooking rabbit stew for tea. All she does is cook and sew. She keeps to herself. The townspeople say her name, Patience, suits her. She scolds me when I'm wicked, but never kisses me when I'm good. Only Father does that. Hestia fancies herself a cook and helps Mother. Prissy is outside with the publican's daughter. She's pushed me into the river twice this week. Don't tell anyone, miss, but I hate her."

"Is your father present?"

"He's coming in from the tavern in his fine new frock coat and breeches. He hoists me into his arms and kisses me. His breath stinks of ale. His beard tickles and makes me laugh. But when he's angry, he frightens me. Father sets me down and pats my bum, saying, 'Sammy, you're my boy.' He kneels, pulls me close, and whispers, 'Come to me in the stables after tea. I have something sweet for you.' Mother enters and gives Father a look. 'You're my boy, Sammy. Don't you forget it,' he says, patting my bum."

"Can you go to the time when you meet your father in the stables?"

Samuel squirmed in his chair. "Yes, miss. When it's dark, I enter the stables carrying a lantern. The horses snort and whinny, and it stinks of straw and poo. I hear a cough and look up to see Father at the edge of the hayloft. 'Come see what I've got for you,' he calls. I climb the ladder afraid Father will hurt me. But I like it when he hugs me and calls me his boy."

"What happens next?"

"Father pulls me to him. His pole is outside his breeches, and it rubs against me. Father sits down in the hay and says, 'Make me happy, Sammy.' I know what I must do. I crawl between his legs and lick his sack. Soon he says, 'That'll do. Move north, lad.' I grasp his pole and lick it up and down, just as he's taught me. I circle the crown with my tongue and stroke the scepter with my hand. Father forces my head down, pushing into my mouth. Tears shoot from my eyes as I try to catch my breath. Father keeps pushing, and I choke. When I can no longer breathe, and think I'll die, he pulls my hair and his pole spits. Father moans, then lifts me over him and says, 'That's my boy, Sammy, you always do as you're told.' He draws me against him and whispers, 'At the sabbat, I'll be inside you and you are to call the spirits.' 'I know,' I say. He wipes the spittle from me with his handkerchief, pulls a sweet from his pocket, and says, 'For you, my sweet. Go inside and tell Mother you've been helping me groom the lame mare.' I hurry down the ladder and run out of the stables, closing the doors behind me."

Samuel began to whimper.

"Are you in pain?" Selena asked.

"No, miss," Samuel said, falling into a spasm of sobs.

"We can stop if the game makes you so sad."

"That's all right, miss," Samuel replied with a plaintive catch in his throat. "I've never told anyone, and I feel better for it. Though some games are more jolly than others, I must say."

"Do you wish to move forward?"

Slats of light illuminated Samuel's tear-stained face as he peeped, "Yes, miss."

"On the count of three, I'd like you to go to the time when you're at the sabbat." Snap!

"I'm given a stinking green potion that makes me dream with my eyes open. Hecuba, the wise woman, says the brew will slip me through the veil. Father carries me over his shoulder, and I see the parishioners hurrying topsy-turvy through the trees holding torches to light the way. Father lays me on the altar of tree stumps so Hecuba can send me into spirit. She waves her arms and screams, then leans over me and stares with her beetle-eyes. 'Go forth and summon the mightiest of fiends, child,' she hisses into my ear. 'Now off be!'

"I break through the veil, which is like crossing the river in a fog. On the other side, I become what they call a Seeker. I search for demons, but only find silly spirits who don't know they're dead. At last I see a fly the size of a stallion with a skull and crossbones on his wings. I beg the Lord of the Flies—Beelzebub, as he's called—to join the sabbat. It's the same as asking the Devil for help. They're praying for the death of the true coven's priestess, and Beelzebub can lend his power. Father opens my legs and shoves his pole in. I scream as the thing pushes inside. I see the rites around me through a thin white curtain. The parishioners, who call each other 'matey,' prance about the altar, chanting, 'Beelzebub! Beelzebub! Come forth tonight!' There are men with men, men mounting women as the horses do, and two women, one putting a black Devil's pole into the other, twisting in the dirt. Father rides me, crushing my shoulders with his hands. Soon a glowing green light runs up my spine and out my brow. It shoots into the kingdom of spirit and makes a path for the demon to follow.

"Hecuba cries, 'Child, you are the door between worlds!' She rubs her hands together, chanting, 'Come forth, Beelzebub, into the night! Appear before us, burning bright! Lend your power, magic's breath, bring about old Mavis' death! With her gone, we assume, our rightful role, old coven's doom.'

"Beelzebub moves through me, and I retch. Everything turns black."

"Can you tell me how the ritual ends?" Selena asked.

"Yes, miss. Father slaps me awake and makes me drink a bitter brew. It's before dawn, and the mates are returning to town. Father carries me through the woods, and I fall into a dream where he and Hecuba are ripped apart by demons. At the inn, I feel my bum dripping. Something's torn there. Father gives me a sleeping potion and puts me to bed. He tells me the pain will be gone when I wake."

"Samuel, will you remain present while I adjust my schedule?"

"Yes, miss."

In the pause that followed, Seth shifted in the chair, as if Samuel were deliberating about whether to continue. When Selena returned her attention to Samuel, she asked, "Can you tell me who your father is?"

"Yes, miss. He's Ambrose Pennington."

"Do you know his family history?"

"His father died when he was six and left him a penniless orphan. At twelve, Father hired on as a groom at the Hell's Ferry Inn, which was built by a Scotsman called Ian McWycke. Father worked hard in the stables. Five years later he was made innkeep so Master McWycke could attend to his other concerns. Father married Mother, and then Father saw the radiant boy."

"Who is that?"

"He's a legend, miss. Some say a tall tale, but I know better. One night after Father became innkeep, he passed out from drink in his room off the stables. He was awakened by a comely spirit child encircled by a ring of light. The boy, a naked angel, really, hovered over Father, then winked at him and disappeared. People say that those who see the radiant boy are themselves lovers of boys. Whoever sees the boy gains vast wealth, only to die a sudden death. Father told me this the first time he took me to the stables."

"Can you move forward to a time after the sabbat?"

"Yes, miss. I'm lying in bed with fever. The blanket hurts my skin. Father's attending to the coaches, and Mother refuses to see me—she knows what Father and I do in the stables. Hestia puts damp tea towels to my forehead, though nothing breaks the heat. She feeds me a broth she's made, but I can't keep it down. Each time I spew, she cleans me up.

"The surgeon arrives, a stout old man in black who smells of rotting flesh. Hestia tells me not to worry, I'm in good hands, for he delivered me into this world. The surgeon examines me, touching me in places only Father ever has. He says, 'Boy, how did you come by that torn backside? Did someone try to harm you? Don't be afraid. You can tell me.'

"I start to cry and say, 'They take me into the woods and dance and sing around me. Then Father rides me until I pass into spirit.'

"The surgeon turns red and tells Hestia, 'Cover your ears, child. The boy is not in his right mind.' He cleans me where it hurts and gives me a tincture that makes me sleep.

"When I wake, the fever's gone and everything's changed. Father works day and night, as more coaches have been added to the run. He acquires the inn from Master McWycke and builds larger quarters for us. The trade makes Father wealthy, and we lack for nothing. All this takes place overnight, as if by magic.

"Father never again takes me to the woods. Now when I lick him in the stables, he says, 'Sammy, if I make one wrong move, they'll 'ave me head.' I don't know what he means until the day we groom the lame mare and Father carries me up to the loft. He pulls down my breeches and pushes his pole inside me. It hurts, and I cry out, but he only pushes harder. A group of town elders, led by the surgeon, throw open the stable doors. The surgeon shouts, 'Ambrose Pennington, you are caught in the act of copulation with your own flesh and blood!' Father spins around as three of the men climb the ladder and fall upon him, throwing him to the floor below. The others bind him hand

and foot and drag him away as he screams, 'I beg you, spare my life!' I sit in the hay, my breeches around my ankles, too afraid to cry."

"What happens next?"

"The surgeon returns and takes me to the levee where the ferries from Banbury dock. A crowd has gathered, as Father sits tied to a chair. Standing behind him is the toothless hangman, arms crossed and grinning. 'Order! Order!'" the surgeon cries. 'I have the witness, and we may proceed.' When I see I must speak against Father, I run. But the surgeon grabs my arm and bloody near rips it off pulling me back to his side. All the while, Father's eyes are searching the crowd.

"The surgeon says, 'The elders thought it fitting to try Ambrose Pennington under God's blue firmament so each of you may bear witness to the crimes of which he stands accused. As people of God, we must condemn the trespasses of the pagan faithless, those who deny our Lord, Jesus Christ. Ambrose Pennington, you stand accused of two unspeakable acts—copulation with your son and consorting with witches. How do you plead?'

" 'Not guilty,' Father mumbles. The crowd yells filthy names at him in reply.

"Still holding my arm, the surgeon asks me if Father and I do certain things together. With each 'Yes,' the townspeople catch their breath. The surgeon turns to Father and asks, 'After hearing this testimony, how do you plead to the charge of unnatural fornication with your son?'

" 'Guilty, your honor,' Father saucily replies, 'if you are to take the word of a child against mine.'

" 'For which you shall be sentenced momentarily,' the surgeon says. 'As for the second crime of consorting with witches, we have no witnesses at present. The court, in its mercy, will ease your sentence if you disclose the identity of those with whom you've cavorted nakedly and lasciviously in the woods, summoning demons for heinous purposes. Breaking the laws of our community brings licentiousness and chaos to our struggle to tame this unforgiving wilderness.'

"A mad grin spreads across Father's face. 'Mercy!' he shouts. 'I'm a dead man whether I give names or not.' He sits up in the chair and addresses the townspeople. 'So it's truth you're after? Some here know the truth as well as I, but are content to let me take the fall.' After a moment, Father says, 'Have no fear, mates. Your secret is safe with me.'

" 'How do you plead to the charge of witchcraft?' the surgeon demands.

"Father looks at the surgeon as if he would murder him and says, 'If truth is what you crave, truth is what you shall have. I was born with nothing, and I shall die a wealthy man. You may kill my body, but I will not forfeit my possessions, I've made sure of that. If I am guilty of summoning demons, even Beelzebub himself, to grant me a comfortable life, so be it! Who here understands what it's like to wake each day not knowing if you will eat or be able to fend off the cold? Who knows the grind of work from dawn until long after nightfall, breaking your back, so another man may prosper? Then a way out appears, whispered by an initiate: 'Conjure unseen powers that work in your favor, my friend. Turn your fortunes around.' Who here knows the amazement at seeing a demon appear from thin air, willing to grant your every wish, and for what price? Your soul, if need be. I say that's a fair trade. Earthly life is a misery, except when mitigated by the grace of gods or demons, what difference does it make? Enjoy yourselves now, my friends, there's no guarantee of heaven despite what the preachers say. You will die and be buried in the sod, and there you will lie for eternity, festering with insects and rats crawling through your bones. So, yes, I did conspire with witches to improve my lot. I did summon demons to gain riches. Who here hasn't wished to possess my lucky charm? If I used ways older than Jesus Christ, and against the word of Jesus Christ, so be it! If the act of fornication with my own flesh joined this world with the next, so be it! My boy had long before seduced me, a man with no impure desires until then, and that is his fate to ponder, not mine. I stand before you with all my sins on view. I dare each of you to do the same.

Then we'll see, as your Bible says, who's worthy of casting the first stone.'

"The elders whisper amongst themselves until the surgeon announces, 'The court finds the accused guilty of both charges, the second by his own admission.' Turning to Father, he says, 'Ambrose Pennington, you will be hanged from the eaves of the Hell's Ferry Inn at sundown.'

"Two of the elders cut Father's bindings. As soon as his legs are free, he swings his fists and knocks the men down. He leaps off the levee and runs upstream through the reeds with his hands bound in front of him. The crowd follows, the surgeon pulling me along by the arm through the river grass. Father's quick, but a few men reach the bend of the river first. They cut him off from above, and the rest surround him from behind in a clearing in the rushes.

"Then, miss, it's as if time stops. Father is trapped. His eyes dart about as his feet sink into the bog. The surgeon, panting for breath, releases my arm and leaps toward Father, grabbing his throat and throttling him. Father can't defend himself because his hands are bound. He struggles in vain as his neck turns purple. His mouth gasps for air, and his eyes bulge. His body goes limp, and his feet give way. The surgeon loosens his hold, and Father falls into the swamp. I run to help him, but there's nothing I can do. I untie his bindings and throw my arms around him. I feel his breath on my face as he gives me a kiss. 'Radiant,' he chokes. 'Radiant—'

"The men stand in silence. I see something no one else is privy to. While Father lies dead in the tide, a wisp of smoke rises from his chest and disappears. I turn and run to warn Mother, for I am certain we will all be killed. I find Mother sewing by the hearth and tell her that we must flee. Mother sighs and, without shedding a tear, says, 'We cannot escape God's will. We are innocent and must entrust ourselves to Him.'

"Trusting no one, I throw clothes into a valise that a coach passenger left behind and nick food from the inn's kitchen. Soon I'm far into the woods, where I come upon the Bear clan's camp. The Chief himself gives me lodging. Hecuba once told me he sees spirits, but I'm too afraid to ask him. I think he understands that I can enter the kingdom of spirit, for he tells me, 'We are brothers, my son.' To help me on my journey, at daybreak he orders one of the braves to ferry me across the river in a hollowed-out barque.

"A fortnight later I arrive in New Amsterdam. I've never seen so many people, miss. I sign on as cabin boy on a mercantile ship that travels to and from the colonies. My sport with Father puts me in right good standing with the captain, whom I serve for the next twenty years, until I die of the pox in the year of our Lord 1767."

A hush fell over the room once Samuel stopped speaking. Selena cleared her throat and asked, "Do you know what became of your family?"

"Yes, miss. Years later, I met one of the parishioners in a tavern in New Amsterdam. He told me that Mother had been hanged for witchcraft—though she affirmed her belief in Jesus Christ—not long after I left home. 'How could Patience Pennington not have known what her husband was doing in the woods?' the reasoning went. The parishioner also told me that Hestia, ever the smart one, ran off, and was taken in by the Bear clan. Prissy, who teased me so, drowned in the river during a flood. A fitting end, I daresay."

"Is there anything more you can tell me?"

"No, miss. I want to go. I fear I've said too much. I can't imagine how you found me. You must be very wise or very foolish to have looked so hard. Try to learn from life and seek the Light. If you fail, you'll find yourself in the same silly muddles again and again. Cheers, miss!"

"Cheers, Samuel. On the count of five, I want you, Seth, to return to consciousness peaceful and integrated. One. Awake and fully conscious. Two. Safely at home in this reality. Three. Leaving behind anything that won't benefit you in your present life. Four. Back in the present. Five. You're here now." Snap!

Seth's body spasmed, his flesh pulled from his skeleton by unseen hands. His face twisted into a misshapen mask as his childish demeanor morphed into a more formal adult appearance. When the contortions stopped, he opened his eyes and surveyed the room. "How long have I been under?" he asked.

"Three hours. We learned a lot."

Seth looked at his watch. "Jesus, I'm late for work! I've got to run." He rose unsteadily from the chair and staggered towards the door.

"Listen to this and call me," Selena said, handing him the session tape. "Be careful. You were under pretty deep. You really should sit here a while longer."

By the time Seth reached the lobby, he was so lightheaded he could barely stand. His flu-like symptoms returned. He walked outside into the balmy fall afternoon and found a pay phone on Central Park West. After calling in sick to work, he leaned against the stone wall that enclosed the park and gazed at the trees. The leaves were starting to turn from green to gold. It took him a quarter of an hour to regain his equilibrium; he then strolled along the park to the subway at Columbus Circle. He intended to listen to the tape, which he clutched in his jacket pocket, as soon as he got home.

ℋ

Cardboard boxes full of books, videotapes, and kitchen utensils blocked Seth's entry into the living room. Shoving the boxes aside, he went to the kitchen, drawn by a loud clanging of pots. He stood in the archway and watched Martin pulling cookware from the cabinets.

"What's going on?" Seth asked.

Martin faced Seth and resolutely replied, "I'm moving out. Aren't you supposed to be at work?"

"You're moving out behind my back?" Seth asked. "Why?"

"Because you're boiling your own urine and being past-life regressed!"

"There must be another reason. I suggested you move out for your safety. Is this your way of breaking up?"

"I'm worried about you and you're making our life together difficult. I need some space. *You* need some space. You've got to pull yourself together, and I've got to keep focused on my writing."

"I'm having a nervous breakdown, and all you can think about is your writing?"

"I've got to have a place to write. To concentrate. You are sucking away all my energy."

"You've already got another apartment?"

"Yes," Martin replied in a calmer tone. "On Broome Street. It's a loft. Come over whenever you want. I've been looking for a month. I happened to get lucky last week."

"I wonder how else you got lucky."

Martin scowled and said, "All I meant was that I found a great place, as if by magic. That rarely happens in New York."

"Thanks for consulting me. I'm thrilled that we made this decision as a couple."

"We can do the same things we always did," Martin said, sounding conciliatory. "We just need to live apart for awhile." Handing Seth the spaghetti pot, he dryly added, "Don't say I didn't leave you a pot to piss in."

Seth threw the pot to the floor and retreated to the living room. "I hope you're not planning on sleeping here tonight!" he yelled before walking into the bedroom and slamming the door.

℘

At first, Seth refused to accept Martin's absence, denying the possibility that his own behavior had contributed to his partner's departure. He moved through the days as if he was grieving, mentally battling anger, bargaining, and depression, until he reached acceptance. When Seth ventured to Martin's SoHo digs for the first time, he walked into a loft with a two-story wall of windows and a stairway leading to a second-floor bedroom and bathroom. The space was furnished with a new sofa, oak bookcases, and stylish chrome lamps.

"Where'd you get the money for this?" Seth asked.

Martin hesitated, then said, "Miraculous gave me an advance."

"You didn't tell me."

"There's a lot of things we've stopped sharing."

Seth regarded Martin suspiciously but said nothing.

Martin gave Seth a tour. Seth stopped before the mantle over the fireplace, where Martin had assembled an assortment of glass pyramids, crystal globes, statues of Egyptian gods, and twiggy magical fetishes in front of a cobalt-blue tapestry of moons, stars, and planets. There were also two silver wine goblets that appeared to be antique.

"Why have you built an altar?" Seth asked.

"I haven't built an altar," Martin stated unequivocally.

"It looks like one to me."

"It's just a bunch of stuff I had in storage."

"I'd ask if you'd gotten back into magic, but from what I saw, I know the answer."

"Then why ask?" Martin replied with an angry flash of his eyes. "It's not as if I didn't walk in on you trying your hand."

"Are you jealous of my connection to the ghost?"

"Of course not."

"Then why were you trying to contact him?"

"You asked me to help you. And he may be able to help me."

"How can a spirit that tried to kill me help you?"

Martin did not reply. Finally, he said, "I can't protect you unless I summon him. And when I do, I want something in return. That's only fair."

"I've been reading up on this stuff, and you're crossing a line. Be careful."

"I am careful. Nothing to worry about, trust me."

Martin took Seth's hand and led him up the stairs to the bedroom, where a newly-purchased bed dominated the space. They clumsily embraced and fell onto the bed, as if after a week apart they'd forgotten how to love each other. Afterwards, they ordered Chinese take-out and ate sprawled across the bedroom floor.

Martin showered, emerging from the bathroom in an ash-colored robe with the hood pulled over his head.

"You look like a medieval necromancer," Seth said.

"I was one in another life."

"I'm not sure how to take that," Seth said sullenly.

"I'm teasing. Don't be so serious."

"This bed doesn't sag in the middle, like our old one. I kind of got used to that."

"Out with the old, in with the new. That's what I want—everything new and shiny. And expensive, once I start making real money."

"Out on the coast?"

"Here or the coast. Wherever they'll pay me."

"I'm staying here, just so you know."

Seth showered and returned to the bedroom to find Martin asleep. He climbed into bed and hugged Martin, who withdrew from the embrace. He lay awake in the unfamiliar surroundings; finally, he descended the stairs in the dark and switched on a lamp in the living room. Sitting on the sofa, he stared at the bare wall adjacent to the bank of windows. *I don't think this is going to work,* ran through his mind. He suppressed the thought, but it only loomed larger. As his eyelids grew heavy, shadowy runes appeared on the wall. The swirling figures looked like the magical symbols in an alchemist's notebook used to indicate metallic compounds and astrological aspects. The images changed shape and pulsated, growing in size to fill the wall's height. He switched the light off and on several times, but the runes remained, even in darkness. Without the light, they dimly glowed. Not daring to question whether the runes were real or imagined, and certain he'd never get any sleep, he dressed and crept out of the apartment as the sun rose in the pale eastern sky.

ℋ

Seth went to sleep on his own the following night. The last thing he recalled as he straddled the sagging bed and drifted into slumber was the weightless sensation of falling through space. Dizzying blackness alternated with blinding starlight until he abruptly hit the earth. He stood up and surveyed the surrounding hills and woodland. Emerging from a thicket of trees were Ambrose Pennington and bug-eyed Hecuba, followed by a group of diaphanous parishioners in colonial garb. "Come back, Samuel!" the parishioners called in thin voices. "You're our cherished one! You belong to us!"

He ran along the banks of a river, moving sluggishly, as if underwater. Rounding a bend, he saw a village in the distance. Unable to gain speed, the parishioners closed in. As they were about to overtake him, he turned and yelled, "I won't come back! I won't let you in!" His screams wrenched him awake. He lay tangled in the sheets, with only his strained breathing and the growl of a garbage truck interrupting the late-night stillness. He remained motionless until his heartbeat returned to normal.

He sat up in bed to shake off the nightmare and experienced a puzzling urge to return to the Orenda Valley, the place he'd sworn he'd never visit again. *Maybe I should listen to Ivy and contact my mother,* he reasoned. *Don't I have rights to some land?*

Keta's voice went off inside his head. "You must release your father. Nothing changes until this is done."

Seth reached for the glass of water on the nightstand. He took a sip and settled onto the mattress. He closed his eyes and thought, *I can find Ajax if I return. I can help him.* The burning scent of dead leaves surfaced, along with the sensation of pressure exerted from above. Seth opened his eyes and cried out, "Are you crazy?"

H

The next night at work, Seth typed "haunted Hope Springs" into the LexisNexis database, and an archived newspaper article appeared on the screen. "The Most Haunted Town in America" began, "Hope Springs, the tourist mecca of historic Freeman County, has a population of 3,500 living souls and at least as many dead ones, for it's widely accepted that the town is home to an uncommonly high number of ghosts. One local paper, the *Wicklow Times*, has proclaimed, 'There are more spirits per capita in Hope Springs than almost anywhere else on the planet.'"

Seth read on. "Hope Springs takes uncommon pride in its unseen inhabitants. The town offers a walking Ghost Tour on Friday and Saturday nights from April through November. The tour begins and ends at the Ferry Inn, affectionately dubbed 'Ghost Central' by residents. Tour proprietor Delia Hazard has a novel explanation for the town's thriving spirit population. 'When the New York artists and writers summered here in the 1920s, they lent their sensitivity to the area, which attracts spirits. That, and the large number of Revolutionary War dead buried in local cemeteries, along with escaped slaves passing through on the Underground Railroad, makes Hope Springs an extremely haunted place.'"

Seth skimmed the rest of the piece, which promoted Freeman County tourism. He went back to his desk, thinking, *If Ambrose Pennington is my ghost, and if Ambrose resided in Hope Springs, then I should take the Ghost Tour.*

Part Three

Harmonic Convergence

Eighteen

The days grew shorter, the air became cooler. As Seth learned more about himself and his past, he saw the summer pass into autumn, even in the gritty urban neighborhoods of Manhattan. One morning he telephoned Martin. "I found out there's a ghost tour of Hope Springs," he said.

"That's for tourists," Martin replied.

"I'm thinking of taking it."

"Why? You said you'd never go back."

"I might be able to find my ghost, now that I know who he is. Do you want to come along? That shouldn't go against Clara's advice about travel."

There was a lull on the line before Martin said, "I could only do it on a weekend."

"The tour's only given on weekends. I can't believe you're willing to go."

"I can't believe you want to go back to Hope Springs."

Seth dialed Richard's number and was greeted by a gruff, "Dam hotline." Upon hearing Seth's request, Richard said, "I'm shacked up with my girlfriend, so stay as long as you like. I'll leave the key under the flower pot next to the front door. You've got to meet Blanca. She's a trip."

Seth made another call and got Selena Moore's answering machine. When she phoned back later that morning, he said, "I finally listened to the tape."

"Do you think that was your ghost?" Selena asked.

"Yes. I'm going to Hope Springs to find him."

"I would strongly advise against it."

"My boyfriend will be with me."

"You'll need more protection than that. You could be placing yourself in danger. I'd like you to call my friend James Pyre. He's the best psychic I know, and he's interested in past-life reconnects, so he might be willing to accompany you. I would feel better if Jim were there."

"I don't want a third party along," Seth said, but Selena insisted. He took Pyre's information and left a message with his answering service. Before he went to work, he phoned the Paranormal Society.

"Ivy?"

"Yes. Seth? What's up?"

"I've been thinking about Raven Grimmsley. If she is my birth mother, I want to meet her."

"I'm not sure how to respond."

"Isn't that what you've wanted?"

"It's not what I want. It's what you want."

"Nevertheless, you've been angling for a confrontation."

"I wouldn't put it that way."

"I'm ready to meet her. I want to find out why she abandoned me. I have a few other questions as well."

"About the land?"

"That's one of them. I'm going to Hope Springs to take the Ghost Tour. Perhaps you can set up a meeting."

"Do you have a date?"

"Not yet. I'll phone you when I do."

"I'll have to consider the best way to tell Raven."

⫸

James Pyre telephoned the following day. After Seth described his spirit encounter, he said, "Selena thought you might have an interest in helping me find the ghost."

"Before I respond," Pyre said, his pronounced New England accent booming out of the receiver, "you must understand something. What you're describing is an earthbound, not a ghost. I'm getting the impression that the Orenda Valley is rife with earthbounds killed during a war."

J.L. Wünberg

"Many Revolutionary War soldiers died and are buried in the area."

"I thought so. Earthbounds can see and hear. They think they're alive, when actually they're trapped in a twilight zone between life and death, reliving scenes that occurred in their lifetime. When you're dealing with earthbounds, you're dealing with energy. We're all energy, when we're alive and after we die. The energy of each being doesn't dissipate. It regroups and takes another physical form. A sensitive person can pick up an earthbound's energy level or vibration."

"I've become aware of supernatural energy since my encounter with the ghost—I mean earthbound."

"Of course you have. I would bet the contact switched on your psychic abilities. What did you have in mind we do once we find this earthbound?"

"I want him to confirm that he was my father. Then I think you should perform an exorcism. He needs to be crossed over."

"Two things," Pyre said, sounding exasperated. "You don't need to communicate with an earthbound to discover if he's connected to you. It will come to you in a dream or mental image, and you'll instinctively know it. The dream will manifest in the brownish color of early photographs or flickering silent movies."

"I had a sepia-colored dream that indicated the ghost was my father."

"You have your answer then. And exorcism is not the way. It throws an earthbound out of the house without giving it a happier place to go. An earthbound must be shown the way home. I'd be willing to perform a rescue, which guides the earthbound to the realm where he can continue his soul's journey. I'm seeing that this will require your participation."

"Since my encounter, I've come to believe that if you contact earthbounds, it should only be to help them."

"Exactly! Helping an earthbound cross over is the only thing one can do, because the rest is selfish misuse and often downright evil."

"What do you charge for your services?"

"I ask that you cover my expenses. A small donation is also accepted. I won't take anything beyond expenses from you because I sense that we have an adventure ahead."

"Thanks."

"One more thing. I'm getting the impression that something's depleting your energy."

"I've been feeling weak lately. I think someone cast a spell."

"Your mother?"

"How did you know?"

"I'll send you some energy now, and we'll address it further on the trip."

"Thanks, Mr. Pyre."

"Call me James."

ℋ

"Ivy?" Seth said into the receiver.

"Yes?"

"I'm taking the Ghost Tour this Saturday."

"That's not a lot of notice."

"I know."

"I haven't spoken to her yet. Let's plan to meet before the tour in the Ferry Inn tavern. I'll let you know if she's agreeable."

ℋ

On Friday, Seth sat in the passenger seat of James Pyre's Audi. Pyre, who was in his late-sixties, complained about the Manhattan traffic. Martin stretched across the back seat with his Walkman headphones clamped over his ears, reading a book called *The Golden Key*. After their phone conversation, Seth bought one of Pyre's books, *Born Again, Together Again*. The jacket bio stated that Pyre was a frequent guest on TV talk shows. Given his expertise in reuniting the living with their dead loved ones, he was also in demand in his private practice. He'd published eight books on a variety of topics: reincarnation, near-death experiences, and past-life reconnections.

They drove down Varick Street towards the Holland Tunnel. "I've figured out the directions using my road atlas," Pyre said over the din of traffic. "You'll have to guide me once we get to Hope Springs." Pyre's silvery hair made him appear luminescent. When he smiled, his chiseled profile and fine bone structure looked almost feminine. His gray-green eyes grew animated when he spoke. "My wife, Stella, is a trance medium," he said. "She wanted to come along, but I told her this was only an exploratory mission. She doesn't like me to be away for too long, which is why I'm leaving tomorrow night after the tour."

As they entered the tunnel, Seth asked, "How did you end up married to a medium?"

"Do you want the short or long answer?"

"The long one, since we've got a two hour drive ahead."

"Well, then, once upon a time I led a Connecticut Gold Coast life. I was an insurance executive, lived in Greenwich, and was a Yuppie before they had Yuppies. When I look back on myself, I get disgusted, but I wouldn't be where I am today if I hadn't started somewhere." The tunnel's greenish light shaded Pyre's skin, giving him the look of an alien being. "Twenty years ago, on a lark, a friend took me to see a psychic. I thought the whole thing was a joke until the psychic, Stephen Majors, told me things about my mother, who'd passed on when I was a teenager. What he revealed, personal traits and bits of family history, couldn't have been known by a stranger. My friend didn't know those details, either. 'Your mother's spirit is present,' Majors told me, 'and wants to give you a message: In order to receive, you must give of yourself. Open your eyes, and see the world in its entirety.'"

"Did you understand what she meant?"

"Eventually I figured it out. After the session, I noticed a pretty blonde woman in the waiting room, and I started to talk to her. I nearly walked out without getting her phone number, but something made me ask. Six months later we were married."

The tunnel gave way to blinding daylight. After passing along a boulevard lined with motels, Central American diners, and gas stations, they drove up a ramp to the interstate highway, with the industrial lowlands of New Jersey spreading out into the distance.

"How did you become a psychic?" Seth asked.

"After seeing Majors, something opened up in me. I could read people's thoughts and foretell events. The turning point came when I sensed the presence of earthbounds. That disturbed me, but I got used to it. When I started conversing with them, I knew I'd reached a deep level of psychic awareness. Then I grasped what my mother was saying. I'd opened my third eye, and was able to see the world in ways I'd never imagined."

"Was being psychic good for the insurance business?"

"Yes and no!" Pyre laughed. "I understood that I could no longer live as I had. After talking with Stella, I left my job and hung out a psychic's shingle. My son from my first marriage, who'd just graduated from the Wharton School of Business, thought I'd gone crazy. A mid-life crisis, he called it. He came over in his three-piece suit and asked, 'How could you give up your career to become a *psychic*?' I told him, 'Because now I'm happy.'"

The car sped along the winding route to Banbury. Autumn was present in a glorious canopy of leaves, fiery reds and oranges and yellows. Seth stared out at the woodland and asked Pyre, "Is there a scientific explanation for why an area is overrun with spirits?"

"The word 'scientific' bothers me, because the great men of science have been slow to accept paranormal phenomena. But after twenty years of observation, I have my own theory."

"Which is?"

"That there are energy columns that penetrate the earth's surface like needles in a pin cushion. In Sedona, Arizona, and parts of Hawaii, the columns are composed of positive energy. But in Dudleytown, Connecticut, the energy's negative. It's at these negative sites that a multitude of spirits exist. I also think most major hauntings take place on or near water. We're all energy—masses of electrical impulses—and electricity is conducted by the trace chemicals and minerals in water. Since spirits are energy forms, too, it's easier for them to break through the veil near water. They need a lot of energy to manifest, and they draw upon the force of water to reveal themselves to us. It's also easier for a psychic to give an accurate reading near water. Living on the Long Island Sound has helped me."

Seth grew agitated, worried about protection from his earthbound.

What's wrong? Pyre mentally inquired.

Seth squirmed as the psychic's words landed in his brain. He looked incredulously at the driver. "Did you say something?"

"Yes," Pyre replied, this time moving his lips. "I asked you what's wrong. You're sending out panicky vibes."

"But I heard you inside my head!"

"That's because I spoke to you mind-to-mind. You're psychically attuned enough to respond in kind. So tell me what's wrong without using the power of speech."

"I don't know how to do that!" Seth protested.

"Try it," Pyre coaxed. *Form your thoughts, focus them like a laser beam, and send them directly into my brain.*

Seth started upon hearing Pyre's words inside his head, thinking, *This is already so weird, what's a little ESP?*

There's nothing weird about non-verbal communication, Pyre telepathically replied. *It's as normal as having a telephone conversation. Three hundred years ago, no one would have thought it possible to communicate over an electrical wire.*

Seth visualized sending his thoughts in a graceful arc into Pyre's head, saying, *I realized I hadn't protected myself, and I thought I'd be in danger once we arrive in Hope Springs. Copy?*

Loud and clear! Pyre exclaimed inside Seth's head. *You must understand that there's nothing non-physical that can harm you. The only way an earthbound can hurt you is if you feed it your negative energy. If you show a spirit your fears—and they pick them up telepathically—they'll use them to make you to believe they have power over you, when they have none. You are protected from a very deep place in your soul. But you must believe that in order for it to work. You mustn't let your fears undermine you, understand?*

I think so. But my earthbound nearly suffocated me. How do you explain that?

It's true that if you're caught off-guard or don't know how to protect yourself, an earthbound can inflict harm.

So there is some danger, then?

Of course. I can safeguard us with a prayer or ritual, if necessary. One more thing. We may need to rely on this telepathic link in Hope Springs, so don't forget how to do it.

They rounded a bend in the road and descended a steep wooded grade. At the bottom of the hill they passed a gas station and entered Banbury, with its run-down shops and restaurants along the main street. "Strange how this place creeps up on you," Seth commented. His stomach tensed, and he wanted to scream, "Why have I come back?"

Pyre glanced at Seth and turned his pale eyes back to the road. *Remember* was the sole word he planted in Seth's brain as he drove the Audi through the town and onto the bridge that spanned the Orenda. The tires grated on the metal roadway, causing the car to vibrate, and rousing Martin. He removed his headphones and asked, "Are we there yet?"

"We're here," Seth replied.

Pyre drove two blocks into downtown Hope Springs and turned into a snarl of cars on River Road. Following Seth's directions, he navigated the tourist traffic on the thoroughfare, turned off toward the river, and parked on the street in front of Richard's cabin. They walked down the dirt path. Martin sprinted ahead, found the key under the flower pot on the porch, and opened the door. Pyre grabbed Seth by the arm and said, "Wait a moment." He called to Martin, "Seth will be right in." He pulled a small plastic flask from his rear pants pocket and said, "I'll make this quick."

"What are you doing?" Seth asked.

"I'm going to bless you, something I learned from a shaman." Pyre scanned the field of wildflowers that surrounded the cabin to make sure they were alone.

"What's in the bottle?"

"Water from a sacred stream. Your energy is under attack."

Pyre positioned Seth in a dirt clearing and spun him around so that Seth's back faced him. He muttered an unintelligible invocation and touched the back of Seth's head, shoulders, the small of his back, and the back of his knees. He turned Seth around and repeated the process to the front of his body. He turned Seth again and took a mouthful of water. Without warning, he sprayed the water onto the back of Seth's head and shoulders. Seth jumped, but remained in place. Pyre spun Seth around, took another swig, and sprayed him again. He said, "May the white light of God bless you and protect you from evil. May the light of the Lord repel all baneful energy. Amen!"

Seth started to wipe the water from his face, but Pyre said, "Let it dry."

"Was that a baptism?"

"Of sorts. You should notice a change in your energy by tomorrow." Pyre clasped Seth's hand and said, "Meet me at the inn at nine. We'll have breakfast and check out the building afterwards." As he walked down the path to the street, he called out, "Don't forget to bring your camera."

ℋ

Seth entered the cabin. Cobwebs hung from the corners of the living room, and anti-dam literature was stacked in piles around the room. A note attached to the refrigerator with a Damn the Dam magnet read: "Help yourself to food. I've left spaghetti and sauce on the counter, and there's lettuce in the fridge. Call me at Blanca's. I'll try to make the Ghost Tour."

Martin walked into the living room and said, "I unpacked. Why don't we have an early dinner? Maybe we can fool around after that."

Seth dropped his overnight bag in the bedroom and returned to the kitchen, where he set a pot of water to boil. He emptied the sauce into a pan, and searched the refrigerator, stocked with beer and cheap white wine, for the lettuce. He also found a few scallions and a single large carrot. Martin rummaged through his duffel bag and disappeared into the bedroom. When the water came to a boil, Seth broke the spaghetti in half and placed it in the pot. He dressed the salad, drained the pasta, and called Martin for dinner. He ladled the sauce onto the steaming spaghetti and called Martin again. After several minutes, Martin appeared.

They carried their plates outside to the screened-in porch and sat on a chaise lounge with moldy plastic cushions that crinkled under their weight. An awkward quiet descended, broken only by the sounds of the breeze in the tree branches and the rushing of the river over stones. The field of wildflowers and the swaying trees that hid the river from view rendered the ramshackle abode bucolic, despite its decrepitude.

Seth went to the kitchen to refill their plates. When he returned to the porch and sat down, a sickly-sweet odor from inside the house drifted past. He sprang up, nearly toppling his food. "Do you smell that?" he asked, his voice cracking. "I think it's a ghost!"

Martin burst out laughing and said, "Jeez, you're jumpy. I lit some incense. It was supposed to be a surprise." He put down his plate, grabbed Seth's hand, and led him along the hallway to the bedroom. Flinging open the door, Martin revealed a glowing chamber illuminated by green, red, and purple pillar candles and numerous red votives. Swirls of incense smoke clouded the air.

"You're going to burn down the house!" Seth said.

Martin bowed grandly and said in a mock-Arabian accent, "Come into my tent." He led Seth into the bedroom, which was as fragrant as a spice market—essence of jasmine, rose, and patchouli predominated. Seth sat on the double bed and said, "How romantic."

"Take off your clothes," Martin said. "I'm going to get the wine."

Seth shed his T-shirt and jeans. He removed the chain with his religious medallions from around his neck and placed it on the dresser next to *The Golden Key*. The book lay open to a chapter called "Drawing Prosperity to You."

Martin rushed back into the room, shirtless and holding the two silver wine goblets from his loft. "Drink this," he said, handing a goblet to Seth. The beverage was scented with cinnamon and apples.

Seth raised his cup and toasted, "To finding the ghost!" He swallowed a mouthful of the tart brew, which intoxicated him as it went down. He studied the contents of the goblet and asked, "What's in this?"

"Wine and some mystery ingredients. You like to get high for sex, don't you?"

"Yes, but I don't want to pass out," Seth said, sipping the drink, which tasted like mulled wine. He reclined on the sagging mattress and drained the goblet. The candlelight generated a flickering golden radiance. The red votives twinkled like stars from every surface. Hypnotized by the flames, he stretched out, and after a few minutes his vision went funny. Colors jumped out at him, bending prismatically away from their source. The pillar candles gave off a three-dimensional glow. Through his dizziness he asked, "Did you put magic mushrooms in the wine?"

"What if I did?" Martin replied. He sat on the bed and leaned over, releasing Seth's cock from his boxer shorts and tasting it with his tongue.

"I just want to know what I'm in for."

"This is what you're in for!" Martin slipped off his jeans and underwear and straddled Seth, rubbing his groin against his lover. He lowered himself over Seth, who rose to kiss him. Their tongues intertwined, the darting, probing motion rousing Seth to hardness. Breaking the kiss, Martin sucked Seth's earlobe, which caused him to buck beneath Martin's weight, generating an electric friction between their cocks.

"Red is for sex," Martin whispered while licking Seth's ear. "Green is for luck. Purple ambition, the red stars for fuck."

"What's that?" Seth murmured. "What are you saying?"

"Green is for money, red for the passion, purple ambition to bring all the cash in. Abundance is green, red for the sex, purple the power to drive home this hex." Martin ground his body against Seth's and twice more chanted the rhyme. He locked Seth in a paralyzing embrace and said in a lust-choked whisper, "Open the channel, my love."

Seth regarded Martin through the gauzy white veil that had descended upon his mind. Martin appeared far away, a subliminal image of himself surrounded by a blazing wall of fire. Martin whispered, "Open up" again and again. Struggling to understand the command through the veil's obscuring haze, Seth responded by removing his shorts and spreading his legs to position his rear against Martin's thrusting cock, but Martin did not penetrate him. Instead, he rolled Seth onto his stomach and tongued his way down his back. With every nibble, every sucking kiss, Seth let out a guttural, "Oh man," until the room reverberated with his groans. For every "Oh, man," Martin joined in, when his greedy lips were free, with, "Open up, Seth. Open the channel, my love." Martin spread Seth's ass and shot his tongue inside the crevice, releasing the musky, sweat-tinged odor to mingle with the candle scents. "Oh, man, honey, that's great," Seth moaned, as Martin jammed his tongue deep inside. "Red is for sex. Green is for gold. Purple ambition to raise my soul," Martin gasped as he licked fire inside Seth's loins.

"Oh, man, honey. That's incredible."

"Open up for *me*, Seth." Martin trailed his cat's tongue down Seth's legs and deployed it against the back of his knees, which sent Seth into a squirming frenzy. "Oh, man, you're gonna make me come," he cried.

"That's the idea." Martin turned Seth over, dove down, and swallowed Seth's cock, moaning as his lips nestled in Seth's pubic bush. He began to suck in earnest, which intensified the effects of the wine. Streaks of liquid gold shot through Seth's brain as he floated in a druggy cocoon. He swung around and shoved Martin's jutting hard-on down his throat. With each cock lodged in the other's mouth like a serpent swallowing its tail, the circle was complete, and the bedroom became supercharged with the power of desire. Seth licked and swallowed, and the repetition of his muffled "Oh, man's" increased, until the words ran together and took on the rhythmic power of a prayer. "Oh, man, oh, man" became "a-men, a-men," a spontaneous hymn to the god of delight. A deeper communion arose between Seth and Martin, spurring them on. Tongues teased, lips engulfed and caressed, while suctioning sounds and moans filled the room.

Seth reached the point where he could no longer hold back. The "a-mens" contracted into a succession of passion-strangled yelps. "Om, om, om," he cried in a high-pitched voice.

"Open the channel and grant my wish!" Martin shouted between fiery licks.

"Om, om, om," Seth hummed, barely able to catch his breath.

"Open the channel, Seth!"

Seth yelled one last "Om!" for Martin had given his cock the final blow. In a moment where time ceased to exist, a vibrant tingling at the base of his spine moved up his back, like a constellation of stars infusing him with electricity. When the electrical current reached his neck and moved into the seat of his brain, he screamed, "Om, om, oh my God, I'm coming!" As he flooded Martin's mouth and Martin did the same to Seth, something coalesced in Seth's awareness. *You are protected,* messaged mind-to-mind by Pyre, shot into his brain. He sank into the lumpen folds of the bed and, with the taste of cock and semen suffusing him, momentarily lost consciousness.

From behind a gauzy white veil, Seth saw himself as if gazing into a mirror. Before him stood a smiling, beatific Keta. He and Keta were now one and the same, twinned by a cosmic orgasmic gnosis of the Divine. Seth's vision was interrupted by Martin calling, "Ajax, instrument of abundance, come forth now!"

𝓜

Ten miles to the north, in the secluded woods of Upper Dark Hollow, Ajax awakened to the call. He spun his immaterial form into his gossamer human self. The dark curls, burning eyes, somber face, and shrouded body became visible to anyone with supernatural sight. He glided through Raven's darkened hallways, searching for the summoner. It wasn't his mistress, who called with recognizable commands and incantations. This was someone new.

A second telepathic command floated into the house, a distant cry in the night. "Serve me now, instrument of abundance! Serve me now!" Accompanying the injunction was a jolt of homoerotic energy. "My boy is here!" the spirit murmured. "He performed this magic with me lifetimes ago. I'd know him anywhere."

Ajax searched the living room and bedrooms, but found nothing. Raven was out, Rah-wing was asleep on his perch, and Stone lay passed out drunk on his bed. Would his boy agree to send him into the Light? He passed through the front door and rose into the air, heading towards Hope Springs. "That's where the summoner calls from," he said to the crisp evening breeze. "Perhaps he awaits me at the inn. Now he will set me free." Soaring through the oak forest, Ajax glimmered with a white radiance, animated by the hope which coursed through his ethereal form.

ℋ

Raven's black Impala sped up the asphalt driveway, tires thrumming as the car approached her house. She was returning from a talk she'd given at the Depot, a former train station transformed into a posh eatery that overlooked the river. She held her "Ghosts in the Orenda Valley" lecture series there every month. Few people showed up, and the series made no money. At best, it promoted her books, but even this income was meager. Devoting herself to raising humanity's awareness of the paranormal had been a losing endeavor. As she approached her sixtieth year, living on the verge of bankruptcy, her patience with her lot was strained. She had been on edge all evening. On the way home, when she rolled down the car window, an odor, like the blood of a wounded animal, wafted in on the breeze. A chill went through her, and she raised the window against the smell. When she turned off the engine and stepped out of the car, she had an intuitive flash: "Seth's back."

The phone rang inside the house, and she flew up the steps and dashed into the living room, stopping only to switch on a lamp. Rah-wing rustled on his perch beside the fireplace.

"Hello!" Raven panted into the receiver.

"Raven, it's Ivy. I'm glad I got you in."

"Do you have any news?"

"That's why I'm calling."

"Don't keep me in the dark! What's going on?"

"He's in Hope Springs to take the Ghost Tour tomorrow night. He wants to meet you."

Raven let out an anguished moan. "I sensed it! You should have given me more warning."

"I just found out."

"The spells certainly haven't worked!" Raven said harshly.

"Spells?"

"Yes, spells. He's well protected. Why is he so keen to meet me?"

"Why does any adopted child want to meet his birth mother?"

"There won't be a happy reunion."

"He knows about the land," Ivy said in a small voice.

"How could he know about the land unless you told him?" Raven said.

"He figured it out. Did research, I guess."

"He wants his inheritance. Well, he's not going to get it."

"He seems reasonable. I think you should meet him."

Raven hesitated before saying, "I want you there to mediate."

"I can come down tomorrow. I'll leave Ali with my mother. Why don't we meet at the Ferry Inn tavern at seven? You'll have an exit strategy, since the tour starts at eight."

"You think of everything."

"I'm just trying to help."

There was a lengthy silence on the line until Raven said, "It's against my better judgment, but I'll meet him. I'm counting on you to ensure that this goes smoothly."

"Trust me, it will be fine."

"It had better be," Raven said before hanging up. She turned and called to Rah-wing, who flew to her outstretched finger. "My son's come back," she said dully.

Rah-wing eyed his mistress and peeped, *Radiant boy,* inside her head.

"Yes, my pet, radiant boy."

If the child returns alive, beware, the mother dies!

Nineteen

Seth slept deeply. When he awoke the next morning, the effects of the wine had worn off. He remembered Martin's strange rhymes, but could only recall that the words dealt with the power inherent in colors. He rolled over to find Martin propped against two pillows engrossed in *The Golden Key*. Except for a slight grin on his lips, Martin's fixed expression indicated that he'd withdrawn into his own world again.

Seth got out of bed and called Beth to tell her he was in town. She insisted on taking the Ghost Tour with him; they decided to meet at the Ferry Inn tavern. He then called Ivy. After several rings, she picked up. "I'm just about to leave the city," she said.

"Can we meet before the tour?"

"Yes. Raven will be with me."

"I never thought this would happen."

"Neither did she. We'll be at the Ferry Inn tavern at seven. Don't mention the land. She's paranoid about it."

"I hope she's not paranoid about me."

"We'll find out."

Seth and Martin dressed and set out for town. The morning air was cool, a foreboding of the winter winds to come. After walking along a deserted stretch of River Road, they entered the tourist zone with its restaurants, boutiques, and antiques emporiums. The Ferry Inn, set on a slight rise above the street, loomed ahead. Seth felt a rush of anticipation tinged with fear as they climbed the brick steps, entered the inn, and passed the formal dining room. They navigated a warren of wood-paneled hallways, walked through the reception area, and entered the atrium restaurant at the back. There they found Pyre at a table drinking a cup of coffee.

A waitress wearing a white cotton blouse and black skirt appeared. She handed Seth and Martin menus and poured them coffee, returning a few minutes later to take their order. While waiting for the food, Pyre said, "I've been mapping out the day. Our agenda should be, first, to explore the inn. After that, we'll walk through town. This evening is the tour. Then perhaps we can get a bite to eat before I head home."

The waitress approached bearing a large tray. She served them and refilled their coffee cups before crossing the room to wait on another table.

"Why did you tell me to bring my camera?" Seth asked.

"Because earthbounds turn up in pictures. As we make the rounds, shoot whatever interests you and we'll see what, ah, develops."

"Okay," Seth said with a laugh.

After breakfast, Pyre led Seth and Martin to the front desk. "Do you mind if we snoop around?" Pyre asked the clerk, whose black-ringed eyes suggested that she hadn't had a full night's sleep in weeks. "We won't disturb any of your lodgers, dead or alive," he added.

"It's against policy," the clerk answered.

"We only want to look around."

"Looking around is fine. Just don't disturb any of the guests."

Seth stepped forward and inquired, "Where I can buy tickets for the Ghost Tour?"

"You can get them here, or you can buy them at the Bell, Book and Candle bookstore down the street. They're ten dollars each."

Seth purchased three tickets, and they ascended the oak staircase that led to the upper storeys. Prompted by Pyre, they stopped on the landing between the first and second floors to view the wedding portrait. The stern couple stared angrily out of the canvas, as if their privacy, or some secret they shared, had been violated. Both wore purple roses, the man in his lapel, the woman on her bodice and in her primly curled hair.

"I noticed this painting yesterday," Pyre said. "Something about it intrigues me."

"They don't look like a happy couple," Seth said.

"True. But I'm sensing that the portrait is related to your earthbound."

While they stood before the picture, the musty scent of decomposing flowers drifted past. Associating the smell with the roses in the portrait come back to life, Seth tensed and was about to bolt down the stairs when Pyre took his arm and steadied him. "It's only a passing spirit," Pyre said. "It can do you no harm."

Martin regarded his companions and said, "I didn't feel anything. You're letting your imaginations run wild."

"That's not the case," Pyre said evenly.

Martin glared at Pyre, but averted his eyes when he could no longer hold the psychic's gaze.

Seth took photos of the portrait from several angles, and leaned in to examine the two grim faces. Upon closer inspection, the couple blurred in and out of focus, their funereal garments rippling to reveal shrouded dimensions beneath the folds. Thinking there was something wrong with his vision, or that he was having a flashback from the night before, he stepped back and glanced at Pyre. The psychic's expression indicated that he, too, was witnessing the undulations that muddied the painting's surface. Seth moved away in alarm when several faces, each a different aspect of the same visage, emerged from the swirling vortex.

"Lose your fear," Pyre advised Seth. Martin looked at both men, confused.

The portrait completed its metamorphosis into a grape-like cluster of faces that dominated the canvas. The central face was covered with creased yellow skin like rotting leather. The eyes, which sank into chasms in the skull, were two black holes that sucked in light. The long nose drooped, and the charred lips pointed downwards in a permanent scowl.

Martin inspected the finely worked gold-leaf frame, oblivious to the painting's mutation, while Seth and Pyre watched the cadaverous face open its mouth to speak. At first no words emerged from the parched hole; then a scratchy telepathic voice demanded, *Who called me? Was it you? Or was it* you? the last question hurled into Martin's brain. He jumped and looked at the painting, but could not distinguish the mutating faces.

No one called you, Pyre telegraphed the grimacing face.

I have been summoned by an unknown sorcerer, the face replied. *Be careful what you call forth, you may get more than you bargain for.*

I am careful, Pyre said. *Therefore, you have no need to warn me.*

One of you covets my services. One of you should mind what he wishes for.

Spirit, if you do not walk in the light of God, begone! Pyre ordered. *Trouble us no more.* He snapped his fingers three times, and the cluster of faces whirled around the canvas before dissolving into a dark mass of paint. The newlyweds gradually returned to view.

"Something spoke inside my head," Martin said shakily.

"Probably one of the heads in the picture," Seth said. "Didn't you see them?"

"No. A shadow fell across the painting, that's all."

"Actually," Pyre said, "the painting underwent a cross-dimensional shift."

"I didn't see anything. Just that weird voice in my head. It seemed to know who I was."

"Let's move on," Pyre said. "We've got a lot of ground to cover."

Seth and Pyre climbed the stairs to the third floor, while Martin lingered in front of the painting. "Ajax, is that you?" Martin whispered. There was no answer, and he followed them upstairs.

The third floor landing was flooded with sunshine pouring through a leaded glass skylight above the stairwell. As they walked down a hallway lined with forest-green wallpaper above mahogany wainscoting, they were chilled by a sudden drop in temperature.

"It's freezing up here," Martin said. "How can they rent these rooms?"

"This is our welcome," Pyre replied, leading Seth and Martin further along the corridor. Near the end, he stopped in front of a door bearing a brass plaque that read "Room 18." A curious look flitted across his face. After a thoughtful pause, he said, "This floor's alive. I can hear its heartbeat. The cold is the exhalation from its lungs. We're standing in a paranormal locus that's manifested especially for us."

Seth rubbed his hands together against the cold, but said nothing.

"If I'm not mistaken," Pyre said, "this is your earthbound's lair."

A shiver passed through Seth. He steadied himself against the wooden ledge that ran above the wainscoting.

Pyre shut his eyes to commune with what was on the other side of the door. He remained silent for several minutes, looking as if he'd fallen into a trance. When he opened his eyes, he said, "There's a very powerful entity inside. Martin, get the front desk clerk. We're going in to see what this spirit's all about."

"If there's something in there, why would we want to contact it?" Martin asked.

"Because that's what I'm here to do," Pyre calmly replied. "Now please get the clerk before we lose the manifestation."

Martin retreated down the hallway, returning a few minutes later with the clerk trailing behind.

"Are there guests in Room 18?" Pyre asked.

"No one ever stays *there* long," the clerk said.

"May we see it if it's unoccupied?"

"It's against policy."

"What policy is that?" Prye asked, reaching for some bills in his wallet. He handed them to the woman, and she removed a set of keys that had been hooked to the pocket of her jacket. She fitted her passkey into the lock, struggling with the dead-bolt until the door opened. "I should warn you—this spirit's as nasty as they come," the clerk said. "He appears in mirrors and as a twinkle of yellow lights. Many guests have run screaming from the room, which is why we only rent it if we're full up. The spirit stinks of rotten eggs. He's tried to strangle several guests, who leave with black-and-blue fingerprints around their neck. Are you sure you want to enter?"

"Yes," Pyre said.

"Then mind the antiques. They come apart at the touch. Close the door on the way out."

They crossed the threshold into Room 18. Sunlight streamed through the lace curtains that hung across the double windows. The dazzling light amplified a milky glow that pervaded the room. It was so cold their breath was visible. Pyre moved to the center of the room. "Start taking pictures," he told Seth. He closed his eyes and stood motionless. His delicate features assumed the rapt tautness of deep concentration. Seth skirted Pyre and shot pictures of the four-poster bed, the inlaid-wood dresser with a spherical brass and pewter mirror above it, and a cherrywood armoire. When he moved further into the room to photograph the writing table that stood between the windows, a sulfurous odor burned his nostrils. His eyes teared, and a fit of nausea overwhelmed him. His windpipe constricted, and an image of Ambrose collapsing into a swamp came into his mind before he crumpled to the floor. "I can't breathe," he choked.

Martin rushed over and helped Seth to his feet. His wide-eyed expression indicated that he could smell the stench.

"Get me out of here," Seth said.

Martin put his arm around Seth and led him into the hallway. Seth slumped against the wall and sat down. "I'll be fine," he said, breathing deeply. He handed the camera and case to Martin and said, "Go back and take pictures."

"Do I have to?"

"Yes."

Martin returned to the room and approached Pyre. "What should I do now?" he asked. Pyre waved him away. He was struggling to contact the entity, and apart from the scent that permeated the chamber, the spirit would not reveal himself. Shooting pictures at random, Martin finished the roll of film.

"He's playing with me," Pyre mumbled.

"It stinks in here," Martin complained as he sat on the bed and reloaded the camera. He took a picture of the suspended nimbus of frozen light that hung below the beamed ceiling.

The air grew heavy and humid, and a voice went off inside Pyre's brain. *Why shouldn't I play with you, old magus? You summoned me, and I wish to see if you're worthy of my service.*

I'm not a magician, Pyre replied, directing his thoughts into the ether. *You are confusing me with someone else.*

Nonsense! the spirit roared inside Pyre's head. *If it wasn't you, perhaps it was the amateur sorcerer beside you.* The spirit's presence manifested as an egg-shaped sphere of black, annihilating energy.

You know him? Pyre asked.

Fleetingly. But I've known his partner Seth for lifetimes, the voice hissed. *If you're so bloody psychic, you should have known.*

I did. I just wanted you to confirm it.

Damn you! the spirit said. *You are an evil magus.*

I am no such thing. I'm here to find the earthbound who contacted Seth. I would like you to confirm something.

I won't confirm or deny anything.

Were you Seth's father in a previous existence?

The spirit released a swooping, high-pitched laugh inside Pyre's head. *Let's just say we were kissin' kin.*

We're here to help you cross over.

You don't think I'd fall for that old trick? I can help myself over anytime I please, thank you very much.

If you haven't made the journey thus far, you will need some assistance.

You underestimate me.

We can help you repent.

I have no shame.

Why did you contact Seth?

Why did you contact me?

To help you and Seth resolve the past.

Bollocks!

Only then can you release the anger that's holding you—

What is this, a therapy session? I'm from the wrong century for that rubbish.

And return home.

Home? What is home? I don't know whether to laugh or cry.

We'll help you over whenever you choose.

Don't hold your breath. Or better yet—do! A fiendish laugh echoed inside Pyre's brain as the spirit turned his attention to Martin. *How may I be of service?* popped into Martin's head.

Martin snapped to attention. With Pyre still in trance, Martin whispered, "Are you Ajax?"

I'm called that by some.

"Can we strike a deal? Come to me when I call and I will outline the terms."

It is I who establish the terms.

"As you wish."

My service does not come cheaply. You may bargain away your soul. I know. I once struck such a deal.

"I'm not afraid."

Very well, then. I will come when I'm called.

The spirit's presence waned. The oppressive air lifted and the chill dissipated. Pyre opened his eyes as the room's frosty glow vanished. "He's gone," Pyre said. He regarded Martin warily. "Martin, there's no need for you to contact the spirit. In fact, I advise against it."

"We should check on Seth," was Martin's curt response.

Pyre inspected the room to make sure they were leaving it in good order. He motioned Martin ahead, and they proceeded into the hallway.

ℋ

"Well?" Seth asked, getting to his feet. He looked expectantly at Pyre.

"It's as you suspected," Pyre replied. "The earthbound was your father in another incarnation."

"Did he say so?"

"Not entirely, but I could sense it. He wants to be helped over, though he denies it."

They walked down the hallway, which had lost its chill, and descended the stairs. As they passed the portrait on the landing, the scratchy voice went off inside Seth's head. *Remember what you must do. Or else you will lose—* Seth grabbed the staircase banister to steady himself, and gripped the railing until he reached the ground floor.

They left the inn by the front entrance and joined the throng of tourists strolling along River Road. They dodged daytrippers who loitered in groups on the sidewalk. The jumble of people with nothing to do but shop, eat, and wander lent the town a celebratory air. Continuing along the thoroughfare with its historic buildings, Seth pointed out the sites to Pyre. Martin lagged behind, pulling a thermos from his shoulder bag.

"What's in that?" Seth called out. Pyre moved ahead to read a plaque on a weathered flagstone house.

"Tonic," Martin replied as he drew nearer.

"Tonic and what else?"

"Tonic and tonic."

"Please don't get drunk."

Martin stared defiantly at Seth and took a sip. "Maybe I'll see spirits if I drink them," he said. "Maybe I'll be able to communicate with them, like you."

"You need a clear head for that. And don't be envious. I never wanted this ability."

Seth and Martin caught up with Pyre, and they strolled into the heart of Hope Springs, where Seth clasped Pyre's arm. With Bell, Book and Candle in view, Seth said, "That's where I met the old woman and the medium. I don't want to go in there."

"There's no need to," Pyre said. "I'm seeing plenty out here. In front of the white mansion across the street is an arc of red, purple, and amber light."

"I don't see anything," Martin said.

"I'm guessing that's a troubled earthbound, since amber is the color of base supernatural energy," Pyre replied. "Take a picture. It's behind the convertible."

Martin grudgingly complied. "I don't know why you can see them and I can't," he said.

"You must attune yourself," Pyre said. "It takes time."

"I thought I had, for years now."

"It helps if your intentions are good."

Seth and Pyre crossed the street while Martin lingered in front of Bell, Book and Candle, drinking from his thermos.

In the next block, they came upon a vacant plot of land surrounded by yellowing maples. Stopping to inspect the leaf-strewn lot, Seth said, "I wonder why nothing's built here. Every other piece of land along the street is developed."

"The ground is overrun with earthbounds," Pyre said. "This is a sad spot, an old burial ground or mass grave."

"How can you tell?" Seth asked.

"I see arms reaching out of the earth, and disembodied hands grasping for the Light. I also hear voices crying for release. Take a picture, Martin."

Martin swigged from his thermos and shot off the remaining pictures on the roll.

They wandered for another two blocks, reaching the town limits. The sidewalk ended, and a two-lane country road replaced the prettified village boulevard. They crossed the street and reversed direction. The afternoon sun slanted at a steep diagonal, bathing River Road in dense, coppery light. The Ferry Inn loomed large in the distance and appeared to float in mid-air. Seth dismissed this as a trick of light and perspective. Yet as they drew closer, the inn continued to hover above its setting on the rise. When they reached the fenced-in grounds of the Parsons Mansion, Pyre stopped.

"Are you seeing what I'm seeing?" Seth asked.

"Yes," Pyre said. "The most incredible energy columns."

Martin strained to ascertain the vision and said, "I don't see anything. What do they look like?"

"Sparkling needles piercing the inn," Pyre replied. "The rays are the color and consistency of milk, and radiate out from the building's core. Don't you see them?"

"No," Martin replied. He barged ahead, saying, "I need a drink! Maybe that will help."

Pyre took in the opaque light shafts. "I'm sorry Martin's missing out," he said.

"He's frustrated," Seth said. "He's always tried to commune with the supernatural."

"That's evident. But he's seeking something in return, when you should only offer assistance. I also think he's afraid. That's a lot of liquid courage he's consuming." Pyre paused, his face registering a look of awe. "I see it!" he said. "In the center of the cannon square."

"What?"

"Spirits rising from the ground into the air. Masses of them, like angels ascending to heaven."

"I can't make it out."

"This spot must be a portal that allows earthbounds to pass between dimensions, where their realm connects with ours."

"I had my vision about Hope Springs being cursed by a shaman near here."

"Then you accidentally passed through the gateway."

Seth and Pyre looked at each other incredulously and followed Martin as he crossed the square and trod along the gravel path beside the Ferry Inn en route to the tavern. Opening the tavern door, Seth and Pyre stepped aside to let two patrons leave. Apart from Martin, who stood at the copper-topped bar, and Beth and Christy, perched on stools, they were the only customers present. Martin mumbled a greeting to the women and barked, "Margaritas all around!"

The bartender appeared more interested in the World Series on the muted TV than in serving customers. "Frozen or on the rocks?" he carelessly inquired.

"Frozen," Martin said.

"Just a glass of water for me," Pyre said as he settled onto a barstool.

Seth hugged his friends and introduced them to Pyre. "What do you think of Hope Springs?" Beth asked Pyre.

"The town is full of earthbounds and manifested energy," Pyre said. "I've never seen anything like it. Not even Dudleytown in Connecticut compares. I'm surprised it isn't more notorious."

"For some it is, and we try to protect ourselves," Christy said. "You must have noticed the town's dark energy."

Martin poured a round of drinks from the pitcher the bartender set before him. He placed a twenty dollar bill on the bar, lifted his glass, and toasted, "To the invisible realm, the key to prosperity."

"And to the mystery behind it," Seth said. He sipped the cocktail, more out of habit than desire. He glanced across the room and saw an amber light glimmering beside the tavern door. The light flickered and brightened, and assumed the silhouette of a shrouded man with eyes of burning coal. A crown of dark curls framing a mournful face appeared, followed by a ring of purple fingerprints encircling a translucent neck. Seth's breathing constricted as the scent of burning leaves filled his nostrils. He leapt from his chair, but was restrained by Pyre's grip on his arm.

"That spirit cannot harm you," Pyre admonished.

Beth and Christy searched the room for the source of Seth's fright. When Christy made out the cadaverous figure, she cried, "That's the ghost from your house!"

"All I see are fuzzy lights," Beth said.

"That's the earthbound from Room 18," Pyre affirmed.

"I see the lights!" Martin slurred. "Ajax, come to me."

I've come for Seth, Ajax said inside Martin's mind. *If you want my assistance, you must be quick.* The spirit glided across the tavern, addressing Seth. *Yes, son, you're the reason I'm here. You must save me. You must return me to the Light. Only you can work the magic, not your psychic friend. That's the law that breaks the curse—accept me, forgive me, set me free. Or pay the consequences.*

Ajax drew nearer, and Seth telegraphed, *I mean you no harm, but I'm not sure how to help you.* The spirit continued to approach. *I mean you no harm. You must ask James to guide you.* A light blazed to life in Seth's mind. The light expanded and intensified into a diamond-white incandescence. *I mean you no harm, but go away.*

Ajax stopped. Pushed by an unseen hand, he retreated to the far side of the bar. *Then you will learn the hard way,* he angrily stammered.

"Thank God it moved away!" Christy said.

Beth laughed nervously, her face ashen. "Now I see why you were so frightened in my house," she whimpered.

"We should calm ourselves," Pyre said. "The tour starts in fifteen minutes. The earthbound will not harm anyone."

Seth slumped onto his barstool. He stared at Ajax across the room and asked, *Are you and Ambrose Pennington—?*

A blast of cold night air interrupted him as Ivy and a flame-haired woman entered through the tavern doorway. Ivy moved towards Seth, hand extended. "Here we are," she said. "Finally!"

Seth introduced Ivy to the others, while Raven hovered in the background. Ivy motioned her forward, saying "Seth, this is Raven Grimmsley."

Raven approached, her gaze fixed on Seth. He recognized her as the woman he met at Beth's party.

"I don't want to be here," Raven stated matter-of-factly.

"I'm glad to meet you," Seth said, as he stood and shook her hand. A kiss or embrace seemed out of the question.

"Raven is Seth's birth mother," Ivy announced to the group.

"That's not been proven," Raven said.

"I think it has," Ivy said.

Raven studied Seth's features and said, "You have your father's face. I hoped never to see it again. And those eyes—"

"There are many questions I'd like to ask," Seth said. "I've considered looking for you, but never thought I'd find you."

He paused, waiting for a reply, then said, "Would you like a drink?"

"No!" Raven said coldly. "If you've come for an inheritance, you may as well know, I'm broke. There's nothing for you."

"I'm more interested in my family background," Seth said cautiously. "What can you tell me about my father?"

"Your father? You don't want to know about your father. He was one of the darkest men who ever lived. Be thankful you escaped him. I am."

"And the McWyckes?"

"What about them?"

"I read something about a bequest at age twenty-one."

"So that's why you're here!" Raven exploded. "You want the one thing that can save me. Well, you won't have it. You could be an impostor."

"Raven, that's not necessary," Ivy said. "Seth is your child. I would think you'd be thrilled to meet him."

"What you think doesn't matter. I'm unclear as to why you talked me into this."

"If he has the family's powers, he may be an asset to our circle."

Raven eyed Ivy and said, "Let me worry about the coven. After all, I'm in charge."

Seth glanced at his watch and said, "The tour's about to begin. I'm in town for another day. Could we meet tomorrow?"

Raven twitched her eyes as if something had caught her attention, some unseen presence. She looked suspiciously around the room, suddenly aware that Ajax was nearby. "I don't see the need," Raven replied. "Once is more than enough."

Seth put his arm around Martin, who tottered beside him, and with his friends following, marched past Raven and Ivy. "Good night, mother," he said as the group left the tavern. They crossed the cobblestone street to the brick square with its weather-worn canon, where they joined the two dozen people waiting for the tour to begin. Ajax followed, gliding like a vapor through the tavern's flagstone wall. In the twilight, he was barely discernible, except for an occasional whiff of sulfur.

Seth surveyed the inn and the Parsons Mansion, trying to detect ghostly presences from his position within the spirit portal. Watching Martin guzzle from his thermos, he caught the scent of burning leaves on the evening breeze. He flinched and fought the urge to run. He whispered to Martin, "There's going to be at least one ghost on the tour."

Twenty

Three women approached the group of people who had assembled in the square. Delia Hazard, the elfin figure in the lead, wore olive-green tights under an embroidered rust-colored tunic. White plastic ghost earrings dangled from her ears. Blanca Naughton and Wanda Morrigan, walking behind her, looked more like storybook witches. Blanca was draped in shawls and diaphanous scarves. Wanda sported an ankle-length black cape with a high-backed collar that framed her poker face. All three women carried lit torches that reeked of kerosene.

Delia addressed the crowd in a shrill voice. "Good evening, ladies and gentlemen. My name is Delia Hazard, and I'll be your guide, along with torchbearers Blanca and Wanda, for tonight's Haunted Hope Springs tour. Before we begin, my assistants will collect your tickets. Please have them ready." Blanca and Wanda circulated among the crowd, taking tickets with one hand while brandishing their torches with the other. Blanca let out a startled cry when she recognized Seth. "Richard's told me about you," she said. "He's going to join us later."

Delia continued with, "Let me preface the evening by saying that Haunted Tours was founded by Freeman County historian and parapsychologist Raven Grimmsley. Ms. Grimmsley's credentials are extensive, as you will discover if you peruse her many books. These are available at Bell, Book and Candle down the street. I can honestly say that each site on the tour has been authenticated by the most scientific methods known to man."

"And ghost," someone interjected, sending a nervous titter through the crowd.

"That's right," Delia said, "and ghost. Because by tour's end, everyone will agree that ghosts are as real as you and I." Looking to see who the jokester was, Delia noticed Seth among the crowd. "Shall we begin?" she said, making her way across the street.

The torchbearers shepherded the group to the Parsons Mansion, where Delia stood wearing a fixed smile. Once her audience had gathered round, she proclaimed, "This grand home was built in 1784 by one of Freeman County's oldest and wealthiest families. Back then, the Parsons clan owned nearly every grain and lumber mill in the county. Over time, the perils of commerce stripped them of their fortune, so that today all that remains is this mansion. While it's always been said that the Parsons Mansion is haunted, proof came during its recent renovation. After photographing the furnishings for insurance purposes, the photographer was surprised to find that none of the pictures came out. He checked the camera and shot more photos, and nothing but a foggy white blur appeared. Then, on a hunch, he asked permission of the resident spirits to take pictures, and the entire roll came out."

"Big deal," Martin mumbled.

"Now if you'll follow me," Delia said, "we'll visit the next site." The guides waved their smoking torches and trudged up a precipitous cobblestone street. The tourists struggled to keep pace, with many of the seniors gasping for breath and falling behind. About half-way up the hill, Delia stopped in front of a dilapidated wood and flagstone home of indeterminate age. With the crowd circled around her, she said, "This dwelling is known as the House of the Possessed Desk. Writers beware!" She laughed at her own joke, which no one else seemed to get. "That's because the man who lived here twenty years ago owned an antique writing desk. Each night before going to bed he'd lock the desk drawers with a key. But whenever he forgot to do so, the drawers opened and shut of their own accord. He would then have to get up and lock each drawer if he wanted to get any sleep."

A teenage boy wearing a Black Sabbath T-shirt asked, "Can we see the desk?"

"I'm afraid not," Delia replied, "since all the houses on the tour are private residences." She cleared her throat to signal a great pronouncement. "By way of explaining the phenomenon of ghosts, Haunted Tours believes that if someone is hugely traumatized, they can leave behind a psychic imprint at the site. Then, sometimes hundreds of years later, those people we call sensitives can re-experience the imprint. This explains why some people see spirits and others, standing in the same spot, do not."

Thrilling to her own performance, Delia cried, "Onward and upward!" She motioned the group to the top of the hill, where the torchbearers herded them toward a canary-yellow Victorian mansion with a surfeit of white gingerbread scrollwork. "This is the Seafarer Inn," she said. "When I stayed here several years ago, early one morning I was awakened by footsteps outside my room. I got up and opened the door. There, standing before me, was a muscular male ghost. I shut the door because I didn't want to call attention to myself. Five minutes later I decided to see if the spirit was still present. When I tried to open the door, I found it was locked from the outside."

"Oh, my!" someone in the crowd exclaimed.

"Since there was no phone in the room," Delia said with a girlish giggle, "I had to bang on the door to get the proprietor to release me. It was most embarrassing."

"What did the ghost look like?" an elderly woman in a pink sweat suit asked.

"He was tall and wore a sailor's uniform. Quite dreamy, actually. Haunted Tours did some research and discovered that a ship's captain had built the house, which explains its name—and its ghost. Now if you'll follow me, we'll take a walk down Ferry Street."

Descending the other side of the hill in the failing twilight, Delia directed the group towards a row of squat stone dwellings reminiscent of British terraced houses. Several people lagged behind, bored or dissatisfied with the tour. Others found buildings of a more general historic interest to view. Waving their torches, Blanca and Wanda rounded up the stragglers before Delia resumed her narrative.

"These cottages were constructed for mill workers in 1783," Delia said, "after Hope Springs, then called Hell's Ferry, burned to the ground in a catastrophic fire. While manifestations have been reported in each of the twelve houses, turn your attention to number forty-two, for there the grisliest haunting occurs." The darkened house, which had a "For Sale" sign nailed to its front door frame, was bereft of life, as cold and uninviting as a graveyard. Seth approached the cottage and grew nauseous. Retreating to the edge of the crowd, he joined Pyre, who kept a skeptical distance from the proceedings.

"Ten years ago," Delia continued, "a couple with a baby girl moved into number forty-two. One night they heard what sounded like crying. The husband went upstairs to calm the baby, but found her fast asleep. This happened several more times, prompting the couple to ask their neighbors if they heard the crying, which they all did. Haunted Tours did some research and discovered the story behind the sounds." Pausing for effect, Delia declared, "The reason we're standing a house away from number forty-two is that some people get a gut-wrenching sensation if they come too close. Others feel cold spots. After some investigation, it was discovered that the home's first occupants were a widowed mill foreman and his beautiful fifteen-year-old daughter. The foreman wanted the girl to marry a Parsons and move up in the world, but as Cupid would have it, she fell in love with a mill worker and became pregnant. One night there was a screaming row. Terrible crashing sounds were heard. In the days, weeks, and years that followed, the daughter was never again seen in public."

"How does that explain the crying?" Christy asked.

"I was just getting to that," Delia said. "After the couple with the baby moved out, the next owner decided to remodel. He tore down a shed in the backyard—" Delia's voice trailed off, "—and discovered two human skulls buried there. Haunted Tours surmises that the mill foreman murdered his daughter and her baby. And to this day, residents hear their mournful cries. Now if you'll follow the torchbearers to the bottom of the hill, we'll visit the Ferry Inn."

⸙

Delia led the group onto the inn's property and handed her torch to Wanda before proceeding up the steps and along the covered porch out of the gusting wind. The torchbearers remained on the gravel path alongside the inn, away from the flammable structure. "We've arrived at the venerable Ferry Inn," Delia announced, "one of the oldest inns in the United States."

Martin whispered, "Oh, God, not another history lesson."

"I hope there's some information on my ghost," Seth said.

Two figures, briefly visible over Martin's shoulder, scurried into the shrubbery below the porch as Delia said, "The inn is referred to by Hope Springs residents as Ghost Central. To recount every spirit inhabitant would take hours, so I'll mention only the most well-known. Several people have witnessed Aaron Burr's ghost descending the staircase, his eye sockets bloodied." Gasps of titillated disgust rippled through the crowd. "A man wearing a stovepipe hat and ruffled shirt periodically leans out of the dining room wall. Several employees have seen him over the years. A soldier in Revolutionary War regalia regularly shows up in photographs taken in Room 8, even though he's not visible to the naked eye. And there's the little girl in a blue pinafore who appears beside the canal in back and along the riverbank."

"How cute!" exclaimed a buxom woman holding her young daughter's hand.

"Not really. I'll explain in a minute. The most disturbing manifestation occurs in Room 18. Numerous guests have seen the face of a handsome, dark-haired man in the mirror above the dresser. Before they can recoil, the man sheds a single tear. He opens his mouth to speak, but no words come out. Only the thought, 'Save me!' transmitted into their minds, is articulated. He then disappears in a puff of smoke."

"That's so sad," the buxom woman said.

"Yes, it is. Now let's walk up to the canal."

The tourists filed off the porch and ambled across the expanse of lawn behind the inn. Led by the torchbearers, they climbed a grassy hillock to a gravel path at the top, which paralleled a canal nearly twenty feet wide. Delia stationed herself before a weeping willow with feathery branches that dipped into the canal. The torchbearers assumed guardian positions on either side of her, their fiery brands dancing in reflection upon the black surface of the water.

"I can now reveal why the girl ghost is not so cute," Delia said. "Of all the inn's spirits, two have been sighted most frequently—the girl, and a woman thought to be her mother. It's believed these spirits were wrongfully killed. It's also believed the woman's husband is present, though he's never been properly authenticated. He may be the ghostly inhabitant of Room 18."

"The husband is Ambrose Pennington," Seth announced. "He's the man in the portrait on the stair landing." The tourists looked at Seth, uncertain if he was part of the entertainment.

"I'm afraid no one's been able to name the ghost family," Delia said. "The only identifying trait has to do with the girl. She's led several people to their deaths in the river and the canal. She lures her victims to the bank and pushes them into the water. This may be an action she repeated in life, and now in death. She's an enraged entity."

The smell of sulfur wafted across the canal. Seth turned to see a faint constellation of lights twinkling above the water. The prismatic display grew brighter and expanded. A flaming figure of a shrouded man with outstretched arms flashed through his mind. *I can't wait any longer,* the man shouted. *If you won't cross me over, you will pay with a life.* The glittering lights morphed into a gaseous ball. *Your search for truth will bring you sorrow. Ambrose Pennington is gone. I remain. Help me, or one of you will die.*

I don't know how, Seth projected into the ether.

The sulfuric stench transmuted into the smell of burning leaves. The odor grew stronger, nearly overwhelming Seth.

Holding onto Martin's arm for support, he said, "Smell that? It proves Ambrose and my ghost are the same."

Martin regarded him quizzically and replied, "I'm not sure it proves anything at all."

ℋ

Raven and Ivy slipped under the willow's branches during Delia's speech. Raven nudged Ivy and pointed a finger towards the canal. "That's Ajax," she whispered. "Let's give Seth a little scare."

"There's no need," Ivy said. "He'll leave in a day, and you won't see him again. Trust me."

"I don't trust you or him."

"That's a fine thing to say."

"I'm up against a wall. I can't waste any more time."

"If you'll follow me," Delia announced to the crowd, "I'll show you the spot beneath the willow where three of the girl's victims drowned."

Hidden beneath the leafy curtain just yards from the approaching tourists, Raven intoned, "Ajax, now my bidding do! Defeat the one who defeated you. Frighten our Seth Davis away, nevermore to return. Today!"

Ivy jostled Raven's arm, whispering, "This isn't necessary!"

Raven's command shot out, an invisible arrow that pierced Ajax's nimbus as he hovered above the canal. The spirit spun into a glowing amber ball and darted towards Seth. Martin, draining the dregs of his thermos into his mouth, stood in Ajax's path. The spirit lunged at him and howled, *Be careful what you wish for!*

Martin jumped. Distracted by a passing breeze, he looked around. "Ajax, is that you?" he murmured. "I'll summon you tomorrow night."

No need, Ajax replied. *You are only in the way. Step aside.* Ajax pushed Martin toward the canal. Martin's knees buckled, sending him down the muddy incline. Tottering like a scarecrow, he landed hard on his ass at the water's edge.

"Instrument of abundance, serve me now!" Martin drunkenly cried.

You have nothing to offer.

Seth spun around to see Martin, a nervous swimmer, falling into the canal. He scrambled down the slope. "Someone's in the water!" he screamed upon reaching the concrete embankment.

A man's voice cried out, "I saw the girl ghost!"

Someone else replied, "It's a hoax."

Delia dropped the willow branch she was raising for the tourists to pass under and ran over to Seth. "Did someone really fall in?" she asked breathlessly.

"Yes! He's gone under."

Christy and Beth scurried down the incline. "What happened?" Christy asked.

"Martin fell in!" Seth cried.

Martin's head appeared above the water and a scream filled the air. Seth tore off his shirt and jeans and jumped into the canal, swimming towards Martin's flailing body. The water froze him and hampered his breathing, but he kept moving forward.

Flitting above the canal as a pale orange fireball, Ajax taunted, *This is how I'll grant your wish!* He darted over Martin and dove into the water, grabbing his feet and pulling him under. Martin disappeared as Seth reached the spot where he'd struggled seconds before.

Be careful what you summon forth! It may control you in the end.

Martin spasmed as water filled his lungs. Propelled by a purely physical reflex, he shot to the surface. His head reared above the water and he drank in air before releasing a horrifying wail. He fell back into the water and choked as water filled his belly, then forced its way up through his throat. He breathed in and exhaled water, not air.

A radiant flash illuminated the black depths, out of which appeared a naked boy wearing a crown of light. The boy extended an iridescent hand and pulled Martin through the canal; his keen ambition, screenplays, magic, and dwindling affection for Seth trailed in his wake. His life slipped away into the water, which embraced him with the beckoning arms, chalk-white face, and dripping fangs of a Gorgon.

$\mathcal{H}$

Seth dove underwater at the spot where Martin had last come up for air. The swampy water stung his eyes, and he was forced to feel about blindly. He came up against nothing but the sluggish current. When he surfaced, he heard a commotion on the bank and saw flashing lights and firemen in full regalia. "Over here!" he shouted, waving his arms.

Two firefighters took off their oxygen tanks and slickers and dove into the canal, swimming up alongside him. "He went down here," Seth said, his teeth chattering, his voice small and wretched.

One of the firemen, with dark glinting eyes, said, "He could be on the bottom." He turned to his partner and asked, "How deep is it?"

"Fifteen feet," the other fireman replied.

"He'll drown if we don't find him!" Seth said.

"We'll dive for him," the fireman replied. "You better get out of the water."

Seth was reluctant to leave, but shivers wracked his body. The divers went under, and Seth swam towards the embankment. They hadn't surfaced when he hoisted himself over the low concrete wall.

Beth and Christy ran over and handed Seth his clothing. "Where's Martin?" Christy cried.

"He's dead," Seth said flatly. "I couldn't reach him in time."

"You don't know that," Beth said.

"Yes, I do," Seth insisted. He fell to his knees, clasping his face with his hands.

Pyre approached and wrapped Seth in a towel bearing the Ferry Indian insignia. "I'm afraid he's gone," Pyre said, cradling the quaking man against him. "There's nothing anyone could do."

ℋ

Delia took charge of the tourists, shepherding them towards the inn. Some thought Martin's drowning had been staged, intended to give them a fright. Delia reassured those who feared that a real accident had occurred with, "The divers will find him in no time." Twenty minutes later, the divers pulled Martin's body from the water and laid him on the gravel path alongside the canal.

Seth stumbled over to Martin and knelt down. The gravel cut into his knees, but the pain barely registered. He shook Martin's shoulders and pleaded, "Martin, come back! Martin, can you hear me?" But the clay-colored lips and lolling, spiritless eyes declared that Martin had vacated his physical body and was not coming back. Seth collapsed onto the corpse, kissing the clammy lips and cheeks. He gathered him in his arms, knowing he'd never hold him again.

The dark-eyed diver approached and put a hand on Seth's shoulder. "I'm sorry," he said. "You better warm up inside. The police will want to talk to you."

Seth rose and left the body where it lay, covered by the diver with a green tarp. He wrapped the towel around his waist and removed his wet boxer shorts, then put on his clothes, which clung to his damp skin. He picked up what sounded like radio waves and telephone conversations coursing through the atmosphere. His mind flooded with a welter of swelling noise. Out of the clamor, the Egyptian regression memory arose: he saw himself as a priest dressed in a white robe and sandals holding an ankh over a corpse, murmuring comforting words and an appeal to the Gods. Golden hieroglyphics streaked through his mind, accompanied by Keta whispering, "Now you are ready. Send your beloved to the Light." Beth approached and hugged him. He surrendered to her embrace, so faint he could barely stand.

Twenty-One

A heavy wind arrived, as if it were a force of sorrow. Leaves tumbled from branches and onto lawns, sidewalks, and the street. The tourists who lingered at the inn were augmented by locals who learned of the accident. As the crowd waited for clarification, the atmosphere grew edgy. Seth roamed the grounds, unable to comprehend that Martin was gone. Beth approached and took him by the hand; she and Christy led him to a police car with its red lights flashing. Pyre consoled him as they sat in the back of the squad car that sped to a station house outside town. He managed to walk from the car to the waiting area in police headquarters, then collapsed onto a wooden bench. Richard rushed into the station house and hugged him, saying, "I'm sorry. I got here as quickly as I could."

A policeman addressed Seth from the other side of a desk covered with stained paper coffee cups and an empty pizza box. The fleshy officer gesticulated meaninglessly, until the words, "You'll have to identify the body at the coroner's office" sunk in.

Seth's friends escorted him outside into the darkness, hands placed in front of their faces as the leaves continued to fall in circular pools of air. Everyone crowded into Richard's Pontiac station wagon, which was littered with crumpled leaflets and placards, and reeked of stale cigarette and marijuana smoke. They drove in silence along a two-lane road illuminated only by the car's headlights. Fifteen minutes later they entered Davistown, the county seat. Richard pulled up in front of a brightly lit fortress with ghostly striations running through its concrete walls; four gothic turrets crowned the structure. He broke the quiet with, "This is the county government building and museum. The coroner's office is in the back."

They walked into a wood-paneled office appointed with 1930s *moderne* sconces and a sleek chrome railing that divided the space into a small visitors' area and a larger employee domain. A rotund, balding man rushed to greet Seth as if he'd been expecting him, yet the man looked disheveled, like he'd been roused from sleep. His rumpled white shirt hung unevenly out of beltless brown trousers, and his greasy gray hair stuck out on one side of his head. "I'm Morty Boardman, the county coroner," the man said, thrusting his pudgy hand toward Seth. Ignoring the rest of the party, Boardman ushered Seth into an office on the other side of the railing and closed the door. He offered Seth a chair facing an oversized desk. Boardman settled into a worn leather chair behind the desk and wheezed, "I'll make this as brief as possible."

Seth kept his composure as he fielded questions about Martin's place of residence, his next of kin, and where the body should be sent. "What's the cause of death?" he asked in a dry voice.

Glancing up from his paperwork, Boardman replied, "Drowning, of course. Nothing's official yet, but an autopsy will confirm it."

"Yes," Seth replied, "he drowned." He told himself, *If someone pushed him into the canal, it was murder.*

"There's one more point of business," Boardman said briskly. "I must ask you to identify the body. If you'll come downstairs to the morgue . . . "

Seth followed Boardman down a flight of stairs to the basement and stopped before a door the coroner had trouble opening. When he finally got his key to work, the sweet stench of formaldehyde rushed from the chamber and nearly caused Seth to retch. He entered the frigid room and faced the wall of stainless-steel crypts.

Boardman eyed the anonymous doors and muttered, "Now which one is it?" He turned the handle on a ground-level door and purred, "Ah, yes," before pulling a rolling metal table into the center of the room. With a grotesque flourish, Boardman whipped the sheet off the corpse to reveal Martin lying naked on a gurney.

Seth stared at Martin, who looked like he'd frozen to death. The rigid purpled extremities indicated the body was starting to decompose. Martin's face, a sickly pale blue, had gone slack, as if he didn't care anymore about his appearance. Seth turned away, and caught Boardman averting his eyes from the gloomy spectacle. "That's Martin Spencer, dead and gone," he said.

"Once you sign the papers upstairs, you're free to go," Boardman said. "We'll have the body transported to New York when we get confirmation from the family."

"I'd like to spend a few minutes with him. Alone."

"That's not allowed," Boardman officiously replied.

"Then make an exception."

"I'm afraid that's not possible, except for next of kin."

"He was my lover!" Seth shouted, which echoed in the thick, refrigerated air.

"I see," Boardman said, his eyes popping out of his doughy face. "Don't be too long, since it's against regulations." Boardman waddled out of the room and shut the door behind him.

Seth stared at the inert body. "A terrible thing's happened, Martin," he said. "I'm so sorry our trip ended like this. I would never have placed you in danger. I want you to know how much I love you, no matter what our disagreements were." He bowed his head in respect and said, "It wasn't supposed to be like this!" His crying shook his body, as his face and limbs flushed hot. Time seemed compressed into torturous split-seconds and elongated into an eternal present. Eventually, he calmed himself and witnessed a cloud-like presence resembling a human body floating beneath the ceiling. The outline of Martin's face was visible, along with a sad smile on his lips. "Martin, do you know how much I love you?"

The pulsating form emitted two sparks of white light in response and floated down to the corpse. As the spirit descended, the Egyptian memory returned. Seth saw himself in a white robe and sandals with his hands outstretched over a body wrapped in burial linen the color of parchment. Moving alongside the gurney, he stretched his hands over Martin's body and prayed, first telepathically, then aloud, "Hear me, spirit! Do you require assistance to cross into the Light?"

The transparent form sparked twice.

"Then heed my words!" Seth declared. "Remain on this plane long enough to say goodbye to your loved ones. You may never see them again on this level of existence or the next, so take proper leave. When you're ready, look to your right. You will see two points of light approaching. The lights will help you make the journey. Feel the warmth, as the lights draw near and embrace you. Move with the lights, and you'll find that an ecstatic reunion awaits. Now go, and may God bless you!"

The flickering essence remained in place, hovering above Martin's body. It sparked twice and rose to the ceiling, where it lingered for a moment before vanishing. Seth kept his eyes on the ceiling and cried, "Maybe we'll meet again. And maybe it'll be better next time."

ℋ

Beth stopped on the weedy path leading to Richard's cabin and embraced Seth. "Try and get some sleep," she said. "I'll call in the morning." Christy took Beth's arm and they walked toward the street, where they disappeared into the darkness. Richard guided Seth towards the cabin, which appeared in silhouette under a dome of stars. Trailing behind, Pyre said, "I should stay. Do you mind if I spend the night?"

"No problem," Richard replied. "You can sleep in the living room."

Seth opened the screen door and crossed the front porch. Martin's possessions, including the wine goblets, were strewn about the cabin. Seth imagined his partner would appear with a towel around his waist, fresh from the shower, until a racking pain in his chest told him otherwise. "I can't stop thinking about Martin," he said. "It's my fault he's dead."

"That's not true," Pyre said.

Richard led Seth to the living room sofa. "I'll be right back," he said. He reappeared with a bottle of Jack Daniels and three shot glasses. "Drink this," he said, handing a glass of whiskey to Seth and Pyre. He raised the glass he had in his hand and toasted, "To Martin, may his life have served a worthy purpose. And to Seth, who must carry on. Down the hatch."

"I don't usually indulge," Pyre protested before knocking back his drink.

Seth swallowed the whiskey in one gulp, the liquid burning a trail from his throat to his stomach.

"Pardon me for asking," Richard said, "but why did you bring a psychic to Hope Springs? The town is full of psychics. Blanca knows several." He looked at Pyre and added, "No offense."

"None taken," Pyre replied.

"Because when I stayed at Beth's in August, I was nearly killed by a ghost," Seth said.

Richard replied with a skeptical snort of laughter. "You guys must have been drinking. And you didn't even invite me over."

"I'm not kidding. The next day I had a vision which showed me that Hope Springs was founded on the theft of native lands and the destruction of the environment. I also understood that Hope Springs is cursed, and the curse must be lifted, otherwise the town and the river will be destroyed. By coming back, I thought I'd kill two birds with one stone. Martin and I would have some time to ourselves, and James could help identify my ghost. Instead, I've managed to kill only one bird." He stopped speaking as tears burned the edges of his eyes. "Isn't it funny that *faygele* is Yiddish for 'little bird'?"

"What's your take on this?" Richard asked Pyre.

"Seth is being tested by the power behind reality—God, the universe, take your pick," Pyre said. "By coming back here, he's walked into a spiritual minefield."

Richard looked at both men as if they were putting him on. He started to say something, but shook his head and refilled the glasses.

Seth picked up his glass and drained it. He poured himself another shot and drank it down. Turning to Richard, he said,

"It's four in the morning, Martin's dead, and I'm finally feeling the whiskey. Let me explain what this is about."

"That would be helpful," Richard said.

"I think Martin's death is intended to scare me away from the Orenda Valley."

"Why?"

"I may own land here that Raven Grimmsley doesn't want to surrender."

"You never mentioned that before!" Richard said. "Is it the land she's selling? How are you connected to Raven?"

"She's my birth mother."

"Your mother? If she's your mother, you have to stop her."

Addressing Pyre, Seth said, "I understand that I will be stuck in a karmic connection to Ambrose Pennington until we resolve our conflict."

Pyre nodded in agreement.

Richard asked for clarification, but Seth said, "Let me finish. It's also dawning on me that Hope Springs is an emblem of out-of-control materialism. The pursuit of individual advancement over the greater good is the norm, and any means to a profitable end is the golden rule."

"What are you basing that on?" Richard asked.

"On what you've told me about your struggle to halt the dam. On what I saw in my vision. And on what I think someone will do to avoid giving land to its rightful owner."

"But why lay this on Hope Springs? This is a small town like any small town."

"Because the Orenda Valley's milky light—its visible energy—sucks away goodness. It's Chief Ferry's curse, which burned down the town in 1783. What's left is the degraded side of human behavior, which is motivated by greed. People will kill to protect what's theirs. Look at Martin. I can't prove it, but I think he was murdered."

"He drowned, Seth."

"He was killed by greed."

"How are you drawing these conclusions?"

"That's what I *saw*. Martin's death has brought it into sharper focus. Absolute greed is what's allowing the destruction of the environment to take place. Short-term, short-sighted profit in exchange for long-term devastation—possibly even extinction of life as we know it. That's what you're fighting against, isn't it?"

"Yes."

Seth lapsed back onto the sofa, spent. "Know your enemy," he hoarsely declared. "It's the same greed that has made the few the powerful, and kept land and wealth in their hands all over this country."

Richard's eyes grew large behind his metal-rimmed spectacles, and his mouth curled into a smirk. "All my life I've tried to understand the world through political and economic paradigms," he said, "so I appreciate your message about greed. Yet even after knowing Blanca, what I can't wrap my head around is the supernatural gibberish that everyone who spends more than a day in this town spouts. That mystifies me." Interrupting himself to light a cigarette, he inhaled the bluish smoke and said, "It's late and you've just suffered the worst shock of your life. We can discuss this when you've calmed down. All I'll say before I send you off to bed is this: use your overactive imagination to write a book, like I've been telling you for years."

"What I saw is real," Seth said. He struggled to his feet and stumbled down the hallway to the bedroom. He collapsed onto the bed without undressing, and passed out as soon as his head hit the pillow.

℘

You've become one, breathed the voice inside Seth's head, interrupting memories of Martin.

One what? Seth asked.

A priest, the voice whispered.

Seth and Pyre were en route to Manhattan. Seth glanced out the car window at the Jersey farmlands that looked depleted in the autumnal light. "A priest of what?" he said aloud.

Use your inner voice, Pyre urged. *A priest of the dead, as a result of your encounter with Martin's spirit.*

How did you know? Seth asked incredulously.

I heard you. The telepathic signal traveled quite clearly.

I guess I shouldn't keep anything from a psychic.

You've assumed the shaman's mantle you're destined to wear.

James! Seth shouted in exasperation. *I'm a typesetter and, on some days, a writer. I live in the late twentieth century in the most unnatural city in the world. What good does it do to be a priest of the dead?*

It's for the good of others that you assume your role. You will benefit richly from such service.

Should I hang out a shingle?

Don't be sarcastic. You know that you were once such a priest. In Egypt, it was the greatest honor to be initiated into the mysteries of the dead. Why do you struggle against your gift?

Because disembodied spirits scare the shit out of me.

Following the signs for New York, Pyre merged onto the turnpike. *It's obvious your current contact with the spirit world is a reconnect to your Egyptian life,* he telegraphed. *It's your soul's birthright coming into play.*

A cascade of golden hieroglyphics shot through Seth's brain in reply.

And man to man, the gay stuff I couldn't care less about. There have always been homosexual shamans who've communed with the dead. The only difference between you and me is our sexual tastes, and that's, as they say, like preferring oranges to apples. Otherwise, we could be spiritual father and son. Our job is to appease the suffering of the dead and lead them back to God.

Seth refused to respond, willfully shutting down his mind.

So be proud to be a gay priest, my boy. It's an old and revered vocation.

ℋ

Seth and Pyre continued their journey in silence. When they emerged from the Holland Tunnel into lower Manhattan, instead of driving north, Pyre proceeded east along Canal Street. Soon they were crawling along the crowded streets of the Lower East Side. "Do you know where you're going?" Seth asked, wondering how a psychic could have such a bad sense of direction.

"I'm confused," Pyre admitted.

They drove along Allen Street, and the building Martin lived in when he and Seth met came into view. Seth glanced up at the sooty brick structure and understood that he'd never again return to Manhattan to be greeted by his partner. Such finality induced a tormented "Oh, God!"

"What's wrong?" Pyre asked.

"We just passed Martin's old apartment."

"You must keep him alive through your love and your actions. I'm afraid that's the best we can do." Pyre looked at Seth and asked, "If I drive to Houston, I'll get to your apartment?"

"Yes. Make a left, cross Sixth Avenue, and bear right on Bedford."

"I remember now."

"If I hadn't insisted on returning to Hope Springs, Martin would be alive and drinking too much, but at least he'd be here."

Conversation ceased until Pyre doubled-parked in front of Seth's building. "Do you want me to come up?" he asked.

"Not unless you can tell me how people survive the loss of love," Seth answered.

"They do so by accepting that every event has a purpose, whether or not we understand it. And they do so by learning to love themselves and God in a deeper way than they had before."

"If they don't go mad first," Seth replied. He got out of the car and retrieved his bag from the trunk. Pyre followed and hugged him as he stood forlornly on the sidewalk. "I'll call you tomorrow," Pyre said.

"Thanks for your help, James. Maybe after the funeral we can contact Martin to make sure he's all right."

"He's all right," Pyre said before getting into the car and pulling away.

I hope he's okay, Seth thought while riding the elevator to the sixth floor. *Otherwise, I'll meet his angry spirit in my dreams.*

ℋ

Seth dropped his bags on the floor of his apartment and took his address book from the metal table beside the captain's bed. He found Clara Cooper's number and dialed it. The answering machine picked up.

"Clara, this is Seth Davis. Something terrible's happened. Please phone me as soon as—"

"Seth. Hi. I'm here," Clara said.

"Martin died. Or was killed."

"I'm so sorry." Clara paused, then said, "Were you away from home when it happened?"

"Yes. We were in the Orenda Valley. I know you said not to travel, but it was a short trip. I didn't think we'd be in danger. He drowned in a canal."

There was silence on the line until Clara said, "You must be very careful. I'm sensing that something's opposing your energy."

"I'm aware of that."

"Is there someone in New York who can advise you about how to break a spell?"

"Yes. I've already enlisted their help."

"Do you trust that person?"

"Yes."

"Good." Clara hesitated before saying, "Under no circumstances should you return to the Orenda Valley."

"Why?"

"Because I'm seeing that you could die, too."

Twenty-Two

Richard sat in the lobby of the Patriot Bed and Breakfast, on the outskirts of Hope Springs, holding a manila envelope containing photocopied newspaper clippings and notes scrawled on a yellow notepad. The building, a former grist mill perched above a tributary of the Orenda, was over two hundred years old. The walls were constructed of rocks dredged from the river. The low, wood-beamed ceiling gave the room the feeling of a wine cellar. Morning sunlight penetrated two leaded-glass windows that overlooked the stream. Richard scanned the premises for a secluded spot. The dining room had a few breakfast stragglers. The bar on the other side of the lobby, with antique muskets on the wall, wasn't open yet. Perhaps he could persuade the concierge to grant him access.

The front door opened, and Raven Grimmsley, wearing dark glasses and a tan trench coat, walked in, searching the room and looking over her shoulder. Richard rose and waved. "Over here," he called.

Raven turned and headed back out the door.

"Wait!" Richard shouted. "We must talk."

Raven reappeared. She removed her glasses; her face was pinched, her red hair limp and unkempt. "I shouldn't have come," she said.

"I'm glad you did. Let me find a place where we can talk." Raven paced the lobby while Richard asked the concierge if they could be served in the bar. Dropping Raven's name seemed to work. The hostess ushered Richard and Raven into the bar, switched on the lights, and showed them to a table.

"I'll just have coffee," Raven said.

"Same for me," Richard said. He handed the hostess a bill and added, "We don't want to be disturbed."

Raven settled into a chair and regarded Richard warily. "I don't know what you want, but if it has to do with Seth Davis, you're on the wrong path. I have no connection to him."

"I'm here to discuss the Starfire plant," Richard said. "I'm not sure what Seth has to do with that."

"He's your friend, isn't he?"

"Yes."

"He appeared out of nowhere in your company."

"So?"

Raven remained silent.

"Why are you so concerned with Seth?"

"He thinks he has rights to family property, but he does not!"

The bar door creaked open, and a waiter carrying a tray entered. He set two coffee cups and a pitcher of cream before them and departed.

"I haven't spoken to Seth since his partner drowned. I'm not aware of any connection he has to you." Richard removed the clippings and notes from the folder and said, "This is what we need to discuss." He handed Raven a map of Freeman County, with several parcels of land circled in green marking pen.

Raven glanced at the map. Her cheeks colored. "Where did you get this?" she demanded.

"The map is from the county museum. What's important are the highlighted areas."

Raven glared at Richard. "Let's not play games. I assume you know that those parcels are McWycke land that is currently for sale."

"Yes. And the parcel along the river at Blithe Point is for lease—to Starfire."

Raven rose and pushed back her chair. "I don't wish to discuss this. It's a private matter." She walked towards the door.

"It's not private if the land use is of public concern."

Raven stopped and turned to face Richard. "Who gave you this information?"

"I read newspaper accounts and started digging around for land deeds in the county archives. It's laborious, but eventually I found what I was looking for."

"Blanca told you, didn't she?" Raven screeched.

"Blanca told me nothing. I've been trying to figure out who owns the Blithe Point land, and by chance and luck I followed the trail to you. Now please sit down."

Raven looked affronted, but complied. She nervously sipped from her cup.

Smiling sympathetically, Richard patted Raven's hand, which she promptly withdrew. He said, "What Blanca *has* described to me is the nature of witchcraft. There's a strong link between the worship of Mother Nature and the movement to save the environment. That impressed me."

"Please, Mr. Abbey, I don't need a lecture. Get to the point, if there is one."

"It would appear that we are on opposite sides of the fence. You intend to lease your land to Starfire. I have been working to halt construction of the plant. But I don't see that we are in opposition."

"How is that?" Raven asked, piqued.

"Because we both wish to serve Mother Nature. We both wish to restore the planet's wounded ecology."

"Oh, really! You are too much. I will not be manipulated by someone who doesn't know the first thing about my faith. My concern with the land is monetary."

"Precisely. You have forgotten, or never learned of, the dangers inherent in nuclear energy. There's no safe way to store the waste. If there's an accident, land and water will be contaminated for millennia, not to mention the loss of human and animal life. There is no way this technology can jibe with your beliefs."

"You may be able to indoctrinate Blanca with your brand of snake oil, but I'm not buying it. Nuclear energy is clean and efficient, and it doesn't pollute the environment."

"It does when there's an accident."

Raven rose and said, "I'm beginning to see the conspiracy at work. Blanca feeds you information and Seth stands in the wings waiting to steal the land from me."

"Blanca has maintained her allegiance to you. She's defended you. And Seth has nothing to do with this."

"I know otherwise. You have not convinced me of anything except to proceed as I've always intended."

"Then I will challenge you in the papers, on TV, in court, everywhere."

"And I will meet your challenge. Good morning, Mr. Abbey." Raven walked out of the bar, donning her sunglasses and slamming the door behind her.

Richard gathered his papers and put them back in the manila folder. "Impossible woman!" he muttered.

ℋ

Blanca awoke at eight, as she did every day she worked at Bell, Book and Candle. She kissed Richard on the cheek and went into the kitchen, where she fixed herself a spartan breakfast of scrambled eggs and coffee, and made sure there was enough coffee for Richard when he rose. She dressed and walked down the hill to River Road. She opened the store at ten, prior to Delia's arrival, and sat at the cashier's station for nearly two hours, serving only a few customers.

At noon the door opened, setting off the tinkling bell above it. Raven stormed in and walked to the cash register. "I must speak with you!" she said.

"Now?" Blanca asked.

"Yes."

"Let me see if Delia can cover the register." Blanca ran to the back of the store, and Delia returned with her.

"Is everything all right?" Delia asked.

"It will be," Raven snapped.

Raven and Blanca walked to the storage room. Raven closed the door and looked accusingly at Blanca. She said, "It appears that you've spilled the beans to your lover."

"What are you talking about?"

"Richard Abbey knows that I own the Blithe Point land. I assume you told him."

"There was an article in the paper that mentioned you selling the land. Based on that, he's been researching land titles. He came up with your name."

"I would wager you pointed him in that direction."

"I may have. But he would have found it on his own."

"You may have!" Raven said. "Either you did or you didn't. Either way, you've betrayed me and the coven. Your time with us is over."

"Raven—" Blanca pleaded.

"If I can't trust you, you cannot remain with us. It's that simple."

"I have kept our secrets, and I've explained your position to Richard—"

"You didn't tell him about my finances?" Raven interrupted.

"I had to, so he would understand your need to lease the land."

"Is nothing sacred? You expose my personal tribulations to just anybody? And what have you told me about Seth Davis? Nothing I don't already know. You're useless to me. You're out! It will be easy enough to find a replacement."

Blanca responded, "Please don't be hasty. I am loyal to you. Remember that you sent me to Richard. I love the coven, but I also respect what Damn the Dam is fighting for. You've put me in the middle."

"Fine. Blame me." Raven regarded Blanca coldly and said, "Let's see how loyal you are. You can help discredit Mr. Abbey by planting drugs in his cabin. A kilo of cocaine should do the trick. I'm told the bikers are rolling in it. When the police receive an anonymous tip about a drug deal, won't he be surprised to be in possession of enough coke to put him behind bars for years. That should stop Damn the Dam for good."

Blanca shook her head from side to side. "Absolutely not," she said.

"You will do this," Raven said quietly, "or something worse will happen."

"I better get back to the register," Blanca said. She left the storage room and closed the door behind her.

⁂

Blanca told Richard about Raven's visit that evening when she got home.

"She's crazy!" Richard said. "If she's broke, what's she going to pay for the coke with?"

"I don't know," Blanca replied. "She threw me out of the coven. After ten years!"

"She'll take you back once she calms down."

"I'm not so sure."

"Do you mind if I stay at the cabin tonight? I should be there in case she tries anything."

"Who cares about the cabin? I want you safe with me."

"The Damn the Dam records are there. I don't want anyone rifling through them or planting false evidence."

"I wish you wouldn't."

"It'll only be for one night. I'll be back in the morning."

"If you must," Blanca said. She kissed Richard long and deeply, then whispered, "I love you," as he headed out the door.

A quarter of an hour later, Richard walked along the path to the cabin. The night was black, with no illumination from the crescent moon that hung low on the horizon. He opened the screen door and crossed the porch in darkness. Switching on the living room light, he looked around. Everything appeared to be as he left it that afternoon. His desk in the corner was covered with leaflets, and the signs he was drawing for an upcoming protest lay on the floor. He opened his filing cabinet and saw no indication of an intruder. The hanging file folders and the papers within were in order.

He went to the kitchen and poured himself a shot of whiskey, then retrieved his blue glass bong from the bedroom. He removed his stash box from the bottom drawer of the filing cabinet, then put it back; better to remain vigilant. Turning on the TV, with its flickery reception, he sat on the sofa, flipping through the channels with the remote.

A branch snapped, and Richard sat up. He heard footsteps. He went to the porch and switched on the light. "Anybody there?" he called. There was no answer, only a flurry of moths and insects around the exterior bulb. He went inside and found his flashlight. Returning to the porch, he stepped outside and scanned the torch across the field of wildflowers and weeds that surrounded the cabin. Nothing moved or scurried away. The torch's light created eerie shapes in the blackness as he canvassed the field.

He went inside and settled in front of the TV, sipping whiskey as he watched a local show on Orenda Valley history. The scenic valley vistas and river views were familiar, as were the shots of Hope Springs' eateries and shops. There was an interview with Delia Hazard, during which she plugged her bookstore and the Ghost Tour. The host introduced a segment on the valley's haunted reputation. His first guest was Raven Grimmsley, who stared directly into the camera and said, "The Orenda Valley is the most haunted locale in the United States, possibly the world. You could be standing next to a ghost anywhere within its environs and may or may not be aware of it. On some days, there are so many spirits present, the air takes on a milky quality, like a mist. This is when paranormal activity is highest."

The phone rang, and Richard jumped. He crossed the room to his desk. "Hello?" he answered shakily.

"It's me, honey," Blanca said. "Just calling to make sure you're okay."

"I'm fine. Nothing's amiss. It's spooky being here, though. I never noticed that before."

"Why don't you come home?"

"I'll be there in the morning. I want to make sure everything's safe."

"Be careful, then. Raven's got me worried. I've never seen her like this."

"She'll come round, once she sees she's on the wrong side of history. She can't be that stupid or that greedy."

"I hope you're right."

"I love you."

"I love you, too. Get some sleep."

Richard hung up and turned off the TV. He knocked back the remaining whiskey and took another look outside. Nothing stirred. He switched off the porch light, locked the front door, and retreated to the bedroom, where he lay across the bed and smoked a cigarette. He heard noises outside—the rustle of the wind in the trees, a branch snapping and falling to the ground, and water rushing in the distance. All were natural sounds, not human or ghostly footsteps.

He remained jittery. To ensure a good night's sleep, he went to the bathroom and took a bottle of Seconal from the medicine chest. He swallowed three pills with a glass of water and lay down on the bed. He was asleep in fifteen minutes.

His awareness returned in the form of a dream. He was a child, in a house that had no connection to his childhood home. He drifted through the dwelling, which had no furnishings. He heard the sound of running water, and felt a sense of dread. He climbed a stairway to the top of the house, where he entered an all-white bathroom. The floor and walls were covered in gleaming marble. Peering into the shadowy depths of the room, he saw that the bathtub was overflowing. Someone had left the water running.

He walked to the tub to shut off the water, but there were no handles. There were only two metal nubs protruding from the wall, which he grazed with his fingers. He could not grasp them, and could not turn off the water. Something was wrong—a dam had cracked and a flood was imminent. Unable to stop the deluge, he called out, "Someone help me!"

He turned and looked up. Coming towards him was a silver-bladed knife. He screamed. The glinting knife elongated as it moved closer. He saw the face of the woman wielding it. Her mouth was open in a menacing O. Her eyes were wild green dots. She had rippling shoulder-length red hair. The woman caught Richard in her gaze and lowered the knife. A horrific series of screams tore from his lungs. The woman yelled, "Damn it! Choke it! Damn the good goddamn!"

Richard sank through watery depths to the sunless bottom of a nameless sea. A peculiar burning odor of dead leaves accompanied by the weight of an ocean pressing down upon him was the last thing that penetrated his consciousness.

❦

Martin's parents had come and gone, denying their son's gayness even after his death. To them, Seth was Martin's friend or roommate, nothing more. The Spencers had relied on Seth to provide a superficial understanding of Martin's life in New York, but would not allow anything personal to be broached. They returned to their home in California with Martin's ashes to make funeral arrangements. Seth was never extended an invitation to attend. He wondered if his adoptive parents would be so cold. He knew his birth mother certainly could be.

It had been a shock to explain Martin's death to friends. No, it wasn't AIDS. No, he wasn't killed because he was gay. He explained it as an accident, a tragic mishap, a freak occurrence, keeping his suspicions of the involvement of magic to the small circle who could accept the possibility of it.

Again, he moved through the stages of grief, only this time he felt grief's power firsthand. For several days he battled insomnia, until he gave into exhaustion and sank into a dream. A tiny stick figure approached from a distance, waving a miniature hand in greeting. The figure drew nearer and assumed normal proportions, and Seth recognized Richard's smile peeking through his beard. Richard reached out and drew him into an enfolding bear hug. He pulled away and bade Seth a wordless farewell before receding into the distance and vanishing. The ringing of the telephone interrupted the dream's fadeout. Groping for the receiver on the nightstand, Seth mumbled, "Hello?"

"It's Beth. Are you sitting down?"

"I was asleep."

"One of my cop friends phoned to say that Richard was found dead in his cabin."

Seth tried to speak, but couldn't.

"The police think it was a drug overdose, possibly a suicide. His heart received some kind of shock and stopped beating. My friend said it was strange, because it looked like he'd been suffocated. Are you there?"

"Yes," Seth said, as tears collected in the corners of his eyes.

"There's more," Beth said wearily. "His front door was broken open and the cops found a stash of cocaine under the sofa. It's a safe bet the media will turn the story into a scandal. You know, Damn the Dam was a front for drug dealing, or was financed by drug money. There's a faction around here that would do anything to discredit the environmentalists."

"A suicide?" was all Seth could utter in response. He sat up in bed dazed.

"That doesn't make sense to me, either. I saw him last week and he seemed upbeat. Knowing him, he did one snort over the line, and it killed him."

"That's so weird, because I was just dreaming that he'd come to say good-bye."

"I guess he had." Beth started to cry. "I've got to go. I'll call back when I know more."

ℋ

The day following Richard's death, Seth pulled out the photos he and Martin had taken on their last visit to Hope Springs. Sitting on the captain's bed, he flipped through the pictures, looking for a good shot of Martin. He stopped when he came upon a photo of the portrait on the Ferry Inn stair landing. Peering out between the dour husband and wife was the monstrous visage he and Pyre had seen. The face was shadowy and indistinct, but it was present. "They do show up in pictures!" he said in amazement.

He examined the remaining photos. A picture of Martin sporting an awkward smile was too poignant to bear, and he turned it over. A shot of the white mansion on River Road showed that Martin had captured the red, purple, and amber rainbow that Pyre described. It appeared as an arc of diaphanous energy trailing several feet down the street. Two pictures later, a shot of the vacant lot revealed thin, ghostly arms emerging from the ground and reaching heavenward, mingling with milky light shafts that riddled the air. Martin, if he were present, might have contended that what appeared was a photographic anomaly, a trick of light, or a printing error. But the photos, many of which Martin had taken, documented the existence of spirits.

Seth phoned Pyre to tell him about the pictures. He left a message with Pyre's service and looked at the photos again. He felt the pull of an invisible arm drawing him back to Hope Springs—one of the limbs reaching up from the empty lot beckoned him. "What is it about that place that won't let go?" he wondered aloud. The only answer he received was the silence that had taken up residence in his apartment.

ℋ

The phone rang as Seth was about to leave for work. He picked up the receiver and said, "James?"

"It's Ivy. How are you doing?"

"As well as can be expected. My friend Richard Abbey died."

"I heard. I'm sorry. Do you think it was a coincidence?"

"What do you mean?"

"His girlfriend was thrown out of the coven for her association with him. And now he's dead."

"First Martin, then Richard."

"I've got some news. I found a document."

"What is it?"

"Your original birth certificate with your birth mother's name."

"How did you find that? I tried years ago and couldn't get my records unsealed."

"I know a high-level police officer. He can access almost anything."

"What's the name on the certificate?"

"Raven McWycke."

"So it's true."

"This changes everything. You can claim the property Raven is selling. You own the power plant land."

"That could take years in court. The plant could be built by the time a judgment is handed down. Besides, I don't have the money for a lawyer. And it may not be a legal issue. It's just a family tradition."

"Perhaps, but a lawsuit can stop construction until ownership is determined. You owe it to Richard."

"Why are you helping me?"

"I have my reasons."

"You've said that before."

"I don't agree with Raven about Starfire."

"That's it?"

"I also want—I want Raven's job."

"She works?"

"As High Priestess."

"How will helping me achieve that? I'm not in the coven."

"She can be pushed into a sudden fall, as an old legend says. And with your pedigree, you could be."

"I'm late for work. I'll phone you when I've thought this through."

"You must confront her before construction starts. With Richard gone, time is crucial."

"Can you get me a copy of the certificate?"

"Of course."

ℋ

When Seth returned home from work, the phone rang, and he heard Pyre start to leave a message. He fumbled for the receiver and said, "I'm here, James. I looked at the photos from Hope Springs. We captured a lot of spirits."

"I'm not surprised," Pyre replied. "How are you doing?"

"Not good. Richard Abbey died."

"I saw it in the papers. I'm sorry."

"I want to go back to Hope Springs."

"Why?"

"To contact the earthbound in Room 18."

"We already did that."

"I need to understand what he wants from me. I want the whole truth."

"No one knows the whole truth. No one sees everything, not even me," Pyre said with a self-deprecating laugh. "Going back could open a Pandora's Box—you'll be placing yourself in danger."

"I know. My astrologer warned me."

"The earthbound may not cooperate. He didn't the last time."

"You'll find a way to make him cooperate," Seth insisted. "And you can protect me with your water ritual."

"It might be wiser to attempt a psychic fly-in, where I contact the earthbound from a distance."

"There's something else. Remember the red-headed woman in the tavern? I will soon have a document that proves she's my birth mother."

"You want to see her? She wasn't happy to meet you."

"I have some business with her that impacts the nuclear power plant construction."

"I see."

"When are you free?"

"I'll be in the city on Friday. Let's meet for lunch and talk then." Pyre shuffled some papers and said, "Monday, the thirty-first. I think we should consider this carefully."

"We're going back, James."

"Only if you agree to send the earthbound into the Light."

Twenty-Three

Seth took Monday, the thirty-first off from work. The front door buzzer sounded a little before eleven, and he rode the elevator to the lobby, fretting, *I can't believe we're going back on Halloween.* Two hours later, Pyre's Audi rumbled across the metal roadway on the bridge between Banbury and Hope Springs and got stuck in traffic on the other side. Once again, he saw the power of a season changing, the evolution now in the thinness of the light, the bare branches of trees, the once-green lawns brown and covered with decaying leaves. A ragtag parade snaked through the cars. Among the adult revelers was a white-sheeted ghost, a skeleton in a black unitard embossed with electric-green bones, ghouls sporting rubbery masks, and a storybook witch and wizard, each in a velvet cloak studded with faux jewels. The celebrants lurched about, performing an impromptu folk dance that morphed into rhythmic steps more fitting to a disco. As he watched the dancing, he felt the absence of Martin; every year they looked forward to creating costumes for a Halloween party they attended in the West Village—Martin always opting for something dark and sinister, Seth wanting something light and glittery. The Audi inched along River Road toward the Ferry Inn, passing yellow corn sheaves tied to lampposts and a banner suspended above the thoroughfare that announced: *Expanded Ghost Tour Tonite. Haunted Hayrides Leave Hourly from Blithe Point. Tickets at Bell, Book and Candle.*

"Do you think it's dangerous being here today?" Seth asked.

"I've already told you what I think," Pyre replied. "We should keep a low profile."

"Isn't Halloween the day that spirits walk the Earth?"

"That's the old belief."

Taking in the crowded thoroughfare, Seth said, "Martin always thought Halloween was the unofficial gay holiday. A day we could be ourselves, or anyone else we wanted to be. It was our very own New Year's Eve party."

"Halloween was the last day of the year in the Celtic calendar, so it *was* New Year's Eve. People believed that on Halloween night wandering spirits returned to their former homes for protection against winter. It was also the time when witches, both male and female, were thought to be out and about."

"Maybe we shouldn't have come back."

Shrugging off Seth's remark, Pyre said, "Once Christianity appropriated the pagan holy days, October thirty-first became the Eve of All Hallows, or All Saints. The veil between the material and spirit worlds is thinnest on Halloween, so it's appropriate we're here today."

"Symbolic, almost."

Pyre turned into the Ferry Inn driveway and parked the car in the rear lot. They walked around to the street entrance, passing the inscrutable Chief Ferry sign, which was festooned with orange and black crepe ribbons, dried maize, and gourds. Seth stopped on the grassy rise in front of the inn to watch the parade, which continued to snarl traffic, but Pyre motioned him on. They entered the inn and approached the reception area. The desk clerk greeted them with startled raccoon eyes and a perplexed half-smile.

They climbed the creaky staircase to the upper floors, passing the somber couple in the portrait. Seth waited in the third-floor hallway while Pyre entered Room 18 and, burning sage incense, cleansed the chamber. Fifteen minutes later, with a cloud of smoke swirling around him, he opened the door and waved Seth inside. He drew the gray draperies across the windows, throwing the room into shadow, and said, "Pay close attention. I'm going to cast two magic circles, one for you and one for me. I will do this using an inner visualization process. Given the earthbound's hostility, I'll chant a mantra that both summons him and protects us. Once the earthbound is present, ask him what you need to know. You must not stray from the subject at hand, otherwise he may try to divert your attention, possibly to harm you. It's imperative that you remain inside your circle. If you step outside its boundaries, I can't guarantee your safety. Understand?"

"Yes," Seth said, his heart thumping. "But you said that non-material beings can't hurt me."

"That's correct, so long as you don't allow them to. Until you master that paradox, you are at risk."

They struggled to move the antique four-poster bed against the far wall. The wooden frame and canopy creaked and shuddered, but did not collapse. Pyre surveyed the area available for magic. "Each circle will be four feet in diameter," he said. "It's not a lot of space, but our circles must not overlap." He positioned Seth near the windows, and stationed himself across the room opposite the bed. "I'm going to summon the earthbound. Stay in your circle no matter what happens." He closed his eyes, and his face tightened into a pale androgynous mask. As he meditated, a wall of cool flames flared up around Seth and rose to the ceiling. Pyre emitted low, drawn-out syllables from the back of his throat. After several minutes of chanting interspersed with rhythmic deep breaths, he opened his eyes and said, "From here on, communicate with me by telepathy. You will need to speak to the earthbound in the same manner."

In a resonant telepathic voice, Pyre said, *Troubled earthbound, I summon you in the name of the love that permeates All That Is. On the count of three, make yourself present. My friend wishes to ask you some questions. We come to help, not harm you.* Pyre counted off the numbers. There was no response. He repeated the count in an imposing baritone, but the earthbound failed to appear.

The air grew dense, and the sound of water rushing, along with the suction of footfalls on the stairs, penetrated the chamber. A cacophony arose, as if all the sounds in the inn had become audible in the room. The noise subsided, and a wave of energy passed through the door, bringing with it the stench of sulfur. The new arrival assumed human form and stood near the bed. He positioned himself equidistant from both magic circles, creating a triangle of power. The creature's drooping garment and aureole of black hair were visible in the subdued light, lending him the air of a fallen angel.

Who are you calling your friend? Ajax asked. *Not this benighted human. For if he's your friend, you're a poorer man for it, and I shall have no fun destroying you both.*

We have summoned you in good faith—faith in the Light that protects us, Pyre asserted. *Your threats cannot harm us.*

That remains to be seen. What is it you wish to ask me, boy?

Who is responsible for the deaths of my friends, Martin and Richard? Seth timidly inquired.

Ajax, a hologram pulsing with yellow light, laughed contemptuously. *Why should I answer? What's in it for me? Do you think me a fortune teller?*

Seth repeated the question with greater authority.

Very well, Ajax said. *Martin was a warning, meant to rouse you to action. As for Richard, my mistress, of course. She gives the orders, and I carry them out.* The response ricocheted around Seth's brain, as if in an echo chamber.

What's her name?

Ajax yawned, affecting boredom. *What's in a name? You've met her.*

I want to know her name.

Why do you ask me this when you already have the answer?

Pyre whispered inside Seth's head, *Shield your thoughts, he's trying to find your weak spot.*

Seth visualized a wall of white light surrounding his mind. *Tell me her name!* he demanded.

After a moment, Ajax mumbled, *Raven Grimmsley.*

Now tell me why you tried to kill me.

Don't be so coy, my beauty. You know that I knew you before. When I lived my last life as a man, you were my son. I used you and paid dearly for it, though it gave me satisfaction. I daresay, you may have enjoyed it, too. Look at the life you now lead and tell me that you didn't take some pleasure in our sport.

There's a world of difference between two men loving each other and a man forcing himself on a boy, his son no less. You violated me. That's evil, pure and simple.

Regardless of what happened between us, you were immensely powerful then, and you've carried that power through lifetimes. When I first sensed you in the tavern with your revolutionary friend, I thought you could be persuaded, by threat of death if need be, to free me from the hell I inhabit. You have no idea what I've suffered because of you. When you repelled me, it put salvation that much farther out of reach.

Whatever you suffered, you brought on yourself.

Now that you've returned, either you send me to the next level, or I'll destroy you, regardless of what your friend says. If I can't live in the Light, neither will you.

Seth's body tensed, and he moved toward the circle's perimeter.

Lose your fear, Pyre telegraphed. *And stay inside the circle!*

Son, I didn't mean to frighten you, Ajax said, *but you must believe me when I say I'm at my wits' end. Imagine what it's like to watch your soul be eaten away by a cancer brought on by others. I was forced to commit atrocity after atrocity by the coven I served. It was never by my own design.*

A pitiful weeping sounded inside Seth's head.

Don't be taken in, Pyre shot into Seth's brain. *It's a ploy for sympathy. He's up to something.*

Since you've summoned me to ascertain the facts, Ajax said in a mesmerizing voice, *there's one question I would ask of you. Why did you abandon me at the hour of my death? Tell me that, and we'll both be standing in the radiant light of truth.*

How can I answer that? Seth replied. *That was lifetimes ago.*

Sammy, surely you remember your Da who's come to take you in his arms.

I'm not Sammy!

But you are, little one. You are. You were my son then, and you're my son now.

I told you, I'm not Sammy!

Come to Father," Ajax chanted with a hypnotic suggestiveness. *Come to Father now.*

I will not! Seth's consciousness fell away as he spoke. He sank into a hole in time unlocked by the spirit's evocation of the past, and slipped into a waking dream of stars streaking across a cobalt sky. The falling motion sickened him as he spiraled downwards at a dizzying rate. Stars blurred into an elongated band of light and exploded. He landed with a thud. When he opened his mouth to speak, a high-pitched child's voice with a flattened British accent emerged. "It's not as you say, Father."

Then tell me what transpired, Ajax coaxed, *for it's a son's duty to avenge his father's death.*

"I ran away thinking, 'Father's dead, he'll never protect me from these men. They'll kill me, too, for what we did in the woods.' I found passage to New Amsterdam and then England, where I could live without fear. You speak of revenge, Father, but I was ten years of age when you died. I knew nothing of a son's duty. That's the truth, I swear it."

The truth is that you were responsible for my demise. If you hadn't flirted so wickedly with me, if you hadn't seduced me with your boyish charms, the elders wouldn't have come upon us, and I would not have been sentenced to death. That is the truth.

Samuel stamped his foot and shouted, "I am not to blame. I never flirted with you!"

If you raise your voice to me again, Ajax communicated, *I shall tear you limb from limb!*

Samuel burst into tears. "Don't hurt me, Father. I never meant you any harm." The circle of astral fire surrounding the boy blazed upwards and sent Ajax's insubstantial form reeling against the wall behind him.

Damn you! Ajax cursed. *There's always someone looking out for you.* Gliding back to his cusp in the triangle of power, he purred, *Don't cry, little one. Da was only playing a game.*

"You scared me, Father," the sniffling child said.

It's just a game, like when I tell you I'm going to take your life for the one you cut short. The Bible says, 'An eye for an eye.' I say, 'A lifetime for a lifetime.'

Samuel began to cry. "I didn't mean to hurt you."

There, child. Come to me. Let us embrace and forget the past.

Seth's inhabited body hovered on the edge of movement. *Stay where you are!* Pyre telegraphed. *It's a trap!*

Don't be afraid, Ajax said. *My anger has passed. I now feel nothing but love. Come and let Father hold you.*

"Don't leave the circle!" Pyre said aloud.

I long to kiss you, Sammy, Ajax said. *Father's missed you so.*

Samuel's eyes brightened as he inched towards the spirit. "So all's forgiven?"

Of course. Come to Father.

Samuel moved to the circle's boundary. His foot rose and lingered in mid-air, on the verge of stepping from the present to the regained past. As Samuel was about to leave the protective ring, Pyre shouted, "Stay right where you are!" Samuel froze in place before crumpling to the floor and breaching the circle with his body. The impact severed the link to the past, startling Seth back into consciousness.

Go back! Go back! Pyre telepathically screamed. Though disoriented, Seth pulled himself inside the magic circle.

You would kill the only one who can help you? Pyre said to Ajax. *Are you so depraved?*

Revenge tempts me, Ajax sighed. The spirit vaporized into a funnel of oily smoke and vanished.

Seth rose and looked around the chamber as the smoke cleared.

The earthbound's still present, Pyre said. *He'd like us to think it's safe to leave our circles, but that's not going to happen.*

Ajax rematerialized in a blaze of ochre light, clad in his drooping shroud.

Thank you for answering Seth's questions, Pyre said. *On the count of three, I want you to take leave of us. Return to your realm in peace. One. Two—*

Wait! Ajax cried. *I have a request. And it's my humble wish that you grant it, since I've done what you've asked.* He hesitated before saying, *Release me from servitude to the McWyckes. Cross me into the Light. This is what I've always needed from you, son. Only you can break the curse.*

Why should we help you, when you've caused so much misery? Seth asked.

Because I've handed you the key to your past. And I have come to regret my actions towards you. I now seek forgiveness.

He's right, Pyre said. *Since he's made his request from the heart, it's our duty to honor it. We must help him over.*

But how can I forgive him? Seth said.

By knowing it's the higher way. To show love instead of vengeance is the path to the Light for us all.

Then you'll help me over? Ajax said.

Yes, Pyre replied. *And we should act quickly. Where did you end your earthly existence? For it's on that spot that we must send you back to God.*

By the river, in a thicket of rushes, Ajax grimly stated.

Lead us there. We'll reenact the deed, and at the moment of your death, we'll direct you towards the Light.

Let us leave at once!

Remain in place, Pyre said. *I must banish the circles first.* He closed his eyes and assumed the mask-like expression he'd worn when invoking the astral fire. Shafts of golden light flashed and dispersed. The circles' cool flames dissipated, engendering a momentary calm. With the circles gone, Ajax's otherworldly radiance prickled the men's skin like nettles.

An insistent knocking sounded. Seth approached the door and said, "Who is it?" The voice on the other side of the door said, "Let me in. We have no time to lose." He turned the handle. "What are you doing here?" he exclaimed.

Twenty-Four

Seth stepped back from the door and Ivy hurried into Room 18. "I came as quickly as I could," she said. "Someone tipped off Raven that you're here. The desk clerk, probably."

"Are you sure it wasn't you?" Seth said. "You're playing both sides against the middle."

Ivy blanched, looking offended. "The clerk called me, too. You're lucky I'm in town for Halloween and got here first."

"You've set me up," Seth said. "You knew I was going to contact Raven after we finished with Ajax. Something's not right."

"You must trust that my intentions are—"

Loud pounding on the door interrupted Ivy. "Open up!" the voice on the other side demanded. Seth opened the door, and Raven stood there scowling.

"Come in, mother," Seth said.

"I'm not your mother!" Raven said. "You have no proof." She crossed the threshold and stopped short when she saw the other occupants. "Colluding with the enemy, Ivy?" she said.

"Seth's not my enemy," Ivy replied.

"Why have you returned?" Raven asked Seth. "What business do you have here? And why is my familiar present?"

"That's why I'm here," Seth said. "Ajax was my father in a previous life—"

"That's preposterous!" Raven said. "Of course I believe in reincarnation, but the idea that my familiar was your father, and that I am your mother is sick. You need help."

"Seth is correct," Pyre said. "At least as far as the earthbound is concerned."

"By what authority do you say that?" Raven said.

"The earthbound has told us. Ask him."

"I will not play this game. Even if he is Seth's long-lost father, I am not his mother in this or any other life."

"Yes, you are," Seth said. "I have proof. And based on that proof, I will work to stop Starfire. Richard's death won't end the struggle."

Raven flushed with anger. "You will not cheat me out of my land!" she cried. "Show me your proof."

Seth hesitated, glancing at Ivy. She stepped forward, reached into her shoulder bag, and extracted a piece of paper, which she unfolded. "Here," Ivy said, handing the paper to Raven. "Take a look."

Raven scanned the paper, clutching her crystal pendent as she read aloud: "Certificate of Live Birth. Maiden Name of Mother: Raven McWycke. Name of Father: Israel—" She screamed and tore the paper into bits before hurling it onto the carpet.

"I have another copy," Ivy said.

"You are a traitor!" Raven yelled at Ivy. "You and Blanca have worked against me. This has nothing to do with Seth, does it? It's all about control of the coven."

"Starfire must not be built," Ivy said. "You cannot endanger the environment because of your selfish needs."

"Hypocrite! All you want is to take my place. I should have seen it before. You're always jockeying for position." Raven turned and faced Seth. "And you! That certificate may say you are my child, but I gave you up once and I can do so again. I reject you. There is no law that requires me to make you my heir, only an outdated family tradition. Go away and never bother me again. No court will rule in your favor."

"You mentioned the tradition in the newspaper article I read," Seth said. "Why is it suddenly off the table? You are my mother. My adoptive parents raised me, but you gave me life." He paused before saying, "Don't you have any feelings for me?"

Raven shuddered. Frustration and anger formed tears in the corners of her eyes. "This won't work, Seth. Why do you pursue someone who gave you up? Doesn't that tell you you were not wanted? What's the use of trying to find something that never was?"

Seth looked into Raven's eyes. "Because I need to understand my heritage," he said. "All adopted children do. I've found my father, for better or worse, in Ajax."

"And you think you've found your mother in someone who rejects you? Your spirit father was a dangerous magician. Your biological father was no better. You should be thankful never to have met him. Go back to your adoptive parents. They are all you have."

"Now I have you."

"All you want is the land."

"That's not true. But I will sue you for ownership, since I can prove my parentage. I'll tie up the land for years. You'll never earn anything from Starfire."

"What a strange world. What are the chances you would know Richard Abbey?"

"I'm as surprised as you. Richard would call it synchronous."

"Richard can no longer speak. Be careful you're not—"

"Nothing is worth that," Ivy cautioned.

"One dark curse or ten makes no difference now," Raven said somberly. "And who's the culprit—an invisible spirit?" Pointing a finger at Ajax, Raven uttered, "Damn it! Choke it! Death bell knell. Send this boy straight to hell. Damn it! Choke it! Demons wail. All will fall, if you fail."

"Raven!" Ivy exclaimed.

Seth looked at Pyre, who telegraphed Ajax, *Do not heed the command. Destroy Seth, and you destroy your chance for the Light.*

Holding the pendent before her to amplify her words, Raven recited, "Glowing child with golden hair, radiant boy, youthful and fair. Mother took his life away. If child returns, mother pays. Kill him now! End his days!"

If you kill him, who will help you over? Pyre said. *We are your last chance!*

Raven shouted, "Kill my son, returned from the dead. Send him back to darkness' stead!"

The air in Room 18 hung stagnant and heavy, like the deadened atmosphere of a tomb. Ajax inched towards Seth. His transparent form filled with tongues of flame as he glided across the carpet. He whispered inside Seth's head, *Let me gather you in my arms, and you'll never leave me again.* Seth's cheeks flushed and his limbs weakened. He backed across the room until he came up against the bed and could go no further. Ajax's fiery figure, leaking sulfur, rose up and towered over him. A powerful grip around the throat lifted him off the carpet. His legs dangled in the air and he swooned, surrendering to a realm devoid of physical sensation. His final thought, before his mind went blank, was that he would now see Martin again.

At the point of asphyxiation, Ajax released Seth, who collapsed to the floor. The spirit darted towards Raven, seizing her by the neck. *Do you think I'd destroy the only one who can save me?* he hissed inside her mind.

"Kill my son!" Raven cried. "I'll free you if you perform this final deed."

Ajax's stranglehold increased, forcing the air from Raven's lungs. Her raspy coughs and muffled cries filled the chamber. "Everyone's turned on me," she gasped. Ajax tightened his grip; with his incorporeal hands, he crushed her neck bones and upper vertebrae as she struggled for breath. *Strange how servant becomes master in the end,* he said. Raven's emerald eyes flashed, and she released a throat-tearing scream. She wilted in Ajax's grasp and toppled to the floor lifeless, a frozen look of shock on her face. Blood trickled from her mouth onto the scraps of the birth certificate left on the carpet.

Seth regained consciousness as Raven died, a life spared for a life taken. A vision of orange flames falling to earth and disintegrating as they hit the ground roused him. He struggled to his feet and stared at the body until a wisp of black smoke rose from Raven's chest. The smoke gave off the sour stench of decomposing leaves. Savage pecking at the window and a rustling of wings preceded a shattering explosion, which sent broken glass and a spray of blood across the room. A shiny black form hurtled past and fell against Raven's body. Rah-wing cawed to his mistress, fierce cries of devotion. The bird twisted as the blood drained from him, and he somersaulted into the air and landed on top of Raven, where he spasmed and ceased moving.

It seems that I'm released from service, Ajax said. *My mistress succumbed to karma delivered by her prisoner.*

Opening her telepathic channel to the spirit's wavelength, a coven privilege granted only to the High Priestess, Ivy said, *Three times over, as is the law. She lost her role as priestess, her pet, and her life in pursuit of wealth. The black magic kick-back will impact her for lifetimes.*

So much like myself the last time around, Ajax said. *With my mistress dead, the McWycke dynasty ends, never again to be made whole. The legend is fulfilled.*

What are you talking about? Ivy said. *According to coven law, I succeed Raven.*

Ajax's face assumed the enraptured look of an oracle. He intoned, *The coming of a fairy boy, radiant in visage and true to himself, brings great fortune and a sudden fall.*

Yes, the radiant boy, Ivy acknowledged.

Seth's the fairy boy, now and when he was my son. My boy's powers made me a wealthy man before I was destroyed by my exploitation of them. Seth's presence has destroyed Raven as well.

But how does that affect the coven?

You'll see at the next full moon. The coven's power is broken.

Raven left instructions that in her absence, I should take command. Nothing's changed. And let me point out that a McWycke descendant lives. Ivy scanned the room and said to the men, "If you'll stay here and keep Raven company, I'll go downstairs and make some calls."

"And become sitting ducks?" Seth said.

"Of course not. You must learn to trust me."

"Trust is earned."

"Then give me time." Ivy took Seth's hand and said, "With Raven gone, the coven needs a new mate."

"Thanks, but it's not my religion."

"Think it over. You may find our group more sympathetic than you imagine." She walked to the corpse and said, "I shouldn't tamper with evidence, but—" as she lifted Raven's head and removed the crystal from around her neck. She turned and left the room.

As the door to Room 18 closed, Pyre telegraphed Ajax, *We must help you over at once. Is there another way out of here?*

Yes, Ajax said. *The fire stairs. The door is alarmed, but I can disengage it.*

Let's go, Pyre said. He opened the door and glanced down the hallway, then motioned his companions to follow. Ajax assumed the lead, gliding to the far end of the hallway, where he stopped before a door with a red alarm box. The spirit paused to extend a diaphanous hand into the alarm, then passed effortlessly through the door. Seth tried the handle, and when no sound went off, opened the door onto an exterior stairway. They descended, treading softly on the metal steps, and followed Ajax's twinkling form a floor below. They reached the ground and scurried along the gravel walkway towards River Road and into the Halloween night.

Twenty-Five

Led by their spirit guide, Seth and Pyre negotiated the costumed throng that paraded along River Road. Seth was properly attired for the event, wearing a ring of painful black-and-blue bruises around his neck, but the chilly night air left him uneasy and suspicious. He stopped to observe the Halloween spectacle. Burning brands and illuminated jack o' lanterns lined the thoroughfare, casting dancing shadows across the masked and painted faces of the revelers. Some marchers shook tambourines and bells, while others chanted praises to the Goddess. The procession, with its surging, turbulent energy, was a modern-day pagan pageant. On this night, the old ways exerted a powerful hold over the popular imagination, as if two millennia of Christian dominance couldn't blot out an earlier, perhaps more primal connection to the Divine.

Pyre urged Seth on, and they followed Ajax, who glimmered in the darkness. They left the town limits and approached the white birch forest that bordered the Orenda. The spirit's translucent form filled with smoke that swirled in dense clouds. He slipped off the blacktop and moved between the tree trunks. He stopped and telegraphed his companions, *I do not wish to be helped over. I'm happiest as I am.*

Don't be foolish, Pyre said. *Crossing over is the best thing you can do.*

Ajax loomed upwards, his prismatic aura mingling with the lower branches. *You will cozen me, I know it, and send me to hell!*

I will do nothing of the kind, Pyre replied.

What makes you think the Light will have the likes of me?

If you've understood your errors, and have repented, you'll be embraced like the best of men.

I have repented, Ajax said, assuming his normal stature. *This way. We're nearly there.* Gliding deeper into the forest, he confessed, *If I dwell upon dying a second time, I won't be able to endure it.*

The ground turned soggy, making the going treacherous. As the trees thinned, supplanted by clumps of reeds the height of a man, the murmur of water rushing over stones could be heard. Ajax stopped and said, *Beyond this wall of grass is the place. I can't bring myself to return.*

We must perform the crossing over exactly where you expired, Pyre insisted.

Ajax edged forward and disappeared behind the rushes. Seth and Pyre parted the tall grass and trudged to the center of a swampy clearing surrounded by a circle of golden reeds. The spirit froze in place as first he, and then Seth and Pyre, were pulled into a past-life loop that replayed the pounding of Ambrose Pennington's heart as he raced through the marsh. Flickering sepia images of Ambrose slashing the rushes with his bound fists followed. Sound and vision merged into a moving picture—the site's psychic imprint—as they saw Ambrose slip, twist his ankle, and yelp in pain. Dogs barked, and the hoarse shouts of men were heard everywhere.

Exposed like a fox in a meadow, Ambrose thought while limping into the clearing. *The river's my only hope.* He dashed through the curtain of reeds towards the shoal, where a canoe glided into view, paddled by two town elders. Standing at the prow holding a musket was the toothless hangman, grinning madly. "We've got you, Pennington," he shouted. "You're a dead man." The hangman growled ominously, and the extrasensory loop encountered cross-dimensional static. It transmitted only impressionistic fragments: stumble back into the reeds; posse smashes through; heart-stopping shock: *There's no escape—here I shall die;* black anger in the surgeon's eyes; fetid breath on my face; iron grip upon my throat.

A synapse snapped in their meshed awareness, pulling all three further inside Ambrose's mind. *Wheezing, gulping, coughing blood. Can't breathe, legs crumple into the tide. World comes and goes with each shiver. Samuel flings his arms about me. Longing to say, "My lovely, the root of all evil is . . ." but only choking, "Radiant." Icy water numbs the pain. Slipping into nothingness—cold, cold bliss.*

Ambrose looked up and saw a circle of distended faces peering down at him. He watched as his soul rose from his chest and hovered over his useless body, waiting for the coven's summons. As he died a second time, an understanding that had eluded his ghost burst into consciousness: *I have been stuck in this moment forever. Now I can move on.* When the coven called, *a lifetime for a lifetime* echoed in Ambrose's mind. Pyre telepathically shouted, *We're here to break that cycle, not renew it.*

Catching Ambrose exactly at the moment of death, Pyre began the crossing over. "I want you to notice the two points of light waiting to guide you to the higher world," he said in a clear, deliberate voice. "Do you see the lights?"

Yes.

"Do you desire my assistance in reaching that destination?"

Seth and Pyre heard *a lifetime for a lifetime* nag at the dead man's soul. When Ambrose failed to respond, Pyre said, "It's now or never."

Two gleaming stars radiating an immaculate white light pulled Ambrose, who appeared in a black frock coat and breeches, in their direction. At last he stammered, *I'm ready to make the crossing. I no longer seek retribution.*

"That's what I hoped to hear," Pyre said. "Seth will now take you home."

Pyre's words exploded inside Seth's head, knocking him out of the telepathic loop. "But I don't know how to do that!" he said.

Speaking serenely within Seth's mind, Pyre asked, *Didn't you help Martin?*

"Yes, but wouldn't it be easier if you did it?"

"That's not the point. I can offer no further instruction. Use what you've learned, and follow your instincts."

Seth pictured Martin's purpled body in the refrigerated morgue, with his pulsing spirit floating overhead, and called upon Keta. *Ancient one, help me, if you will, in setting this soul free.* Keta appeared in his mind, hobbling with the aid of a wooden staff. *I'm with you,* Keta said. *Proceed.*

I want you to notice the warmth of love that exists all around you, Seth said to Ambrose. *Can you feel the Divine spark?*

Yes, Ambrose replied. *My cold flesh is warmed by a glow from some invisible fire.*

That's the primordial flame that pervades all existence. As the warmth enfolds you, I want you to focus on the two points of light to your right. These are messengers from the next world, sent to help you cross the river. The lights have always been there, but they've been obscured from your vision until now.

I see the lights approaching.

Then release your hold on your previous existence and go with the lights. They'll lead you to a realm where you can continue your soul's journey. Are you ready?

Yes, child, Ambrose said, his voice cracking.

Go with love in your heart, knowing you'll encounter a peace you've forgotten existed. Go with the lights, Seth urged.

An all-encompassing radiance beckoned. Before Ambrose surrendered to the flow, he cried, *Can you find it in your heart to forgive me?*

Through the veil of memory, Seth recalled the sorrow of Samuel's life. *Yes, Father, I can let go of that existence,* he replied. *But it's harder to accept the deaths of my lover and my friend.*

Forgiveness is the key, Keta reminded Seth. *He's asked yours. Now you must honor his request. It's the only way to heal the wound that exists between you.*

Seth regarded Ambrose, who had bent his head in supplication. *As much as I know how,* he said, *I forgive you. Now go forth into the Light.*

Ambrose lifted his arm in farewell. Father and son observed each other across the swampy expanse, and an umbilical cord of pulsing white light sprang up between them, connecting them heart to heart. The healing bond glowed brightly and sparked as Keta addressed Seth and Ambrose, saying, *Love and forgiveness have cleansed your past-life transgressions. Willful dark magic is not the way. You are now free to begin anew.* The bond dimmed as Ambrose moved across the Orenda. On the river's far side, his eerie shape flickered and vanished.

The instant Ambrose disappeared, the events in Seth's life flashed before his eyes and piled up one upon the other. He understood that everything in the world that has ever taken place or will ever take place occurs in a single eternal moment. A vision came upon him filling the sapphire sky. He saw a winged water nymph clad in sea-green drapery dart overhead and dive into the river, searching for something in its depths. The silvery mermaid emerged from the water and alighted on a log, addressing Seth in a sinuous tongue he could not understand. He looked at her with a puzzled expression, and she implanted her meaning directly into his brain.

I am Astarte, the river's rightful ruler. Your good intentions, now and in the future, have released me from bondage. You will help restore the balance. The river will continue to flow to the sea. For this, I give you my blessing, you who are by nature a water creature. You must discover your faith in Gaia, mother of us all. Astarte trilled and flitted off the log. *By allowing me to return to my rightful place, you have lifted the curse from the valley. Once I find my lair, I'll gladly leave this disorderly realm. Who would want to be human? What a mess you make! Always remember that the universe is one vast emanation of love. Farewell!*

The hallucination faded into weathered sepia snapshots of a piece of rope, a child's arm, and a vial of forest-green liquid. *Let it go!* Keta commanded. *The detritus of this life and the other lives, let it go. Only then can you begin the new age of your existence.* A soft sigh filled Seth's head before Keta suggested, *The rope that bound Ambrose? Samuel's arm gripped protectively by the surgeon? The potion used to put the child in trance, or one of Set's sacred tinctures, perhaps? What does it matter, so long as you loosen your grip on the past, and it loosens its stranglehold on you.*

Seth looked to his right and saw two points of light, which didn't beckon but simply shone their radiance on him. He smiled peacefully, and the vision dissolved. Then there was nothing but Pyre gently grinning in the failing twilight. Seth scanned the clearing to get his bearings. The tall reeds were mere shadows against the black sky. The invisible river gurgled beyond the wall of rushes, which enclosed them in darkness. All that remained of Ambrose was an intoxicating odor of frankincense mixed with the aromatic scent of roses.

Epilogue
True Religion

Twenty-Six

Seth and Pyre walked through the woods with only the light of the moon to guide them. Upon reaching the road, they followed the glare of bonfires and streetlights into town. They saw no police presence at the Ferry Inn until they opened the door to Room 18 and found Ivy and two officers from the Hope Springs police department. The room had been searched. Seth and Pyre's overnight bags were rifled through and tossed onto the bed, and the desk drawers and armoire doors were pulled open. Raven and Rah-wing were missing. The only evidence of the dead was a blackening bloodstain on the carpet.

Ivy introduced officers Green and Gartside. "They won't take much of your time," she said, "since you were *out* during the unfortunate incident."

Green, the heavyset officer who interviewed Seth the night Martin died, lumbered forward. "Gentlemen," he said, "there's no need to read you your rights, since I just want to ask you a couple of questions. State your names for the record."

They complied, and Gartside, tall and lean in his blue uniform, scribbled the information onto a steno pad.

"Pass Officer Gartside a driver's license or photo ID with your current address on it," Green ordered.

Seth and Pyre fumbled for their wallets and handed over their licenses.

Green eyed Seth, his gaze lingering on the bruises around Seth's neck, and asked, "What brings you to Hope Springs?"

"We're ghost hunting," Seth replied.

"You certainly picked the right night," Gartside said as he jotted down Seth's response.

Green gave his partner a disapproving glance and asked Seth, "Have you ever met Raven Grimmsley of Upper Dark Hollow?"

"Yes, last summer at Roger Prince's July Fourth party."

Green narrowed his eyes and said, "Where were you this afternoon between the hours of five and seven?"

"We were in the woods helping an earthbound cross over," Pyre interjected.

"You mean a ghost?" Gartside gushed. "Was there ectoplasm and shit like in *Ghostbangers*?"

"*Ghostbusters*," Seth corrected.

"Yeah, that's the one."

Giving his associate another dirty look, Green continued, "So you were not present when Raven Grimmsley was strangled to death—murdered—right here in your room?"

Before Seth or Pyre could reply, Ivy said, "No, Bert, they were nowhere near here."

"I *know* that," Green testily replied. "I just want their answers for the record." He swiveled his head in Gartside's direction and said, "You're taking this down, right?"

"Um-hum."

"Then for the record," Pyre said, "we were along the river about a mile north of town."

"Are there any witnesses who can corroborate your whereabouts?"

"Only the spirit," Pyre answered.

Gartside chuckled, "That's a good one! Only the spirit!"

"And he's no longer with us. Not even in spirit."

Clearing his throat, Green said, "That's all I need. Give them back their IDs, Bill."

"Um-hum."

Seth smiled meekly as he took his license from Gartside. He walked to the bed to retrieve his overnight bag.

Green's face flushed crimson. "Just a minute!" he barked.

Seth turned and faced the sheriff.

"In case you think we're a couple of country bumpkins who don't know their ass from their elbow," Green said, "let me tell you something. This is the second time you've been connected to a corpse in Hope Springs. If anything suspicious arises from the autopsy, you'll be hauled back here so fast you won't have time to catch your breath. Interesting that both you and Mrs. Grimmsley have bruises around your necks."

"I think Seth gets the point," Ivy said. As she ushered the officers out the door, she told them, "I'll meet you in the lobby."

Ivy turned and faced Seth and Pyre. "That was the hardest thing I've ever pulled off," she said.

"What did you tell them?" Seth asked.

"That Raven was killed by her familiar spirit."

"And they believed it?"

"It's Hope Springs, Seth."

ℋ

Seth and Pyre vacated the formerly haunted Room 18 and checked out. Pyre navigated the Audi along the narrow drive from the parking lot to River Road, where Seth caught sight of Chief Ferry lounging effeminately on the inn's orange-and-yellow floodlit sign. The Chief wore his flapper's headdress and smoked a long white pipe, but where he had once seemed inscrutable, he now appeared to be smiling conspiratorially. He looked beatific, like a meditating brown Buddha. Seth glanced back through the rear window. The torches, jack o' lanterns, and bonfires that bathed the town in a flickering amber glow distorted his view of the Chief—was his broad grin real, or an effect of the lights?

The car's tires grated on the metal roadway as it sped across the bridge that spanned the Orenda. On the Jersey side, Pyre gunned the engine and careened along the winding two-lane route back to Manhattan.

"Like a bat out of hell," Seth said, to which Pyre telepathically replied, *Exactly!*

They sat quietly, each with his own thoughts, while passing through expanses of farmland and darkened towns. For the moment, there was nothing more to say. The silence was broken only when they emerged from the Holland Tunnel and Pyre asked for directions. As they pulled up in front of Seth's building, Pyre said, "Call me tomorrow and we'll compare notes."

"Thanks, James," Seth said.

"No need for that. It was my duty to the dead and the living."

Leaning across the front seat, Seth gave Pyre a clumsy hug before getting out of the car and going upstairs.

ℋ

An unnatural stillness greeted Seth as he entered his apartment, as if no one had lived there in years. To create the illusion of human habitation, he turned on all the lights, but Martin's remaining books and videotapes scuttled the effect, and the ringing emptiness persisted.

Seth brewed a pot of mint tea. He sat on the captain's bed, leafing through *The New Yorker* and sipping from his mug until nearly four in the morning. Only then did the previous day's adrenaline give way to exhaustion. After he brushed his teeth, he studied his reflection in the bathroom mirror. Small lines had materialized around his mouth, and his face looked tense and somehow older—his features had lost the sensuous fleshiness of youth. His cheekbones were pronounced rather than chiseled, and the skin was tautly drawn across his face. His green eyes glinted in the glass. They had lightened in color to become more luminescent, more feline. There was a streak of white-gray in his chestnut hair that had never been there before. That, along with the ring of bluish fingerprints encircling his neck, gave him the look of a specter. *I'll never again catch a movement, a light, or a shadow out of the corner of my eye without thinking, 'Is that a ghost?'* he mused.

A haunting loneliness surfaced. He was on his own again, abandoned by those he loved through circumstances beyond his control. This was the foundling's fate. He climbed into bed as the sun rose, thinking, *It's the first dawn of the Celtic New Year.*

It was also All Saints Day, and he glimpsed himself as a holy fool preaching belief in the supernatural. Struggling to remain awake, he envisioned Jesus with a shining star of light between his eyes. He began to pray:

Sweet Jesus, Great Goddess, my Sweet Lord,

Thank you for being there for me when all I could do was lie on this bed and call out your name and say, "Save me, Jesus!"

Thank you for shining the beautiful white light of the Lord God on me in my darkest hour.

Please keep me humble in your sight.

And please allow me to walk on this Earth with humility and love and compassion in my heart.

Thank you for blessing me with the gift of this lifetime.

And thank you for blessing me with the gift of my other lifetimes.

Thank you for blessing me with the gift of life itself,

Even though sometimes it seems so sad and difficult and painful and lonely.

And other times it's full of the most amazing joy,

And the love of friends, and learning about love through friends.

Thank you for blessing me with the Yin and Yang of my life.

And thank you for blessing me with the challenges and changes I need in order to grow and develop my spirit and my soul.

Please help me open my heart to the joy and love of the universe.

And please help me understand that the universe provides what I truly need.

This is the light of the Lord God.

This is the light of my Sweet Jesus.

This is the light of Jehovah and Allah and the Amazing Krishna.

This is the light of the Illuminated Ones and the Awakened Ones.

This is the light of the male and female Tibetan Buddhas.

This is the light of the Great Goddess,

The Divine Mother of us all.
This is the light of the native religions,
Which see the beauty and the interconnection and the harmony in all that exists.
And which know that the divine spark of God inhabits everything on this plane.
Sweet Jesus, Great Goddess, my Sweet Lord,
Please protect me from evil spirits.
And please protect me from evil humans.
Thank you for shining the beautiful white light of God on me.
Thank you. I love you. Good night.

♍

Seth rose from a deathlike slumber before noon, remembering that he had to go to work later that day. He moved from the bedroom to the living room to the kitchen, an apparition of his former self looking for some sign of his future existence. All he detected was an undefined shining whiteness ahead, just out of reach.

To reanimate himself, he turned on the shower taps, and with the steaming water running down his body, he awakened. The water revitalized him, baptizing him in a new understanding. *I've seen the Light as well as the dark side, which few people do and survive. I'm sure the hidden world's been revealed to me so I can share it with others. Why else would I receive such wisdom if not to pass it on?* He dried off and dressed, experiencing a heightened mental clarity and buoyancy of spirit that came from having acknowledged his higher calling. He perceived his life in all its complexity, layer upon layer of significance and connection, and believed he could make absolute sense of it.

He decided to make a shopping run before going to work. He rode the elevator to the lobby and charged up the street, powered by an electrifying supernatural energy. He seemed to glide rather than walk, and felt the brisk November air pass through him, as if breathing were no longer necessary.

He turned onto Sixth Avenue, intending to visit Balducci's market, but as he was about to pass the Catholic church at Washington Place, he was compelled to stop. His eyes were drawn to the medieval portrait of Jesus that remained in place behind the Plexiglas display window. He moved closer to get a better view of the serene likeness. The huge pitying eyes were infused with a blissful calm and a profound acceptance of all that is. They also seemed to be on the verge of releasing a torrent of merciful tears.

Seth leaned forward and touched the window. "I understand now," he said. "I'm your child." He stood in place gasping and trembling as his tears fell like hot rain to the pavement. He struggled to compose himself and, with lowered eyes, touched the window and murmured a simple prayer of gratitude.

"Thank you, Jesus."

Feeling himself bathed in a nimbus of golden light, Seth started and looked up. The mysterious portrait once again beckoned. The graceful, refined countenance appeared to come to life and whisper, "This is where you begin."

Twenty-Seven

Seth walked through the halls of the Port Authority and rode two escalators to the top floor, where the bus to the Orenda Valley idled. He stowed his overnight bag in the luggage hold and boarded, settling into a window seat towards the back. The bus pulled out of its berth and drove through the grimy glare of the Lincoln Tunnel, emerging into New Jersey. The passage from one state into another reminded him of the similar journeys he made with Martin, but there was no new Martin in his life. Six months later, he remained single, with no immediate desire to change his status.

The bus drove deeper into the Jersey countryside, and signs of an early spring were visible from the window. Fresh green leaves, not a week old, were emerging on the trees and shrubs. White and pink blossoms covering formerly barren branches suggested the rebirth of warmth and sunlight. This couldn't come soon enough for Seth. The death of the light, and the corresponding loss of hope, during the winter months had been painful to endure.

To what was he returning, on this long Easter weekend, with Martin, Richard, Raven, and Ajax gone? He would stay with Beth in her apartment along the river in Banbury, now that her house was sold. He had found a true friend in her. He would see Christy, perhaps. He was returning to answer a summons, from without and within. Blanca had assumed leadership of Damn the Dam, and she asked him to join the struggle, both to honor Richard's memory and as the presumptive owner of the Starfire land. He would have to fight Raven's estate to claim the McWycke legacy, but he was willing. With the help of the

Damn the Dam lawyers, he could tie up construction in court. If he won the land rights, he would do something he and Blanca had discussed—establish a conservancy prohibiting the use of the land for anything but solar and wind power. His goal was to leave the land, as much as possible, in its natural state, subject only to the changing seasons.

There was another reason for his return. He'd visited Ivy at the Paranormal Society during the winter, and she'd lent him books on the Old Religion. He was initially reluctant to study a faith which seemed foreign and outdated. Yet as he read, he found a correspondence between Old Religion nature worship and regard for the planet and what he considered the paramount issue of the time—the restoration of the earth's ecology. If man continued to degrade the planet at the current rate, all life would be imperiled and possibly extinguished. This could not be allowed to happen.

Seth stared out the window and toyed with the Herkimer crystal in the double-moon pendant that hung around his neck, recalling Ivy's requests to join the Circle of Light coven. He had deflected them for months, then one day acquiesced. Aligning himself with a group of nature worshippers might be an odd choice but—along with joining Damn the Dam—would set him on the path to ecological activism.

The bus pulled up to the Mobil station in Hope Springs, and Seth stepped outside into the mild springtime air. Ivy stood there waiting. "I'm so glad to see you," she said. "This is an auspicious day. My car's parked in town. Let's have a drink at the inn, and I'll drive you to Beth's."

"Sounds good," Seth said, taking in the trees and flagstone homes that lined River Road. "It's strange to be back." They strolled along, bathed in warm, clear light. "I'm a bit shaky about the coven thing."

"There's no need."

"I must admit, there are parts of your religious practices that I find silly, for lack of a better word."

"You'll get past that once you're initiated. You'll see that the rites make sense—symbolically, emotionally, and intellectually."

"Still—"

"Remember, you're Raven's son. You are fulfilling the line of familial succession. This is your spiritual birthright."

"I never thought of it that way."

"You may also tap into the power of your birth father. I've heard he was something else."

"In a good way?"

"You'll see."

"Maybe I'll become a gay priest of the dead, like James said."

"A priest of the living would be a better choice."

"Perhaps a priest of the True Religion."

"What's that?"

"It won't be Christianity."

"I should hope not."

"The new religion, what I call the True Religion, will include Jesus' love and compassion for every living soul. But the possession of the Earth for profit and power that arose during Christ's two thousand year reign can no longer be condoned if the planet is to survive."

"What about the Old Religion?"

"It won't be Wicca, either, though the veneration of nature should be carried forward."

"Let me remind you that you are about to join a coven."

"The new religion should be an amalgam of every prior religion, since all religious awareness is founded upon the celebration of God's presence in the universe."

"True enough."

"But unlike previous faiths, the new religion will be based on the understanding that our planet is a single living organism, with each tree, river, ocean, animal, human, and elemental spirit an integral part of its body."

Ivy looked questioningly at Seth.

"The worship and protection of Gaia—planet Earth—will be the new religion's focus. The restoration of the planet's ecology, stemming from a psychic connection between all of Earth's inhabitants, will be its goal. Practicing the True Religion will result in the telepathic union of all beings. Once this occurs, Gaia will be fully activated, and Mother Earth will become the living Goddess. Only then will mankind move into the New Age."

"Is this what you've thought about all winter?"

"The books you gave me stimulated my imagination."

They walked past the Parsons Mansion. Seth looked up at the weathervane on the front lawn, and Keta's voice went off in his head. *You've found your path, my child. Always keep your eyes open and trust yourself. You have a long journey ahead.*

Ivy and Seth climbed the brick steps leading to the Ferry Inn. They stopped on the grassy front landing to admire the view of the rustic town with the river and cliffs golden in the sunlight. The river, which had existed since the beginning of time; the river, which ran over a miraculous crystal bedrock; the river, which was a primal force for man, beast, and spirit alike; this river would run unobstructed to the sea. This was what Seth had vowed to work for.

Ivy took Seth's hand and led him through the inn's front door. Smiling tenderly, she said, "Welcome home." She clasped the crystal pendant around her neck and said, "Now let's work some real magic."

Acknowledgments

While a novel is usually written in solitary confinement, for the sake of both the writer and society at large, a novel is rarely published without the kind assistance of many individuals. Several friends and colleagues contributed to the development and publication of this book, and to each I am grateful. Bonnie Knight provided the initial inspiration, along with constant critical feedback as the book evolved. Bobbie Hodges assisted with my paranormal research, and also provided an insightful critique of an early draft. Craig R. Carey gave the manuscript a kick-ass edit (yeah, my ass). Fellow writer Bev Jafek offered comprehensive advice about the twin processes of writing and securing a publisher, and gave me the suggestion that led to the book's publication. Patrick Merla, who has mentored numerous writers, offered his time, industry insights, editorial expertise, and marketing and legal knowledge, all of which helped advance the book towards publication. The same kindness was extended to me by Chelsea Station Editions author David Pratt. Robert Kent graciously provided legal counsel. Finally, my publisher, Jameson Currier, offered expert editorial guidance, without which this book would not exist in its present form. A heartfelt thanks to them all.

About the Author

J.L. Weinberg was born and raised in San Francisco. He moved to New York City to become a film critic, but was sidetracked by stints as a model and actor. He returned to movie journalism, writing for *New York, Premiere, The Village Voice, Interview, American Cinematographer, The Advocate,* and *The New York Native. True Religion* is his first novel.